TORTURES
OF THE
DAMNED

TORTURES
OF THE
DAMNED

HUNTER SHEA

PINNACLE BOOKS
Kensington Publishing Corp.
www.kensingtonbooks.com

PINNACLE BOOKS are published by

Kensington Publishing Corp.
119 West 40th Street
New York, NY 10018

All Kensington titles, imprints, and distributed lines are available at special quantity discounts for bulk purchases for sales promotions, premiums, fund-raising, educational, or institutional use. Special book excerpts or customized printings can also be created to fit specific needs. For details, write or phone the office of the Kensington sales manager: Kensington Publishing Corp., 119 West 40th Street, New York, NY 10018, attn: Sales Department; phone 1-800-221-2647.

This book is a work of fiction. Names, characters, businesses, organizations, places, events, and incidents either are the product of the author's imagination or are used fictitiously. Any resemblance to actual persons, living or dead, events, or locales is entirely coincidental.

ISBN-13: 978-0-7860-3477-2
ISBN-10: 0-7860-3477-7

First printing: August 2015

10 9 8 7 6 5 4 3 2 1

Printed in the United States of America

First electronic edition: August 2015

ISBN-13: 978-0-7860-3478-9
ISBN-10: 0-7860-3478-5

For Mom and MIL,
The ladies who keep us all in line.

1

The trio of explosions ripped the biting January night air in two. Daniel Padilla was dozing between commercials when the sky exploded. He bolted from his recliner, as did his wife, meeting in the middle of the living room.

"I think the furnace exploded," Elizabeth shouted, balling her fists tight at her sides.

"We wouldn't be standing here if it did," Daniel shot back. A framed picture of the family at last summer's picnic at Orchard Beach crashed to the floor, making them jump. That last explosion shook everything in the house.

Footsteps thumped above them. The kids ran down the stairs.

"Mom, Dad, did something just blow up?" Rey asked. His youngest brother, Miguel, clung to his leg.

Daniel motioned with his hands for them all to calm down. "I'm going to check outside. It sounded like a plane. Everyone just sit tight."

Max, Gabriela, and Miguel crowded around Elizabeth on the couch. Gabby's cheeks were smeared with tears, her stuffed koala, Cody, tucked under her arm.

He ran to the closet and threw on the first coat he found.

It was a track jacket that belonged to his middle son, Max. It was a size too big for Daniel, but it would do.

"I'm coming with you," Rey said, slipping into the sneakers that he kept by the front door. He must have been lying in bed listening to his iPod because his short, jet-black hair was flattened on one side. His earbuds dangled around his neck.

There was no sense arguing. Rey was a senior in high school now. Some days he was more man than boy. "Okay," Daniel said.

The frigid air stung his face and shocked his lungs when he opened the door. Lights were on in every house in the neighborhood. A good number of porches were filled with people searching the sky.

No one spoke.

There wasn't a sound to be heard. Even the wind had stopped. Daniel didn't feel the powdery snow around his bare feet.

He looked up and down the street and over the houses opposite them. With his high front porch, he had a clear sight line to the Bronx border. All he saw were stars blinking in a clear, black sky.

When Rey spoke, Daniel's heart did a triple beat. "How come there aren't any sirens?"

He was right. Whatever had happened sounded as if something massive had been blown to bits. The screech of police, fire engine, and ambulance sirens should be echoing around them.

"I don't know. Go inside and see if there's anything on the news."

It was still a half hour until the eleven o'clock news, but Daniel was sure this would be breaking news on the local channels.

Buck, his next-door neighbor, was on his tiny porch dressed in full winter gear and wearing his cowboy hat. He was a solid guy in his early sixties with, as he himself

claimed, a body made by good beer and medium-rare steaks. "Holy shit, Dan. What the hell do you think that was?"

The silence was becoming more disturbing than the initial blasts. Daniel wiped a sweaty palm over his face. "I have no clue, Buck. I thought for sure it was another plane going down."

They'd both worked in lower Manhattan on 9-11. Neither would ever forget the sounds those planes made when they hit the Towers.

"I'm gonna call a friend of mine on the force," Buck said. "I'll come over and let you know what he says. In the meantime, you might want to put something on your feet."

Daniel looked down at his snow-covered feet. The sight finally made him feel the cold. He shook each foot, flicking snowflakes, and went back into the house.

2

"There's nothing on TV," Elizabeth said to Daniel the moment he stepped back inside. She was worrying at her auburn curls, twisting the strands tightly around her fingers.

"What about the radio? Sometimes they're quicker."

Max held up the small transistor radio Daniel kept around to listen to Mets games when he worked in the garage. Puttering around, fixing things, and getting covered by grease and grime was always made better by baseball, even when the Mets lost—which was more times than most. "I've been listening to every station, but all they have is commercials or guys talking about politics."

Daniel took the radio and ruffled his hair. "Buck is calling one of his cop friends. I wonder if it was an earthquake."

Elizabeth stroked Gabby's hair, keeping her calm. "Remember the one in the eighties?" she said. "I was staying at my grandparents' house in the Bronx with my brother when it happened. My grandfather came rushing out of the bedroom in a panic. He thought the old boiler had exploded, too. When the house had started rumbling, my brother woke up and immediately shouted, 'Earthquake!' He pulled me to the doorway between the living room and dining room. I thought he was crazy at the time, but he was the only one who knew exactly what was happening."

"But it sounded like it came from above us," Rey said. He flipped through every channel, looking for any kind of news report.

"It was hard to tell," Daniel said. "It happened so fast. And it was so *loud*."

"Are we going to be all right?" Miguel asked in his high, quiet voice. He sat with his knees pulled close to his chest, his big, brown eyes watching, waiting for cues to panic or calm down.

Daniel sat next to him and pulled him onto his lap. "Of course we are. You're all right now, aren't you?"

He reluctantly nodded his head.

"And that's just the way you're going to stay," Daniel said, kissing his forehead.

"Do you promise, Dad?" Gabby asked, reaching out for him. He held her hand atop his wife's belly.

"I promise, pumpkin. It was just a loud noise. Now I'm just curious what caused it. There's nothing to be afraid of. In fact, we might as well make a little party out of it. Why don't you, Miguel, and Max go in the kitchen and make us all ice cream sundaes?"

Gabby's eyes lit up. "Really?"

Elizabeth gave him a warning look. "Dan, it's late."

He kissed her cheek. "They don't have school tomorrow. I think ice cream is exactly what we all need."

She saw the hidden message in his gaze. *Anything to take their minds off it.* She sighed and nudged Gabby off the couch. "Make mine with extra cherries," she said.

The kids tramped to the kitchen, Max hanging back, visibly upset that he, their fourteen-year-old, had been lumped in with Gabby and Miguel. Someone had to keep relative order in the kitchen. Not to mention, Max's stomach was a bottomless pit. He practically lived with his head in the refrigerator. The clanking of bowls and spoons rang out, along with cabinet doors opening and closing.

The local news started, and Rey turned the sound up.

They began with a days-old story about a train derailment in lower Connecticut. Daniel put his arm around Elizabeth. She could feel the tension in his taut muscles. Four stories later, there was no mention of the explosions. They teased a story about one of the Kardashians and went to commercial.

"That doesn't make sense," Rey said. He changed to the other two local stations. No one was talking about it.

"Maybe they need time to get the reporters on the scene," Elizabeth said.

Daniel shook his head. "Maybe. But you'd think in this day and age . . ."

Rey put the remote on the coffee table and dove into his phone. "I'll see if anyone's talking about it on Twitter or Facebook."

That was a damn good idea. Daniel was always amazed by how resilient his kids could be. He'd never think of doing something like that. Then again, he only used social media sparingly to promote his business. He wasn't one for sharing pictures or broadcasting to the world when he was going to the gym.

The doorbell rang.

"That must be Buck," Daniel said, rising from the couch.

3

Buck Clarke strode into the house, larger than life. His sizable beer gut hung well over his belt. He had to duck as he walked through the foyer to avoid tipping his hat off his head.

"Fucking fireworks," he announced. "Can you believe it?"

Daniel watched Elizabeth bite her lip. He'd learned long ago there was no sense asking Buck to tone it down because kids were around. Buck was what Buck was.

"That didn't sound anything like fireworks," Daniel said.

"My buddy said someone got ahold of professional-grade fireworks, loaded them in several steel drums over in an abandoned lot in Mount Vernon, and set them off, one after the other. He said the concussion blew out windows for a ten-block radius."

"Is your friend with the Mount Vernon Police?" Rey asked.

"Nah. He's a state trooper. They all talk to each other."

"But we didn't hear any sirens," Daniel said.

Buck's eyebrows went as high as they could go. "That's because it happened way the hell on the other side of Mount Vernon. Guess we're out of range."

Gabby and the boys came in carrying bowls of ice

cream smothered in whipped cream, chocolate syrup, and cherries.

"Do you want a sundae, Buck?" she asked.

He gave a short laugh and scratched his stomach. "I'd love to, but Alexiana might kill me if I came home with ice cream on my collar. That sure does look good, though."

Elizabeth got off the couch and stood close to Buck and Daniel. "How come it isn't on the news? I mean, it shook the whole house."

Buck shook his head. He spoke lower. "I'm just as suspicious as you are. Fireworks don't make much sense to me, either. The little news blackout doesn't make it easier to swallow. I believe what my buddy tells me, but for all I know, he's being fed a line of horseshit."

"I don't think we'll be sleeping for a while," Elizabeth said. "Hopefully someone says something soon."

Buck turned to leave.

"I'll keep my ear to the ground. Just remember, don't believe everything you see and hear."

4

All was revealed the next day on the morning edition of the news. As Buck had said, the cause of the massive explosions *was* fireworks. Channel 4 News panned around the empty lot, rotted lumber sticking out from mounds of black and yellow snow. The camera settled on the twisted remains of a green ash can. Brightly colored police tape kept the news crews from trampling the scene.

"Elizabeth, look," Daniel said through a mouthful of bagel. He pointed at the small TV screen tucked away in a corner of the kitchen counter.

"Shouldn't there be more than one?" Elizabeth asked.

He shrugged his shoulders.

"Maybe the others are totally destroyed or the police took them for evidence. They said it could be heard all the way up to Connecticut and as far east as Long Island."

The exceedingly cold reporter with red, cracked lips talked about the local damage to windows—both car and home—and how the 911 lines were jammed with calls. For residents in the area, it sounded and felt like a main gas line explosion or an earthquake.

Elizabeth poured a cup of coffee in her BEST MOM EVER mug. Miguel and Gabby had made it for her last Mother's

Day from a kit Daniel bought them in the supermarket. "I hope they catch the *cabrón* who did it. That scared the hell out of the kids. Miguel talked my ear off until three. I heard you snoring down the hall the entire time."

She gave him a playful slap on the back of his head.

"I think that ice cream made me crash."

Elizabeth wagged a finger at him. "That's what happens to middle-aged men. Your kids, however, got a nice sugar high."

When the kids came down for breakfast, Daniel explained what had happened and let them watch one of the reports. By the time they got to the mall later that morning, all was forgotten.

For Miguel and Gabby, it would simply be remembered as the night they had ice cream sundaes before bed.

5

Rey's favorite season was the spring, and not for the usual reasons such as the renewal of life, warmer weather, or it being a prelude to summer, which meant two months without school.

Spring was when he tagged along with his friend Nick after school to the paddocks at Yonkers Raceway. Nick's father was a horse trainer. He'd worked at Yonkers, Monticello, and Freehold since he was around Rey's age. When spring came, he allowed the boys to help him out every now and then. Stalls needed to be shoveled, new hay thrown down, horses had to be fed and groomed.

With senior year coming to a merciful end—Rey was not one thinking high school was the best years of his life—he and Nick were on an early dismissal schedule. That gave them more time to spend at the track. In just a couple of weeks, school would be over and he could come here every day. There was even the promise of being paid this summer. That money would come in handy to buy books when he started at Fordham University in the fall.

Today, Nick's father was working with three horses: Bam-Bam Hanover, Shining Shamrock, and Run Scotty Run.

The names sounded absurd, but they came out like music when the announcer called the races.

The paddocks were bustling. Almost every stall was full. Men and horses were in constant motion. The smell of sweet hay did little to mask the heavy, clinging odors of sweat and road apples. Rey's mother hated when he went to the track. She said he made the whole house smell like a barn. His father, on the other hand, was glad to see he'd taken such an interest. "Boys can get into far worse things at his age," he'd tell his mother.

He was right. Most seventeen-year-olds in Rey's class spent their time smoking weed, Snapchatting ridiculous stunts or naked-ass shots, or having "Skype sex" when they weren't actually messing around with any girl who would give them the time of day. Three girls in his class had gotten pregnant this year. Two dropped out. One said she didn't give a shit what people thought and was proud to have her baby, even though the father, a sophomore, refused to even acknowledge it was his.

Here he was, feeding Bam-Bam some carrots, feeling the sun warm the back of his neck. A little stink was a fair trade-off.

"Slow down, Bam-Bam. You'll give yourself a stomachache."

The black-maned, chestnut stallion snorted, blowing Rey's hair from his forehead.

"Gee, thanks. Your breath could melt wallpaper."

Nick's father walked by, leading Run Scotty Run by his bridle. "Got another one for you and Nick in a few minutes."

Rey waved a hand to swat away a cyclone of flies. "Got it."

He patted Bam-Bam's nose and double-checked to make sure he had enough fresh water.

Now he just had to find Nick. Odds were, he'd be hovering around the race office, hoping to catch a glimpse of

Dakota, the hot secretary who had all the guys in heat. Rey laughed. As if Nick even had a shot.

The piercing screech of tires spinning on asphalt brought Bam-Bam and most of the other horses into hysterics. Trotters were notoriously high-strung. An unexpected loud noise like that easily set them on edge.

Someone yelled, "Hey, who the hell did that?"

In seconds, it was pandemonium.

Bam-Bam reared on his hind legs with a high-pitched whinny.

"It's okay. It's okay," Rey said to the horse, keeping his voice as calm as possible.

All he could see was the white of Bam-Bam's eyes.

Rey tripped backward as he desperately attempted to move out from under the massive, frightened animal.

6

The bus ride home from School 7 always felt like it took hours to Gabby. Going to school was the opposite. She'd barely have time to tell her friend Cynthia about last night's episode of *American Idol* before the dreaded, big brick building loomed outside the bus doors.

Today was worse than ever. Her mother had promised to take her out to look for a dress for this Friday's daddy-daughter dance. She couldn't wait to try on dresses and shoes, and if she was lucky, she could convince her mom she needed the new Selena Gomez perfume. Cynthia got a bottle for Christmas, and Gabby had been green with envy ever since.

The bus was its usual riotous self. Ed, the bus driver, was deaf in one ear and didn't mind the noise. He was one of the few cool grown-ups.

"Do you know what color you want?" Cynthia asked.

A stray ball of paper bounced off the top of Gabby's hair, landing on Timmy Doyle behind her. He whizzed it over her head, just missing Jerry Adams.

"Definitely purple," Gabby replied, ignoring the paper war. "I saw this awesome dress in a Forever 21 catalog."

Cynthia raised an eyebrow. "They only sell clothes for

teens and adults, Gabby. They won't have dresses in your size at Forever 21."

That's exactly what her mother had said to her. Gabby remained confident. She might be ten, but she was tall for her age.

"You'll see," she said to her friend.

The bus crashed into a pothole and the girls bounced in their seats. All of the kids gave a cheer. Some shouted for Ed to do it again. The old bus groaned in reply.

Gabby checked her watch. Still at least twenty minutes until her stop.

Come on, come on. Why couldn't this be a day when a lot of kids were sick and there were less stops?

Her little brother, Miguel, came up the aisle, swaying from side to side in rhythm with the bus's overworked suspension. He looked pale and his eyes were wide.

"What's wrong?" Gabby asked him.

Up close, she could hear him wheeze.

"Where's your inhaler?"

He shook his head. Escalating fear shone in his eyes.

"Hold on. Sit down." Gabby got up and guided him to her seat. Taking a knee, she fumbled with her backpack. Miguel was always losing things, even the one that was so important it meant life or death. When Gabby was eight, like him, she hadn't been so forgetful. Now at age ten, she often had to play the role of mommy when they were at school.

She found the blue plastic inhaler in her backpack's side pocket. Giving it a quick shake, she placed it in his mouth and gave him two quick puffs. His breathing regulated almost immediately. The color slowly returned to his normally walnut cheeks.

"You feel better?"

Cynthia had placed a protective arm over his shoulders. Miguel smiled, taking a deep breath.

"Lots," he said.

"Sit between us until we get home. I'll grab your bag on the way out," Gabby said.

The bus came to a jerky stop. The doors opened so three kids in Miguel's grade could get out. Two mothers and one dad stood on the curb waiting, receiving hugs, and waving to Ed.

Miguel nudged Gabby's side. "Look. There's a big fire."

"Where?" Cynthia asked.

He pointed at the window opposite them. A big, black, roiling cloud billowed high into the sky. It was hard to tell how far away it was. Other kids saw the smoke, as well, quieting down long enough for the distant blare of fire engines to be heard.

"I wonder if it's coming from the apartment buildings on Bronx River Road," Gabby said.

"I bet it's a car fire on the parkway," Miguel said. "I wish we could drive there and see."

Like most boys his age, Miguel wanted to be a fireman. He was hooked the day the local fire department showed up at school last year and let him ride in the fire truck. He'd gotten himself so excited that day, he'd had to use his inhaler twice.

The ebony plumes of smoke looked sinister, like an evil, living villain straight out of a Disney cartoon.

Gabby had no desire to see what was causing such a terrifying thing to blot out the blue, cloudless sky.

7

Today was not Max's day. And things didn't look like they were going to get any better.

"Give me your iPod," his mother said, her arm thrust out, palm flat.

"But it wasn't my fault," he pleaded, knowing it was a losing cause.

"I don't care whose fault it was. This is the second time this semester I've had to get you from the principal's office for fighting. Did you not listen to a word your father and I told you the last time?" He could hear her grinding her teeth. "Well, did you?"

He flinched when she shouted.

"I did," he mumbled into his chest.

"What?"

Max looked up, but couldn't go so far as to meet his mother's eyes. "I did."

He pulled his iPod out of his pocket and handed it over. She snatched it away, jamming it into her pocketbook.

"You can forget seeing that for the next month."

A protest died in his throat, withering under her stare.

"And that's just the start of your punishment. When your

father gets home, we'll talk about what else will be in store for you. When we're through, you'll think twice before fighting again, I promise you."

Max stared at the black-and-white tiled floor. He felt hollow inside. The knuckles on his right hand hurt from punching Chris Nichols in the forehead—he was aiming for the jackwad's nose—but he knew better than to ask for ice right now. His mother had to talk herself down first.

"Do you understand me?"

"Yes."

"I don't know what's gotten into you this year. You think because you filled out a little you have the right to push other kids around?"

"Chris is a jerk. He's picked on everyone in the ninth grade, even the girls. Someone had to stand up to him."

His mother put her hands on her hips. "Are you going to tell me you were defending a girl?"

If he said yes, he knew she'd go easier on him. What actually happened was far, far worse, and not something he could readily tell his mom. It would be embarrassing. It might even hurt her.

No. He wasn't going to lie. But he wasn't going to tell her everything, either.

Before he could answer, a loud, piercing wail sounded from outside. It was like a thousand penny rockets going off at once. Even his mother stopped, her mouth half-open.

They both ran to the kitchen window, looking up.

"I don't see anything," his mother said.

"Me, either. Maybe it's coming from another direction."

The back door slammed behind them as they stepped into the yard, turning in slow circles, scanning the sky.

The screeching grew louder, coming closer with each passing second.

8

Daniel Padilla was putting the finishing touches on a new web design project for a national car rental company when the lights in the four-man office flickered.

"Don't you die on me," he pleaded with his computer. All he needed was another two seconds to save his work.

His partner, Tim Giordano, popped his head over the partition. "I think that's a sign," he said.

"Oh yeah, of what?"

Tim ran his fingers through his unruly hair. They'd met working at a major design company in the city in the late nineties. Eight years ago, they broke free from working for The Man and started their own company. A handful of clients followed, and word of mouth spread.

"When the lights start to go out, it's time to go home. Especially on a nice day like today," Tim said.

The beauty of being your own boss was that they could pick up and leave any time they wanted. Two junior designers, Vinod and Uday, worked part-time and weren't in the office today. The biggest project they had was now done. Tim had a point. After all, they'd gone out on their own so they could strike a better work-life balance.

Daniel pocketed the thumb drive and made a second

backup. This one would go in the small fireproof safe tucked under his desk.

"I think you're right. I have to take Miguel to Little League practice in an hour anyway," Daniel said.

Tim let out a long groan. "Lucky me, I just remembered that Stacey wants me to do the food shopping." He pulled a list out of his shirt pocket. "Maybe I'll stay here a little bit longer."

Daniel laughed. "You can't hide here forever. Might as well get it over with."

"Yeah, but it's only three thirty. Every blue hair with a walker will be clogging the aisles. It's like stepping into a zombie flick."

He patted Tim on the shoulder. "Hey, don't knock them. You'll be one of those doddering old folks sooner than you think. Some young guy will be stuck behind you, fuming that you can't decide which brand of prune juice to buy."

"Laugh it up now, Dan. You're only two years behind me."

Daniel hit the lights and was locking the door when a deep, drawn-out rumble of thunder reverberated through the building.

"Sun storm?" Tim said.

The key was in the lock, but Daniel had yet to give it the final turn. He stood still as a stone, listening.

It started again, sounding closer. The doorknob vibrated in his hand.

"I don't think that's thunder," Dan whispered.

Turning the key, he bolted down the hall, stopping at the big window overlooking the parking lot.

Towers of black smoke loomed in the horizon.

Tim bumped into him, breathless. "What the fuck?"

They saw a flash of white arc across the sky. It exploded in a brilliant blaze of sparks and flame over what appeared to be the center of Yonkers. Daniel's eyes slammed shut, the image of the fireball burned onto his retinas.

He and Tim both turned away from the window, shielding their faces.

The building went eerily quiet. The lights shut off, as well as the air-circulation system.

"Jesus Christ, we're under attack," Tim said, rubbing his eyes.

Grabbing his shirt, Daniel led him to the stairs. "Come on, we have to get home!"

Running down the emergency stairwell, Dan fumbled for his cell phone.

I have to call Elizabeth. Please, God, let the kids be home. I'll tell her to take them all to the basement and stay calm. I'll be there in five minutes.

The phone was dead. It had been sitting in its charger all day.

Tim hit the steel door to the parking lot. A few people were standing around, looking to the sky.

"Is your phone working, Tim?"

Tim looked at his smartphone. "No. How the hell can that be?"

"I'll call you from my landline phone when I get home, make sure you and the family are okay."

They ran to their cars, Daniel clipping a portly man in a disheveled suit who was mesmerized by the sky's horrid tableau.

"I don't have a landline phone anymore, Dan. I'll plug my phone in when I get home. Call me on that."

"Be safe!" Dan shouted, pressing the entry button for his car. The car didn't chirp back and his door didn't unlock. The keys felt like lead weights in his fingers. He managed to slip the correct one into the door lock. It was the first time he'd ever used the key to get into his car.

He jumped behind the wheel, praying to God his family was safe and to guide him home to them.

9

Rey rolled out from under a terrified Bam-Bam a second before the horse brought its powerful legs down on the very spot where he'd fallen. He scrambled to his feet, running a safe distance from the riled horse.

The paddocks had erupted into a melee of screaming horses and shouting men. Rey was terrified; they were surrounded by one-thousand-pound animals that could easily crush a man.

Something crashed to the ground on the other side of the paddocks with a dull *thud*. Rey could feel it in his chest more than he could hear it. The ground shook, and he almost lost his footing again.

Where was Nick?

He knew he should probably help the trainers settle the horses down, but he was rooted to the spot.

The secretaries poured out of the race office, staring wide-eyed at the chaotic scene.

Someone shouted at them, "Get back inside!"

Like Rey, the secretaries couldn't move.

A cloud of thick, white smoke wafted over the paddocks. The breeze carried its scent to Rey. It smelled sweet, with an underlying scent of something sharp and metallic, like an overheated blow-dryer.

"Are we on fire?" he heard one of the secretaries say.

"It looks like it. Come on, get your purse, and let's get out of here," another one replied, her voice high and trembling. Rey looked. There was no sign of Dakota. Was she still in the office?

A man shrieked, "Fire! Fire!"

Horses broke free from their stalls, splintering wooden barricades like they were made of toothpicks. They ran full tilt in every direction, nipping at anyone in their path. Men dove for cover. Rey watched in horror as a horse sideswiped Old Joe, a semi-retired trainer who liked to give Ray and Nick tips about who would win a couple of that night's races. Of course, they were too young to bet, but Rey always checked the next day's racing form and Old Joe would be right most of the time.

The old trainer went down, skidding on his back into a bale of hay. The horse wasn't done with him. It turned back, reared on its hind legs, and came down full-force on Old Joe's chest.

Rey shouted, "Nooooooo!"

A fountain of blood geysered from Old Joe's mouth. The horse dipped its long head, opened its mouth wide, and bit off his face. With one quick jerk of its neck, Old Joe's crimson skull was revealed.

Rey wanted to throw up. Men streamed past him. Even Nick's father headed for the parking lot, not bothering to give him a second look. Someone who looked like Nick was right behind him.

"Nick!" Rey shouted. His friend didn't even glance back.

If he stayed here much longer, it would just be him and the horses. Another one kicked a man in the small of his back, folding him in half.

He looked into the open race office door. What if Dakota was still in there? He hadn't seen her come out yet.

Breaking his paralysis, he sprinted to the office. A pair of black horses taller than any man spotted his sudden movement and galloped for him like twin heat-seeking missiles.

10

Gabby knew something was wrong when she saw her mother and Max waiting for them at the bus stop. Their house was only two short blocks from the stop. Gabby had been allowed to walk home with Miguel since last year.

In fact, all of the parents were there, looking very worried.

After they'd spotted the boiling clouds of smoke, all playing and talking on the bus had stopped. When they heard the first explosion overhead, the littler kids started crying. Everyone, even the older kids, just wanted to be home.

Ed drove faster than usual and the bumps weren't funny at all.

"Mommy!" Miguel cried, jumping into her waiting arms.

Max took Gabby's backpack and hefted it onto his shoulder. "Come on, we have to get back home," he said. He sounded calm, but something in his tone said he was not to be questioned. Her mother was already turning toward the house with Miguel pulled to her chest.

"Mom, what's going on?" Gabby asked as they jogged down the block. People were out staring at the sky, clogging the streets. Sirens pealed in every direction.

"I don't know, honey. We have to get home and wait for your brother and father. We'll be safe at home."

Max grabbed her hand. His palm was cold and sweaty.

Something shrieked high in the sky. There was a tremendous *boom*, and for a moment, it was as if there were two suns burning down on them.

Gabby clapped her hands to her ears. Everyone stopped.

"Was that a bomb?" Max asked.

"Let's keep going," her mother replied.

They jumped at the sound of cars crashing at the intersection behind them. Gabby turned around. All of the cars were rolling to a stop. It was like the drivers no longer had control. Intersecting lines of cars piled up at the light, which had gone dark.

Cynthia!

She hoped the school bus was all right. Cynthia's stop was only five blocks away.

Gabby was afraid. She could see that Max and her mother were just as scared, and that made it even worse.

They ran.

Their two-story house with the gray shingles and white trim was just half a block away. They had to zigzag around everyone like football players. The whole neighborhood was out, some talking excitedly, most in silent awe.

Somebody was attacking Yonkers. Maybe they were bombing all of New York. Maybe even the whole country.

A surge of tears sprang to Gabby's eyes, streaking across her cheeks as she ran. She looked over at Miguel. He was crying, too, burying his face in their mother's shoulder.

Charging into the house, her mother shouted, "Rey! Daniel! Are you here?"

Miguel refused to be put down.

"Stand in the doorway," her mother said.

"Why?" Max asked.

"Just stay there for now, please. Where's my cell phone?"

Miguel pointed with a tiny finger at the living room table.

She snatched it up, then whispered a long string of curses in Spanish.

"Max, let me have your phone."

He took it from his back pocket. She fumbled with the screen and looked ready to throw it on the ground.

"It's dead, too," she said, rubbing Miguel's back. She gently handed him over to Max. Miguel fussed until Gabby began stroking his hair.

She watched her mother dash to the kitchen and try the old-time phone on the wall. She dialed, waited a moment, hung up, and dialed again. Taking a moment to compose herself, she gingerly placed the phone back on the cradle.

"Is it over yet?" Gabby asked.

Since they'd been inside, there hadn't been any more explosions. Even the sirens had gone silent.

Her mother took a long, deep breath. She suddenly looked so tired. She motioned for her to come closer, pulling her to her side and kissing the top of her head.

"I don't know, baby. I just don't know."

11

Daniel and Tim popped out of their cars at the same time.

"Damn thing won't start," Tim said, casting a wary glance at the sky. There were just a few glittering remains of whatever had detonated over the city. Dark clouds spilled across the sky, a blossoming tide of oily smoke reaching for the sun.

"Same here," Daniel said, punching the roof. He looked at Kimball Avenue and saw at least a dozen stalled cars, their doors opened and people milling about the road.

His heart was racing. *I have to get home. I have to get home!*

It was a little over a mile to his house on the Yonkers-Bronx border. Tim lived at the midway point. They'd often joked about how lazy they'd become, driving to an office they could walk to in no time. It looked like their lazy days had come to an abrupt halt.

"We're gonna have to hoof it," Tim said, tossing his briefcase in the trunk.

Daniel slipped the strap of his briefcase over his chest and shoulder. He started running. "Come on!"

Their office was in a converted three-floor apartment building opposite the outdoor Cross County Shopping

Center. Daniel would have to practically run the length of Kimball Avenue to get to his house. It'd been a long time since he'd run for anything. He hoped his legs and lungs would hold out, because his heart and brain were going to push them as far as they could go.

He and Tim ran abreast of one another, separating every ten feet or so to avoid crashing into one of the many people who were outside wondering what was going on. Thankfully, there were no more explosions, but the growing plumes of smoke did little to allay his fears.

"I never thought I'd . . . live to see this happen again," Tim said, struggling to keep his breath.

"But why here?" Daniel said. "Why target Yonkers?"

Neither needed to say the word *terrorists*. No matter how complacent New Yorkers seemed after 9-11, the very real possibility of experiencing another terror attack was always at the back of their minds. Any intelligent person knew there was no way to prevent every asshole with a political or religious agenda from blowing shit up. To Daniel, it always seemed a matter of where and when.

The where was never, in his mind, Yonkers. And the when, that was always a mystery, one that he hoped would never come to light.

"Maybe we're . . . just . . . collateral damage," Tim replied. The tip of his shoe caught in a crack in the sidewalk. He stumbled a few feet, arms pinwheeling, but managed to keep his feet. "The city is only a few miles away. Those motherfuckers."

Daniel decided it was better to save his breath than get into a verbal rage.

They came to an intersection with a dead stoplight. Two cars had crashed head-on into one another. The drivers were too busy yelling at one another to notice that their world had just been turned upside down.

The absence of the everyday noise of traffic and planes

overhead was unsettling. It was as if the explosions had devoured everything capable of sound, except people like the ones in the intersection screaming about who was at fault and demanding insurance cards.

They came to the corner of Ranier Place and Kimball and stopped. Tim put his hands on Daniel's shoulders. Both were panting, sweat ringing their collars and underarms.

"Look, Dan, get home safe. Try to call me if you can."

"Jesus, Tim, what the hell is happening?"

"All we can hope for is that it's over. Get your family and hunker down in the basement. You know what to do."

"Right."

As Daniel turned to go, Tim called out, "Hey, check this out."

Daniel watched as Tim jumped a row of low hedges. He ran back to the sidewalk carrying a bicycle. "Use this," he said. "I can tell you're gassed. It'll get you home quicker."

"I can't take a kid's bike."

"You can. Bring it back when everything settles down. Trust me, whoever owns this isn't going to be using it."

Wrestling with his conscience, Daniel thought about Elizabeth and the kids and how terrified they must be at this moment. He took the bike from Tim.

"Thanks. I'll see you . . . soon."

Tim sprinted down his street the moment Daniel put his feet on the pedals.

12

Unlike everyone else, Buck Clarke was not outside sky gazing, waiting for the next explosion. He'd been home, just like every day since his retirement from IBM two years ago, working in his wood shop, when everything went to hell.

His live-in girlfriend, Alexiana DeCarlo, twenty years his junior and the best woman he'd ever come across, shouted down to him from the kitchen.

"Buck! We're being attacked! Buck!"

He dropped the carved duck he was making as a weather vane for the yard and ran up the stairs.

Several concussions in the distance made the house vibrate. Pushing the blinds aside, he looked out the front bay window. The top of a sizable smoke cloud bubbled up by the Yonkers–Mount Vernon border.

He muttered, "Holy shit."

Alexiana grabbed his arm. "We have to get downstairs now, Buck." She had straightened her long blond hair and was wearing a tight tee and short-shorts that hugged her sumptuous curves in anticipation of a little afternoon delight. It wasn't going to happen now.

"Wait. What are they saying on the TV and radio?"

She nervously fiddled with the remote control, dropping it twice onto the couch. The flat screen blipped to life, showing a woman potting plants in her DYI Zen garden. Alexiana changed the channel to the network news.

Every station was in commercial. It was half past the hour.

"Goddamn advertising," Buck grumbled. "The fucking place is coming down around our heads, and they have to make sure they give Dunkin' Donuts their airtime." He stormed out of the living room and found the battery-operated radio he kept on his dresser. Alexiana followed him into the bedroom. She was shivering. Buck placed a protective arm around her.

"I'm scared," she said. Her eyes were wet with fresh tears.

"I know, honey, I know. Right now, everyone is."

He had more success with the radio.

"There have been reports of several large detonations in lower Westchester County and possibly New York City. As of this time, we're not sure of the nature of the explosions. We . . ."

Buck and Alexiana held their breath.

"Come on, *we what?*" Buck shouted.

The DJ cleared his throat. "We just got word that authorities have confirmed the launch of at least half a dozen surface-to-air missiles. They're attempting to locate the source of the missiles. It's important that—"

There was a high screech over the house, followed by a tremendous *crack*. Alexiana jumped with a terrified yelp. The radio immediately died in Buck's hands. He shook it, turned the knob to look for more stations, but came up empty. There wasn't even static.

Tossing the radio on their bed, he went back to the living room. The TV was in the same condition as the radio. Buck flicked the light switch on the wall. Zip. Everything electronic was fried.

He cupped Alexiana's face in his calloused hands. "Alex, I need you to go downstairs now."

"You're coming with me," she pleaded. The tips of her hair were wet with her tears as she sluiced them off her face with the edge of her hand.

"I will. I need to do something first. You remember the code, right?"

She nodded. Her hands were trembling so badly, he wondered if she'd be able to operate the control panel.

He kissed her softly on the lips, tasting the salt of her tears. "I'll be right back. You just sit tight."

Because her legs were so shaky, he walked her down the stairs.

"I love you," she said, clinging to his shirt.

Buck grabbed his cowboy hat from the peg by his workbench, swatting the bits of sawdust from the brim. "I love you, too. Just remember the code, and I'll be back in a few minutes."

Buck jogged up the stairs, wishing he'd cut down on all that red meat. He was winded by the time he stepped out of the back door.

13

Daniel couldn't believe what he was seeing. The big intersection at Yonkers and Kimball Avenues was completely clogged with stalled cars and people. Rolling down the incline, he frantically searched for a gap that would fit him and the bicycle.

Unlike the people he'd already passed who were milling about in stunned silence, the road ahead was chaos. Men, women, and children were streaming out of cars and buses, as well as the bank, diner, Walgreens, and all of the dozen shops in the immediate area. They were in a blind panic. The rush of frantic voices chilled Daniel's blood.

He pulled on the hand brakes, slowing down as much as he could without stopping. The only way to his house was through the throng.

Why are they all gathering in the middle of the road? Daniel thought. They were like a school of frightened fish, clumping together in an undulating mass. Except schools of fish acted like one mind, instinctually driven to swim *from* danger. There was no confusion on their part. Sense danger—swim in the opposite direction!

Maybe man had become too complex to function as simply and elegantly as fish.

Dan spotted an opening between a garbage truck and an SUV. If he carefully wound through the shifting tide of humanity, he could shoot through it to the other side. His house was only six blocks from that point.

He coasted down Kimball Avenue, bracing himself as he entered the throng. He made a quick right turn, narrowly avoiding a stroller with a crying baby, then clipped his shoulder into a burly man's back. Veering left, back on course to the garbage truck, he had to come to a full stop. A woman no younger than eighty fell flat on her back. Her watched her mouth open, crying out, but he couldn't hear her through the cacophony.

"Are you all right?" he shouted.

Someone pushed him sideways. He toppled over the bike, his shoulder taking the brunt of the fall. Daniel saw stars as lightning bolts of pain radiated from his shoulder to his neck and back. He turned over in time to watch a man in a suit pedal away with the bike.

Wincing as he rolled to his other side, he came face-to-face with the old woman. She struggled to get up. A large, sneakered foot just missed mashing her hand.

"Let me help you," he said, getting to his knees and placing a hand under each of her armpits. As he stood, she came with him. She felt lighter than a bag of cat litter.

"Thank you so much. God bless you," she said. She was very unsteady on her feet, so Daniel kept an arm around her, guiding them through the mob.

He spotted the chipped blue garbage truck and pushed forward. The woman was saying something to him, but he couldn't hear a word. All he could focus on was getting them both out of this madness.

"We're almost there," he said.

Her paper-thin hand held tightly onto his own. Other people had spotted the gap and were squeezing through one at a time. The other side of the intersection was clear sailing all the way to where Kimball Avenue went on the incline, leading to the reservoir.

They had just stepped between the garbage truck and the SUV, an expensive Escalade that was now as useful as a doorstop, when Daniel felt a crush of people at his back.

"Hold on! Hold on! Just let us get through!" he shouted to no one and everyone.

The old woman tottered, and he lost his grip on her. Her hip smashed into the lip of the loading bay of the garbage truck. Daniel went to grab her, but he was pushed through the narrow opening.

"Stop! You're hurting her!"

The old woman's mouth opened and closed as the hysterical mob forced the air from her lungs. Daniel tried to fight the tide. A woman elbowed him in the chin, a toddler tucked under her arm like a football.

"What the hell is wrong with all of you?" He looked over his shoulder at two converging clouds in the sky—one black as night, the other white as cotton. No one knew what was in those clouds, and they didn't want to be around when they were overhead. The fear of it was driving them into a frenzy.

Two men wearing hard hats hit Daniel square in the chest as they barreled past. He went down again. Dozens of legs scampered over him. He tucked his head under his raised arms. He was lucky. No one stepped on him during their escape.

When the rush subsided, he rolled back onto his feet. Most of the crowd had left. He saw them sprinting in every direction.

His heart lodged in his throat when he looked to the garbage truck. The top half of the old woman was bent over into the truck's loading bay at an impossible angle. The crush of people must have snapped her back in two. He ran over to check on her, feeling for a pulse at her neck. Her eyes were open, wide in shock and the final agony of death.

He lifted her out of the truck and carried her over to a patch of grass by the firehouse. The big doors were open, but there were no trucks inside. They must have hit the road the moment the first explosion hit.

No one's final resting place should be in the putrid belly of a garbage truck. Daniel made the sign of the cross over her and said a quick, silent prayer.

I'll call the police when I get home.

It was the right thing to do, but he had a sinking feeling the old standards of right and wrong had been upended for the foreseeable future.

14

Elizabeth stared at the front door, surrounded by Gabriela, Max, and Miguel. She clutched the rosary her grandmother had given her for her confirmation to her chest.

Please, Rey, please, Daniel, come home.

As much as she wanted to, she couldn't cry. Miguel and Gabby sobbed into her sides. Max tried to comfort his little brother, but she could see the fear in his own eyes, hear it in the way his voice shook.

Max, her little warrior whose body was outpacing his maturity. She ran a hand through his thick hair, hoping he couldn't feel the tremors that had overtaken her.

She let out a startled gasp when there was a knock at the back door.

"You in there, Liz? Dan?"

It was Buck. She extracted herself from Gabby and Miguel's grasp. "Just stay here," she said. Keeping to the archway between the dining room and kitchen seemed like the safest place to be, should there be another explosion. It took her three attempts to pull back the latch on the back door.

Buck stood outside the screen door, panting under his black cowboy hat.

"You okay?" he asked.

She nodded. "So far."

"The kids all home and safe?"

"I'm still waiting for Rey. And Daniel."

Buck let out a pained groan. "I was afraid of that. Look, I need you and the kids to head on over to my house. Go down the open doorway in the kitchen. At the bottom of the steps, you'll see a steel door. Knock once, pause, then three times rapidly. Alex will let you in."

"What?" She clasped her hands together to keep them from trembling.

"Look, Liz, I have a bomb shelter, a big one. Alex is already safe inside. I've made preparations for us and your family. It's the safest place to be right now."

Elizabeth took a step back. "But I can't go. Not without my son and Daniel."

Buck took off his hat and wiped his brow. "You can. You have three kids who need you right now. I'll wait here for Rey and Dan."

She noticed the butt of a gun sticking out of his pocket. He followed her gaze. "Until I know what's going on, I feel safer with it." He looked up and said, "Liz, we don't have time to debate. You have to get the kids to the shelter right now."

The screen door squeaked when she opened it. She saw the black and white clouds rumbling toward one another.

Buck said, "I don't know what the hell that is, but I can tell you it's not good. Now, get your kids and go!"

15

Rey heard a scream and instinctively pulled up, banging his thigh into the corner of a desk.

Dakota Charles stood ten feet in front of him, looking over his shoulder and pointing. Her burgundy hair, normally flawless and cascading over her shoulders like an Eden-esque waterfall, was a matted nest covering half her face, as if she had been tugging at it in a fugue of madness.

He turned in time to see a pair of angry stallions attempt to gallop full-bore into the narrow doorway of the race office. One of them was Bill's Little Dividend, a five-year-old that most times finished in the money. He couldn't make out the one on its heels.

The office shook as if it were on the center of a fault line as the horses smashed into the doorway. They were far too big to actually make it inside. Rey recoiled at the sound Bill's Little Dividend's skull made as it opened like an egg against the lintel. A splash of blood and something gray and spongy rocketed from its skull, hitting Rey in the face. He immediately gagged, dry-heaving until his stomach hurt.

Dakota kept screaming even though both horses were down, twitching in the throes of fast-approaching death.

Clutching his stomach with one hand and wiping the gore

from his face with the other, Rey said, "It's all right, Dakota. They can't hurt us. You hear me, Dakota?"

He kept repeating her name because it looked as if she were in shock. He'd read somewhere that when a person is in shock, you should say their name over and over until they come out of it. The connection with their name was like a lifeline to normalcy. It didn't appear to be working as well as the article had promised. When Rey took a step toward her, she scrabbled backward, nearly falling over a chair on casters.

Holding out his hands, he said, "Dakota, it's all right. I need you to calm down, okay?"

The next scream died a gurgling death in her throat. For the first time since he'd run into the office, her eyes fixed on him. She gave a jerky nod.

"Is there anyone else in the office?"

Aside from the central area that housed four desks, there were three offices, each with their door closed.

"N-no," Dakota stammered. "They all left me."

Rey saw dense, pale smoke, like a fog rising from the damp marshes in a horror movie, gather outside the window behind Dakota.

"We have to get out of here," he said, offering his hand.

Dakota turned, saw the smoke, and hurried to him. "Did something blow up out there?"

Rey sighed. "I don't know. Come on, I don't think it's safe to be here."

She took his hand. If something this momentous had happened just five minutes earlier, Rey would have considered himself the luckiest guy in the world. Whole elaborate fantasies would have been constructed around the simple act of feeling Dakota's hand willingly in his own.

Holding her tight, he helped her to gingerly step around the still horses. Dakota's heels slipped in a pool of warm blood and almost took them both down atop Bill's Little Dividend's sweaty haunches.

"Where's your car?" Rey asked.

"Over there," she said with an upward flick of her chin.

Rey's stomach threatened to go into spasms again.

There was no way they were going to get to Dakota's car.

The parking lot that lay between them and the exit was a nightmarish killing field. Cars were stalled in crazy angles. They had stopped in the process of fleeing the track.

The horses, driven insane by God knows what, had descended on the stranded people and cars like a surge of battle-crazed warriors. Men lay in bloodied, trampled heaps. Those who remained in their cars cowered as horses built like tanks rained blows on rooftops and windshields. The moment they had access into the cars, the horses thrust their mighty heads inside, tearing at the occupants with teeth strong enough to snap bone in two.

The traffic along Yonkers Avenue had stopped, as well. Horses chased people down the main road and side streets. Human wails and horse whinnies rang like a chorus from Hell.

"Oh my God!" Dakota squealed, turning into Rey's shoulder.

"There's a shortcut to my house," Rey said. "Are you okay to run?"

Dakota kicked off her shoes and nodded.

They went back toward the paddocks, where the smoke was creeping. Skirting it as much as they could, they climbed over a chest-high wall and ran across the quarter-mile track. The air smelled strange.

"We have to climb that fence ahead of us," Rey told Dakota, who kept an even pace with him. It was clear she was a runner. "That'll take us to the reservoir. We'll run along it for a little bit and come to another fence. My house is a few blocks past that."

Before they came to the reservoir fence, a peninsula of alabaster smoke overtook them. Rey's lungs felt as if they would seize up, but he kept running, faster now to get out from under the noxious cloud. Dakota made the fence first, clambering up it like a spider.

16

The last few blocks were a blur to Daniel. The shock of seeing a stampeding mob kill the old woman brought a cold numbness to his brain as well as his extremities. He ran up the steepest part of Kimball Avenue with ease. If he was tired or winded, his mind was oblivious.

It had only taken ten minutes for the world to come unglued, for people to degenerate to frightened animals.

Where were the police? Was there no one in charge? And what about the air-raid sirens? They'd been reduced to testing them once a year—it used to be monthly when he was a kid growing up in the Bronx around the corner from one of them. Did no one see this coming?

Cresting Kimball Avenue, he turned down Churchill, pumping his legs even faster knowing he was so close to home. He ignored the people around him, some of them running, as well, though in different directions.

Shadows stretched out before him as he veered into his street. He dared to look up. The sun was slowly being obliterated by the foaming clouds left in the wake of the explosions.

When he saw his house, he gave everything he had left to his legs.

"Elizabeth!" he shouted.

The houses around his own were strangely silent. It was as if the madness that had gripped the rest of Yonkers refused to enter his block.

He turned the knob of his front door, giving silent thanks that it wasn't locked. He wasn't sure his hands could function well enough to fish for his keys and insert them in the lock.

"Elizabeth! Gabriela! Max! Rey! Miguel!"

Silence echoed back to him.

Where the hell were they? Had something happened to them? Did the kids even make it back from school? Elizabeth could be out now, searching for them down streets littered with dead school buses.

He was about to run upstairs when a voice called out from the kitchen.

"That you, Dan?"

Buck stepped into the living room. He was pale, beads of sweat dotting his upper lip.

"Where's my family?"

"They're safe over at my house. I told Liz I'd wait for you."

Dan felt an enormous pressure deflate from his chest. He had to fight back a surge of tears.

"Thank you, Buck. I don't know what I would have done . . ."

"You don't have to thank me. I have a bomb shelter beneath my house. They're all in there with Alexiana. If you want, you can join them while I wait for Rey."

Daniel's heart stopped. "Rey? He's not home yet?"

Buck shook his head.

Daniel thought hard. Was today the day when he tutored the freshmen after school? Did he still practice intramural baseball? No. *He said where he was going to be at breakfast.* Elizabeth would know.

As if he were reading his mind, Buck said, "Elizabeth told

me he was at the track helping out with the horses. It's just over the way. He should be home soon."

Daniel turned to the front door. "Buck, you have no idea what it's like out there. I . . . I saw a woman get killed because she was too old and frail to get out of people's way. The sky is turning black with smoke. Nothing works. It's like the end of the world."

Buck put a hand on his upper arm. "Just sit tight. Rey's a smart kid. He'll get here."

"And if he doesn't?"

"Then you and me both will find him."

17

Miguel had his mommy, but he wanted his daddy, too. And Rey. Max was nice, but Rey was the coolest person in his world. Rey could drive, often taking Miguel to his favorite park in the Bronx on weekends, and he was going to be in college. He was like an adult, but he still knew how to have fun. He and Gabby sat on a cot while his mother talked to Alexiana, both of them pacing.

Buck had called this place a bomb shelter. It was like an underground fort, with multiple rooms and all kinds of supplies stacked everywhere. Max was in one of those side rooms now, using—what did Alexiana call it?—a chemical toilet. It sounded dangerous to him. Why would Max want to sit on a toilet full of chemicals?

Miguel guessed the ceiling of the shelter was about six and a half feet high. His dad was six feet tall, and it looked like there would be just enough room for him to stand without hitting his head. The main room was stacked with crates of canned food and big jugs of water. There was a folding table with some chairs around it. One end of the table had plastic bags filled with plates and cups and utensils. There was even a shelf loaded with board games and decks of playing cards. He spotted a few coloring books and a box of crayons. He thought of asking Gabby to color with him, but she would probably say no. And there was no way Max would do it. Not now, at least.

A pair of bare lightbulbs in the ceiling, those curly ones that he was told never to touch, provided more than enough light to see everything. If he weren't so scared, Miguel would have loved looking in every nook and cranny of the bomb shelter.

If they were in a bomb shelter, that meant what they all heard before was bombs. Bad people were bombing them.

Why?

He knew from school and listening to Buck sometimes when they barbecued that bad people attacked good people all the time. It was usually because they wanted something they couldn't have themselves. If they couldn't have it, no one else could. Miguel felt like that sometimes when Max would get a toy for older kids that he really wanted, too. When he was feeling really brave, he hid them from Max. That way, Max couldn't play with it in front of him, which would only make his desire to have the same toy hurt that much more.

"Is Daddy coming soon?" he said. Gabby sniffled beside him.

His mother wiped his tears from his cheeks. "Soon, baby. Very soon."

She exchanged a look with Alexiana that made him think otherwise. She didn't know when Daddy and Rey would be back. They were both as scared as he was.

He looked up at the sound of a dull *thud*. The floor and walls shook briefly. His mother's hands flew to her mouth as she stifled a cry. Alexiana pulled her into a tight hug.

"Why won't the bad men stop?" he asked Gabby.

She turned away from him, sobbing.

18

A high black fence separated the track around the reservoir from the water itself. Patrol cars used the gravel track to patrol the area on a 24/7 rotation. When Rey was really little, the area around the reservoir had been open to the public. People jogged around it, had picnics in the vast grassy areas, and rode sleds down the hill when it snowed.

After the suicide skyjackings on 9-11, the reservoir had been sealed up and fortified with armed guards. Something as large and easy to access as a major water source became a potential target to be protected at any cost.

Rey remembered seeing the fences go up, new perimeters established, and the host of uniformed men and women who guarded it night and day. At the time, when he was in first grade, he said it looked like they had put the reservoir in jail.

Despite the intense security measures, Rey's curiosity compelled him to find a way in, which he did, without getting caught. He'd come through the res a handful of times, especially when he was running late helping Nick at the track and had to get his butt home for dinner. Those other times, he kept away from the gravel track, skirting the bottom of the hill and hiding behind trees when the patrols rolled past.

Still holding Dakota's hand, he looked back and saw a ton

of security forces gathering by the fence that separated the res perimeter from the racetrack. He hoped they stayed there.

"How much farther?" Dakota asked, her toned legs pumping so hard, she was starting to pull away.

"Not far. You'll see the fence by the exit soon."

The air here was cleaner, untainted by the strange fog. That was a very good thing. Rey wasn't sure he could hold back his bile if they stayed under the fog much longer.

He couldn't help noticing how Dakota's full breasts jiggled underneath her tight blouse. It was jaw-dropping. Again, another moment that would have held far greater importance if not for the fact that their world had been flipped on its ass.

Struggling to keep pace with her, lest their hold on one another break, he focused on getting home.

"You're . . . pretty fast," he said.

She didn't reply. Her mouth was pulled into a tight line. He had to be ten years younger than her and he was gasping. She was still able to breathe through her nose.

They ran. The blinding afternoon sun was turning a deathly, liver-spotted gray. He spied a massive black cloud coming from the east. They were headed right for it. His house was somewhere between them and the cloud. They had to keep going, no matter what.

Dakota shrieked and let go of his hand, swatting at the air, though still running.

A bat had swooped down and gotten its claws tangled in her hair.

"Get it off me!" she yelped, slowing down.

"Hold still."

They stopped. The bat chittered angrily, its flapping wings battering her head and the sides of her face.

What was a bat doing out in the middle of the day? The explosions must have driven it from whatever dark place it hung upside down in.

Rey jabbed a hand at the bat in an attempt to shoo it away.

The bat tried to avoid him, but was still stuck in her hair. She let out a sound that sounded like a distressed, deaf cat.

"Just . . . just cover your face with your hands," Rey ordered.

He didn't want the bat to scratch her eyes.

The more he tried to get it out, the more tangled it became, twitching and fluttering like mad.

"Just stop!" he yelled at the bat.

Without thinking, he made a fist, reared back, and punched it in its silver dollar–sized head. The bat immediately went still. Unconscious or dead, he didn't care which. He was just glad he was able to untangle it from Dakota's hair.

He placed it carefully in the grass. Dakota skittered away from it, squealing.

"Oh Jesus, I thought nothing could freak me out more than what happened back at the track," she said.

"We'd better keep going," Rey said, pointing at the black cloud. "I want to get to my house before that comes over us."

She didn't need to be told twice. They were off and running again.

He spotted the fence that faced Kimball Avenue. Almost there!

There was a sharp *crack* behind them, followed by a kicked-up clod of grass and dirt in front of them. Rey whipped his head around. One of the guards had gotten out of his truck and was shooting at them. There was absolutely no cover between them and the fence.

Another *crack*.

A bloom of wet heat broke out on his arm. He shouted in pain, skidding to his knees. Dakota turned around. He didn't have time to tell her to get down before two more shots sounded out.

19

Daniel heard the shots and ran to the window. With the absence of normal, everyday sounds, the rifle shots sounded as loud as cannons.

"You see anything?" Buck asked, coming up behind him.

"Nothing in the front, at least."

Buck sucked on his teeth. "People are going to turn on each other fast, Dan. If the cars and TVs and radios are dead, there's gonna be panic. And that's when the situation gets real bad, real fast."

Rey's chest ached.

His son was out there.

Out where the bad people were ready to take to the streets. He'd been around long enough to know how it went. Even things as simple and temporary as a blackout led to looting and beatings and far, far worse.

"I can't just stay here," Daniel said, making for the door. Buck held him back.

"When you go out there, which way are you gonna go? You have four choices. You make the wrong one, and you have no chance of running into Rey."

"Those gunshots sounded close."

Buck nodded. "They did."

Daniel feigned resignation long enough for Buck to let go of his arm. The second he was free, he bolted out the door. Buck came after him, but even on his best day would never be able to keep up.

"Please, Buck, stay here and keep waiting for Rey," Daniel said at the bottom of the stairs. "I just have to see if he's close, for my own peace of mind."

The day was morphing into an unnatural night. There was very little blue sky left. It looked like the entire city was burning. There wasn't a soul outside. Every window and door in the houses around him was locked tight.

Another shot pinged down the street. "It's coming from there," Daniel said, pointing to the blocks between his house and the reservoir.

Buck jogged down the stairs. "At least take this." He jammed a gun in his hand. It was heavy and cold. "If some asshole is already taking potshots, you'd better be prepared to defend yourself."

Daniel offered it back. "I can't. I only fired a gun once, on a range, during my honeymoon at the resort twenty years ago."

Buck stepped back. "You can. Now, go check it out and I'll keep an eye out for Rey. Come right back."

Daniel nodded and ran down the street.

20

Dakota was screaming and still on her feet, which was a good thing. Rey thought for sure she'd be lying in the grass, dead or dying. The hand he'd placed on his burning upper arm came back crimson. He couldn't see through his tattered shirt exactly where he'd been shot. Luckily, the pain wasn't so bad.

"Hurry, get up!" Dakota implored, waving her hands frantically. "We don't have much time."

Rey got to his feet and turned to face their attacker.

The security guard was still at the top of the hill, but now he was struggling with what looked like a golden retriever. The golden-coated dog had its front paws on the man's shoulders, snapping viciously at his face. During the struggle, his gun had fallen from his hand.

Rey urged Dakota toward the gate. "Go, go, go!"

He kept an eye on the struggle between man and beast. The retriever's muzzle was stained red.

"Why was he shooting at us?" Dakota said as she scaled the fence.

"I don't know. Maybe he thinks we're the ones who did it."

The why of it didn't matter to Rey. He'd been shot, but not

fatally, and a dog—a golden retriever, of all breeds—had come to their rescue. Someone wanted them to keep going.

Dakota landed hard on the other side of the fence, flopping to her hands and knees. Normally, the fence wasn't even an obstacle, but it hurt bad when Rey stretched his arm out, the skin pulling away from where the bullet had hit. Still, he made it over rather quickly and landed on his feet.

He helped her up, again inappropriately thrilling at her touch.

"My house is just down the block," he said. "Once we get there, you can call someone to let them know you're okay."

She winced when she saw his arm. "We have to get that checked out."

"My mother used to be a nurse. I'll be fine."

Maybe it was shock that gave him the bravado. His arm had gone a little numb and the bleeding wasn't as bad as he thought it would be. He thought, *Is the bullet still inside me?* He hoped not. He'd watched enough cop shows to realize it was always better when the bullet went clean through.

As they turned to run the final two blocks, he heard someone shout, "Rey!"

He was too choked up to reply. Pulling Dakota along, he ran to his father.

21

Each passing minute was an agonizing eternity for Elizabeth. Alexiana was talking to her, but she couldn't hear a word. Miguel had fallen asleep on Gabby's lap. Max sat on one of the folding chairs, staring at the door, like her, waiting.

"What?" Elizabeth said, catching the tail end of Alexiana's rambling.

"All this time, I thought Buck was crazy. You can't imagine the amount of money and planning and daily maintenance, what with the rotation of water and food, he's put into this. All I can say now is thank God for that man. I want to apologize for doubting him, you know? He was right. We were stupid to be lulled back into our safe little worlds. Something like this was always around the corner."

Elizabeth put a gentle hand on Alexiana's. She whispered, "Please, I don't want to get the children more upset than they already are."

She sensed where her neighbor's mind was going and wanted to cut her off before she started expounding on terrorists and sleeper cells and doomsday. They'd had a few conversations over the years, especially on summer nights in the yard with tiki torches around them and plenty of frozen margaritas in them, about the state of the world and how New York would always be a hard target. Over a decade without a follow-up attack was giving them a false sense of security, Buck would say.

Amazingly, he'd never let on about the bomb shelter. It was a considerable shelter, stocked to the ceiling with supplies and enough room to accommodate all of them—when everyone was finally safe inside.

His own girlfriend of fifteen years had thought he was nuts. Elizabeth guessed he didn't want them thinking that, too.

Max spoke for the first time since they'd come into the shelter. "Do you think it's stopped?"

Elizabeth was ardently praying it had. "I think so."

"Then Pop and Rey should be here soon."

He said it with an assurance that infected her, gave her hope.

"Gabby, are you all right, sweetie? Do you need anything?" Alexiana asked. Gabby shook her head, lightly stroking her brother's cheek while he slept.

"It seems very quiet now," Elizabeth said.

"This shelter has so many layers around it, it would be hard to hear a rock concert if it happened right above us."

They sat in silence.

Elizabeth said, "Maybe I should go up and wait with Buck."

Alexiana motioned for her to stay calm. "You need to be here with your children, Liz. I'd go, but other than Buck, I'm the only one who knows how to get in or out of the shelter." She checked her watch, a pretty rose-colored Fossil with little jewels around the watch face. "Trust me, Buck will be here very soon, even if it's just to report in. He has everything planned down to the last detail. If either of us isn't in the shelter but nearby, we have to check in at the top and bottom of every hour. It's almost four thirty."

Elizabeth was having a hard time with everything. A little over an hour ago, she was waiting for her children to get off the bus and planning a punishment for Max. Now God knew how many bombs had been dropped on the city, and she was waiting in an underground shelter for her husband and oldest son to make it there alive.

"What did we do to make you so angry with us?" she murmured.

"What was that?" Alexiana asked.

Elizabeth had to keep from crying when she felt the pressure of Max's hand on her back.

22

Buck let out a long, exhausted sigh when he spotted Daniel, Rey, and a pretty-yet-disheveled girl running to the house. He stepped outside to greet them under a low, black sky.

"At least something's gone right today," Buck said.

Daniel was smiling despite their dire situation.

"You should lock up your house tight, Dan. No telling how long we'll have to wait things out. And pack a bag with one change of clothes for each of you. I'll take Rey and the little lady to my house and wait for you there."

Rey was reluctant to leave his father. He shot him a look of total confusion.

"Buck has a bomb shelter under his house," Daniel explained. "Your mother and brothers and sister are there already. Go!"

Buck led them to his house while Daniel started locking the front windows. Buck was glad he'd made calculations for the Padillas and at least two unexpected guests.

"My name's Buck Clarke," he said to the girl, offering his hand. She really was a looker. He wondered how she and Rey came to be attached to one another. She held Rey's hand like it was a lifeline. Then he noticed the blood on the boy's shirt.

"I'm Dakota. Dakota Charles." She shook his hand weakly.

"You all right, Rey?"

"I think so. One of the res cops started shooting at us."

Buck shook his head. Cutting through the reservoir during a meltdown had been a bad idea. The res was filled with armed guards dreading a day like today. Their nerves were on high alert, which made for itchy trigger fingers.

"You good enough to help load some extra things and bring them downstairs?" Buck asked.

"Yeah."

Once they entered the kitchen, Buck told them to hold still while he ran to the linen closet. He grabbed a handful of fresh pillowcases. He tossed one to Rey and one to Dakota.

"Rey, I need you to go in my pantry and fill yours with anything edible you find in a can. Dakota, fill yours with the water bottles from the fridge."

They got to work without any questions. Buck opened one of the drawers and scooped his hand inside. It was filled with unopened bags of cookies and boxes of crackers. Once they were in the bag, he dropped in a jar of peanut butter.

"Almost forgot," he said, ambling into the living room. "I think we're gonna need this."

He made sure not to crush the cookies and crackers under the bottles of tequila, Wild Turkey, Johnnie Walker, and vodka. For all he knew, these might be the last drinkable bottles of alcohol he'd ever see. No sense wasting them.

By the time he was done, Daniel was back, holding a couple of bulging bags. Buck locked the back door and double-checked the front.

"You might want to help Rey out," he said. The boy was having a little trouble holding the can-laden pillowcase.

He swept his free hand toward the door leading to the cellar. "After you."

23

Buck gave a series of knocks, and there was a lot of clicking and whirring before the door opened. Elizabeth nearly knocked Rey over when she saw him.

"Thank you, God, oh, thank you," she cried, pulling her son to her by his neck.

Buck ushered them all inside. They had to go down a few steps before they were on level ground. Alexiana threw her arms around Buck. Gabby and a sleepy-eyed Miguel rushed to hug Daniel's legs.

"We were so worried, Dad," Gabby said.

Daniel kissed them all, wiping tears from Gabby's cheeks.

"It's going to be all right," he said. "Now that we're all together."

"Oh my God!" Elizabeth exclaimed. She forced Rey into a chair. "Alexiana, do you have a first aid kit?"

"We have more than one."

"What happened to you?"

"Some asshole shot him," Dakota said.

Despite everything that had happened, Miguel and Gabby stood openmouthed.

Alexiana handed Elizabeth a blue plastic box. She cracked it open, taking out the scissors and cutting Rey's blood-soaked sleeve away. Everyone looked at the angry red gash that ran vertically across his bicep.

"I always said you were lucky," Elizabeth said. "The bullet only grazed you."

She applied antiseptic to the wound. It fizzed and bubbled with white foam. Rey hissed in pain. "Jeez, Ma, that stings."

"It's supposed to. Sit still and let it work."

She asked Daniel to hold two sterile pads to the wound while she wrapped gauze around his arm. She said to Buck, "I know this sounds crazy, but is there any chance you have antibiotics?"

Buck went to an olive cabinet on the wall. "I have everything we need in here." He gave her a bottle of amoxicillin and a bottle of water from the bag Dakota had brought.

Elizabeth gave the items to Rey. He washed the horse pill down. "I'll give you two a day for the next couple of days just to be safe."

With the immediate need addressed and everyone finally together, a long, uncomfortable silence filled the underground shelter. There was so much to say, so many questions to ask, too many fears to discuss. It all formed a bottleneck in each of their throats. After the chaos of the past hour—could it have only been that long?—maybe silence was exactly what they needed to regroup.

Max was the one to mercifully break it.

"Were there any more explosions?"

Rey answered, "None that I could hear, no."

"Did you see anything blow up? Was anything on fire?" Max continued. Daniel knew his son. Max always needed to *know*. He craved facts. He was their deep thinker, and lately their fearless brawler.

Rey looked to his father, then Dakota and Buck.

"Actually . . . no. Someone at the track was screaming about a fire, but I didn't see any actual flames. Did you, Dad?"

Daniel thought about it, replaying his sprint from the office and the awful incident with the old lady. He had seen something explode in the sky, but that was it. The whole panic came about from a series of chest-shaking concussions and a lot of smoke.

"Come to think of it, no, I didn't. There's smoke every-where," he said.

"Then what happened?" Max asked.

The adults looked to one another, then focused on Buck. Their neighbor, who had obviously spent a considerable amount of time and money preparing for a day like this, should have a better idea than most.

He lifted the cowboy hat from his head and smoothed his sweat-soaked hair back.

"I have a couple of theories," he said. "But before I start thinking out loud, why don't we get the kids settled into the other room."

24

After a back-and-forth in hushed tones, Rey was permitted to remain with the adults. The humiliation of being tucked in what Buck called the bunkhouse with Max, Gabby, and Miguel would have been unbearable. He didn't want to appear any younger in front of Dakota than he already was. After what they'd been through, he also felt he deserved to be part of the conversation. Thankfully, his father relented.

When they asked him what had happened at the track, he and Dakota spent a lot of time stepping over each other's sentences. When they got to the part about the horses going wild and attacking people, going so far as to eat some of them, the adults took a collective breath.

"Even a horse scared near to death won't go feral like that," Buck said, tipping his hat back so he could rub his forehead. "That's not natural."

When Rey went into greater details about the carnage, his mother stopped him by changing the subject. It was obvious she was overloaded.

"I can't believe the size of this shelter," Elizabeth said. "I counted ten cots back there." There were five sets of bunk beds in the bunkhouse. Crates of supplies had been crammed under each bed. No space was left unused.

"It's the reason I bought the house back in '95. The main structure under the house was already here. It'd been installed in the sixties, back when the Cold War was in full swing. My ex-wife and I lived over in Fort Lee when the car bombing in the World Trade Center garage happened. We both worked in the city at the time. She was in Midtown and I was down in Chelsea. That day opened my eyes. That was followed by the bombing of the *Cole*, then U.S. embassies around the world. You could see where things were heading if you had your eyes and ears open. Too many people were making too much money at the time to give a rat's ass."

Buck reached into the pillowcase he'd brought down and pulled out a bottle of vodka. Alexiana got a few glasses out of a nearby crate. "We might as well have a drink. No one's going anywhere for a while."

"Are we safe down here?" Rey asked. Everyone had a glass but him.

"Other than some heavy-duty military bunkers, you're in the safest place you can be, kiddo," Buck said. "I expanded on the shelter, extending it into the yard. It's shielded to protect us from nuclear fallout and any other nasty crap the enemy can throw at us."

Daniel said, "So you and your wife moved to Yonkers after the garage bombing?"

"Nah. We got divorced two years later. I caught her cheating on me with some younger guy in her law firm. He was one of those whatchyacallit metrosexuals, though at the time, I just assumed he was gay. All those business trips they went on with me sitting at home without a care in the world. Goes to show you never know."

"If it wasn't for him, you'd have never met me," Alexiana said, draining her glass and pouring another. Her hands shook, the bottle's neck clinking off the rim of the glass.

He rubbed her knee. "That's right. Which is why I'm not the least bit bitter. Anyway, I came out here after the divorce to get away from the new happy couple. They'd bought a house just a block away. I had no desire to be their neighbor. When I was looking for a place, I told my Realtor I wanted one with a damn good bomb shelter. There weren't that many on the market. This was the biggest one I found, and I had room to make it even bigger. I'd just had the cap relined when you all moved in next door."

Elizabeth took a sip of vodka and winced. "How can we be sure there are any enemies? Maybe something happened to the power stations. Like a chain reaction."

Shaking his head, Buck said, "No, we were definitely attacked by some*one*, not some*thing*. Right now the questions are who did it, what did they hit us with, and why?"

Unlike the adults, Rey didn't have alcohol to help take the edge off things. It felt like every nerve in his body was humming. He inched forward in his seat, his elbows propped on his knees. "So, what do you think, Buck?"

Buck swallowed slowly. "In my opinion, the who of it all is a short list. I figure it's either the Russians, the Chinese, or some Muslim terrorist cell. Or maybe all three working together. This was big. Maybe bigger than some sleeper cell could accomplish by itself. You know, the first attempt at bringing down the Towers started right here in Yonkers. Mohammed something, can't remember his last name, owned a gas station where the auto body shop now is at the end of Yonkers Avenue. They filled up hundreds of gallons of gas to make the bomb that took out the garage. When shit is brewing right where you live, you have to be wary."

He tipped the bottle into his glass, filling it with the remaining vodka. "From what I can tell, whoever it is hit us with a Chinese buffet of bad shit. They could have blown up parts of the infrastructure with your typical homemade stuff. You wouldn't believe how big a bang you can get with the right store-bought materials. But . . . there was also a lot of surface-to-air missiles. What was in them? Could be a mix of nuclear dirty bombs, biochemical stuff that could do all sorts of short- and long-term damage to everything living. The big one that I had especially prepared for and I'm sure they set off was an EMP bomb."

Dakota cleared her throat. "What's an EMP bomb?"

"That, darlin', is the one that'll set us right back into the Stone Age."

25

Miguel had said he wanted to go back to sleep and that he was tired. Gabby knew her little brother well enough to understand that he was scared and wanted to get away from everything the only way he knew how. She had tried rocking him to sleep while the adults talked in the next room, but he insisted that Max lie down with him.

Max's mood confused her. Everyone else, even Mom and Dad, were frightened and nervous. But Max, he seemed . . . angry. Not at anyone in particular, but he was definitely very agitated.

Maybe he was upset that there was no one he could lash out at this time. She'd watched the change in her older brother over the past year. He used to be shy, kind of quiet, happier with a book than horsing around with his friends. Over the summer break, he'd had a heck of a growth spurt. When he went back to school in the fall, he was suddenly someone other kids wanted to be around—like a planet pulling moons and space debris into its orbit.

It'd been a year of sudden and stark change. Max was still trying to figure things out.

Now both Max and Miguel were asleep in one of the bottom bunks.

There was no way Gabby could sleep. She was too busy listening for more explosions, waiting for the lights to turn off.

If that happens, I'll freak out, she thought. *It'll be like getting sealed into a coffin in the ground.*

The more she thought about it, swearing she could feel the weight of the earth above her on her shoulders, the thicker the air became.

Were they getting enough air?

And where was the air coming from? Was it safe to breathe?

Her chest tightened. It felt just like that time she went on the Manta roller coaster in Sea World. It had gone so fast, her breath had been knocked out of her lungs on each loop.

She had to calm herself down. Buck was smart. He wouldn't have them all down here if he didn't know what he was doing.

It was hard to believe this had been under their feet all the time. When Buck would break out the sprinkler and let them run around his yard, a whole other house had been inches below their bare soles, waiting for a day like today.

Remembering what her religious instruction teacher, Sister Margaret, always told them to do in stressful times, she prayed. First an Our Father, then five Hail Marys. When she came to the end, she found her chest feeling a little lighter, so she said another five, mumbling the words so she could drown out what Buck was saying in the next room.

Unlike most kids, she didn't want to know.

26

Daniel was both bone-tired and wired. He was still reeling, as they all were, over what had happened. Add to that the incredible revelation that his friend and neighbor had been preparing for this, and keeping his family in his plans, was almost overwhelming.

Why the hell didn't we move to Vermont, or North Dakota, or even Canada? Daniel thought, silently punishing himself for not taking better care of his family. *You knew New York wasn't safe anymore, and you didn't have the guts to break away. You had to stay in your comfort zone. Even after Mom and Dad had passed, you were still too afraid to leave the nest.*

When Buck mentioned the possibility of an EMP bomb detonation, a score of puzzle pieces suddenly locked into place, breaking his self-flagellation.

He said, "That would explain the phones and cars. Jesus, if there were any planes in the area when they went off."

Buck looked at them all gravely. "That might account for some of the later explosions when the planes hit the ground."

Elizabeth said, "Will one of you please tell us what an EMP bomb is? Is it nuclear?"

"No," Daniel answered. "In some ways, it's worse. EMP stands for electromagnetic pulse. Just about everything we rely on today is electronic."

Buck interjected, "Shit, people even need electronic devices to read a damn book now. No one carries cash anymore. Why? Because we have credit and debit cards. This country is full of gadget geeks who think they're the smartest nerd on the block because they've integrated their entire lives with smartphones and tablets and cars that can be turned on while you're landing in a jet."

Daniel swiveled in his chair to face his wife. "There have been a lot of people in the IT community who have voiced concerns that we've become so dependent on our machines that we've left ourselves wide open for a devastating attack. But this one wouldn't come with suicide hijackers or flames or unstable nuclear devices. An EMP explosive device lets out a brief but powerful electromagnetic pulse that virtually fries everything electronic within its detonation range. People and infrastructure are left unharmed."

Alexiana let out a long sigh. "Well, at least that's good."

Buck held up a finger. "Initially, it sounds like we dodged a bullet. However, if EMP bombs are strategically placed, they effectively knock out all of our communications and banking, as well as our power grids. Right now, we could all be penniless and cut off from the rest of the world."

"What about people in hospitals and homes hooked to monitors and different machines?" Alexiana asked.

"I'm afraid there wouldn't be much hope for them," Buck said. His face had gone pale.

"If one of those went off, wouldn't your lights down here be out, too?" Rey asked.

Daniel noticed how Dakota leaned closer to him, her hand almost touching his. If they were all going to be in close quarters for an extended period of time, he'd have to keep an eye on that. Rey was a minor, after all, and Dakota was too much woman for a boy to resist.

"Like I said, I'd prepared for that. The shelter is completely shielded and grounded. I also made sure I replaced anything electronic with devices that had been hardened, which means they're impervious to an EM pulse. Even the air-filtration system I installed can't be taken out. I know quite a few people have shelters, but I'll bet you a million bucks almost none of them were set up for this. What most folks haven't realized is that the fundamentals of war have changed.

"Various countries and terrorist organizations have been targeting the Internet and massive databases in the U.S. over the past few years. I'm sure your father knows a lot about that."

Daniel nodded. The government and private companies were investing millions, possibly billions, into safeguarding against professional hackers. The hackers themselves were being trained and financially compensated by their own countries. He'd read an article about a recent attempt by an Al-Qaeda operative working out of Canada who had attempted to worm his way into the NSA's database. Luckily, he was clumsy and the Feds had been able to trace it back to him. He was facing a long stint in Guantanamo Bay for his efforts.

Buck said, "There's been a lot of chatter about leaps in EMP weaponry, especially in Russia. Nuclear war is a losing game. Mutually assured destruction makes winners of no one. This is more insidious. It rips centuries of development right out from under us. If you can't communicate, you can't organize. An unorganized people is easy to conquer, the land isn't toxic, and there will be plenty of spoils to plunder."

Daniel looked to the door leading to the bunkhouse section of the shelter. He hoped the kids weren't listening in.

There were already more than enough difficult things they would need to explain to them.

While Buck continued talking, he closed his eyes for a moment. *We're safe down here, but for how long? When we open that door, what are we going to see? How did this happen?*

"Daniel?" Elizabeth said, gently rocking his knee. "Are you all right?"

He took a deep breath that did little to calm his fears. Daniel managed to put on a weak smile. "Yeah, I'm fine. Just trying to wrap my head around everything." He kissed the tip of her nose, caressing her cheek.

"So, what do we do now?" Rey asked. Despite his wound, he looked keyed up enough to run a marathon. Daniel wondered if he should have let him have a little bit of vodka. Drinking age laws had obviously been suspended for the foreseeable future.

Buck looked at the main shelter door. "We sit tight, and we wait."

27

A lone low-wattage bulb burned in the ceiling in the bunkhouse. Buck had an old windup clock sitting on a trunk. It ticked with the passing of each second. Elizabeth lay in a bottom bunk, staring up at the metal meshwork that supported Daniel's mattress.

Across from her, Max and Miguel were in a bottom bunk, facing away from one another. Gabby was above them, mouth open slightly, knees drawn up to her stomach. Rey had a bunk bed to himself. His bandaged arm had come out from under the thin blanket and hung off the side of the bed.

All of her miracles. And then there was the miracle of this place, and the incredible kindness of their neighbor who had secretly taken it upon himself to make sure the Padilla family was safe.

Elizabeth counted the ticks of the clock between each of Buck's thunderous snores.

Six seconds.

It was a wonder anyone could sleep with the amount of noise coming from Buck's throat.

They'd all decided it was best to go to bed after Buck had spent the good part of an hour first cranking his portable radio to give it a charge, then shuffling all up and down the dial, searching for any kind of signal. The radio was hooked up to an antenna that he said went to the surface.

There had been nothing but dead air and static. It was as if the world above them had simply blinked out of existence. There wasn't much to say after that, so they each picked their bunks and closed their eyes. Tomorrow had to be a better day.

The bed above her shifted, springs squeaking. Elizabeth stretched her leg up, softly pushing her foot against the mattress.

"Daniel, you awake?" she whispered.

She heard him roll to the edge of the bed. His head popped over the side. He looked at her upside down.

"I can't shut my brain down," he whispered back. "I could have used more vodka."

"I can't help thinking about camp," she said. "My parents sent me to Camp Keewanna up in Maine for two summers. I feel guilty thinking about the fun I had at camp after . . ."

He reached a hand out to her. She took it, reassured by the warmth and strength in his grip. "There's nothing to feel guilty about. Close your eyes and go to camp. It's better than the alternative. When you come to your first kiss behind the canoes, feel free to replace Harold Sanders with me."

She squeezed his hand. "I love you."

"I love you, too. Try to sleep. There's nothing we can do for now. And I don't think this place is going to be conducive to naps, not with all of us crammed in here. So get it while you can."

Stretching his neck, he kissed the back of her hand. His head and arm disappeared and he settled back into bed. She knew he was getting himself into his comfort position, resting on his right side, one hand under his pillow, the other flat against his leg, knees slightly bent. She'd watched him fall asleep like that almost every night for twenty years.

Elizabeth closed her eyes, conjuring up images of Camp

Keewanna, chasing a moment of sleep that did its best to elude her.

She wondered about Harold Sanders. She hadn't seen him since that last day of camp. Was he married with a family, like her? Where were they now? Did the same nightmare play out there, as well? Were Harold and his family as lucky as they had been?

Were they even still alive?

28

Dakota woke up in a panic. She sat straight up in bed, taking in the row of bunk beds across the room. For a moment, she couldn't remember where she was or who the people were around her.

She took a breath, and the nightmare that had jolted her awake in the first place faded into oblivion.

She was in a bomb shelter. The man who owned it was named Buck. She tried to remember his girlfriend's name but came up blank.

What time was it?

It looked the same as it had when they stumbled off to try to catch some sleep. Her eyes found the alarm clock. The hands glowed in the low light.

Almost five.

Did that mean five in the morning, or five at night?

How long would they be down here before they lost all sense of day or night? Maybe it had already happened.

Cradling her head in her hands, she suppressed the urge to cry. First, she didn't want to wake up the kids. Second, she was pretty sure if she started, it would be impossible to stop.

Carefully, she crept out of her bunk. She spotted Rey sleeping in a bunk next to the rest of his family. If it weren't for him, she would have most likely hidden in the closet in the race office. She recalled the sound the horses made when they tried to muscle into the building. Her jaw clamped down tight. She'd heard the term "paralyzed with fear," had read those words often in the suspense novels she devoured, but she'd never truly understood it until yesterday. When the bombs or whatever they were went off and everything went bat shit crazy at the track, she literally couldn't move or speak—not even when all of the other secretaries tried to pull her along with them to their cars.

Cars that wouldn't start.

She replayed what she saw in the track's parking lot. How the horses assaulted everyone in sight.

That could have been her.

Tiptoeing into the main room, she sat down at the table. Fishing for her cell phone in her pants pocket, she placed it on the table, giving it a few spins. Even if it worked and she wasn't hiding under the earth like a frightened rabbit, there wouldn't have been anyone to call.

Her parents had died driving to her college graduation. It had rained the night before, and according to the police, her father had hydroplaned over a massive puddle. He lost control and ended up in the oncoming lane right in the path of a bread delivery truck.

Mom had died instantly, but Dad clung to life for another painful two weeks.

When she buried her parents, she also buried every hope and dream she had conceived when they were alive. She'd never gone back to pick up her diploma. Her degree in economics held no fascination for her.

The insurance money and the sale of the house left her enough to drift for a while. She didn't make friends because there was no point. When she tired of a place, which didn't take long, she'd disappear and the people she'd met there would be out of her life.

In fact, she had just been thinking about picking up stakes in Yonkers and going north, maybe to Boston.

Buck had said that if an EMP bomb had been used, they were now penniless. All she had was twelve dollars in her pocket. The rest was in the bank. There had been three hundred thousand left, from her last account.

All of it, gone.

And now she was in a hole, with strangers. No one knew what actually happened. Was it safe to go out today?

She bit her lower lip to stifle the tears that started to fall.

Just appreciate the fact that you're not alone, for once. These people will take care of you.

But for how long? They didn't know her. If supplies ran low, would they ask her to leave?

Maybe it was best to go now.

29

Alexiana heard a dull *thunk* and was instantly awake.

Someone's trying to get in the shelter!

Everyone else was still asleep. She scooted out of her bed and went to shake Buck awake.

She and Buck hadn't told the Padillas about the gun safe tucked away in the back of the bunkhouse. In it were several pistols, four rifles, two shotguns, and enough ammunition to hold off a small army, which Buck had been prepared to do if need be.

The safe had a combination lock that required six numbers, each in a specific sequence. No one was getting in there who shouldn't.

When Buck wakes up, I'll go to the safe.

Her boyfriend was sleeping on his side with his back to her. His snoring was at a lull.

Wait, Buck has his .38 under the pillow. No need to break out the rest.

Her heart banged against her chest walls. She was jumpy as hell, but she had a damn good reason for it.

Just as she placed her hand on Buck's shoulder, she saw Dakota at the door, trying to get out.

She pulled her hand back and sighed, expelling a good dose of her fuel-injected nervous energy.

Quietly shuffling out of the bunkhouse, she stopped short of the door and said, "It's as difficult to get out as it is to get in."

Dakota whipped her head around. Her eyes were red and swollen, a pool of tears barely contained within her lower lids.

"Can you help me, then?" Dakota said.

Alexiana shook her head.

"Why not?"

"Because I don't know what's on the other side. For all we know, opening that door will let in toxic gas or nuclear fallout. I'm not gonna take that chance."

Eyeing the keypad on the wall, Dakota said, "You don't even know me. There's no reason to keep me here."

Alexiana unfolded one of the chairs and sat down, crossing one leg over the other. "I just gave you a very good reason to keep you here. And here's another one. You're part of us now. You're here for a purpose, even if you don't know what it is at the moment."

The girl slumped against the door. "I'm here because of dumb luck. If Rey hadn't found me in the race office, I'd still be there, or in my apartment, or maybe the school down the block from me. I remember reading in the paper that it was one of the city's fallout shelters."

Reaching under the table, Alexiana rummaged through a crate until she found a two-cup coffeemaker. "You want to get me some water?" she asked, pointing at the two watercoolers.

Dakota got back to her feet, dusting off the back of her slacks.

"You'll need this," Alexiana said, holding out the little glass pot.

She took it and filled it.

Alexiana flipped a switch and an orange light blazed on the coffeemaker. "Battery-powered. We have an electric one, too, but it's best to save the generator as much as we can."

In silence, they made their coffee, both drinking it black with no sugar.

Alexiana moved a straggly lock of hair from Dakota's face while she drank. Their unexpected guest smiled. By the end of their first cup, her tears had dried.

30

No one talked much the next day, not even Miguel, who was usually a nonstop chatterbox. Max played two games of Chutes and Ladders with him after a breakfast of granola bars and a powdered orange drink that didn't taste so bad once everything dissolved.

After that, Gabby agreed to color with him. They were both on the bunkhouse floor, a box full of crayons between them.

All of the adults were around the big table, talking in that special low way that meant they didn't want the kids to hear. Even the pretty girl whom Rey had brought with him was with them, sitting between Alexiana and their mother.

Max sat on a bunk opposite Rey, who was reading some kind of manual that Buck had given him.

"This is crazy," Max said.

Rey looked over the manual. "Which part?"

"All of it. I want to go outside. I can't stay down here like a friggin' mole."

"You're not going anywhere, so don't talk like a tough guy."

"But what if everything's okay now?"

"It's not. If it was, there'd be someone on the radio. That's why Buck asked me to read up on this."

Max read the cover. "How can they make a radio out of ham? That's just dumb."

Rey shook his head. "I hope you're just trying to be funny. It's like a kind of phone, or the way cops talk to the station in their cars. I'm going to see if I can talk to anyone, find out what's going on. Buck said this is a real old-fashioned way to communicate and there might not be many people left who even own a ham radio, but it's worth a try."

"Let me see that," Max said, plucking the book from his brother's hands.

Rey started to protest, then broke out in a coughing fit.

"Dude, cover your mouth."

Gabby looked up from the picture of a frog she'd been coloring. "Are you okay?"

Rey nodded, swallowing back the tail end of a cough. "I think I just swallowed funny."

Their mother said from the other room, "I hope you're not coming down with something. You just got over that cold last week."

Buck said, "Well, if he does have a cold, get ready to have it, too. In these close quarters, it's one for all and all for one in the sickness department."

Max didn't care about colds or ham radios. He tossed the book on Rey's bed.

There had to be something going on up there. It wasn't like someone had dropped a nuclear bomb on them. He was sure plenty of people had made it through in one piece.

"You wanna arm-wrestle?" he asked Rey.

"Why don't you do some push-ups or something? Burn off some of your energy."

Max got to his feet, scattering the crayons as he walked between his brother and sister.

"Hey, cut it out, jerk!" Gabby yelled.

She threw a crayon. It bounced off his back.

"Guys, keep it down," their father said.

Max went to the end of the bunkhouse and laid his palm against the steel wall. Would he be able to feel the vibration of a passing car or people walking on the lawn?

He should be grateful that he and his family were safe. But he couldn't stop the tingling in his brain, radiating throughout his entire body. It was a current of nervous energy, the likes of which he'd never felt before. Logically, he knew he was probably in the best place he could be.

Logic worked very hard to hold sway over the claustro-phobic sense that it wouldn't take long for him to lose his mind buried alive in a bunker with board games and warm orange drinks.

31

Buck said he kept track of the days on a pocket calendar.

"How many days do you think we'll be down here?" Elizabeth asked. She looked tired. They were all tired. Aside from the stress, their biorhythms had been thrown completely off, living without sight of the sun or moon.

"I don't know. I keep hoping we'll get something on the radio. The absence of any kind of signal concerns me."

So far, he'd checked off two days on his calendar. Two days without a single sound from the outside world.

Daniel's stomach grumbled. He stared at an open box of energy bars.

Alexiana pushed the box across the table toward him. "You can have one if you want."

Jesus. He couldn't even hide his hunger pangs down here. He waved her off. "I'm fine. I'll survive until dinner."

The military MREs (Meals Ready to Eat) weren't half-bad. They weren't half-good, either, but it would quiet his stomach down.

As much as he wanted the energy bar, he had to be disciplined. Sure, it looked like they had more than enough food now, but what if they were trapped in the shelter for weeks, or months? The energy bar he ate now would be one less thing to feed his kids.

He thought of the life that had once been ahead of them, how Gabby wanted to be a nurse like her mom, Miguel a fireman, Rey a database developer, and Max, well, his future profession changed each day. Last time they spoke, he'd said he wanted to be an MMA fighter, and if that didn't pan out, he'd settle for boxing promoter. Daniel had just sighed at the time.

Now what lay ahead of them?

The scrape of a chair against the concrete floor made him jump.

"I'm gonna get sick," Dakota announced.

Buck hurriedly found a thick plastic bag. "Use this."

She ran to the small area designated for the chemical toilet and washbasin. They could all hear her retching.

Miguel crinkled his nose. "Ewwww."

"Shh!" said Elizabeth.

Rey stood outside the drawn curtain. "You okay?"

She spit several times. "Yeah. I'll be all right."

You okay?

Seems they'd been saying that a lot.

Everyone said yes.

And everyone knew it was a lie.

32

On the fourth day, Elizabeth started crying after breakfast. No matter how hard she tried, she couldn't stop.

She felt Daniel's arm over her heaving shoulders, Alexiana's hand around hers.

No one said a word. Not even the kids.

Pull yourself together! You're going to scare the kids.

She opened her eyes and saw Max and Gabby through the blur of tears, crackers in their hands, dread on their faces. Elizabeth couldn't remember if she'd ever cried in front of the children. Of course, there had been tears of joy, the occasional maudlin movie that hit her the right way, but she'd never broken down like this.

"Don't cry, Mommy," Gabby said.

Hearing the pained concern in her daughter's voice only made it worse. She had to bury her face in Daniel's chest, hoping to muffle her weeping.

She cried until her throat hurt, until her eyes were sore, until she could no longer breathe out of her nose.

When the wave passed and she looked up, everyone but Daniel was gone. She'd clung to him as if he were a life preserver.

He wiped her tears with the cuff of his sleeves.

"Feel a little better?" he said.

"Not really. Just tired now."

"With the way things are, that'll qualify as better. You want to lie down for a bit? I'll set a game up for the kids."

"Only if you stay with me."

He kissed her lips. "We're not going to be down here forever. Just think, we could pop up and see that everything's back to normal."

"But what about the radio? How come no one is on the air?"

"Maybe the radio is broken. It's technology. It's not perfect. Maybe it wasn't hardened correctly for an EM pulse and it's fried. Anything's possible at this point."

She pushed her hair back, tying it in a ponytail. "If everything is all right, will you take us to Rosita's for dinner?" She smiled, but not without effort.

Daniel helped her up. "I'll even let the kids order their own appetizers. And double orders of fried ice cream."

"You know that'll make Miguel sick all night. How about Roma's for pizza instead?"

"And wine for the chaperones?" Daniel asked.

"Of course wine for the chaperones. I need a table by the window. I have to see the sky," Elizabeth said.

He walked her to the crowded bunkhouse.

"We'll get outta your way, Lizzie," Buck said. "Everyone needs a little time to themselves. In fact, maybe we should work out shifts."

"Probably a good idea," Daniel said.

33

Buck had accounted for everything except the boredom.

Keeping nine people from going stir-crazy while searching for any sign that it was safe to go out was no easy task. After they'd gotten over the initial shock and came to grips with the fact that they were going to have to coexist in the shelter for who knew how long, finding ways to fill up the days—days in a theoretical sense, since the clock was their only proof when it was morning or afternoon—was the biggest challenge of all.

The kids were getting snippy with one another. Even the adults had their moments. The utter lack of privacy, sleep deprivation (because everyone's circadian rhythm was smashed to bits), and omnipresent fear of the unknown above had put everyone on edge. Simple bodily functions could lead to sharp words and cutting glances if one forgot to excuse themselves after a burp.

Tense. Yep, that described the mood. Tense as a small condom on a porn star's prick.

Buck sipped on a juice box, watching Miguel color the last picture in the last coloring book. Good thing he had plenty of blank paper and notebooks. Miguel would draw his own pictures and color them when he was done.

"Can you please pass me the headphones?" Buck asked Alexiana. She walked listlessly into the bunkhouse and handed him the white Sony headphones. He plugged them into the radio. Maybe with the headphones, he could discern something amid the static.

Aside from Miguel, the rest of the Padillas were in the bunkhouse. He could hear Max grunting as he did sit-ups. The kid reminded him of a poodle he'd had when he was first married. The dog had enough energy to send a rocket to Saturn. They eventually had to give him to a couple he knew from work because they had more space for the crazy dog to run around.

Dakota leaned on the table next to Buck, staring at Miguel with a wan smile.

"Wish me luck," he said.

She gave him a thumbs-up, but there was little hope in her eyes.

He gave the radio's crank a dozen turns, charging it up. The moment he flipped the On switch, he was greeted by static. Turning the knob slowly with his thumb and fore-finger, he went up the AM band, searching for even the tiniest snippet of a human voice.

By the time he scrolled past 1010, the home of the leg-endary New York news station, he felt defeat settle into his gut.

Maybe I should just go outside and check tomorrow. If anything, it will give us some answers. This not knowing is what's going to drive us all crazy.

Even though he had plenty of water and cleaning supplies, he was sure they were all getting a little ripe. The chemical toilet was working overtime, as well, and there were bags of solid waste that he'd love to get out of the shelter.

What did you do to us?

He wasn't sure who the *you* was, but he'd give his right leg to know whom he needed to channel his hate against.

Maybe tomorrow.

The dial hit the end of the AM band. He switched it to FM and worked his way down.

34

While his family played another game of Crazy Eights, Rey slipped into a top bunk, pulling the blanket up to his chin. Gabby was accusing Max of cheating. His mother made a halfhearted attempt to settle her down. Max told Gabby to stick her head in the toilet.

To conserve the generator, Buck had shut off the two lights. A battery-operated lantern hung on one of the bunk posts, bathing the bunkhouse in cold, blue light.

"You skipping out on us?" Max asked, a crazy grin on his face, satisfied that he'd pissed Gabby off.

"I think I've played enough Crazy Eights to last two lifetimes," Rey said.

"We can play something else," his mother said.

"No, you guys play. I think I'm going to take a nap."

In a way, Rey was grateful for the light restriction. Under the strange lantern light, his parents couldn't see how pale his skin had become overnight. He'd seen it for himself in the mirror by the toilet, just before Buck went into power-saving mode.

He shivered under the blanket. His lungs hitched, desperate to cough, but he held it in. The last thing he needed to do was to start spewing his germs everywhere. If he was lucky, a nice long nap would leave him feeling better.

Doubling the pillow under his head, he could see Dakota sitting at the head of the table in the other room. She was reading an old paperback. He couldn't see what was on the cover. Buck had a couple dozen books that weren't survival guides. None of them had appealed to Rey. There were dark circles under her eyes and pin drops of sweat dotted the sides of her face. She coughed softly into her hand, turned the page, and brought the book closer to her face.

Dakota had spent the better part of the last day reading. She'd barely spoken to anyone. He couldn't tell if she was depressed or angry or if this was just how she always was when she wasn't a secretary at the race office. What he knew about teen girls he could fit in a thimble. That towered in comparison to what he knew about women.

Funny, he'd been no farther than ten feet from her for a week now, and he still found it difficult to summon up the courage to talk to her.

Rey felt another cough coming on and held his breath. His body shook with exertion, but no sound came out.

He needed air. Fresh, clean air. Everything down here seemed stale, reused, recycled, reconstituted until all the good stuff had been stripped away. He'd seen movies where people survived the apocalypse by securing themselves in bomb shelters. At the time, it looked awesome. To outlive Armageddon by hunkering down in a fully stocked bunker and emerge to start a new civilization was the stuff of fantasies.

This was no fantasy. This was a horror movie, one of those flicks from the seventies where there was no happy ending.

Because even if they made it out of Buck's shelter in one piece, what was out there waiting for them?

You may be the last man on earth even close to Dakota's age and you still can't untie your tongue, he thought.

Between the fever he knew was raging in his system, his swirling brain, and his whirling hormones, he didn't think he'd be able to actually sleep.

Sometime during his sister's pronouncement that she was the winner and Max could go stick *his head* in the toilet, the darkness overtook him.

35

"How is she doing?"

Alexiana shook the thermometer down. "Her fever is just under a hundred and three."

Daniel watched Elizabeth press a cold washcloth to Dakota's forehead. She took a pained sip of orange drink and lay back on the bed.

"Rey was around the same," he said.

Buck opened one of the medical boxes he'd mounted to the walls and pulled out an amber bottle. "Here, give them each a couple of these and some Tylenol," he said to Alexiana.

"Those different antibiotics?" Daniel asked.

"Yep. I ordered three hundred of them from a Canadian company over the Internet. In fact, most of the pills I have are from Canada. It was either there or Cuba. They should take the fever down and knock out whatever's in them."

Miguel nudged his way onto Daniel's lap. "Is Rey going to have to go to the hospital?"

Daniel hugged him close. "No, he'll be fine. He just needs medicine."

"I hope he doesn't get me sick," Max said.

"Don't be such a creep," Gabby said.

"Chill out, guys," Daniel said. "Rey and Dakota need their rest. Just keep it down."

Tears streaked down Miguel's cheeks. "I don't want Rey to be sick."

"Oh, come on, Miguel. Stop being a baby," Max said.

Daniel shot his son a warning look. He silently approved when Gabby backhanded her older brother's chest. Max had become quite the tormentor over the past week, to the point where Daniel wanted to treat him like a little kid and spank him in front of everyone. The humiliation might do wonders.

Buck said, "I'll change the air filter. Don't want the same old germs circulating, you know."

"Any luck with the radio today?" Daniel asked, rocking Miguel on his lap.

"Same as every other day," Buck sighed.

"I think it's time we at least took a peek."

Buck fiddled with the brim of his cowboy hat. "I'm not so much worried about what's outside the door as I am about what can make its way inside the shelter."

"Don't you have a way of checking?"

"Not from in here. I can give everyone potassium iodide tablets to take. It'll protect from low-level radiation, should there even be any."

Daniel said, "What if you and I got out quick? A few seconds with the door open shouldn't be dangerous."

"If you go, I want to go," Max said.

"Not a chance," Daniel quickly replied.

"Look, I know you're worried about Rey. I have all the meds he'd get from a doctor. We don't have to act rashly," Buck said.

Daniel had to fight the sudden impulse to punch his neighbor in the face hard enough to knock the stupid cowboy hat off his head.

Where the hell did that come from?

In the blink of an eye, Buck had gone from an incredible

friend who had saved his family to a smug jailer who refused to let them go free. Daniel knew the thought was completely irrational.

So why after taking a few deep breaths did he still want to hit the man?

36

It hurt like hell to swallow the antibiotic capsule. Dakota felt the pill stick to the back of her throat and panicked. Sitting up as fast as she could, she brought the water glass to her lips with a trembling hand and swallowed hard.

Mercifully, the pill went with the downward tide.

"Sorry," she said. "I thought I was going to choke."

Elizabeth took the glass before she spilled the rest all over herself. "You scared me for a second there."

"That makes two of us," she said, smiling weakly. It had been a long time since she'd had someone wait on her. She had to admit it was kind of nice, being mothered by Elizabeth, even though the woman was closer to being an older sister. What wasn't nice was the way she'd been feeling. The medication didn't seem to be working. Her fever had yet to break, and there was a fluid rattle in her lungs when she breathed or coughed. Worst was the cramps. She hurt all over. It was as if she'd been tossed from a speeding car.

"How's Rey?" Dakota asked.

Elizabeth cast a quick glance at his cot. The lantern was on low, making it difficult for Dakota to see for herself. Her teenage savior had gone through a ferocious coughing fit an hour earlier. He'd been silent ever since.

"Sleeping, which is what you should probably do."

At first, it had been difficult, sleeping amid perfect strangers who were never more than a few feet away. Now she was so bone-tired, all she needed to do was close her eyes and she was out.

"Still with the fever?" Dakota said.

Elizabeth craned her head back, loosening the muscles in her neck. She closed her eyes and took a moment to answer. "Yes, but it's a little lower today. I keep waiting for the other kids to come down with it. I worry about Miguel. With his asthma . . ." She let the words trail off.

Dakota reached out and wrapped her hand around Elizabeth's wrist. The woman's skin felt cool and soothing compared to her own burning palm. "I don't think he can catch what we have."

"What do you mean?"

"I keep thinking back to when Rey and I ran from the track and through the reservoir. Something was burning, but we couldn't see any flames. At one point, we ran into this low cloud of smoke. It smelled strange, like nothing I've ever smelled before. I keep wondering, what was in that smoke?"

Elizabeth crouched closer to her face. "What makes you think it was the smoke that made you sick?"

"We've been sick for days. If we had a cold or flu, at least one of you would have gotten it by now, especially your little one. But it's just us. You were a nurse. Could there have been some kind of chemical that we breathed in? Like what got into the lungs of the first responders on nine-eleven? I met a woman in Pennsylvania who lost her husband to some kind of lung infection. He was a firefighter in the Bronx when the Towers went down. He worked at Ground Zero for six solid weeks."

"I don't know. With them, symptoms didn't show for months, or even years."

Dakota felt the heavy tug of fevered sleep pull on her. "It's something to think about. I could be wrong. I hope I'm wrong."

The dark room lost focus for a moment.

"But if I'm right, what if whatever made us sick is still out there?"

37

Things were getting to the tipping point. Buck kept the lights on for most of the day, if only to combat a blanket of depression that had settled over all of them. Man was not made to live in the dark.

The little kids were beyond antsy, given to prolonged bouts of crying for no reason. He'd known Gabby since she was an infant, and she'd never been much of a crier. Now, she couldn't stop.

It didn't help that Rey and Dakota weren't getting any better. Supplies were running low, and even though he knew he was used to it, the smell was getting worse.

Elizabeth had brought Dakota's theory to him and Daniel and Alexiana the day before.

"Fucking chemical warfare," he hissed, eyeing a sealed plastic container that supported two boxes of MREs. "I don't have anything that can detect something like that."

"It might not be that," Daniel said. "If something blew up, it could have been burning plastics or those damn CFL bulbs. Those things are so toxic, you have to clear the room if one breaks."

Elizabeth said, "Either way, they need a doctor. Whatever it is has settled into their lungs and is resistant to the antibiotics we have. We have to leave the shelter."

Buck had to couch his reply. He'd been sensing their frustration with him. Everyone wanted to get out. Naturally, he was the bad guy, keeping them all cooped up in a high-tech tomb.

If he could hear just one person on either of the radios.

With Rey and Dakota sick, they'd run out of time waiting for news that the coast was clear.

"I'm not gonna argue with you, Lizzie. I'm not dumb enough to come between a mother and her sick child. I'll go and scout around."

"We'll go," Daniel said.

"Not a good idea. One of us should stay here."

"Don't go male chauvinist on us," Alexiana said. "We can take care of ourselves." She shot him a warning look.

Buck pushed back from the table. "Max, can you help me for a sec?"

Max came from the bunkhouse and lifted the MRE boxes off the container, stacking them on the table. Buck lifted the plastic lid and pulled out a pair of black backpacks.

"What's in those?" Max asked.

"These are what I call Bugout for the Dugout bags. I have four already made. There are six more on the bottom that you all should fill. I'll give you a list of what you need. This is just in case. Once I open the shelter, we have to be ready for anything."

He unzipped the bag. All of the contents had been neatly arranged inside.

"Holy crap," Max said.

"Watch your mouth," his mother scolded.

Daniel stood over the bag, looking over everything.

Buck said, "Each has your basic survival necessities: freeze-dried food, water and water purifiers, first aid kit, map of the tristate area and country, light sticks, fire starter, waterproof poncho, duct tape, scissors, face masks, flashlight and penlight, batteries, rope, blanket, and my favorite"—he extracted a large, silver blade from a leather holster—"you can't go anywhere without a good bowie knife."

He disappeared into the bunkhouse while everyone carefully went through the Bugout for the Dugout bag. When he came back, he placed two silver pistols and two shotguns on the table.

"Whoa, isn't that a little extreme?" Daniel said. He smacked Max's hand when he went to touch one of the shotguns.

"Dan, we don't know what the hell we're going to find when we leave here. If power hasn't been restored, order sure as hell hasn't, either. Your best friend can be your worst enemy. We're not going anywhere unless we're able to defend ourselves. We have a lot of precious cargo we need to care for."

Elizabeth palmed one of the pistols. "It's so heavy."

"That's a Beretta 92FS. One of the most reliable guns ever made. Each can hold fifteen nine-millimeter rounds. They're easy to shoot and will put an immediate stop to a bad situation."

"Or make it worse," Elizabeth said.

Daniel held the shotgun, hefting it as if he was guessing its weight. "If we have the Berettas, isn't this overkill?"

Buck took his cowboy hat from the peg on the wall and squashed it on his head.

"No such thing as overkill anymore, Dan. I say we head out now." He checked his watch. "We'll have eight hours of daylight. Max, hand me that box over there."

"What's that?" Elizabeth asked.

"Geiger counter," Buck replied, taking out a black box with a handle built into the top and a glass display. "If there's any radiation out there, this will warn us. If we end up right back inside, it's because this thing will be wailing off the charts."

Daniel stared at the bags and guns for a moment. He looked to his wife and son, then at Rey in his bed and Gabby and Miguel playing checkers on the floor of the bunkhouse. Slipping the backpack over his shoulder, he said, "Where should I put the guns?"

38

"You have to close the door behind us as fast as possible," Buck said to Alexiana.

She and Elizabeth stood by the door wearing multipurpose respirator masks. Buck and Daniel had their bags slung over their shoulders, shotguns in hand. The children had been ushered into the bunkhouse after Daniel made the rounds saying good-bye and promising to be back very soon.

Buck and Daniel wore military gas masks with large visors that covered their eyes and noses. A black canister protruded from the mouthpiece. Each also held a full, black plastic trash bag filled with garbage and some of the waste from the chemical toilet. It would do wonders to relieve the cloying smell of the shelter.

Despite the mask, Alexiana could hear her boyfriend quite well.

"There's no telling what's still in the air, so the less you let in, the better," he said.

"I know," she said.

Elizabeth's eyes were shiny, but she'd been able to hold back her tears as she stroked Daniel's hand.

"Who knows, we may go out there and find everyone

having a block party," Daniel said, his grin lifting the mask higher on his face. "We might scare the crap out of them."

Elizabeth gave him a faltering smile.

"You ready, Dan?" Buck asked.

He lifted the shotgun level with his waist. Buck jumped to the side. "Keep it pointed at the ground! Last thing I need is to be taken down by friendly fire."

"Sorry. Maybe I should just stick with the pistol."

"Keep it," Buck said. "Only point it at something you want to shoot and you'll be fine."

Buck gave Alexiana a big nod. She punched the final digit in the locking code, turned the handle, and opened the door wide enough to let them through. Buck and Daniel ran out the door as fast as they could. The second they were out, she closed the door with a loud, metallic *bang* and reentered the locking code.

"You see any changes on the Geiger counter?" she asked Elizabeth.

"The needle didn't even move."

"Well, that's one thing in our favor. We were due that."

39

Daniel followed Buck as he bounded up the basement stairs. The big man moved better than usual. He remembered Buck getting winded when he mowed the lawn with his power mower. A couple of weeks of food rationing had obviously done him some good. They'd all lost weight, but Buck seemed to have shed the most pounds. Beer guts tended to wither away when there was no more beer to feed the beast.

They stopped in the kitchen. The cheese sandwich Alexiana had made before the bombs hit was still on the plate by the sink, the bread green and blue with mold. A warm can of Pepsi was on the table.

He thought about stories of ghost ships found floating in deep waters, the crew and passengers gone, tables set with half-eaten dinners, glasses of wine waiting to be finished. He could feel the ghosts of their former lives all around them.

Daniel flipped the light switch on the wall. Nothing happened. Buck opened the refrigerator. The light didn't come on inside and the air flowing from it was room temperature.

"Power hasn't come back on," Buck said. "It's a shame. I had five pounds of filet mignon in the freezer."

He parted the white curtains decorated with apples over the sink with the shotgun.

It was only eleven in the morning, but the skies were dark. Heavy, gray clouds lumbered overhead.

"Storm clouds or smoke?" Daniel asked. The flesh of his face beneath the heavy gas mask was already beaded with sweat.

"Looks like a big storm to me." Buck turned on his Geiger counter, waving the box around the room. Daniel had seen enough war and sci-fi movies to know how they worked and the soft ticks they made. The readings remained relatively silent.

"We good?"

Somehow, Buck had been able to cram his cowboy hat over his gas mask. The two accessories made his head look three times its normal size.

"All good in here," he said.

He handed the box to Daniel and went to work undoing the four locks on the back door.

It opened with a low, elongated squeal.

"Think you need to grease those hinges," Daniel said.

"I'll add it to my list. You ready?"

Daniel nodded. They stepped into the yard. It could have been the suppression of sound by the gas masks, but Daniel had never heard the neighborhood so silent.

They opened the lids of Buck's garbage cans and dropped the trash bags inside. "If anything, that really needed to be done," Buck said. "Think I'll skip dragging the cans to the curb, though."

Nothing looked disturbed. The houses still stood, lawns were green, no signs of fire or destruction. Daniel spotted Gabby's pink bike leaning against his house. Miguel's scooter was right behind it, exactly where they'd left it.

Cautiously walking off Buck's patio, their feet made a squishing sound when they stepped onto the grass.

"Must have been raining a lot," Daniel said. He checked the Geiger counter's monitor, relieved to see the needle holding still at the low end.

"That could be good or bad. Good if it's washed away any toxins, bad if it's seeded with the stuff, whatever that stuff may be."

They crept between their houses, vigilant for any sights or sounds of life.

"Where the hell is everybody?" Daniel asked, licking salty sweat from his upper lip.

Buck's head swiveled from side to side. "Either gone or in hiding."

They stopped on the front sidewalk, looking up and down the block. All of the houses were dark. The streetlights that should have been on were off. A low rumble of thunder warned of impending rain.

Daniel shouted, "Hello! Is anybody here?"

Buck swatted his hand up and down, cutting him off. "No one will be able to hear you with the mask on. I don't want to call attention to ourselves just yet, either."

Daniel turned to his wife's Corolla. He'd taken his and her key rings before he left the shelter.

"I'll see if the car will start," he said.

The sound of the car door opening was like a gunshot in the dead of night. He was sure it could be heard for miles. He got behind the wheel, saw her rosary beads hung over the rearview mirror, the curled picture of them all at a family reunion tucked into a seam in the dashboard.

He put the key in the ignition and turned.

40

"Where are Dad and Buck?"

Rey startled Elizabeth and Alexiana. He leaned against the bunkhouse door frame. He looked so frail. Elizabeth could see his pulse pounding on the side of his neck.

"You shouldn't be up," she said, helping him to a seat. She placed her hand on his forehead. He was still burning up, even though she'd given him Tylenol just two hours ago.

"Did they go out?" he insisted.

Alexiana said, "Yes, about ten minutes ago. They wanted to see how things were and whether it was safe for all of us to leave the shelter."

He used his finger to pick at a groove in the table's surface. "They went to see if there was anyone around to help me and Dakota."

Elizabeth wrapped an arm around his shoulders. She could feel his bones beneath his simmering skin. "What makes you say that?"

He turned to her with bloodshot, glassy eyes. "I'm not always sleeping. I can hear what's going on. I'm not saying them going out there for us is a bad thing, Ma. Dakota is real sick, sicker than me. Maybe they can find different medicine if they can't find a doctor. I just wish I could have gone with them."

"Even if you weren't sick, Buck wouldn't have let you go," Alexiana said. Before Rey could protest, she added, "He thinks it's important to leave a man in charge. He's kind of old-fashioned that way. Until him and your dad get back, that's you."

Rey was hit with a coughing fit that left him gasping for air. Elizabeth rubbed his back, trying to keep him calm. She thought of giving him a puff from one of Miguel's inhalers, but he settled down on his own.

"We got anything to eat?" he asked.

Elizabeth gave her neighbor a look of silent thanks, then searched for an MRE and some water.

41

Buck watched Daniel turn the key again and again. When nothing happened, not even the *click* of the alternator, he slammed the wheel with his palms and got out of the car.

"Maybe it's been sitting around too long," he said.

"I'll try my truck next." Buck went to his driveway and opened the door to his Explorer.

"Zippo," he said. "This thing's deader than Saddam. I suspect none of the cars out here are gonna start. More to add to the case of an EMP explosive being at least one of the little surprises."

Daniel moved the shotgun from his left to his right hand. The man looked supremely uncomfortable handling the firearm. Buck wondered if he'd been wrong to make him carry it. He worried Dan would shoot himself by accident in the act of defending himself. Even before today, that was something he'd worried about. The Padillas were good people, not exactly straight from *The Donna Reed Show*, but damn close. Did they have what it would take to survive? Daniel was a nice guy, but a little soft. Buck hoped somewhere inside the man were some hard edges, waiting to surface.

Light patters of rain started to come down, obscuring his view out of the plastic visor of the gas mask.

"These Bugout for the Dugout bags waterproof?" Daniel asked.

"Yep."

"Good. I want to at least walk to Dr. Manetti's office over on Kimball, see if there's a chance he's still there and okay. If he is, we can either bring him to Rey and Dakota or them to him."

Buck grunted. "Shit, Dan, doctors didn't make house calls before everything went to hell. We should look around for anything that'll make it easy to take Rey and the girl to him, like a wheelbarrow. They don't seem up to much walking."

Daniel scratched at his neck, turned, and started walking up the street.

Most of the houses they passed had drawn blinds. The entire neighborhood was comprised of one- and two-family houses, all stacked in neat little rows. One thing Buck liked about it was that no two were exactly alike. No cookie cutters here. Tudors, Capes, ranches, you name it, they all lived in architecturally disjointed harmony.

It had been the middle of a pretty nice day when everything happened. If their neighbors had fled, they wouldn't have taken the time to close the blinds. Buck wondered how many sets of eyes were secretly following them. They had to know it was him. How many other people in Yonkers walked around with a cowboy hat?

There was that one guy who lived by the diner, but he always wore a white hat with a tan band. Sometimes he'd stick a hawk's feather under the band.

"Dan, hold on a sec. I want to check in on Mrs. Fumarelli."

Mrs. Fumarelli was one of their oldest neighbors and the last remaining member of the original families that had moved in when the neighborhood was constructed. A widow of over twenty years, she lived with Bruce, her mutt of an attack dog that was an ornery son of a bitch to everyone but his elderly owner.

"We should have taken her to the shelter," Dan said as they walked up her brick steps.

"No sense looking for regrets. There wasn't time to think."

Buck knocked on the door. He waited, then knocked again, harder and longer. Usually, if anyone so much as stepped onto her front porch, Bruce set off like a hell hound, barking at the door.

"I'll check around back," Daniel said.

Stepping onto the porch, Buck tried to peer between the blinds. All he could see was the lower back end of a couch and an area rug that looked to be as thin as loose-leaf paper. He tapped on the window with the barrel of the shotgun.

He was about to see if he could lift the window when Daniel shouted, followed by the distinctive blast of the shotgun.

42

"I have to go," Miguel pleaded outside the curtain.

"I'll be out in a minute," Max barked.

Jesus, it's impossible to have even a second to yourself in this pit, Max thought. The only time he didn't have his brother and sister attached to him was when he was in the makeshift bathroom, and even then, Miguel would inevitably need to go the moment he closed the curtain.

Max turned the battery-powered lantern so he could study the bowie knife better. The blade was long, going from the tips of his fingers to well past his wrist. It was wide, too, almost as wide as his palm.

He'd pocketed the knife when he was helping the adults put more of those survival backpacks together. He knew there was no way they'd ever put one in any of the kids' packs.

Buck had the knives in a long piece of cloth with pockets sewn in to hold each knife. There were eight in all, and no two were exactly alike.

How bad did Buck think things were going to get?

The man had socked away a lot of guns and knives. It was as if he had prepared himself to wage a one-man war.

But the war had already started, hadn't it? Whoever had thrown the first punch was definitely in the lead—for now. Max imagined every awful scenario that could be waiting for them when they eventually left the shelter. He'd even tried to come to grips with what he thought was the worst possible outcome—that they would stay down here forever, occasionally going out to gather more supplies, the shelter being the only safe place left for them to live out a meaningless existence.

"I'm going to pee my pants, Max."

Max slipped the knife into his pocket, careful not to jab the tip into his leg.

Miguel had had his first accident in years last night, and the pants he had on now were his last pair until the others dried, which took forever down here.

He couldn't let his brother spend the rest of the day bottomless.

43

"Dan, you all right?"

He heard Buck round the corner into the yard and gave a shaky, "Yeah, I'm fine."

Mrs. Fumarelli's dog, Bruce, lay in a bloody, crumpled heap. The shotgun had almost split the dog in half. Daniel had been shocked at the kick of the gun and how far Bruce skidded across the patio when the shells tore into him.

Buck whistled. "Holy crap, why'd you kill Bruce? He was more bark than bite. Come to think of it, I didn't even hear him barking."

The shotgun shuddered in Daniel's hands.

"He didn't. I came back and knocked on the door. I even pressed my ear against it to see if I could hear Mrs. Fumarelli shuffling around inside. When I didn't hear anything, I was going to go out front when I saw Bruce slowly coming out from behind the garbage pails. You had to see him, Buck. Something was wrong. Really wrong. His eyes were red. I'm not talking bloodshot. They were the deepest red I've ever seen. Blood was leaking out of them."

They looked at the dog's carcass. Blood was everywhere, including the sides of its muzzle. It was impossible to tell what it had looked like before.

"Did he attack you?"

Daniel fought back a burp that was sure to lead to worse things.

"I was waiting for him to do his usual song and dance. I thought it might get Mrs. Fumarelli's attention, if she heard him barking and growling. Instead, he just showed his teeth, reared back, and jumped at me. I don't even remember pulling the trigger. It happened so fast. One second he was there, looking mean as hell and sick or something, the next he was dead."

Buck scratched his head under his hat. "Might have been sick with hunger if he's been out here this whole time. He was a loyal dog. Maybe he didn't want to go far from her, so he stuck around, getting hungrier and hungrier. When you came around, you must have looked like a walking pork chop." He slapped Daniel's back, hard. "Don't beat yourself up about it. You had to defend yourself. If he got ahold of you, you'd have been a sorry mess."

Daniel looked at the surrounding houses. Despite the deafening shotgun blast, no one had come out or even gone to their windows to see what was happening. He craned his neck up, staring into the oncoming raindrops.

"You hear that?" he said.

Buck shook his head.

"This time of year, when storms roll in, all you hear are birds flying away from it. I haven't heard one since we left the house. I can see why there might not be any people around, but where the hell are the birds?"

Buck kicked a rock across the patio. "I haven't a clue. Come on, let's go inside and make sure Mrs. Fumarelli is okay."

As they walked, Daniel thought about what Rey and Dakota had said about the horses, and the dog that had attacked the guard at the reservoir. Those weren't separate, random events. Like the power, something had affected the animals—but what?

They climbed the steps to the front porch, and Buck used the butt of his shotgun to break out one of the windows. He crawled inside, his belly catching on the lip of the windowsill for a second before he flopped onto the floor. "Guess I'll never have a career as a cat burglar," he said, wiping bits of glass from his shirt and pants. Daniel followed him inside with a little more grace.

The house was dark and dusty. The wall behind the small tube television was crammed with framed photographs of Mrs. Fumarelli's family. She had five children, and Daniel had lost count of how many grandchildren he'd seen visiting.

"Mrs. Fumarelli, it's Buck Clarke and Daniel Padilla," Buck shouted, trying to make his voice carry through the gas mask. "We want to make sure you're all right. We have a safer place where you can stay."

The house remained silent.

Buck tilted his head toward the stairs. "I'll check upstairs." His footfalls sounded like an elephant stomping on wood. If Mrs. Fumarelli hadn't reacted to the shotgun blast, broken window, or his ascent, Daniel held out little hope of her being in the house.

Her dining room table was bare except for a tidy stack of mail. She had a beautiful breakfront with fine bone china on display. Little knickknacks from a full life were amid the dinner plates and serving bowls. There was a pewter barrel from Niagara Falls, an ashtray that had never seen a cigarette butt from a Poconos resort, figurines of flamenco dancers from Madrid. There was even a photo of her and a man, he assumed it was her husband, holding each other underneath the Eiffel Tower at night. They looked to be in their forties, smiling, in love.

He thought of all the times Elizabeth had asked him to go to Europe. His fear of flying kept them grounded in

America, though he had taken her to Mexico, by car, for their second anniversary. It'd been a hell of a drive and not likely to be repeated.

The floor creaked overhead as Buck went from room to room.

Daniel continued into the kitchen.

His knees locked when he turned to the left.

Mrs. Fumarelli was sitting at the kitchen table. Her head had slumped forward, resting on its side, her milky, vacant eyes boring into him. He didn't need to feel her pulse to know she was dead. A pool of dried blood spread out beneath her open mouth.

"Buck! Buck! I found her!"

44

Buck draped a clean sheet over Mrs. Fumarelli's body, then went downstairs to find some wood and nails. Daniel came down with him.

"What are you doing?" he asked.

Buck said, "I'm going to board up that window we broke. I don't want any stray animals coming in here and having a go at Mrs. Fumarelli."

They found what they needed in the garage and made quick work of sealing up the window.

While they worked, Buck considered what had killed the poor woman. Probably her heart, though that didn't explain the blood. She could have had a heart attack or a stroke and hit her face on the tabletop. It was just a shame that with so much of her family nearby, she had to die alone. Even Bruce was outside when it happened.

They went out the back door. It was the kind that locked itself when you shut it.

"You still want to check out that doctor's office?" he asked.

Daniel surprised him with his sure answer. "I have to try. It doesn't look hopeful, but we haven't gone very far."

They walked side by side in the middle of the street,

stealing glances at the houses. A sun-faded drawing of a Disney princess was taped to the inside of a front window. That's where the Parker twins lived, four-year-old girls who rambled their scooters up and down the block any day the sun was out. A handcart leaned against Mr. Otello's house across the street. The man was always carting something as he endlessly worked on his pristine house. Where was everyone?

"We must look terrifying," Daniel said. "If I saw us, I'd pull back the blinds and wait for us to pass."

"Well, I'm not taking this mask off just to make people feel better. Better to be feared than dead."

The rain started to come down in earnest by the time they made it to the end of the street. They had to go two blocks, make a left, and walk down three more to get to the doctor's office. Buck wasn't relishing the fact that he'd be soaked down to his underwear by the time they were done.

Daniel pointed at a brown Tudor house to their left. "Did you see that?"

Buck looked over. "No."

"I thought I saw those curtains in the bottom left window move, like someone either walked past them or quickly pulled them shut."

"It's good to know someone is around. I'd hate to think we missed a mass rescue. Our neighbors could be sipping mai tais in Cancún for all we know."

"More like they're in some cramped gym taken over by the military, eating bad food and stiffening up from sleeping on cots."

Buck smiled. "It's good to see your cynicism, Dan. You're going to need it from here on out."

Daniel stopped. "There it goes again!"

Indeed, the curtain was moving. Suddenly, it was jerked to the side. A girl, she couldn't be more than twenty, pressed her face to the window. They moved closer, stopping at the fence outside the house. Daniel held up a hand in greeting.

Buck had seen her from time to time in the corner store, though he'd never spoken to her. He remembered her ears had always been plugged with earbuds so she could listen to music while she bought energy drinks.

The girl looked terrible. Her skin was paler than milk. Dark bruises hung under each eye. Her hair was greasy and matted to her skull.

She held up a hand, asking them to wait. Her head bent down. It looked like she was doing something with her hands that were out of sight. She paused and looked up at the gray sky.

The patter of raindrops splashing on Buck's hat was picking up the tempo. Rain sluiced down his visor, distorting everything he saw.

The girl lifted a sketch pad to the window.

It said: *DON'T COME IN HERE. WE'RE ALL SICK.*

She turned it around. *YOU HAVE TO RUN AND FIND A SAFE PLACE. NOW!*

Buck turned to Daniel. His stomach tightened into a knot.

"Why do we have to run?" Buck shouted. He wasn't sure she'd be able to hear him. Daniel did his best to pantomime *why?*

She pulled the pad away and scribbled quickly. The windowpane made a vibrating *thud* when she smacked the pad against it.

RATS!!!

"Rats?" Buck said. "What the heck does she mean?"

Daniel turned on his heel and tugged on Buck's arm. When Buck spun around, he understood.

Dozens of rats poured out of the sewer opening across the street. The same was happening all up and down the block.

And they were all headed for him and Daniel.

45

The sick girl at the window had disappeared. Daniel yanked Buck's arm, leading him back down the street and away from the onslaught of sewage- and rain-soaked rats.

"Come on, Buck, we have to get back to your house!"

As far as he could see, black and brown furry bodies, some bigger than kittens, scurried out of every sewer opening and drainpipe.

The rain must have been flooding them out of their dark hiding places. It was coming down in drenching buckets. Steady, riverlike streams ran down his visor, branches connecting until they emptied onto his shirt.

"I don't believe this," Buck said.

Daniel pulled hard. "Hurry!"

A pink-eyed rodent came up to Daniel's shoe, attempting to nibble on his heel. He kicked backward, sending the rat flying into the gathering mob.

Buck flinched when one tried to climb up his pants leg. He knocked it off with his shotgun. It also snapped his inertia.

They ran, followed closely by a tight-knit pack of undulating bodies. So many were up ahead, seemingly on a crash course with them, that Daniel considered jumping off the sidewalk and smashing in the door of a nearby house.

"Maybe we should get on the roof of one of the cars," he said, panting heavily.

Buck urged him on. "They can easily climb up a car. Just keep going."

Lightning flashed, affording a terrifying glimpse into the true hell gathering around them. It was immediately followed by a heavy crash of thunder. The rainfall intensified, smearing his vision. At this rate, when there was no lightning to bring everything into stark contrast, Daniel could barely see.

Maybe that's a good thing, he thought.

Where the hell were all these rats coming from? Were there always this many just below their feet?

And rats were normally afraid of people, scurrying away the moment they'd been spotted.

Not this swarm. It was as if they'd been intentionally starved and the storm was the dinner bell. Daniel pumped his legs harder. He'd be damned to survive the bombing of the city only to become a vermin's main course.

He cast a quick glance behind him to make sure Buck wasn't too far behind. He could just make out the big man's outline.

When he turned back, his shoulder clipped a tree. He spun sideways, losing his balance and hitting the concrete hard. Buck's hand dragged him up before he could regain his bearings.

"I can't see in this thing!" Daniel barked.

"Just keep going straight."

Aside from the lack of vision, his heavy panting was making it almost impossible to breathe in the gas mask. Frustrated, he ripped it from his head, letting it dangle along his back.

"Are you crazy?" Buck shouted.

Daniel was immediately baptized by the storm.

The rats took up every square inch between them and Buck's house, which was only a couple of hundred feet away.

He shivered, thinking he could hear their chorus of starved chitters amid the howling storm.

"Just shoot and stomp," Buck ordered.

"What?"

"Clear a path. Whatever you don't hit, squash. Don't slow down. Shit, I wish I'd brought the grenades."

Daniel jumped when Buck's shotgun erupted. A cone of crimson rats rose from the pack, flopping their entrails over their advancing brethren.

Something made a wet *pop* under Daniel's foot and he almost lost his balance again. Looking down, he saw three rats working their way up his pants, mouths chomping with yellow teeth. He smacked them off with the butt of the shotgun, leveled it at the ground, and pulled the trigger. More rats went flying, pieces scattering in every direction. Buck took another shot, as well.

They carved a path as best they could, but it was impossible to avoid squishing them by the dozens, as well.

He shoved his revulsion to the darkest recess of his mind, veering from the sidewalk to the side of Buck's house as fast as his legs would take him.

46

The pounding at the door put everyone on high alert. Alexiana grabbed the .38 she'd taken from the gun locker and ran to the shelter door.

"Is it them?" Elizabeth asked. Miguel ran into her arms, clutching her as if she were all that stood between him and the omnipotent pull of a black hole.

"This whole shelter is soundproof, so I can't hear. If they don't give the knock code, I can't open the door."

There was more frantic rapping.

Gabby and Max remained by Rey's side. He had managed to pull himself out of bed, though his legs looked very unsteady.

Alexiana made a fist and knocked on the door twice, paused, then three rapid knocks.

The rapping stopped.

Elizabeth jumped at the answering knocks. Three knocks, a pause, then two.

"It's them!" Alexiana cried, entering the code and unlocking the door.

Buck leapt into the room first. He was soaked through. His cowboy hat flew from his head when he slammed his legs into the table.

Daniel was next. Elizabeth's heart rocketed into her throat when she saw her husband wasn't wearing his gas mask. Had something happened?

"Close the door! Close the door!" Daniel barked.

Alexiana screamed. The gun fell from her hand. She tried to close the door but it wouldn't shut all the way.

Buck shouted, "Everyone, grab a bag! Liz, help me get Dakota and Rey!"

Elizabeth looked to Daniel, then Buck, Miguel fastened to her breast. "What's going on? Daniel, what happened?"

When Alexiana jumped onto a chair, Elizabeth finally looked to the door and understood.

Hundreds and hundreds of rats galloped inside, leaping over each other's bodies.

Still holding on to her son, she slipped two of the survival bags over her shoulder. "Gabby, Max, grab a bag and run! Follow your father!"

Daniel took their hands, running against the tide of rats. The eager rodents made clumsy bounds at them, trying to hold on with claws and teeth.

These rats weren't running *from* something. They were running *to* them.

"Alexiana, help me!"

Her neighbor stared at her, past her, refusing to get off the chair. Elizabeth ran to the bunkhouse. Buck had a huge canvas bag over one shoulder, Rey leaning on his other. "Can you run for a spell?" he shouted. Rey nodded.

"You go ahead of us, Lizzie," Buck said. "I'll guard the rear."

Dakota had gotten out of the bed, the haze of her fever taking a backseat to the sea of rats at her feet. She hopped and squealed, shaking them from her legs. Elizabeth wrapped her arm around the girl's waist, pulling her along. Miguel kept his face to her chest, refusing to look. It was best he didn't.

As she passed Alexiana, she shouted, "Alexiana, get off the damn chair and move your ass out of here! Now!"

Alexiana blinked hard, looked at the mounds of rats invading the shelter, and jumped off the chair. She landed atop a half-dozen rats.

Elizabeth ran up the stairs with Miguel and Dakota, her ankles slipping and twisting, threatening to give way and spill her into the mass of chittering vermin. The rats were like a brown, furry waterfall pouring down the stairs at an alarming rate.

Keep running! Keep running!

Something sharp bit into Elizabeth's ankle.

Then another at her calf.

She ran, reaching the kitchen and wondering where her husband and children had gone.

47

As they bolted up the stairs to the second floor, Max saw two rats climbing along his sister's shirt. She was so busy trying to keep up with their father that she didn't notice.

Max snatched them off her shirt, throwing them hard down the stairs. His hand was left wet and slimy. As one ran along the banister, he brought a heavy fist down on its head. It broke into spasms, falling to the carpeted steps.

Thankfully, so many rats had zeroed in on the basement that few bothered to follow them up.

"In there!" their father shouted.

They followed him into a bedroom. Max slammed the door behind them.

"Daniel!"

"It's Mom," Gabby cried. She'd jumped onto the bed, pressing her back against the wall.

"We're upstairs, first room on the left!"

Footfalls pounded up the stairs.

Max opened the door the moment he heard them hit the landing. His mother rushed into the room with Miguel and Dakota. She tossed the survival bags on the floor. Dakota slipped from her grasp, landing on the edge of the bed.

Gabby darted forward to keep her from crumpling to the floor.

A few rats had tailed them as they fled the first floor. Instead of closing the door, Max stepped into the hall, kicking each square in the snout, sending them across the hallway like furry kick balls.

"Close the door, Max!" his father shouted.

He took a second to make sure no other rats were lurking about. Funny, despite all of the madness that had just overtaken them, he'd never been frightened. In fact, it felt good to finally be out of the shelter.

Maybe, Max thought, *the rats just did us a favor*.

48

The rats reminded Rey of the incoming tide at Orchard Beach the day after a storm, when the water churned brown and ugly. Buck pulled him along the way his father used to hold on to him, letting the small waves break over his scrawny stomach.

"Let's go, Alexiana," Buck shouted. "Keep running up and don't look back. We'll be right behind you."

She screamed as her feet came down on fur and flesh and almost fell over. Buck snatched her arm before she could. Alexiana ran for the stairs, hollering as if her hair were on fire.

Buck handed Rey one of the red fire extinguishers that were mounted on the wall by the shelter door.

"Blast them with this," he said. "That'll clear them the hell out."

He hustled them both up the stairs, taking two at a time. The kitchen looked like something from a bad drive-in movie. The floor was crawling with frenzied, sewage-soaked rats.

Buck and Rey pulled back on the extinguisher triggers. Twin clouds of white foam cut into the tide of rats. Sure enough, they scampered over one another to avoid the onrush of carbon dioxide and powder. Up in the kitchen, Alexiana had positioned herself on one of the countertops.

"Ahh!" Rey yelped.

A pair of rats had taken meaty bites from his ankles. He flicked them across the room, then showered them with the extinguisher.

The sharp pain of the bites shattered the fever fugue that had spun around him like a cocoon the past few days, so much that he knew he could stand on his own. He pulled away from Buck, who made a wide circle around them with the extinguisher. The rats were held at bay, but it wouldn't last long.

"Where do we go now?" Rey said.

Something thumped above them.

Buck flung his girlfriend over his shoulder. "You good enough to make one more sprint?" he asked Rey.

"Hell, yes."

"Follow me."

Charging into the dining room, where there were far fewer rodents, they made a sharp turn up the stairs. One of the bedroom doors was already closed. Rey turned around.

"They're still coming," Rey said, astounded by the sheer number of rats. What the hell did they want? Why were they chasing them?

He pointed the extinguisher at the stairs and yanked the trigger. A puff of smoke and foam burped out, then it was empty. He threw the metal canister at the horde, taking out at least a dozen in the process.

"Get in here," Buck hollered, standing in the doorway of another room.

Rey turned to his left and saw his brother's face in the narrow opening of the other door. "Stay inside," he said. "They're all coming this way."

Max slammed the door shut as Rey ran toward Buck and Alexiana. Buck and Rey pushed the door closed with their backs. They could feel the vibration of the rats throwing themselves at the door.

Their high-pitched squeals drowned out the pained wheezing of Rey's lungs as they fought for air. Buck sounded like he was about to pop, his face reddening from the strain of running with Alexiana up the stairs.

"Can they get under the door?" Alexiana said, her eyes wide and staring.

Buck shook his head, gulping air in between ragged exhalations. "Remember, I put those guards on before the winter to keep heat from escaping. Even those jelly-boned fuckers couldn't squeeze under there." He turned to Rey. "Thanks, kid."

Rey patted his arm and closed his eyes. Lack of oxygen made it difficult to talk.

Thump, thump, thump, thump.

The rats threw themselves at the door without ceasing, like zombies on the trail of living flesh. Rey flexed his feet, the fire from their bites making him wince.

His heart thudded.

Did they have rabies? How long did it take to die if you had rabies? Was it painful?

Because if they had transmitted the disease to him, he was positive help was not nearby or on its way.

49

Daniel turned to the wall separating the two bedrooms when he heard someone knocking. Buck's muffled voice said, "You all present and accounted for?"

"All except Rey," Daniel said. He kept his eyes on the door. He and Max had turned over a dresser, jamming it against the door. If any rats somehow made it through, they had golf clubs they'd found in the closet.

"He's in here with us," Buck replied. "Everyone okay? Anyone get bit?"

Elizabeth had torn two pillowcases into strips and was tending to the bite wounds on Dakota and Gabby. Both lay on the bed, Dakota sheened in sweat. The only one who hadn't been bitten was Miguel. He sat by his sister's side, holding her hands as she winced when her mother applied antiseptic cream from the first aid kit in her backpack.

"Yeah. Elizabeth is patching us up."

Several sparks of lightning lit up the room. The ferocity of the rain was growing weaker by the minute as the storm passed, leaving a tremendous light show in its wake.

"Might want to take some of the antibiotics, just in case," Buck said.

Daniel looked to the bed, the contents of one of the

Bugout for the Dugout bags spilled all over the comforter. Elizabeth had already made them each take a pill. She didn't say out loud what they both feared. Antibiotics wouldn't do a thing to help them if the rats were rabid—just as they hadn't been able to stop the sickness that was burning Rey and Dakota from the inside out.

"Hey, Dad, how are Max, Gabby, and Miguel?" Rey called out.

"They're good. How are you holding up?"

His heart felt lighter just hearing his son's voice. He was so sick. Running from an army of rats couldn't have done him any good.

"Tired, but I'll be fine. These rats won't give up."

The wet *thunk* of bodies crashing into the doors had become steady white noise. Daniel kept picturing wood rat traps, a truckload of them, thrown atop the ceaseless rats. The hard *thwack* of thousands of metal bars snapping shut on heads, bodies, and tails of the filthy vermin would be music to his ears.

"Any of them bite you?" Daniel asked.

"A couple. Alexiana fixed me up."

"Take it easy for a while. We're safe now."

Daniel heard some shuffling, but there was no reply. Max eyed the door, ready to pounce.

"Max, let your mother look at that leg."

"It can wait."

"Nothing's coming through. I'll keep an eye on the door."

Elizabeth said, "Lift up your pants legs so I can see."

Max sighed, reluctantly abandoning his post. "I'm fine, Mom."

Daniel tapped the club's head in the palm of his hand. A lover of nature shows, he tried recalling any case where a mass of animals as low on the food chain as rats ever pursued larger prey with this kind of single-minded purpose. He kept coming up empty.

When he and Buck had entered the house, they thought they were in the clear. He guessed the door didn't close all the way behind them, leaving a wide-open invitation for the rats. They never would have let Alexiana open the door if they knew the rats were in the house. One second Daniel was knocking, Buck telling him there was a code, the next Alexiana had cracked it open and Daniel saw the horde undulating down the stairs. Now the creatures had flushed them out of the safest place they could be.

There was just so much in the way of supplies in the backpacks. They would run out sooner rather than later.

Thwack! Thump! Thump!

The rats propelled their bodies against the door, mindless battering rams with seemingly limitless stores of energy.

50

Despite the horrible reason for being locked in Buck's bedroom, Gabriela felt strangely relieved. Just to be able to see the sky, even one gray with storm clouds, made her feel lighter.

While her father and brother kept their focus on the door and her mother told stories to Miguel about funny things he used to do as a baby, she stared out the window, looking over the neighborhood. It was dark, even more so without the streetlights that normally would have come on during a storm this bad. Cars remained in parking spots and no one was outside, which looked normal for a day filled with rain, thunder, and lightning. It wouldn't take much to convince herself that it was an ordinary rainy afternoon. When the storm blew away, the block would come to life again, just like it always did.

Don't be stupid, she thought.

If things were normal, they wouldn't have been attacked by rats. Lights and TVs and iPods would work. Her father and Buck wouldn't have gone outside wearing those scary masks to protect them from stuff in the air.

The gas masks!

"Daddy," she said, her heart starting to pound like the backbeat of a P!nk song.

"Yeah?" He was so busy worrying about the door, she was surprised he even heard her.

"Is it safe to breathe the air?"

He gave her a questioning look. "What do you mean, honey?"

Her finger picked at a chip in the windowsill's paint. "Buck made you wear those masks before, but we don't have any now."

It took him a moment to consider his reply. Her mother stopped her storytelling, looking to him with a face Gabby knew well—concern. It was the look her mother gave her when she fell off her bike and needed four stitches just above her eye, or when she said a science test was harder than she thought it would be.

"We were just being overcautious," he finally replied. "It looks like it's rained a lot since we went into the shelter. If anything was ever in the air, it's gone now."

Gabriela looked to Dakota, who was mumbling something in her sleep. The skin of her face was pulled tight over her skull. She was looking less and less like a real person, and more like a wax figure, her flesh so pale and always shiny. Something *had* been in the air. Dakota and Rey both breathed it in. And now they were sick.

The tiny punctures where the rats' teeth had broken the skin itched and burned at the same time.

A dark, fast-moving shape caught the corner of her eye. She gazed at the backyard.

"They're leaving!" She excitedly pointed out the window.

Her mother and father stepped beside her.

"I'll be damned," her father said. He placed his hand atop her head.

The rats fled from the house as one, a sickening mass that blotted out grass and concrete as they headed back to the sewers.

Her father pounded on the wall. "Buck, look out your window!"

51

Buck opened the door a crack to make sure there were no furry sentinels waiting to get inside the room. "We're clear," he whispered, creeping into the hall. A few of the rats lay on their sides in the hall, dead from bashing their skulls while trying to get in the door.

Alexiana helped Rey to his feet. Heat came off his flesh in steady waves. The poor kid looked like a gentle breeze would knock him over. She helped him to the master bedroom and knocked on the door. She heard furniture scrape against the floor and the door opened. A smile broke out on Daniel's face as he pulled his son to him.

"Where's Buck?" he asked.

"Making sure they're really gone. He said to stay here until he gave the all clear."

He ushered Alexiana into her own room. She felt as if she had stepped into some sort of dream where everything was familiar but yet she was still a stranger. "Better you wait in here with the rest of us," Daniel said.

Daniel and Max kept watch by the door, gripping Buck's golf clubs. She couldn't remember the last time Buck had gone to the Dunwoodie course. He'd taken up golf when he took early retirement, but decided it wasn't for him. If he wanted fresh air and cocktails, he said he'd prefer to have them with her in their yard.

No one spoke while they waited for Buck. Occasionally, the floor protested as he walked about the house. One time, he knocked something over in the kitchen.

Alexiana sat next to Elizabeth on the bed.

"How many bites?" Elizabeth asked, looking down at the rips in her jeans.

"We each got a few. I disinfected and dressed them up the best I could."

The house had grown eerily silent.

Where was Buck? He was a big man and the veritable bull in a china shop. Stealth had never been one of his strong points. Alexiana worried at her fingernails, carving bits off with her teeth.

"I can't just sit here," she said, storming over to Max and plucking the club from his hands.

Daniel reached out to stop her but she scampered away. "Buck said to wait here."

"Do you think I do everything Buck tells me?" she spat, heading for the stairs.

"Wait, you shouldn't go alone," he said.

She stopped and saw him hand his club to Max. "Keep the door closed until we get back."

Max did as he was told and Daniel took the stairs in front of her. "Stay behind me and try not to hit me."

The thought almost made her chuckle.

Everywhere she looked, the floors were smeared with filth and dirty water, the greasy residue of the rat horde. Her carpets were destroyed. The only way to get them clean would be by bonfire.

She kept her fingers on Daniel's back, afraid to lose contact with him as they crept into the living room.

"Buck," she called out, softly but loud enough to be heard in another room.

The back door was wide open, the bottom half of the screen door dented from the rush of rat bodies. Daniel looked outside. "Buck!"

A steady patter of rain dripping from the roof onto an aluminum drain echoed in the alley between their two houses.

"Down here."

They spun around. His voice had come from the basement. Alexiana broke away from her human shield and jogged down the stairs. Buck was in the shelter, kicking a crate across the room. It looked like the place had been ransacked by looters.

"How the hell did a bunch of rats do all this damage?" she said.

He grabbed an enormous nylon bag off the table. "There's a lot about what just happened that's going to bother me until the day I die. Those fuckers managed to get into any food that wasn't in a can. Shit, they even ate through a couple of the water jugs."

She looked down and saw he was standing in a half inch of water.

Daniel took the bag from Buck. "I guess we should take what's good and bring it upstairs. If it's not safe to be out, it's too late now."

Alexiana took a box of MREs from the top of a stack. A corner of the box had been chewed but they hadn't gotten inside. "I'll take this in the kitchen, then let Elizabeth know they can all come out."

52

Buck and Daniel spent the night in the living room. The women and children took the upstairs bedrooms, three in all. They'd brought up some of the mattresses from the cots so everyone had a relatively comfortable place to sleep.

The men had agreed to take turns on watch. Even though Daniel said he'd take the first shift, Buck couldn't sleep a wink. It was impossible to shut his brain down, even for a few minutes.

With the absence of electricity and the moon obscured by clouds, the house was doused in complete darkness. They had flashlights, but agreed to use them only in case of emergency.

"You don't want the rats to know we're still here?" Daniel half-joked.

"It's not the rats I worry about."

Buck peeled back the lid on a can of sardines, pinching one out and laying it on a cracker. Last year, the doctor had put him on blood pressure meds, advising him to cut out salt, change his diet completely, and exercise. After all the small-portioned meals and cardio from running around, he'd earned a little treat.

Besides, he thought, *you probably outlived the doctor.*

"You see anything?" Buck asked.

Daniel was at the front window, his shadow a shade lighter than the pitch around them.

"Nothing but a cat that ran across Yanick's yard. We know we're not the only ones around. I expected to see a candle lit in a few windows. Where the hell is everyone?"

Buck swallowed his treat down with a swig from a bottle of Jack Daniel's. He said, "Come tomorrow, we're going to have to make some decisions."

Daniel shuffled around, but Buck couldn't tell where. "There has to be a triage set up somewhere. I'm not even asking for a functioning hospital. Rey and Dakota need professional help. And we all need rabies shots, just to be on the safe side."

"Which means we can't stay here," Buck said.

He let that sink in for a while.

Buck continued, "You and I are going to have to find a way to transport your son and that girl. We can try local doctors' offices first. If no one's home, we can always head to that new medical center over at Ridge Hill. It's closer than St. John's Hospital. Even if the doctors have scattered, maybe your wife can find what we need. And then there's the chance the military or FEMA or some other agency has boots on the ground and relief centers. But we're not gonna know until we get out there."

"And what if those damn rats come out again?"

"We bust the door down on the nearest house and hold them off. That's the good thing about Yonkers. Everywhere you look, there're houses. We'll always be just a few steps from shelter."

Daniel grunted as he plopped onto the couch next to Buck. "Sardine and Saltine?"

"That's all yours," Daniel said.

Chewing the salty combination, Buck said, "It might get ugly out there, Dan. You and I have family to protect. I need to know that you're willing to do whatever it takes to keep them safe."

Daniel didn't hesitate, answering, "Don't you worry about me. I'm the guy that blew a dog away, remember?"

Buck patted Daniel's leg.

He believed him. Daniel might have been a quiet man who spent most of his time staring at a computer screen. But he was a good man who loved his family and was smart enough to realize how deep they were in the shit.

Tomorrow they'd get to wade in that shit, chest-deep if necessary.

53

The next day, after a breakfast of cheese and crackers and dried cranberries, Max was shocked when his father announced they would be heading out in search of a doctor for Rey and Dakota, who were upstairs sleeping at the time.

"I know you're scared, being exposed, but it has to be done."

Max scratched at one of the rat bites. He knew this wasn't just for his brother and Dakota. Everyone except Miguel had been bitten. They all needed medical attention.

His mother hugged his father as they stood hip to hip. It was her less-than-subtle way to show they were on the same page. It was the end of the world as they knew it and they were still cornballs. His friends used to joke that his family was the San Juan Bradys. The crack never amused him.

"The problem we have to solve right now is how to transport Rey and Dakota. They're not up for any long walks."

"Or running," Max added. His mother narrowed her eyes at him.

Buck said, "I have a wheelbarrow in my shed, but it's not the most stable thing in the world. One misstep and it could tip, spilling them out."

Miguel, who had been picking a cranberry apart quietly, said, "How about our bikes?"

"We can take yours and Gabby's bikes," his father said. "But I don't think Rey and Dakota would be able to pedal very far."

Max pushed away from the table. "I know what we need and where to get it. Mr. Burnes around the corner has a bunch of shopping carts he takes from Stop and Shop and ShopRite. He uses them to move his gardening stuff around. We can take them."

His mother looked to his father, then Buck. "What if he needs them as much as we do?"

Max sighed. "They're not his, Ma. He stole them."

Buck said, "We can check and see if he's home, give him a hand if he needs one."

"Can anyone think of a better way?" Alexiana said.

After a long, painful silence, his father said, "All right, Max and I will get the carts. We'll be back in five minutes."

He took a shotgun from the small arsenal that Buck had arranged on the dining room table and handed Max a bat.

"That's all I get?" Max protested.

"That's all you need. Come on."

Buck locked the door behind them. Max took a deep breath. The air smelled good, crisp, not acrid like he'd expected. Down in the shelter, his mind had conjured up all sorts of images, sounds, and smells of what their neighborhood would be like after the attacks. This was counter to everything. It almost bordered on serene.

They jogged around the block, their footfalls sounding like anvil strikes in the silent street. Max couldn't help eyeing the sewers they passed, waiting for their furry friends to come gushing out.

54

Mr. Burnes was a seventy-year-old bachelor who lived on the biggest plot of property in the neighborhood. His one-story house was also the smallest. He was an avid gardener. In the summer, people came from miles around to see his rose garden.

For a man who loved nature, he was not enamored of his own kind. Daniel had spoken haltingly to him a few times and couldn't remember the man ever looking him in the eye. Any conversation seemed like an inconvenience. He'd rather run his hands through fertilizer than say good morning. It was a miracle he allowed perfect strangers to admire his roses.

Daniel and Max spotted one of the pilfered shopping carts sitting by the shed. It was filled with bags of fresh topsoil. Two more carts rested against the rear of the house. One was filled to the top with clippers, trowels, multiple pairs of well-worn gloves, a hedge trimmer, two green plastic watering cans, digging forks, and other tools Daniel couldn't even name. He was no suburban farmer himself. The other cart housed empty plastic flowerpots.

"See, I told you." Max beamed, throwing the flowerpots out of the cart.

"Hold on," Daniel said. "Let's see if Mr. Burnes is home before we ransack his yard."

Max let a pot fall from his hand back into the cart with a look that screamed *why bother*?

Daniel rapped a few times on the back door. When there was no answer, he tried the front, again to no avail. He half-expected to at least see one of Mr. Burnes's neighbors poking their head by a window just to see who was breaking the cone of silence that had taken permanent residence over the block. Nothing.

"Is he home?" Max asked.

"Not as far as I can tell," Daniel replied, hopping to look in the windows. Inside was dark and deserted. He thought of Mrs. Fumarelli and stopped looking. If the man was dead, did he really want to see his second corpse in two days?

He helped his son empty out his cart. "Let's go out the other side where it's paved. That'll make pushing these easier." Before he could maneuver his cart, Max had shoved ahead, taking the lead, the cart in one hand and his bat in the other. Daniel laid his gun in the front bucket, recalling the countless times he'd placed his children in the small seat when they were younger.

An image of a three-year-old Max came to mind, his then-pudgy legs poking out of the tiny plastic holes, hands grabbing for anything they could find on the supermarket shelves. How many times had they gotten to the car, only to extricate Max from the cart and find a pack of batteries, small bottle of spice, candy, or anything else his sticky little hands could get ahold of without their looking, tucking it under his legs? Daniel and Elizabeth took turns trudging back to the store to either return or pay for their son's private stash. And there was Max, smiling away in his car seat, unaware that he was the most skilled thief in the county.

The memory came to an abrupt end when Daniel's cart collided with the back of Max's legs.

"Jesus, I'm sorry, Max. Did I hurt you?"

Max didn't move. He just slowly shook his head from side to side.

Daniel grabbed the shotgun. "What is it?"

His son pointed at the ground to their left. When Daniel saw what had stopped Max, he put the shotgun back in the cart. "Don't look, Max."

Mr. Burnes lay on the pavement, one milky eye staring up at them. One arm stretched out as if he'd tried to arrest his fall by grabbing on to one of the resin chairs he kept at the side of the house. His skin was an ashy blue. Daniel would have thought the man just fell down and died if he wasn't missing the lower half of his body.

Max said, "It's okay, Dad. I've seen dead bodies before."

And he had, at wakes for several older family members. Seeing a professionally prepared corpse in a coffin was one thing. Finding half a neighbor sprawled out by their house was an entirely different experience. Dried, red ropes straggled out from where his stomach should be, looking like the man had been made of shredded cabbage.

"Just keep going," Daniel said. "We have to get back with the carts before everyone starts to worry."

"But what about Mr. Burnes? We can't just leave him here like that. Can we?"

Daniel gripped the shopping cart's handle. In essence, they could, but since Max had brought it up, he had to do something. He looked back into the yard.

"Hold on."

He came back with a blue tarp that had been held by bricks on the top of the shed. They laid it over Mr. Burnes, securing the ends with the bricks.

"Do you think someone will come along and eventually bury him?" Max asked as they pushed the carts down the hill. Daniel's had a squeaky wheel that would have to be oiled before they set out.

"To be honest, I don't know."

55

The moment Max and Daniel returned with the carts, the boy blurted out what they'd found at the side of the old man's house. Dakota had been given a brief respite by the fever gods and was sitting at the kitchen table when they barged through the door. She was sipping a warm bottle of water and nibbling on a cracker.

She'd been out of it for so long, she wasn't sure if what she was seeing was even real. Crazy thoughts and images had been floating through her head day and night. Most times, she couldn't tell if she was dreaming or awake. For all she knew, she was never awake.

When she asked why they weren't in the shelter, Elizabeth had explained everything. Rats? Who ever heard of rats attacking people?

It did little to assure her that she was indeed awake, even when Elizabeth showed her a pair of bites under bandages on her calves.

Even if this was a dream, it wasn't necessarily a bad one. At least she wasn't still in that dank shelter.

Alexiana said, "We'll cushion the carts," and ran up the stairs.

Buck said, "We'll add some water and food in the carts with them. I can tie a couple of packs to the carts, too."

The next few minutes were a flurry of activity. All the while, Dakota watched them in a semi-daze, trying to quell the rumbling in her stomach. At one point, she turned to her right and saw Rey at the table next to her. He looked as bad as she felt.

"Hey," he said. "Nice to see you up."

She gave him a smile. Or did she imagine smiling? It was too tiring to figure out.

"You look like hell," she said to him.

He tried to straighten in his seat and push his hair back. "We can't all be as pretty as you," he said low, looking around to see if anyone else had heard.

"You're sweet," she said, or thought. Was there an echo when she spoke?

Dakota felt a pair of hands slip under her armpits. Next thing she knew, she was standing. Her head swam. It felt as if she'd had four martinis.

"You all right to walk a little?" a voice, Alexiana's voice, said close to her ear.

Dakota tried taking a step. Her knees felt like rubber. Yep, this was definitely four martinis on an empty stomach land. "Sure, I can walk."

"I think I'll keep hold of you, just in case."

She watched Rey push himself from the seat, using the tabletop to balance himself. He took a rifle from a pile of guns—where the hell did those guns come from?—using it as a sort of cane as he followed them out the door.

"I've got her, baby," Buck said before lifting her and placing her in a mound of fluffy blankets in what looked like a shopping cart. When she moved her legs, bottles of water made plastic crunches. "I'll drive," he said.

Her body vibrated as if she were sitting on the world's biggest pocket rocket as the man with the cowboy hat pushed her down the middle of the street. The two kids scooted by them on a pair of bikes.

"Slow down," their father said. "I don't want you more than a few feet ahead of us."

Dakota meant to ask where they were going, but things went kind of gray. She thought of rats, twitching pink noses, whiskers flicking this way and that.

Oh please, let this be the dream part.

She was so tired. She prayed the rats would go away so she could sleep in peace.

56

They'd gone three blocks without seeing another person. Daniel asked them to stop at the corner, jogging up the hill to a house across the street. He shouted hello a few times, jumping a hedge to knock on a window. When no one answered, he came back.

"Guess they're gone," he said to Elizabeth, and resumed pushing the cart with Rey and their supplies. Elizabeth took one end of the handle, as well.

"Who's gone?" she asked.

"There was a girl in there yesterday. She's the one who warned us about the rats. She looked real sick."

They looked at Rey, who was awake, cradling a rifle that he kept pointed at the ground in the jouncing shopping cart. Droplets of sweat dotted his hairline and upper lip. She'd given him Tylenol and another antibiotic an hour ago, but she might as well have had him swallow Cheerios.

"Daniel, where is everybody?"

"I don't know. It was like this yesterday. At least it's not raining. And teeming with damn rats."

Buck looked over at them and said, "If those little fuckers come out again, I have a surprise this time."

Elizabeth was afraid to ask. Her heart fluttered when she

spotted Dr. Manetti's office. Kimball Avenue was littered with abandoned cars under a hazy, gray sky. And here, on a bigger and busier street, was something else they hadn't seen before—big splotches of what looked like deep maroon paint in the streets and sidewalk. If it was blood, then where were the bodies?

"Do you think there's any chance he's there?" she asked.

"It can't hurt to look. At the very least, he should have some different meds we can try."

Gabby and Miguel rode their bikes in lazy circles around them.

Pulling up outside the doctor's office, Daniel and Buck tried the front door. It was locked. No one answered.

"We didn't come here for nothing," Buck said, kicking at the door with all his might. The lock broke away from the frame on the fifth blow. "If anyone was asleep inside, they're awake now."

Daniel took Elizabeth's hand. "We'll check."

Buck waved them through, then went back to Alexiana and the kids. Max tapped the head of the bat in his palm, looking up and down the street, expecting trouble.

"Hello, Dr. Manetti?" Elizabeth said as she stepped into the dark, empty waiting room. Daniel tried the light switch on the wall.

"It was worth a shot."

Everything looked as it should on a day when the doctor wasn't in. Nothing was out of place. When things went south, Elizabeth expected places like doctor's offices and pharmacies to be ransacked. Anyplace that housed drugs was a target for looters or people like them in need.

Somehow, his office had been overlooked. Maybe it was because his shingle had been torn off the side of the house during Superstorm Sandy and he'd said it wasn't worth replacing. "If people need me, they'll find me," he'd told her one day, clicking his pen incessantly as he always did.

They crept past the reception desk, making their way toward the corridor in the back. There were three examination rooms down there, as well as the doctor's office. Inside the first examination room was a large glass cabinet, two chairs, and an adjustable bed.

"He had a key to open that," Elizabeth said, pointing at the cabinet. "That's where all the samples are."

To her surprise, Daniel smashed the butt of the shotgun into the glass.

"No sense wasting time looking for a key," he said.

Elizabeth found her hands were shaking. This was stealing. No matter what had happened, she couldn't simply wash away decades of a good, Catholic upbringing.

Then she thought of Rey and Dakota, crammed in those shopping carts. And what if they all started to get sick? There hadn't been enough gas masks to go around and they'd already been exposed when they had to flee the shelter.

Opening drawer after drawer, she searched for anything that might come in handy. She grabbed a white coat from a peg on the back of the door and tossed a few items into it, including iodine, alcohol, and aspirin, as well as some bandages.

"Let's try the next exam room," she said.

After Daniel repeated breaking the cabinet glass, she hit the jackpot. Inside were some heavy-duty antibiotics, including cefepime, levofloxacin, and a generic of penicillin. There were also alprazolam, also known as Xanax, an antianxiety medication; Percocet, a potent painkiller; and Ultram, a nerve blocker. She threw those in the coat, wrapping it up like a hobo's bindle, filling it with more from the next room.

When they were done, Daniel placed the haul on Rey's lap. Buck produced a plastic bag. "Gotta keep them dry in case it rains."

Elizabeth tried closing the doctor's door, but the hinges were warped from Buck's battering. She wrote a quick note that said: *We're sorry, but we needed the medication. Our child is sick. Please forgive us.* She put it on the floor inside the doorway.

Everyone silently waited for her. She joined Daniel's side at the cart, and they pushed their way to one of the main streets in the city, McLean Avenue.

57

Alexiana first realized how famous McLean Avenue was, or infamous, depending on your point of view, when she went on a business trip to London seven years ago. After a day of training the new hires in her company's latest European office, they all headed out for drinks at the Rose and Crown Pub, a local dive that was the perfect spot for what had turned out to be a rowdy bunch.

They loved her American accent, and she went through countless rounds of "say '*ball*'" or "say '*forget about it*' like a gangster!" One of the pub's regulars heard her New York–ese, turned on his stool, and asked, "You wouldn't by any chance live by McLean Avenue, would ya, miss?"

"I actually live just two blocks away," she'd replied, wondering where the conversation was heading.

He gave her a toothy grin and said, "Well, what are you doing here, then? You have all you need back home!"

If all she needed was a vast selection of bars and restaurants, he was absolutely right. McLean Avenue was a two-mile stretch packed with them, especially the end by the Bronx border that was home to more Irish people straight from Ireland than there were in some of its counties.

Along with the bars were hundreds of shops, several

parks, schools, apartment buildings, repair stations, and supermarkets. The streets were always filled with people and cars, at least until closing time at the bars.

They stopped underneath the dark stoplight strung above the intersection of Kimball and McLean Avenues. There wasn't a living soul to be seen in either direction. Alexiana shivered.

"I thought of all the places, there'd at least be someone here," she said.

Buck pushed the cart with Dakota around the open door of an abandoned Honda Civic. "I did, too," he said. "Things this bad, I'd hoped the bars would show some signs of life."

Daniel pushed his cart next to them. "Maybe we'll find some people in the bars. We can give a quick check inside each as we go by."

Gabby pedaled too far ahead of them, weaving around cars and delivery trucks left in the middle of the street. Daniel shouted at her to stop.

"The military has to have someone in charge somewhere," Alexiana said to Buck. "If I were in charge, I'd try to set up bases in the main thoroughfares. That could be Central Avenue, Saw Mill River Road, Miles Square Road, or here."

"There're a couple on the south side they could use, too, like South Broadway," he said.

"A lot of people on South Broadway," Dakota said, startling them. They thought she'd fallen asleep again. "I went there all the time to get White Castle. God, I'd kill for one of those burgers right about now."

Alexiana's stomach grumbled in agreement. She hadn't had a murder burger in over a decade, but nothing sounded better at the moment.

A dog yelped somewhere to their left, behind a three-story apartment building. Everyone stopped, including the kids on their bikes.

"It's some sign of life that isn't from a sewer," Alexiana said. She looked at the windows of the apartment building. Normally, air conditioners would be running or older residents would be sitting by open windows, watching everyone move about. Some were open, but the only things moving within were curtains flowing with the slight breeze.

The echo of other dogs barking chimed in.

"Sounds like when we go to the pet store," Miguel said. He had one foot on the street, the other on the bike's pedal.

The barking turned to angry snarls, the volume rising quickly, becoming more violent.

"They must be right back there," Rey said, pointing with the rifle to the alley between the apartment building and the adjacent empty lot.

"They're coming closer," Elizabeth said. She stepped between Miguel and Gabriela, placing a hand on each of their shoulders.

"We should get going," Alexiana said. The sounds of the fighting pack of dogs chilled her blood.

Buck resumed pushing the cart. "You're right. Come on, everyone, let's move."

They took four steps before the wild dogs came bursting from the alleyway, howling like creatures birthed in Hell.

58

Rey was the first to react. His vision had grown fuzzy the more he struggled to stay awake, but it was impossible to miss the angry pack of dogs. There had to be at least a dozen of varying breeds. Almost all wore collars, and some were trailing leashes. Even the smallest of the bunch, a black and gray poodle, looked like it could rip their throats out.

These weren't stray dogs looking for the scraps left behind. These were once somebody's pets, driven to a level of savagery he was sure their owners would never have dreamed possible.

A Doberman, its fur stained with blood, especially around its mouth, led the pack. Its eyes were locked on Rey's sister. Just as his father jerked the cart forward, Rey pulled the rifle's trigger. The shot went wide right, plowing into the chest of a three-legged pit bull. The dog yelped and flopped backward, the rest of the pack trampling it.

He fired again, this time with the cart in motion, catching the Doberman on the side of the head. It skidded to a stop, its left eye and ear missing, leaving a depression of wet gore.

"Go! Go! Go!" his mother shouted, pushing Miguel and Gabby forward. Everyone was in a panic. They were so busy running, they failed to realize there was no way they could outpace the dogs.

Alexiana shot into the center of the pack with her Beretta. One of the dogs let out a pained whine. She fired off four more shots, spraying bullets across the front-runners. One dog, no bigger than a Chihuahua but hairier, darted at her leg, taking a quick bite before scampering away.

The shopping cart vibrated so hard, Rey's teeth clacked together, sending bolts of pain into the top of his head. He angled his body as best as he could in the cart, hoping to get some clear shots behind them.

"Watch where you point that!" his father shouted.

Rey leaned over the side of the cart, saw some kind of mutt that could pass for a pony, and fired. The round took out the dog's front legs, but it still struggled to remain upright, thick saliva spraying from its black-gummed mouth.

It seemed that more dogs, hearing the commotion, had joined the fray. For every dog they took down, two more took their place.

Maybe Miguel and Gabby could get away, if they pedaled their bikes faster than they ever had before. But Rey and Dakota and the carts were slowing the rest down. It wouldn't be long before they'd be swarmed under by the pack.

Rey pulled the trigger but nothing happened. *Dammit!*

Buck shouted, "Everyone, get into Rourke's!"

Rourke's Pub was just up ahead and to their right. The front door was open, the chalkboard that listed the day's specials lying on the ground.

Rey's stomach dropped when he saw the big step to get into the bar. There was no way the cart could get over the step. And they didn't have time to extricate him and Dakota without leaving their backs open to the dogs.

Miguel and Gabby jumped off their moving bikes. Miguel ran inside the bar, but Gabby had frozen still.

"Gabriela, get inside!" Rey screamed. "Go with Mom, now!"

Her eyes were locked on the throng of mad dogs. Her lower lip trembled, but she wouldn't move.

Max leapt in front of her, knocking her to the ground in an attempt to protect her from the pack. "You heard Rey, go!" he said.

Gabby stumbled on hands and knees, slipping into the dark pub.

Rey's father, not seeing the extra step into Rourke's, slammed the cart, toppling it forward and ejecting Rey onto the floor. Now the cart was blocking the entrance.

Judging by the escalating squeals from the dogs, they had gotten their prey.

59

When Max saw Rey's cart take that nasty spill, his father's chest slamming into the handle, knocking the wind out of him, he knew they were done for. Buck couldn't get Dakota out *and* maneuver her past the wreckage, along with Alexiana.

There was only one thing to do.

He stopped, turned, and faced the oncoming pack.

Flexing his hands around the handle of the bat, he cocked it over his shoulders, waving the bat head in the air. Last summer in Babe Ruth League, he'd knocked the cover off the ball, leading the team in home runs. It was a huge leap from the previous year when he was a reed-thin singles hitter who did whatever he could to get on base so he could steal second and third.

Holy shit, there were a lot of dogs. They looked more like crazed hyenas. One of them, a pale husky, even looked familiar. Was that Mr. Dobson's dog? Max saw him walking it around McLean Avenue all the time. Had the dog turned on Mr. Dobson while they were huddled in the shelter? What had happened to all of the people, and why were the animals acting crazy?

There was no doubt that they wanted to get every tooth and claw they could in him and everyone else.

Max hissed, "David Wright turns on a fastball!"

He swung the bat even with his waist in a savage arc that brought the bat head in contact with five dogs. They went down fast, one of them being carried by its momentum and smashing into his shin.

Like a pendulum, he brought the bat back around, battering the next wave of dogs. Back and forth he went, hitting everything within range. The bat thrummed in his hand, jostling the marrow in his bones. Still dogs made it past his bat, taking their pound of flesh where they could. With adrenaline firing through his system, he barely felt the nips at his flesh.

Shots rang out beside him. He didn't dare take his eyes from the attacking dogs. He felt the bodies of the ones that had fallen around him twitch and struggle to regain their footing.

"Max!" his father shouted.

He pulled the bat back, ready to bring it down on the head of a sheepdog whose fur was caked with mud, when something pulled him back. Losing his balance, he toppled over the prone body of one of the maimed dogs. When he looked up, he saw his father standing where he'd been, pumping rounds into the dogs with the shotgun.

"Get inside, now!" he yelled.

The pack was thinning. Alexiana and Buck were emptying their guns into them now, too. Dakota was stuck in the cart, eyes wide and terrified. Max chucked the bat into the bar and ran to her cart.

An Irish setter leaped to wrap its mouth around his arm. Max ripped the bowie knife from his pocket, slamming it into the dog's shoulder. The crazed beast ran off, the knife's handle jiggling with its stride.

There goes my knife, Max thought, cursing the dog.

He lifted Dakota out roughly, momentarily holding on to a breast before shifting her weight. A bloodred Pomeranian soared over the leaking body of a boxer. It sank its teeth into Dakota's side. She squealed with agony, her eyes rolling in her head like dice. "Get the fuck off her!" Max shouted, ramming his knee into the dog and dislodging it from Dakota. Blood dripped onto his hand, making it difficult to carry her.

Another dog bashed into his back. Max staggered, nearly dropping Dakota. A shot rang out and the dog flipped over itself. Buck howled, "Get your asses inside!" turning the gun back on the advancing dogs.

Carrying Dakota into the bar, he handed her to his mother. Miguel and Gabby were huddled in a booth, eyes glued to the front door.

"You got her?" he said.

His mother's head bobbed up and down frantically. He headed back for the door.

"Max, stay here!" she shouted.

He scooped up the bat and jumped over the cart blocking the exit.

60

If Daniel hadn't seen it with his own eyes, he wouldn't have believed it. His fourteen-year-old son had taken on a multitude of frenzied dogs and saved his family and friends—all with just a baseball bat!

Alexiana fired her last bullet into a German shepherd and let out a deep, guttural cry. Droplets of blood and gore dotted her clothes and face. She and Buck had hit a lot of the dogs at point-blank range and were, unhappily, wearing the results.

Max bumped into Daniel when he reemerged from the bar, bat held high.

The few dogs that were left turned tail and ran back behind the apartment building. Spread out before them in a grotesque semicircle were the broken and bleeding bodies of almost two dozen dogs. The smell of blood and perforated organs was enough to make him gag.

Daniel wanted to say something to his son, to pull him into a hug, happy he was unhurt and proud as hell for what he'd done. He could see that Max was still humming, his chest heaving, eyes fixed on the dogs' escape route. Instead, he clapped him on the back.

"Thanks, Max."

The boy muttered something in return, a barely audible grunt.

"Buck, Alexiana, you okay?" Daniel said.

Buck tipped his hat with his pistol.

"Just a few bites, nothing serious. Looks like we all got a little jacked up. Holy shit, Dan, what the hell was that all about? I don't think they attacked us because they're hungry."

"Let's get inside, then we can talk," Alexiana said.

They picked up Rey's cart and everything that had been in it, rolling it into the safety of the bar. They did the same with Dakota's cart and shut the heavy oak door. Daniel grabbed a few chairs and jammed one under the knob, piling the rest between the door and the wall of the foyer.

Seeing Rey, Elizabeth, Miguel, Gabriela, and Dakota shaken but safe gave him a reason to finally exhale.

With only a couple of windows facing a dark alley and wood paneling covering every inch of the bar, Rourke's was almost as gloomy as the bomb shelter. A large, U-shaped bar presided in the center of the tavern; it was flanked by dining booths, with an elevated common room reserved for bar overflow, dancing, and local bands.

"I figured as much," Buck said, leaning over the bar. "This place has been wiped out."

Daniel looked at the empty liquor display racks. The glasses still hung from metal racks over the bar, but there was nothing to pour into them. He wasn't a big drinker by any means, but knowing he was locked in Rourke's with no access to a drink made him desperate for two fingers of Scotch or even a beer. Anything to help settle his nerves.

"Was anyone bitten?" Elizabeth asked. "I can't tell with all the blood on your clothes."

Daniel, Max, Buck, and Alexiana nodded. "Just a few small bites here and there," Daniel said.

"Now we really have to worry about rabies," Max said.

"I'll look you all over and dress your wounds," Elizabeth said, her face pinched.

Rey and Dakota were spread out on the padded benches of adjoining booths. "Too bad we didn't film my entrance. I could have been a YouTube sensation," Rey said. Dakota gave a quick laugh before cradling her head in her hands.

"You shouldn't joke about that," Elizabeth said.

Rey used his elbows to prop himself up a little higher. "Why not? Everyone around us has disappeared and what's left is mad crazy. First rats, now dogs." He looked like he wanted to say more, but he was overcome by a phlegmy coughing fit.

Seeing Rey's and Dakota's waxen faces, circles under their eyes so dark it looked as if they hadn't slept in a year, Daniel knew they needed to find a way to keep going, rats and dogs be damned. There had to be medical help somewhere in a city of millions. There was no way they could just be abandoned.

Buck tossed a dirty rag to him. "You got a little blood and stuff on your neck."

Alexiana was pouring the dregs of a glass of water onto another rag to wipe her face and hands clean.

A couple of dogs howled outside. Were they mourning the loss of their brothers and sisters, or calling for more to ferret out the humans trapped in the bar?

Daniel said, "I think we need to stay here for tonight, rest up. We've had enough excitement for today. First light in the morning, we need to try again. We'll have to be more methodical with how we proceed."

Order. Forethought. Consistency. Daniel lived and worked by excelling at each. This world they'd emerged into might be chaos, but there had to be a way to find order within it.

"I'm with you," Buck said. "You and I should check around, make sure the place is secure." He fished a box of fresh shells from a canvas bag he'd tucked under Dakota's cart. "When there's a lull, reload."

Daniel was feeding his shotgun when Max called out from somewhere in the dark recesses of the bar.

"Dad, Buck, come here!"

As Daniel ran, following the sound of his son's voice, his veins turned into twisting icicles when he heard Max say, "Don't move or I swear I'll hit you."

61

Buck helped pull the man to his feet. Max stepped aside, ready with his bat should the guy make a move.

He was in sorry shape. His clothes were tattered and filthy. He smelled like it had been a week since his last shower. He looked to be in his early thirties. His crew-cut hair was littered with bits of dust and dirt, and the flesh around his eyes was speckled with tiny red dots, what looked like burst capillaries.

Wobbling on his feet, they all took a step back when he started coughing. Daniel pulled a bar stool over and slid it beneath him so he could sit.

"You need a drink or something?" Daniel asked.

"Why the hell do you think I came here?" he shot back, wiping the drool from his mouth with his forearm. "Found some beers and half a bottle of Turkey a couple of days ago. I fell asleep after I finished 'em, and when I woke up, I was too fucking weak to try Mulligan's across the street. You want to put that bat down, kid?" He reached into his back pocket, extracting his wallet. He opened it to show them his badge and Bronx P.D. ID card. "Assaulting an officer can get you some serious jail time."

He laughed so hard, he broke into another coughing jag.

"You're a cop?" Buck said.

The man swallowed hard, cleared his throat. "Am, was, I don't even know anymore."

Daniel said, "Then you must know what happened."

Wiping tears from his eyes, he replied, "I know a lot of shit blew up from here to the city and north of us."

"How far did the attack go? Who did it? Do you know what we were hit with?" Buck asked in rapid fire.

"I don't have a fucking clue, man. Everything happened so fast. Before we knew it, all communications cut out. Then the power went. I was on my beat over on Katonah Avenue when it went down. It was fucking bedlam. There was nothing I could do. They all thought I had the answers, like you. I knew as much as they did."

Buck's heart sank.

"You all look in pretty good shape," the man said, then eyed Rey and Dakota. He called over to them, "Did you see the white smoke?"

Dakota replied, "Yes. We were in the middle of it, like a fog." Her flesh was bathed in sweat.

He motioned for Daniel and Buck to come closer, then lowered his voice. "I don't know what was in that smoke, but it's lethal. I got a whiff of it before I holed up in someone's basement. Guess that's why I outlasted most others."

Daniel had to restrain himself from grabbing the man's shirt. "What do you mean *outlasted most others*?"

He straightened up as best he could on the stool and stared at them incredulously. "You've been out there. They're all dead, man. Those who aren't, like me, are just waiting. And the way I feel now, I hope it comes soon."

62

When Elizabeth overheard the man talking to Daniel and Buck, her heart felt as if it had stopped beating, filling with blood until it was about to burst.

No! Rey was not going to die. What did he mean about white smoke?

"Stay here with your brother," she said to Gabriela and Miguel. They shifted into a booth next to Rey. Alexiana had found a few bags of chips. She gave them to the children and then held Elizabeth's hand as they made their way to the sick policeman. Max stayed by the front door, out of earshot.

Thank God for that, Elizabeth thought. She was worried enough about him and what he'd been forced to do outside.

Elizabeth strode up to the man. He looked as if he was about to slip off the stool. "You can't mean everyone is dead or dying. There has to be help somewhere."

He lowered his eyes. "Ma'am, I'm sorry for saying that so loud. Those your kids?"

"Yes."

"Look, I don't know who attacked us or what they dropped on us, but there was something laced in the heavy, white smoke that's killing everyone who was exposed to it."

"If that was the case, we'd see more bodies. We walked at

least ten blocks and didn't see a single one," Daniel said. She wrapped her arm around his waist.

The man swallowed hard. "It doesn't do it right away. From what I gather, the more you breathed in, the quicker it works. Most people ran to their homes when everything went to hell. I'll bet that if you checked in the houses and apartment buildings, you'd see more than your fair share of bodies."

She thought of what Daniel had told her about Mrs. Fumarelli and the old man around the block. The acid tinge of bile bit the back of her throat.

"If that's the case, the military has to have some triage units set up somewhere," Buck said, steadying the man and offering him a bottle of water. He took three loud gulps.

"Who the fuck knows," he said. "The only way to find out is to either walk until you see it for yourself, or run into someone who's been there. We're deaf, dumb, and blind now. Whoever did this just turned us into cavemen. Sick fucking cavemen."

Elizabeth considered the antibiotics she'd taken from the doctor's office. She ran to the bag, emptying out a couple of the most potent pills. She gave one each to Rey and Dakota. If people were too sick to leave their houses, they weren't able to get medical attention. She had to pray that being able to get some potent drugs into Rey and Dakota would make all the difference in the world.

"Here," she said to the cop. "Take this."

"What is it?"

"It's a very strong antibiotic. Doctors use it when all others fail. Kind of a last resort."

He bounced the pill in his palm. "It can't hurt at this point." The pill was thick and chalky and he almost coughed it back up. She also gave him three Tylenol. She didn't need to feel his forehead to know he was burning with fever.

Now her other concern was contagion. People exposed

to the white smoke were infected, but could they in turn infect others?

"Where were you folks headed?" he asked, his eyelids fluttering. Sleep was tugging at him hard.

"We don't know," Daniel said. "We were hoping to find some kind of base of operations so we could get proper medical attention."

"Dan, help me set him down," Buck said. The two men gently laid him down on the floor. Buck kicked the padded cushion off a bar stool and placed it under his head.

"If you go back out there, be careful," the cop said, turning to his side, a small burst of coughing shaking his fragile frame. "It's not just the dogs. Shit, if it was just them—"

Elizabeth knelt beside him. "What else do we need to be careful about?"

He was out. She tried tapping his hot cheeks but couldn't rouse him.

Daniel put a hand on her shoulder and squeezed. "He even admitted he doesn't know everything. There has to be someone out there who knows what happened."

A single tear leaked from the corner of her eye. Tilting her head, she wiped it on her husband's hand as they watched the sick cop sleep.

Suddenly, Miguel said, "Mom, where's Max?

63

Slipping outside had been easier than he thought it would be. His parents were so into that weird guy, they hadn't looked his way. He'd even been able to lift a gun out of the bag that Buck had brought.

His logic was simple. They had to leave the bar, sooner rather than later. Rey was sick, maybe even dying. Everyone could see that, even if they didn't want to admit it. Dakota was in even worse shape.

If they were going to resume walking, they had to make sure that whole insanity with the dogs wouldn't happen again. Max had watched the survivors run behind the apartment building. Back outside, he could kind of hear them, grunting and growling.

He'd proven he could protect his family and friends. Now what he needed to do was catch the rest of those dogs when they weren't looking and finish them off. That way, they could safely get back on the road.

He ran across the street, angling between two stalled cars.

It smelled like rain. Looking up, he saw massive gray clouds moving in. It seemed like it had rained a lot since the day they ran into the shelter. What had happened that was so powerful, it could even alter the weather?

Dashing to the front of the apartment building, he paused with his back against the brick façade. Looking to his left, he saw the empty store that sold auto parts. His father used to take him there when he was just a little kid and let him choose an air freshener for the car while he bought motor oil and air filters. The place had been empty a long time. It was no longer alone in its state of abandonment.

Taking a deep breath, Max turned the corner, stealthily making his way down the alley. His friend from sixth grade, Dana Marone, had lived in this building. They had played in the little courtyard out back when they were in third grade. It wasn't much, just a square plot of grass alongside a tomato garden the super, a Russian man they called Mountain, planted every year.

He stopped at the corner to the courtyard. Yes, the dogs were definitely there. Their smell alone gave them away. It was wet dog plus raw, rancid meat times ten—a stomach-churning combination.

Max poked his head around the corner. His mouth dropped open.

The dogs—there were four now—greedily pulled their share of meat from a strange-looking pile. Long, spaghetti-like strips of flesh and tendon stretched from their muzzles to the pile, snapping when pulled too far. The dogs hungrily gobbled up the crimson strips of carnage.

The pile itself consisted of several bodies—human bodies. Max saw bloody drag marks leading to the mound of rancid meat.

Holy shit! They must be finding dead people in unlocked houses or on the street and bringing them here.

Max felt all the bravado bleed from him in a torrent.

An upturned hand, the fingers curled, lay by his feet. Worse still, the hand was small and delicate, like a toddler's.

Staring at the hand with revulsion, he felt something staring right back at him. He looked up and over to the gathered remains.

The dogs met his gaze, muzzles dripping with blood and torn muscle.

64

Buck had to restrain Daniel from running out of the bar unarmed. If Max had slipped outside, he couldn't have gone far, but those damn dogs were still out there.

"Dan, take this," he said, handing him the shotgun. "Just hold up a second."

He tore open the canvas bag he'd stuffed under Dakota's cart, blindly searching for what he should have had on him in the first place. Something cold and metallic slid into his palm. He stuffed it into his pocket.

"Okay, let's go," Buck said. "Alexiana, stay here and keep watch at the door."

"You be careful," she said, jogging to take her position.

He was damn proud of her. Back in the shelter, when the days seemed to go on forever and the whole not-knowing-what-awaited-them felt like an impending biopsy result, he wondered if she had the mettle to face a world that might be forever changed. She was smart as hell and physically strong, but she'd experienced very little hardship in her life. So far, she'd proved she could handle anything that was thrown at them, and it was a boatload of high strangeness.

Maybe all of his worrying about everyone had been for

nothing. Alexiana and the Padillas, even Dakota, were tougher than a cheap, overcooked steak.

Daniel kicked the door open, revealing an overcast sky. They had to hurdle over the ring of dead dogs.

"Max! Where are you? Max!" Daniel shouted.

Taking his rifle from his shoulder, Buck joined in. "Hey, Max, say something if you can hear us!"

There was no sense worrying about keeping a low profile. If the cop was right, there were very few people left to hear them, and they were probably too sick to respond.

If more dogs or even rats were around, they'd smell them well before they'd hear them shouting for the boy.

Daniel jogged up the street a bit, calling out for his son. Buck stayed close to the bar's entrance, keeping his eyes peeled for any signs of life.

"Where the hell could he have gone?" Daniel said. His face was flush with desperate concern and a hint of anger.

"Maybe he's still in the bar. He might have gone downstairs to the kitchen."

Buck kept waiting for Alexiana or Liz to open the door and tell them they'd found him. He looked up at the massive clouds. It was going to start pouring any minute now. He shouted as loud as he could. "Max! Max!"

He froze when he heard a dog howl, then another, and another.

Daniel ran back to him, his shotgun aimed at the apartment building. "It's coming from back there," he said. "Do you think—"

Buck shook his head. "No, Max is fine."

Another dog let out an eardrum-thrumming wail. It was the sound of an animal on the hunt, or hurt, or both.

Reaching into his pocket, Buck motioned to Daniel to follow him. If there were more dogs around, there was no sense waiting for them to attack again. No, this time, they had to be on the offensive.

He hoped like hell that the kid was down in that kitchen, scrounging up something to eat. This was no place for a fourteen-year-old, no matter how big and strong he'd become.

A shadowy movement caught his eyes in the deepening gloom. He said to Daniel, "Don't shoot. Just put your finger on the trigger guard for now."

He could hear his neighbor breathing heavy, see the barrel of the shotgun waver in his unsteady hands. Daniel didn't reply.

Buck squinted his eyes, trying to make out the slow-moving shadow in the alley across the street. One of the dogs, a small one by the sound of it, tore off with a long series of angry yips.

They were getting closer.

Something shifted in the alley.

Daniel fired his shotgun. Bits of brick exploded.

They heard a pained scream.

Max!

65

Daniel's heart and stomach plummeted to the floor.

I shot my son!

Max fell from the shadows, landing hard on his back, clutching his arm. Daniel ran to him, his pulse whooshing, making it impossible to hear what Buck was shouting to him.

He slid on the concrete like a baseball player stealing a base, stopping just shy of his wounded son. There was blood on the sidewalk and seeping from between Max's fingers.

"Oh, Jesus Christ," Daniel moaned, careful not to move Max too hard. He cradled his head in his lap. Max's eyes were shut tight, grimacing with pain.

"My arm burns," he said.

"Let's get you back inside."

Daniel wanted to say he was sorry, to plead for forgiveness, but the words formed a logjam in his throat. His whole body trembled as he attempted to get Max to his feet. The boy let out a sharp cry of pain when Daniel accidentally grabbed his wounded arm.

"Wait," Max said.

"We have to get you off the street."

Just focus on getting him inside so Elizabeth can take care of him. She'll know what to do. She worked in the ER in St. Joe's. They had gunshot wounds all the time.

Struggling, Max managed to stand. Buck pulled up beside him. Max pointed down the alley.

"The dogs," he said. "They . . . they're eating people."

The first canine, a bloody Labrador, crept from the alley, its head low, spooked by Daniel's shotgun blast.

"How many are there?" Buck asked.

"Four . . . no, wait, a few more came from another yard. Seven, maybe," Max sputtered.

A couple more heads peeked out from behind the Lab.

Buck picked up Max's bat and said, "Both of you get to the bar. I've got this."

He fired a shot at the dogs, missing, but it was enough to get them to scrabble back into the alley. Daniel saw the grenade in the man's hand. He pulled the pin and tossed it in the alley.

"Run!" Buck shouted.

Daniel looped his arm around Max's waist and sprinted to the bar. Despite being shot, Max was able to hop over the bodies, but he slipped on something pink and gray that had spilled from one of the dogs. They both went down, cracking their tailbones.

Buck came barreling over the dogs, skidding into the closed door of the bar.

Before Daniel could move, there was a tremendous explosion. The pressure made his ears pop, followed by a high-pitched whine and an unnatural, muffled silence.

66

Alexiana threw the door open the moment she heard the blast. It shook the foundation of the tavern, knocking glasses from their perch above the bar. She pushed her shoulder into the door and was met by heavy resistance. Something was blocking it.

What the hell had just happened? Was the bombing starting all over again? Was whoever had done this not happy with just under a one hundred percent casualty rate?

She shoved the door again, and this time it flew right open.

Relief flooded her when she saw Buck helping Daniel and Max to their feet. It was short-lived once she saw the blood running down Max's arm. She stepped aside so they could get him into the tavern and shut the door behind them.

Rey yelled, "What happened? Is everyone all right?"

"Just took care of the rest of the dogs," Buck replied. "Lizzy, we're going to need your help."

Elizabeth ran to Max.

"Oh, my baby. Oh, my baby," she cried, over and over.

Her hands fluttered over Max. Daniel helped him into the booth next to Rey.

"Did Max get bit?" Rey said, standing on wobbly legs, leaning over the table to take his brother's hand.

Max's face was pale as seashells. His eyes were glassy and he was shivering. Alexiana grabbed a blanket from one of the shopping carts and handed it to Daniel, who gingerly placed it over his shoulders.

"I was shot," Max said, grimacing when Elizabeth touched the arm that was bleeding. The fabric of the light sweat jacket he was wearing was torn by his upper arm.

"Do you think you can take your jacket off?" his mother asked him.

He nodded.

It was obvious he was biting back tears while his mother and father helped get it off him. She pulled back the sleeve of his shirt.

"I need a light," she said.

Alexiana handed her one of the lanterns, then rushed to get the medical kit.

If Max had been shot, that could only mean he'd been shot by Buck or Daniel. She felt like she was going to be sick. Unless there were other survivors in the area, armed and dangerous.

"Just look at me, bro," Rey said. "Let Ma take care of your arm."

Even Dakota had managed to get up, sidling next to Rey. Elizabeth turned the lantern as high as it would go, studying the wound while pressing a thick gauze pad under the wound to catch the flow of blood.

"Alexiana, can you hand me the peroxide?" she said. Before she tipped the bottle over the nasty gash in his arm, she warned him, "This is really going to sting. I need you to stay still and let it do its job."

She poured the peroxide on his arm. The wound instantly turned white with fizzing foam. Max reared his head back, banging the table with his good fist. Elizabeth let the peroxide soak in for a minute, then cleaned it off gently with another pad.

"The good news is, this is no bullet wound. I just need to clean out the bits of rock and we can apply pressure to stop the bleeding. You're lucky. I don't think you'll need stitches."

Alexiana saw the color return to Daniel's face and his shoulders slump. She understood, and her heart ached for the poor man. He wasn't a trained soldier. He worked with computers, raised a family the best he could, and took them to church every Sunday.

While Elizabeth patched up her son, Alexiana sat with Gabby and Miguel, stroking their hair as they looked on. No one said a word.

Thunder rumbled as fat raindrops pelted the stained-glass windows. Aside from the lantern next to Max, the rest of the tavern had grown dark.

67

Gabriela wanted to hug Max after her mother put his bandages on, but thought better of it. Hugs from her big brother didn't come often, especially the last couple of years. Now he was too cool for anything like that, especially with Gabby.

I bet he wouldn't mind hugging Myrna Castro . . . a lot, she thought. Myrna lived two blocks from their house and had been in Max's class since they were in second grade. He'd had a crush on her forever. There was a time when he used to talk to Gabby about things like that.

Why did boys have to get so stupid when they got older?

The adults didn't say much, other than her father announcing that they would spend the night in the tavern. She didn't like the idea. It smelled weird and there were too many odd shadows cast on the walls from the lanterns. At least the benches in the booths were comfortable.

Her mother was sitting at the bar with her father, Buck, and Alexiana. She tugged on her mother's shirt.

"Can I give the policeman some water?" Gabby asked.

Rey, Dakota, and Max were already asleep, and Miguel was playing with some bottle caps he'd found. She needed something to do. After everything that had happened that day, she was too wound up to just sit and watch her little brother flick bottle caps around.

"Only if he's awake," her mother said. "He's sick and needs his sleep. Here, you can take this bottle."

Her mother kissed her forehead and returned to the hushed grown-up conversation. A gust of wind hammered the rain against the windows. It sounded like it was coming down hard enough to break the glass.

When it rained before, those rats had come, chasing them out of the shelter. Rourke's wasn't half as safe and secure as Buck's shelter. What would they do if the rats came out again and knew they were hiding in here?

Her heart quickened at the thought and for a moment, she felt like crying.

There was no reason to cry, though. Not now. Not just because she let her mind take her to a scary place.

No. The rats couldn't know they were here. It's not like they were super-smart. The last time, they'd followed her dad and Buck into the shelter. This time, everyone was inside, safe, and dry.

What she wouldn't give for her iPod right now. Just an hour to tune out the rain, to close her eyes and pretend she was back home in her room and it was a normal day after school, waiting for her father to come home and dinner to be on the table. To forget that Rey, Dakota, and the policeman were so sick, and Max was hurt, and that they needed guns and grenades just to walk down the same streets where she went shopping with her mother or skipped down when they were home to parades and fairs.

She walked to the other side of the bar where they'd set up the policeman. A blanket was pulled up to his chin. She tiptoed beside him, clutching the bottle of water.

His mouth hung open, but he wasn't snoring like her dad did every morning. The light from the lantern only lit up one side of his face. His skin was so pale, he looked like a mannequin.

A blinding bolt of lightning, followed by a great clap of thunder, startled her. She dropped the water bottle right on the policeman's chest.

Oh no, Mom said not to wake him up!

But the bottle only rolled off him, tumbling across the floor and stopping at her feet. He hadn't so much as moved a muscle.

Bending slowly, carefully, she leaned as close as she could to his open mouth without actually coming in contact with him. Holding her hair up with one hand and turning her head to the side, she tried to calm her breathing and listened.

No sounds came from his mouth.

She waited, moving so close her ear touched his cold lips. She should at least feel the warm breath of his exhalations against her ear.

Gabby quickly pulled away, scooting back from the policeman.

He wasn't breathing. Her ear had touched a dead man!

"Daddy!"

68

Buck looked on while Elizabeth checked the cop.

We never even got his name. I know it was on the ID, but we never got far enough to read it or ask him.

She held his wrist with one hand and pressed her fingers to the side of his neck with the other.

"Is he gone?" Alexiana asked.

Elizabeth nodded, gently laying his arm down.

"I don't want to stay here tonight," Gabby said from the other side of the bar. She was perched on her knees atop a bar stool, peering over at them. Buck could just make out the top of Miguel's head next to her.

"Why don't you kids sit with your brothers," Buck said. Max and Rey were awake now, keeping away from the body so the littler kids would feel safe with them.

Gabby and Miguel's heads ducked out of sight.

"What should we do with him?" Elizabeth asked. "We can't just leave him here."

That was true. Buck couldn't blame Gabby. What child would want to sleep in the same room, a bar no less, with a dead man? The storm wasn't letting up at all, and they didn't have a shovel, so burying him out back wasn't an option.

Daniel said, "What about the kitchen? They have to have

a walk-in fridge or freezer. Buck and I can take him down there. Once we close the door, he'll also be safe from any scavengers roaming around."

Tilting his hat back, Buck said, "It's the closest thing he's going to get to a burial. Alexiana, hand me that tablecloth over there, will you? We'll wrap him up as best we can and carry him downstairs."

With all four of them helping roll the man to his side so they could slip the tablecloth beneath him, they made fast work of getting him ready for transport. He was surprisingly light. Buck guessed the man hadn't eaten for a good long while as the sickness took its toll.

Daniel took the lead down the stairs, bearing the brunt of the dead weight. They smacked the body against the steps a few times, cringing each time, but made it down without any disasters.

Daniel stopped at the final step and laid the body down. He called up the stairs. "Elizabeth, can you bring down a flashlight and the shotgun?"

Buck tensed. "You hear something?"

"We're going to a basement where there's a kitchen. If there are any rats around, I want to be armed."

Buck said, "Good point. I know I'm wiped out when I'm missing something important as that."

Elizabeth scooted around the shrouded body and handed a Maglite and the shotgun to her husband. He swept the beam across the entire kitchen before giving the all clear, handing the flashlight back to her.

With Elizabeth standing to the side providing much-needed light, they huffed and puffed their way to the back of the kitchen where the walk-in sat. The pungent aroma of spoiled food was strong enough to make their eyes water. They quickly placed the body in the center of the walk-in and closed the door tight.

"Might as well look for food while we're down here,"

Buck said. "We need to keep up our strength." *Especially if I'm going to be hauling any more bodies*, he thought. His legs felt like rubber and his lungs burned.

They stuck to the canned goods. Elizabeth found a manual can opener. They carried their haul upstairs, setting everything in a line on the bar. Daniel had even remembered to bring up spoons and forks. Alexiana went back down with Elizabeth to fetch some bowls.

Everyone ate at the bar, even Rey and Dakota, both of them coughing as much as they chewed. Buck noticed how Gabby kept flicking glances at the spot where the cop had died. He stabbed a fork into the peach she was about to eat. She shot him a quizzical look.

"I call dibs," he said, smiling.

"You can't call dibs on food in my bowl," she said.

He popped the peach in his mouth. "You want it back?" A dribble of juice rolled down his chin.

Gabby gave a short laugh, then plucked a pear from his bowl. They went back and forth for the rest of the meal, stealing each other's food and laughing.

"There's no safe base in dibs," Buck said, noting how she had stopped looking across the room. "You've just been schooled, little girl."

Gabby plucked the last morsel in his bowl—a sliced carrot—and crammed it in her mouth.

"I win," she said, showing him her empty bowl.

Everyone laughed, giving her a small round of applause while Buck tipped his hat to her.

When they were done, Elizabeth did the best she could turning the booths into beds with the sheets and blankets they had stuffed in the shopping carts. Daniel found a bottle of Corona behind the cash register. He popped it open with a foamy hiss, took a long sip, and handed it to Buck.

Buck took a pull of the warm, skunky beer and offered it to Alexiana.

"You know we have to leave here tomorrow," he said.

"Let's hope the rain stops," Daniel said, staring at the front door.

Buck imagined the bodies of all the dogs outside, their gore being washed by the lashing rain. Maggots would have a field day. The stench would be unbearable in a day or two.

Even if it rained enough to resurrect Noah, they had to get moving.

69

Dakota woke up the next day feeling better than she had in a week. For the first time, she didn't feel like shutting her eyes and going right back to sleep. Maybe that medicine Elizabeth had given her was working.

"Can I have another one of those pills?" she asked as everyone packed up to leave.

"Sure. Take it with this," Elizabeth said, giving her three Tylenol, as well.

"I want to walk for a while," she said.

When Elizabeth returned with a concerned look, she added, "I need to walk. I'll feel less miserable." *And less like a burden*, she neglected to add.

Rey stretched, swallowing the last mouthful of white potatoes he'd had for breakfast. "Me, too. I gotta move my legs."

Elizabeth felt his forehead, then pressed her lips to his pale flesh. "Your fever is down a bit."

"If you get tired, you can ride my bike," Miguel said, beaming at his big brother.

Dakota's heart melted. Miguel obviously idolized his oldest brother. Rey's illness had probably worried him more than everything else that had happened. Seeing him up and wanting to walk was lifting two spirits for the price of one.

Buck opened the door and went outside with Daniel, shotguns drawn. They came back inside and he said, "We're good. Sun looks like it might come out, too."

Rey and Dakota asked to push the carts. They acted like walkers for them, helping to keep them from falling forward should their weakened legs give out. The sight of the dead dogs, flies buzzing like static on a blaring radio, made Dakota's stomach roll. She was happy to put them behind her.

Because there were so many cars in the road, they kept to the sidewalk, passing the Irish-themed dollar store, garage, and McNulty's Pub. Dakota never understood the meaning of "deafening silence" until now. There should be people and moving cars everywhere. The only things moving besides their party were the front and back pages of a newspaper flipping over itself in the cooling wind.

"It doesn't even feel like summer anymore," Gabby said, pedaling her bike close to her mother.

"Must be all the clouds keeping the sun out," Buck said.

Dakota steered her cart around a skateboard. *I wonder where the kid is who left it here. Is he already dead? Or is he sick, holed up somewhere, waiting for someone to save him?*

The thought made her turn to Rey. He looked as if he'd aged fifteen years. His clothes hung off his already-slender frame.

"Thank you," she said to him.

"For what?" he replied, slowly pushing his cart.

"For saving me. If you hadn't come into the race office, I don't know what would have happened to me."

He bowed his head. "Yeah, but we got sick just the same."

She thought about the cop in the bar. Maybe, thanks to Elizabeth, they wouldn't share the same fate.

"But we're still here. And for the first time in a long while, I feel like I'm part of a family." Before he could say anything, she leaned over and kissed his cheek. Despite being dreadfully sick, he blushed.

Miguel rode his bike between their carts and announced, "Mommy, Dakota kissed Rey."

Rey shook his head, embarrassed.

Dakota was getting tired, but she would be damned if she was going to crawl into her cart and ask Buck or Daniel to take the wheel.

Just walk and enjoy the moment. I don't think there will be many good ones ahead.

70

While Buck and Alexiana took the lead as they slowly made their way down McLean Avenue, Daniel and Elizabeth covered their group's rear. Daniel wanted to make sure his kids were in their sight at all times.

"This is so strange," Elizabeth said. She gripped a Beretta in her right hand, barrel pointed at the ground. "I keep feeling like we're in a bad dream. How many times have I driven down this road? Hundreds? A thousand? The trip from our house to here would take a few minutes, yet here we are on day two."

Daniel paused, thinking he'd heard something move beside the deli to his left. His muscles tensed as he kept one eye on Miguel on his bike and the other on the deli, its front door open, leading to darkness within.

First the horses Rey witnessed go berserk at the track, then the rats and now dogs. Unlike the people, the animals were alive and thriving, but something had altered their behavior. Was it rabies? Could a terrorist infect an entire city with rabies through some kind of chemical weapon? Or had they infected the water supply?

If it was rabies and they didn't find professional medical

help soon, all but Miguel were the walking dead. Only he had escaped the rats' bites as they fled the bomb shelter.

Seeing that the deli was clear, he turned to Elizabeth. "I can't believe it myself. I can't shake this feeling that everywhere we go will be like this. I've never felt so cut off, so completely alone."

Gabby rode a circle around them, her face grim. Daniel reached out to touch the fleeting ends of her hair. She pedaled next to Max. They said something to one another but he couldn't make out the words.

"If it wasn't for Rey, Dakota, and the bites we all got, I'd say we should find a secure place, forage for everything we need, and hole up until the cavalry arrives," he said, kicking aside an empty soda bottle.

"Those are more than enough reasons to keep going," Elizabeth said, nudging his side. "I think I know what day today is."

"You got me. I lost track a while ago."

"Care to take a guess?"

"I don't know. Wednesday?"

"Not just that. The date."

"Now that's asking too much. I mean how—"

She met his gaze with a sad, quivering smile.

"Happy anniversary," she said.

Daniel leaned close and kissed her, savoring her soft lips and the taste of her. "That reminds me, I have reservations at Bolo in the city tonight," he said.

"I've been wanting to go there for years. You think the reservation still stands?"

"If Manhattan is anything like this, I think they can squeeze us in. Of course, I can't guarantee the food will be fresh."

He startled her when he dashed off to a little park at the corner of McLean and Central Avenue. Spotting a cluster of red and purple flowers—he was no horticulturist and had no idea what kind they were—he pulled them up and brought them over to his wife.

"Happy anniversary," he said.

She bent close to smell them.

"Be careful," he said. "No telling what's on them. Could be remnants of the stuff that made everyone sick."

She took a long sniff anyway. "With all the rain, they're clean. Thank you, Daniel."

Elizabeth was an image of opposing factions—a gun in one hand, flowers in the other. Was it wrong to be slightly turned on? No, it was never wrong to have the hots for your wife, especially after two decades of marriage. For all he knew, they were the oldest married couple in all of Yonkers.

They followed the downward turn of McLean and came to a light. About a dozen cars were lined up on either side. They still hadn't seen a soul, not even someone peeking from one of the surrounding apartment buildings. However, there had been a disturbing number of dried red stains on the concrete and asphalt, along with bits of shredded clothing and an odd shoe or two. All were signs of a struggle, or slaughter, with little else to show.

Buck turned to them. "You wanna keep following McLean, or skirt Tibbetts Park?"

"We should go past Tibbetts," Daniel said. "From there we can either follow Yonkers Avenue to St. Joseph's Hospital or take the Saw Mill Parkway to St. John's."

"Tibbetts it is," Buck said. "But not until Rey and Dakota get back in the carts. You both look like you could use the rest."

They made feeble replies, but their eyes flashed with an eagerness to get off their feet.

"We'll push," Daniel said.

"Can you hold these for me?" Elizabeth asked Dakota.

"They're so pretty," Dakota said. "Kind of makes me wish I had a husband to be with me for the end of the world."

They pushed on, the sunlight diffusing through the trees within the park that lined Midland Avenue.

Daniel considered himself a lucky man. His family was still together for a reason. They would find help.

It was just a matter of time.

71

Buck wasn't so sure they'd made the right decision.

On the left was the preserved nature of Tibbetts Brook Park. When he was a teenager, he'd worked as a parking lot attendant there, guiding anxious swimmers into one of the three available lots. Sometimes, he was allowed to collect the parking fee—fifty cents a car—which was a high honor because he'd get to stay in the little air-conditioned booth. It was a much-coveted position on sweltering summer days.

The park was home to the largest public swimming pool in the county, ponds, playing fields, vast picnic and barbecue areas, and an almost-two-mile circular walking/running path.

On the right were rows of one- and two-family houses, each one as dark and still as the one before it.

It had been slow going. He wasn't sure if they could make it to one of the hospitals by nightfall.

And now his biggest fear was nature itself. Tibbetts was home to swans, ducks, geese, squirrels, raccoons, skunks, stray cats, and sometimes even deer, not to mention every kind of rodent that scampered on four legs. If they had been affected like the rats and dogs they'd encountered, they'd have to smash their way into one of the houses and hold them back. And there was no telling what awaited them in the homes they passed. If the cop was right, each was an above-ground grave, an eternal resting place for untold corpses.

They were damned at either turn. Their only hope was to make it to the other side of the road that led to the main thoroughfare of Yonkers Avenue without incident.

He kept two grenades in his pocket. He was glad Alexiana hadn't asked him where he'd gotten them. She, like the rest, was probably just grateful he had them. He wondered if the Vietnam vet who ran the army surplus store in White Plains had made it through everything alive. He was most likely still camped in his shelter, happy to bide his time.

"Keep your eyes on the trees," he whispered to Alexiana.

"Why? Do you see something?"

"No. It's just a feeling that if there are any surprises waiting for us, they'll come from there."

"Maybe we should have stuck to McLean." She readjusted her grip on the pistol.

"It's too late for that now. We need to get through here as fast as we can. If I remember, this part of Midland is a little under three-quarters of a mile. If we pick up our pace, everyone else will, too."

The squeaking wheels of the shopping carts sounded like a clanging dinner bell to Buck. He didn't like this at all.

He looked back at Max, his crimson-stained bat leaning against his shoulder. He looked like a soldier marching with his rifle. The kid was tough, but he'd lost some of his immortality yesterday. He was tempted to give him a gun, but he knew Daniel would be dead-set against it. At least Rey, crammed in the cart, could and would shoot.

Gabby pulled her bike slightly ahead of them and skidded to a stop. "Look," she said, pointing up.

A lone hawk circled high overhead, probably searching for a tasty morsel in the trees and fields of the park.

Where would the ducks go when no one came around to feed them? Buck suddenly thought.

As if reading his mind, Alexiana said, "We should have brought some stale bread."

When the weather was nice, they often fed the ducks at Tibbetts, despite the signs telling them not to.

"Hey, if we can't have bread, neither can they," he replied with a half smile.

Gabby stopped again.

"Are those all hawks?" she asked.

Buck looked up.

The sky was awash with the large gliding bodies of dozens of hawks.

"Where the hell did so many come from?" he said, craning his neck back as far as it could go.

"You think something's dead in the park?" Max said.

"For a dinner party that big, I'd say so," Buck said.

The sky was split by the screeching of the hawks. They rode the air currents, a lazy dervish of keen-eyed predators.

Everyone had stopped walking to take in the aerial display.

"You ever see anything like that?" Daniel said.

They were too spellbound to reply.

A lone hawk spun from the group, venturing outside of the park's perimeter. It swooped low, skimming over the tops of the trees. It let out a piercing wail, angling down the side of an evergreen tree and pulling up at a ninety-degree angle. It made a pass over them, no less than thirty feet overhead, flapped its incredibly large wings, and headed for the circling mass.

"Shit," Buck spat.

He looked to the nearest house, a split-level ranch with iron bars over the windows.

Bet the door is reinforced, too.

"I think we'd better get moving," he said.

The swarm of hawks started to move, descending rapidly in a single, deadly formation.

72

"They're coming!" Rey shouted. He aimed his rifle in the air, peeling off a shot. There was no way to tell if any of the approaching hawks had been hit. They'd formed an undulating, sinking cloud of brown feathers and fury.

"Save your bullets," Buck said, pulling Gabby to him. Alexiana did the same with Miguel. "We have to take cover in there!"

He pointed at a tan shingled house to their right. It had a large bay window and a porch just big enough for two resin chairs and a blue cooler between them. They ran as hard as they could for the house. The wheels of Rey's cart chattered in protest. His teeth clacked together when his father tilted the front up to hop over the curb, slamming back down on the sidewalk and lifting the rear.

The collective cries of the hawks were unlike anything he'd ever heard. All he wanted to do was hop out of the cart and save his father the arduous task of pushing him to safety, but his legs felt like overcooked spaghetti after walking so long.

Gabby let loose with an eardrum-rattling cry as one of the hawks swooped over her and Buck's heads. Buck pulled her from her bicycle, jogging up the small lawn to the front porch.

"Max, look out!" Rey cried.

His brother turned in time to connect the barrel of his bat with a hawk that looked strong enough to carry a full-grown pit bull. The hawk spun to the ground, dead or stunned.

His mother pulled ahead of them, ramming the cart into the front step. Buck and Alexiana were already on the covered porch with Gabby and Miguel. Buck gave the doorknob a savage kick.

"Dammit!"

Rey's father pitched to the side as a hawk grazed his head with its talons. A trio of jagged, bloody lines erupted on his cheek. Gathering himself, he tucked his hands under Rey's armpits and yanked him from the cart. His mother did the same with Dakota.

The aluminum awning over the porch sang with the heavy thumps of dozens of hawks as they dove, their desire to attack blinding them to the barrier. Something heavy hit Rey from behind. His back felt as if it were on fire.

He turned to see two hawks heading right for Max. Rey fired over Max's head. One of the hawks exploded, dousing Max with crimson feathers and tissue.

There was another loud *crack*. Rey turned in time to watch Buck kick the door open after blasting the lock with his shotgun. He practically threw his brother and sister inside.

Suddenly, Dakota screamed. A hawk had gotten its talons tangled in her hair and was attempting to lift her up. His mother swung wildly at the hawk, but it was joined by another, then another.

"Dakota!"

There was no way he could shoot them without hitting Dakota. His father pushed him along, tipping the cart forward carefully at the foot of the steps so Rey could get out. Rey stumbled up the three steps onto the porch, his forward momentum carrying him inside the dark and strange house. Miguel and Gabby rushed to his side. As much as he wanted to be outside helping his parents and brother, there was simply no gas left in his tank to make the effort. Keeping awake, despite the mayhem around him, had suddenly and scarily become a problem.

He turned onto his back and stared at the absolute horror. The hawks were everywhere. And they were winning.

73

Alexiana rushed back outside after telling Miguel and Gabby to help Rey into the living room. The front door was wide open. She prayed that none of the hawks flew inside.

Dakota's feet were several inches off the ground. Her screams were so loud, so shrill, Alexiana thought she was moments away from severing her vocal cords. Elizabeth fought as hard as she could, but she had been knocked down by a massive hawk as it knifed into the small of her back.

Buck and Daniel turned their shoguns around in their hands and swung at the hawks caught up in Dakota's hair. The only problem was that concentrating on Dakota left themselves wide open for attack. Their shirts were torn, revealing blood-slicked flesh. One hawk grabbed hold of Buck's cowboy hat, gliding away with it.

"You son of a bitch!" he yowled. He flipped his shotgun and took a parting shot, missing the hawk with his hat but hitting another.

Alexiana found a thick tree branch by the porch and grabbed it. She joined Max in trying to swat them away from

Elizabeth, who was having a hard time getting up. She must have hit her head when she was bowled over.

"Get the fuck away from my mother," Max howled, swinging the bat as he had with the dogs.

It was madness. She didn't know this many hawks lived in all of Westchester.

Alexiana looked to her left and saw a steady stream of blood running down Dakota's face as her hair started to pull away from her scalp. Daniel locked an arm around her waist, keeping her grounded while Buck slammed a hawk in the beak with the butt of his shotgun.

Something raked the top of Alexiana's shoulder and she nearly dropped the branch.

It hurt like hell. She felt the hot wetness of her blood as it ran down her arm.

Max flipped onto his back as a pair of hawks went straight for his chest. His bat rolled away.

It was a hellish nightmare of flapping wings, wild screeches, and blood. The unbelievably strong force of a hawk snapped Alexiana's neck forward as it found purchase with her hair. She screamed, but everyone else was too pinned down to help her.

I'm going to die!

Falling to her knees, she was sandwiched between two swooping hawks, each latching on to her shirt, pecking at her. She instinctively brought her hands to her face, desperate to save her eyes.

A loud, earsplitting squeal drowned out the mad shrieking of the hawks. Alexiana dropped onto her chest on the cold, wet grass. Dazed, she turned to find the source of the noise.

The hawks were leaving. Everyone had fallen to the ground, gasping.

Alexiana pushed herself up on her elbows.

A man wearing an oxygen mask stood on the porch next door to them. He held an air horn in one hand and the handle of a portable oxygen tank in another. Pressing the air horn again and again with two-second bursts, he drove the hawks back into the murky sky.

74

"Is everyone all right?" the old man gasped through the clear plastic mask over his nose and mouth.

Elizabeth struggled to her feet, then helped Daniel get Dakota upright. The girl was like a dead weight between them. Her eyes kept rolling to the top of her head. The poor girl was about to pass out.

"I think so," Buck answered. "Here, let me help." He took Dakota from her and he and Daniel walked her into the house. All of them were covered in deep scratches and blood, but Dakota looked to have taken the worst of it.

Max touched his mother's shoulder. She pulled him into a grateful hug, thanking God for getting them through and sending help. To her surprise, Max gave her a fierce hug back.

"I thought they were going to take you and Dakota," he said into her neck. "I'm sorry I couldn't stop them."

She broke their embrace, holding his gaze. "You have nothing to be sorry about. Only one person could have helped us, and he did."

They pivoted to face the man next door. He leaned against the doorway, breathing hard.

"We'd better go over there," Alexiana said. The three of

them hopped over the low hedges separating the properties. Elizabeth made it to him first, offering the old man a hand to help him inside.

He waved her off. "I'm fine. Been locked up inside so long, it's nice to get some fresh air." He pulled the mask from his face. An elastic band kept it pinned to his neck.

"We can't thank you enough for saving us," Elizabeth said. "I don't know what would have happened to us if you hadn't come out."

He nodded. "I know what. You would have been carried off like the others. The hawks like to take them high and drop them in the park, like the way seagulls drop clams to break them open. It'd been a few days since I last saw someone. Didn't think there were any more left."

"Hawks?" Alexiana asked.

"People."

Elizabeth noted that he didn't exhibit any of the signs of illness that Rey, Dakota, and the policeman had.

"You better lie low inside the Stevensons' for a while," he said. "Those damn hawks will be back. Them and all the others in the park. Found out the air horn puts a real scare into them, but not for long. Until they find other prey, they'll just circle right on back. I used it to chase that damn flock away from flying off with a young couple a week ago. I couldn't believe it actually worked."

Max said, "So they're all right, too?"

The man put the mask back over his mouth. "Not anymore. They were already pretty sick. They holed up and I assume died right over there." He pointed to a multi-family house behind his own.

"What's your name?" Elizabeth asked. "Are you alone? I'm Elizabeth Padilla and this is my son, Max. My neighbor, Alexiana."

He shook her hand with a weak grip. "Ed Richards. Happy

to see a smiling face that isn't flush with fever. My wife, she's inside."

"I'd be happy to meet her. I'm a nurse. Does she need any medical attention?" She wasn't sure exactly what she could give, considering the state they were all in. If she was sick, she could give her some antibiotics. But that would also mean less for her son and Dakota.

You don't get to choose who lives and dies, she admonished herself.

She pictured Rey with his sweat-soaked skin and hacking cough. Yes, she would choose, and the choice was simple.

"I'm afraid she's past that. She was in the garden when they hit us with the gas. She hung on for as long as she could. I'm keeping her in our bedroom until my oxygen runs out. Then I think I'll just lie down and join her."

He said it so matter-of-factly. It broke Elizabeth's heart.

"I'm so sorry," Alexiana said.

"She's better off. I don't know what the hell happened or who did it, though I have plenty of theories. What's left is no place for people. If you're not sick, you're just walking bait for everything else that's out there. I'm beginning to think my crazy sister and her Bible thumping about the end of days was right." He shuffled his feet, leaning heavily on his oxygen. "Who ever heard of an attack out of the blue where no one, and I mean not a single overpaid public servant or self-serving broadcast network, can tell you a goddamned thing? Men, women, and children die and the damn animals are in control? Maybe it wasn't some country or half-wit jihadists. Maybe it was God cleaning the slate, giving nature a chance to reclaim its place. And maybe I'm just an old man hoping that an act of kindness in the little time I have left will get me to a better place."

Elizabeth didn't know what to say. She didn't want to acknowledge the small part of her that thought he could be right. She'd been a devout Catholic all her life, and it wasn't as if the Church hadn't warned them of a time like this.

"We're holding out hope that there's some order in this chaos, somewhere," Alexiana said. "There has to be."

The old man started to move back into his house.

"For your sake, and your kids', I hope you're right. Like I said, lie low for a few hours. If you don't see them in the sky anymore, you can head out again. But stick close to the houses in case you need to make a fast retreat."

"Why don't you come with us?" Max asked in earnest.

He smiled. "If I was younger and stronger, I sure would. My days for adventure have come and gone. You all stay safe, and God bless you."

The door closed with a gentle *click*.

"Come on, let's go," Elizabeth said, sad for Ed but encouraged by one thing.

He hadn't been sick. Maybe because he was on oxygen, the chemical or toxin hadn't gotten into his system. He couldn't be the only one.

75

When Elizabeth, Alexiana, and Max walked in the door, Daniel jumped off the easy chair and ran to them.

"How bad are you hurt?" he said.

Elizabeth's nose crinkled. She touched the nasty scratches on the side of his head. "About as much as everyone. What's that smell?" Miguel rushed over, wrapping his arms around her legs, almost knocking her down.

"We would have gone over with you to thank the old man, but we had to deal with something else first. Miguel, can you please go sit with your sister for a second?"

The little boy reluctantly ambled back to Gabby, who was sitting by the empty fireplace, staring into it with vacant eyes.

"Buck and I had to remove a body that was lying on the couch," Daniel whispered.

"Oh my God, did the kids see?"

"Unfortunately, yes. They were in here with it the whole time we were fighting off the hawks. I had Miguel take a couple of puffs from his inhaler. He was pretty upset. We put the body in another room down the hall. Just avoid the couch. The corpse was . . . leaking."

Elizabeth's hands flew to her mouth.

Daniel's stomach churned thinking about it. The smell had seared an impression into his nose, deep into his brain.

"Buck found some sealed gallons of water. We should probably all clean up in the kitchen."

"I also found a lot of cans of soup. I'll start up the gas grill in back and heat them up," Buck added, kissing the top of Alexiana's head.

"I think we need to start with Dakota," Daniel said. "She's out right now. It's probably for the best. Hopefully she sleeps through getting those wounds disinfected."

He put his hand on Max's shoulder. For the second time in two days, he'd been in the thick of things, defending his family. They could all take a cue from him. The poor kid was covered in blood and other unidentifiable stuff. "You okay, Max?"

His burly middle son nodded. "I'm fine. Some of those scratches burn, though. Did you see the one that Rey shot? That was pretty badass," he said to Rey, who was sitting on the floor looking like death warmed over.

"I didn't play all that *Call of Duty* for nothing," Rey said before sputtering into another coughing fit.

Daniel said to Max, "First, you need to take some of that water and go clean up in the bathroom. I saw one down the hall. I'll look around for any clothes that might fit you."

Elizabeth said, "Oh, Buck, the man next door said we need to stay inside because the hawks will circle back if they can't find anything else to, well, you know."

"I wouldn't exactly mind the hawk that took my hat coming back with it," he said, giving her a tired wink.

Daniel watched Elizabeth tend to Dakota, who was passed out in a plush chair. He could see the pink flesh beneath her scalp. The girl was already in bad enough shape. She didn't need this heaped on top.

We're going to have to do whatever it takes to survive, he thought. *Nothing is going to be easy or make much sense. No*

*one's going to get a break, no matter how shitty things get.
We'll just keep pushing.*

Daniel went upstairs and rifled through the drawers. The
man who had died on the couch must have been single. There
were no traces of a woman's touch anywhere. He found a pair
of sweatpants and a pullover that should fit Max. He spotted
a small stack of picture books by the side of the man's
dresser.

Maybe he had kids. Divorced? Or maybe nieces and
nephews.

He grabbed the books, as well. They were for younger
kids, but Miguel needed a comforting distraction. Gabby,
too, though she might thumb her nose at a picture book.

Buck had eight cans of soup on the outdoor grill, watching them from the safety of the closed patio door. Someone
had jammed the coffee table against the front door to keep it
closed. Dakota groaned in her sleep as Elizabeth dabbed her
scalp with a moist cotton ball.

They were a sorry mess.

Daniel dreaded going back out there, but he knew it had
to be done.

"I'm going to look around the house," he said to Elizabeth.

"Let me look at your face first," she said.

"You can do me last," he said, and set off to explore every
inch of the bachelor's house.

76

After eating soup with Saltines and two bags of chips, washing everything down with warm bottles of Pepsi and Mountain Dew, everyone stayed in the kitchen. The smell in the living room, and now the room down the hall, seemed to get worse the longer they stayed inside. Max even opened the windows to get some cross-ventilation, but nothing short of a bonfire could expel the stench.

It was starting to get dark outside. Alexiana had spotted a trio of hawks making lazy loops overhead. It looked like they were stuck for now.

"We can't stay here tonight," Max's mother said.

There was no sense anyone asking why. Death had woven itself into the fibers of the house.

"You think the old man would let us crash at his place?" Buck asked.

"His wife is dead in their bedroom," Alexiana said. "Six of one, half a dozen of the other. Besides, I think he wants to be left alone with her. If he wanted us there, he would have asked."

Max said, "You heard what that cop at the bar said. There's probably a dead person in every house."

"Max," his mother snapped, eyeing Miguel and Gabby,

who were staring into their empty soup bowls, on the brink of falling asleep. Everyone was exhausted.

He raised his hands in resignation. His brother and sister had had to sit next to a dead body just a few hours ago. What was the sense of trying to protect them from reality at this point?

"We'll be fine here tonight," Max's father said, striding into the room. He'd gobbled his food and left the table to continue looking around the house. "We can stay in the garage. I'll need a little help pushing the car outside to make room. The owner was a camper and a sports nut. We have what we need for tonight and tomorrow. Best part is, the smell hasn't gotten there yet. Anyone want to lend a hand?"

Max pushed away from the table. "I got it."

Rey said, "I'm in."

"Maybe you should sit this one out, Rey. Buck can help."

Max interjected, "Rey's good. Mom gave him some pills. He can spread out a sleeping bag, right?"

Rey smirked. "Right. Someone has to pick up your slack."

His father sighed, seemed to consider putting his foot down, then said, "All right, follow me."

Thankfully, the garage door was one of those manual kinds and easy to open. Rey put the car in neutral and they backed it into the driveway. Max kept his eyes peeled on the sky. A pair of hawks zigged overhead but didn't seem to notice them.

The man who lived here must have gone camping a lot with friends and family. Old, well-worn camping gear was stacked with brand-new sleeping bags and tents and a camp stove still in the box.

They found rubber mats and laid them out, placing a sleeping bag on top of each. Max went back inside and found just enough pillows for everyone. There were even foil packets of camp food, like freeze-dried ice cream and granola. Rey pitched in as best he could, helping them make the garage as comfortable and inviting as possible.

After the last couple of days, they all needed a nice place to rest. Max spotted two heavy-duty lanterns and placed them in the middle of the circular arrangement of sleeping bags.

"Like a campfire," he said.

His father laid his arm over his shoulders. "Nice work, guys. Call everyone in. Oh, and bring those kids' books I found. I can read everyone a bedtime story."

Max gave a short laugh and headed to the kitchen.

At least for one night, they could pretend that the world outside hadn't gone to hell and a dead man wasn't rotting down the hall.

77

Buck woke up before everyone. He'd always been an early riser. A few years of retirement hadn't changed things a bit. Stretching and yawning, he had to admit it was the best night's sleep he'd had in a while, at least since everything had gone to the shitter.

I guess spending days being attacked by dogs and hawks is good medicine to cure insomnia.

Daniel and his boys had done a bang-up job making the garage comfortable and just shy of homey. They'd done so well, it was tempting to stay there a few days to rest up and fully recover, maybe even stick around until the troops came by to set things right again.

Dakota and Rey slept next to one another. Even in sleep, they looked pained.

Jesus, God, you gotta give us a hand here. They need serious help. Those pills Liz is giving them are only slowing things down. If we don't find help soon—

Padding to the kitchen, he found half a box of Wheaties and several packets of oatmeal. Turning the grill on again, he filled two pots with water and put them on. One was for making oatmeal, the other for coffee. He used paper towels as a filter for the grounds.

No sooner had he poured the first cup when Alexiana came into the kitchen, followed by Daniel.

"That smells so . . . normal," she said, taking the offered cup.

"No cream, but we do have sugar," Buck said.

"I'll drink mine in the garage," Daniel said. "I don't want the smell out here spoiling it."

There was a serving tray on top of the refrigerator. Buck filled some bowls with cereal and oatmeal and carried it all to the garage, along with a pocket full of spoons. Everyone was up, including Dakota, her head bandaged with violet-stained gauze.

"Breakfast of champions," he announced, setting the tray on the floor.

Daniel called him over to the corner of the garage that was filled by two big trunks. While everyone ate, they sipped their coffees.

"What's in there?" Buck asked.

"Protection," Daniel said, flipping the lid of one of the trunks open. The inside was crammed with baseballs, footballs, pucks, tennis rackets, and best of all, helmets. There were at least half a dozen football and hockey helmets.

"Hot damn," Buck said, whistling.

"Check this one out."

The other trunk had rows of protective gear, from shin guards to shoulder pads.

Buck said, "We'll outfit the kids first, and then take what's left. Unless the elephants from the fucking Bronx Zoo are on the loose, we should be in pretty good shape."

Daniel plucked a hockey helmet from the trunk and squared it on his head. It had a clear visor and looked like it'd seen its fair share of ice time. "I don't like the way it dampens my hearing, but it's better than nothing."

Buck tapped the top of the helmet. "I'll step outside, check the unfriendly skies. If our luck holds out, those hawks are long gone and we can test out our new duds. We can make St. Joe's by early afternoon, barring any delays."

He didn't even want to think what else might be waiting for them outside.

At least they'd had a good night's sleep, food, and a form of protection. For one day, they could allow their hopes to ride high.

78

Gabby had a hard time moving her head from side to side. The hockey helmet her father had made her wear was two sizes too big for her head, but it was the smallest in the trunk. He also had her put on shin guards and elbow pads.

She didn't complain. It was, after all, added protection. After what they'd seen over the past few days, they needed all they could get. While everyone else got ready, she stared down the empty driveway, into the woods of Tibbetts Park. There were no hawks to be seen, so far. Alexiana kept watching the sky for their return. But what else was waiting for them in the park?

She'd been there plenty of times and knew it was filled with all sorts of animals. Something had changed them. Whatever had made all the people sick and killed them had done something to the animals. Even coming upon a kitten was a scary thought.

For as long as she could remember, Gabby had begged her parents for a dog or a cat.

Once this was over, she'd never ask again.

"Hey, Gabby, look at me!"

Miguel pulled up next to her. He wore a New York Jets helmet and shoulder pads that made him a little wobbly on his bike. He also had on shin guards and leather batting gloves. Their father had wedged a tennis racket under his seat.

"I can barely see your face," she said.

Within the vast confines of the helmet was a smile. "I even have a tennis racket in case I have to swat a bird or something away."

With the sun shining for the first time and the air so clear, it was hard to believe anything bad could be waiting out there. Miguel seemed unafraid and more impressed with his new suit of armor. She had to restrain herself from reminding him exactly what they were setting out into. It was best to let him remain happy for the moment.

"Mom?" she called out.

Her mother came rushing over. She also wore a hockey helmet with hard plastic leg pads, like a baseball catcher would wear.

"What is it, sweetie? Did you see anything?"

"No. I, well, I want to know—"

The question had been nagging her ever since her father announced that they would be leaving. She was happy to put the house behind her, knowing a dead body was just a few doors away. She'd never forget the man's face or the sallow color of his skin. Or worse, the awful smell.

Her mother went to one knee so they were eye to eye. "What do you want to know, Gabby?"

She looked back at her father, who was talking to Buck while they put a chest pad on Dakota and a batting helmet on Rey.

"Can I have a gun?" she asked, the last word coming out so softly, she could barely hear it.

Her mother stroked her shoulders. "Look, I know you're scared, but you're too young to have a gun. We won't let Max have one, either. If something happens, we'll protect you. I promise, we won't let anything hurt you."

Gabby had suspected as much and promised herself she wouldn't make a scene when her mother said no. Only babies made scenes.

"Okay," she replied, looking at the concrete between her feet. "I just want to be able to help if . . . if something bad happens again."

"You can help by doing exactly what we tell you. Why don't you walk with me? We can hook your bike on the end of Dakota's cart. You can help me push."

It was impossible to resist her mother's warm smile. It was the smile that got her to do her homework when she was tired and fed up, or help rake the yard when all she wanted to do was watch TV.

Gabby smiled back, and received a big kiss on her forehead in return.

"Everyone ready?" her father said.

They looked like a mash-up of every sport imaginable, like modern knights that got their armor from the Sports Authority. Any other time or place, they would have looked ridiculous.

Here and now, it looked and felt right.

Dakota patted Gabby's head as she took one end of the cart and pushed it down the driveway.

79

Rey insisted that he walk despite looking horrid. The circles under his eyes were getting darker and the flesh of his face pulled tighter over his skull. Daniel relented, but on the condition that Rey hold on to the cart.

Dakota didn't even make the attempt this morning. It was probably best. Elizabeth had given them each an antibiotic before they left. Dakota said the pills gave her terrible stomach cramps. In anticipation of what could come, Elizabeth asked Rey to find as much toilet paper as he could. Luckily, there'd been a full twelve pack of double rolls in the linen closet.

"What a picture we make," Daniel said to his wife. He tapped the shotgun's barrel against his batting helmet.

"I've seen you wear worse when you mow the lawn," she replied, nudging his side with her elbow.

"What do you mean by that? I *lawn ranger* in style."

"Honey, jean cutoffs belong on teenage girls . . . in the eighties. You add your dress socks and sandals to the mix and you have an epic fashion faux pas. It's why I always left the house to go shopping when you broke out the lawn mower."

Daniel snorted.

He said, "Gabby, you think you can handle pushing the cart all by yourself for a bit?"

Her lips set in a grim line. "Of course I can."

His heart broke. She'd aged at least five years in just two days. He feared that the innocent daughter he took to Chuck E. Cheese's just a couple of weeks ago was lost forever.

Sighing, he pulled Elizabeth aside.

"With everyone so close, we haven't had a moment to talk," he said.

"Much less think," she added.

"The old man, you said you didn't think he was sick. Did he mention having a shelter, too?"

"He didn't. I thought about it, and I realized why he was well and his wife wasn't. It was the oxygen. When everyone else was breathing in whatever toxins were released in the air, he was connected to pure oxygen. The poison never made it into his lungs where it could spread."

"So what we have left are the lucky few who made it to their shelters and the sick?"

She shook her head. "People like him won't last long. Only until their oxygen supply runs out. No one's left to restock their canisters."

Something skittered in the bushes, crunching leaves. Everyone stopped, those with guns pointing them at the source of the sound. They waited a minute, and when nothing popped out, started walking again.

"What about the animals? You're the only one here with any kind of medical background. What the hell happened to them?" Daniel said, easing the shotgun back to face the ground.

"That has to be something different. We had to have been hit with multiple chemical weapons. They took out our electronics and communication, infected everyone, and turned nature against us. For all we know, even the soil is contaminated. Rey and Dakota are sick now because they were directly exposed to the smoke. God knows what we're being exposed to now."

Buck called out, "Almost there!"

Sure enough, a hundred yards ahead the trees gave way to Yonkers Avenue, the Cross County Parkway running over it.

Daniel felt his shoulders sag as he exhaled. He hadn't realized how tense he'd been walking alongside the park and whatever creatures it held.

"We should follow Yonkers to St. Joe's," Elizabeth said. "It'll be faster, and once we get past Ashburton, mostly downhill. Let's hope the powers that be set up some kind of station on Yonkers Avenue."

"If we keep this pace up, we can be there just after noon. If no one's home, it should at least be a safe place to hole up for the night."

Elizabeth reached out for his hand.

"For Rey's sake, let's pray someone answers when we knock."

80

Max used the bat as a cane, tapping the end of the barrel down hard on the street with every other step. His mother had asked him to stop, and he had, but he was back at it. It was weird the way each strike echoed. This time of day, this whole area should be crammed with revving cars on the road and the parkway. The cars were there, just dead, like everything and everyone else.

If this were a normal day, he'd have his glove looped onto the bat, his cleats clacking on the pavement. When he got home, his mother would ask him, as always, how he managed to get his uniform so dirty. He'd wolf down two bananas and a Hot Pocket along with a bottle of Gatorade before heading to his room to do his homework before dinner.

Nothing came after them from Tibbetts Park. He couldn't decide whether he appreciated the eventless walk or not. He'd decided to look at things like he was living in a video game, one of those badass ones where you have to survive a zombie apocalypse or something.

"Can I check the radio?" he asked Buck.

"Sure. Just hold on tight. Don't want it to drop."

Buck took the radio out of the canvas bag that held the guns and other stuff and handed it over.

Max turned it on and was met with the same static they'd been hearing for weeks. Tucking the bat under his armpit, he worked the dial as slowly as possible, hoping to catch even a whiff of a live signal.

"You hear anything, bro?" Rey said behind him.

God, he looked bad. He reminded Max of a TV special he'd had to watch on the dangers of smoking. It ended with the stories of five people who had terminal cancer from smoking cigarettes. When the credits rolled, they were given the dates when each of the five had died. Rey looked just about as horrible as they had.

"Not yet," he said. "Just more white noise."

"Keep at it. Someone has to be broadcasting from some-where."

That's what we keep telling ourselves. What if it's like this from New York to California?

Miguel rode by his side, asking, "Can I try?"

"No way. You can't ride your bike and check the radio at the same time."

"What if you ride my bike and I use the radio?"

"You're too clumsy. If you break it, we're screwed."

"Language," his mother called out.

"You're a stupid head," Miguel said, his brows knit close together. "I'm not clumsy. You just don't wanna share."

He reached for the radio. Max lifted it over his own head, well out of reach. "Don't go grabbing. That's a good way to break it."

"Mom!" Miguel wailed.

"Leave Max and the radio alone. Come here and stay with me," she said.

"Check it out," Rey said, pointing to a wooden commu-nity board by the bus stop. Instead of the usual fliers for tag sales, maid services, and private tutors, beneath the glass were dozens of notes, tacked on with tape and push-pins. Some were on full sheets of paper, others on index cards, most scribbled on scraps of newspaper or discarded wrappers.

His mother and father paused to read the notes. Max read them over his mother's shoulder.

"My God, this is heartbreaking," his mother said, fingers pressed to her lips.

One of them read:

MY FAMILY IS GONE. SICK FOR A WEEK, THEN LOST THEM ONE BY ONE. I'M NOT GOING TO WAIT TO GO OUT LIKE THAT. YOU'LL FIND MY BODY NEXT TO MY FAMILY AT 175 WINDMERE WAY. AND IF YOU'RE ONE OF THE PEOPLE WHO DID THIS TO US, I HOPE YOU ROT IN HELL.

His father read another aloud. "Andrea, if you get this far, we're going to follow the parkway north. I think it will be better the farther we get from the city. Harold is all right. We both got a couple of bites. Stay away from any animals. There's something wrong with them. We'll leave as many signs as we can so you can follow us. I love you. Bree."

Buck said, "There must have been a lot of hurt and confused people walking around the first week or so. Jesus, will you look at some of these."

Max pointed out one that said:

THIS IS DETECTIVE LEONARD DANWORTH WITH THE WESTCHESTER COUNTY POLICE DEPARTMENT. IF YOU READ THIS, SEEK SHELTER. IT'S NO LONGER SAFE TO BE OUTSIDE. THIS WAS A FULL-SCALE TERROR ATTACK, PLANNED OVER A LONG PERIOD OF TIME. THE AIR IS TOXIC. IT KILLS PEOPLE, BUT IT IS MAKING THE ANIMALS—ALL ANIMALS— VIOLENT. STAY IN YOUR HOMES OR ANYWHERE

*THAT HAS DOORS THAT CAN LOCK AND
PROVISIONS. HELP WILL COME.*

His father gasped, twisting the little knob and opening the glass door. He ripped an index card off the board.

"It's from Tim," he said. Max remembered his dad saying how they had run home together on the day everything went down.

"What does it say?" his mother asked.

"It just says, 'Tim Giordano, with my daughter, Sky, and son, Tyson. Please pray for us.'"

The muscles in his father's jaws worked as if he were chewing something rubbery. Tears dripped down his mother's face.

"He didn't write Diane or Annie," she said.

Max felt sick to his stomach. The Giordanos were closer to them than most of their blood relatives. Mrs. Giordano was one of the nicest women on the planet. Annie was his age, already making plans to go to NYU in a few years. He remembered the night they kissed playing Spin the Bottle when they were eleven. It was just a quick peck, but he'd always secretly hoped he'd get another chance and show her what a real kiss was like.

Tucking the index card into his shirt pocket, his father said, "Let's go."

Buck whispered, "I'm real sorry, Dan."

They walked in a single line under the parkway overpass, each lost in their own thoughts, haunted by the message board. There was a large mound up ahead. Buck and Alexiana came to it first and called for everyone to step around it.

"Don't look, kids," Alexiana said.

But they did. It was impossible not to.

The bloated corpse of a man lay on the sidewalk. It was apparent that various animals had been taking pieces from his cold flesh. Scattered bits of refuse had gathered around him—a few yellowed pages of a newspaper, a cardboard cup, an empty pack of matches, and scraps of paper and leaves. He lay facedown, his arms straight at his side. It looked as if he'd passed out so fast, he didn't even have the wherewithal to break his fall.

They gave the body a wide berth, stepping out from under the overpass and back into the sun. Ahead was the gas station, the pumps idle, fuel prices unchanging.

"We just have to follow this to the hospital," his father said.

Max saw something ahead, on the crest of the hill. It flashed black, a darting shadow. It could have been a trick of the light, or the scurried movement of a dog.

Please, no more dogs.

There it was again!

"Hey, do you guys see that?" Max said, pointing.

It was hard to miss. The shadow was joined by another, then two more, then a half dozen. It was difficult to discern them against the glaring sun.

But one thing was for sure.

They were coming right for them.

81

Every muscle in Buck's body tensed. His hands went ice-cold as his blood rushed to surround his vital organs.

He pumped the shotgun.

"Dan, I need you up here," he said, his eyes never wavering from the approaching figures. They were coming fast, whatever the hell they were.

"More animals?" Dan said, huffing more from tension than exhaustion.

Alexiana reached into the canvas bag under Dakota's cart for a second pistol.

"I don't think so," Buck said.

"Step a little to your left," Rey said to Alexiana. "I don't want to accidentally shoot you."

The barrel of his rifle rested on the edge of the cart. Elizabeth gathered Miguel and Gabby to her, gripping her Beretta. Max flexed his hands around the bat handle.

"It's kids . . . on bikes," Max said.

As the shadows advanced down the hill, Buck saw that Max was right. Though he wasn't so sure about them being kids.

There were about a dozen in all, maybe in their late teens, early twenties. They rode expensive BMX bicycles. Each had a black bandanna covering the lower half of their face like old Western bank robbers. From thirty or so yards away, it was clear they were not friendly.

"Oh shit," Rey said. "It's the Nine Judges."

"Are you sure?" Buck asked.

"Yeah."

"What are the Nine Judges?" Daniel asked.

Buck sucked hard on his teeth. "From what I've read in the papers, they're the newest gang to settle into South Yonkers. After the YPD and FBI anti-gang task forces cleared the streets two years ago, other smaller gangs have been vying to fill the void. Whatever you do, don't lower your gun."

The gang members hit their brakes, coming to skidding halts. Buck saw pistols tucked in the waistbands of their jeans.

Both sides looked one another over, neither speaking. Taking steady, shallow breaths, Buck waited, his finger tensed over the trigger.

Finally, one of them spoke. He was tall and dark as night with a close-shaved head. His eyes were slits, staring hard at them, *into* them.

"Why the fuck you pointing gats at us?" he said. His voice was cold, flat, devoid of kindness or malice.

"We just want to pass," Buck replied. He could feel everyone's tension like a static charge.

"It's a free country. No need to go around pointing guns at people who haven't done shit to you." He leaned his forearms on his handlebars. "What are you, half a hockey team and half a football team? Where do you think you're *passing* to? Ain't nothing over there."

"Nothing back there, either," Buck said, cocking his head to the way they'd come.

Another one of the gang members, a stocky guy wearing a Cincinnati Reds hat, said, "How come you ain't all sick like them two?"

"That's none of your business," Daniel shot back. Buck placed a steadying hand on his arm.

"They were caught in the smoke when the bombs dropped," Buck said. "I might ask you the same question."

The first one huffed. "We got a crib safer than Fort Knox. Arab fucks that did this can't touch us."

Alexiana asked, "How do you know it was Arabs?"

Another one replied. He'd pulled his gun from his jeans, but kept it pointed at the ground. "Who the fuck else you think would do something like this? Fucking terrorists think they got everyone, but we have a surprise for them if they want to step on over here and think they settle their asses into our cribs."

The gang grunted, cheering him on.

"Is the hospital open? Are there any authorities in charge?" Elizabeth asked.

Wrong word, Buck thought, cringing. The last thing these kids wanted to hear about was anything that dealt with authority.

A slight Hispanic kid glided on his bike to her. The sides of his long, dark hair flickered over the bandanna mask. Buck followed him with the barrel of his rifle.

The kid leaned close to her and said, "We're the authority now."

82

To her credit, Elizabeth didn't break the kid's hard gaze. Suddenly, he laughed behind his bandanna.

"Holy shit, did you see the looks on their faces?" he said. His brothers-in-arms broke into hysterical laughter.

Dakota watched the slow escalation from the shopping cart. Unbeknownst to Buck, she'd secreted one of his guns, hiding it amid the jumble of other items in the cart. Since the gang members had shown up, she held the gun but kept it out of sight. The initial jolt of fear had cleared the cobwebs woven by the disease that felt as if it were eating her alive.

She'd been ready to pull the trigger if the masked gang made any move to attack Elizabeth or the kids.

The first one who had spoken was the first to stop laughing. "Now, put your guns down before we get really offended and have to take out ours. I can guarantee we have more experience with shit like this than you. It won't end nicely."

Buck and Daniel looked to one another. Dakota watched Buck's shoulders rise, then fall as he pointed the shotgun down. Daniel, Alexiana, Elizabeth, and Rey did the same. Max still held on to his bat.

"That's better. You all have a nice walk."

He pedaled over to Dakota's cart. "Damn, I bet you were fine before you got all sick and shit."

"Leave her alone," Gabby said.

"It's okay," Dakota said. "He's just giving me a compliment." She wished she could see more than his eyes.

"That's right, little girlie. Fine-lookin' ladies like to be told how fine they are. Who fucked up your head?"

Other members of the gang now surrounded her cart, blocking Elizabeth and the kids with their bikes.

"You can see she's sick," Daniel said. "Leave her be."

A long, dirty finger touched her cheek. "I seen plenty others like this. She ain't got much time left. She'll have a whole lotta time to be left alone when she's dead."

His finger traced its way down her lips, her chin, and her neck. Dakota couldn't stop herself from trembling. The weight of the gun pressed to the side of her thigh suddenly felt hot, sharp, urgent. She heard a few shouts and scuffling, but couldn't see past the tight ring of gang members gawking at her.

83

Daniel almost collapsed when a bicycle tire rammed into the back of his knee. Two kids converged on Buck, guns drawn. Alexiana made an attempt to go to Dakota, but she was stopped when two bikes blocked her way.

"Why is everyone getting so excited?" the one pawing at Dakota said. "This here's the last time she's gonna get this kind of attention. What you think I'm gonna do, toss her salad or something? Bitch is sick. I don't need that on me."

Casting a quick glance at Elizabeth and the kids, Daniel felt his stomach drop. They were outnumbered and out-gunned. The best they could hope for was that the gang would lose interest and continue on their way. Unless they were an advance party sent to prevent them from going any farther.

"Besides," the gang leader continued, "why bother with her when you have a couple of MILFs on your hands? You both cougars?"

Elizabeth and Alexiana didn't answer.

No, this can't be happening, Daniel thought. *I've got to get their attention off of them.*

He took one step forward before the hard barrel of a pistol was pressed to his side. The kid holding the gun had sick, yellow eyes. Maybe not all of them had made it to the safety of their fortified crib before the smoke descended.

"The world goes to shit and this is what you do with the time you have left?" Daniel said.

All heads turned to him. With the bandannas over their faces, he couldn't see if they were smiling or sneering.

"The fuck you say?"

"Leave them alone. We didn't come here to pick a fight. We just want to be on our way."

A tall, gangly gang member riding a bright orange BMX wheeled in front of him. "You picked a fight the moment you pointed your guns at us."

He knew it would do no good to voice the reasoning behind it. Gangs operated on a logic that was all their own. Daniel was drowning in waters he'd never treaded. His heart hammered in his chest. How the hell could he get them out of this?

"You got nothing to say to that?" The kid lifted the bandanna away from his mouth and spat on Daniel's boots. "I thought so."

The gang leader turned his attention back to Elizabeth. "Now, I like my MILFs with a little light chocolate. You got some nice titties. Does your man tell you that?"

Elizabeth shot daggers at him with her stare.

"You don't get titties like that at no surgeon. Those are baby titties. All natural and smooth like coffee and cream. Why don't you show us what you got?"

Daniel and Buck were restrained, their arms pinned at their backs before they could make a move.

The gang leader swiveled his head to Max. "Don't even think of swinging that fucking bat. My boy here will drop you like a bitch." He turned back to Elizabeth. "Now, unbutton that shirt and pop those titties out of your bra. When you're done, we'll check out the white MILF."

"No," Elizabeth said.

"Excuse me?" he said with an exaggerated cocking of his head.

"I said no," she replied, her voice soft and shaky.

He flicked his wrist, pointing the gun at Gabby's head. She gasped. "Mommy!"

"I don't have all day," he said. "Yonkers is running pretty low on bitches. You don't take off your shirt now and there'll be one less bitch-in-training."

Daniel exploded. "Get the fuck away from my wife and daughter, you piece of shit!"

His breath burst from his lungs as he took a knee to his midsection. He collapsed to the dirty ground, dry-heaving.

"Now, show me your titties before I start getting really mad."

Elizabeth's fingers fluttered as she worked at the top button of her shirt. She had a hard time getting it through the loop. Daniel watched her from the pavement. His head was spinning from lack of oxygen.

"Please, don't," he said, barely above a whisper.

When Elizabeth had undone all of the buttons, with Miguel and Gabby crying at her sides, the gang leader said, "Nice. Now the bra."

Elizabeth choked back a sob. She reached behind her back to undo the clasp.

The eruption that followed brought everyone to their knees.

84

Rey watched openmouthed as Dakota fired nearly point-blank into the gang leader's chest. He staggered backward, blood cascading from the front and back of the open wound.

She pulled the trigger two more times, hitting the men on either side.

The sudden and violent cracks of the gun had everyone ducking. Rey fumbled for his rifle and aimed between the latticework of the cart, catching another gang member in the shoulder as he crouched beside his father.

There was a flash of brown and a dull *thud* as Max swung as hard as he could at the gangbanger next to him, flipping him off his bike.

Regaining their senses, two of the gang opened fire.

Rey watched in horror as Dakota's body jerked and spasmed, each bullet burrowing into her fevered flesh. A geyser of blood spurted from her mouth.

His mother screamed, dragging Miguel and Gabby to the ground and covering them with her body.

"No!" his father shouted, scrambling for his shotgun.

Someone shot his father from behind, a fat kid wearing a shirt that couldn't cover his porcine belly. It made a target hard to miss. Rey shot him just above his enormous belly button and he collapsed upon himself.

Gunfire, shouting, and screaming ruptured the silent morning air.

Buck turned around and caught the one behind him in the chest with his bowie knife, bathing him in crimson.

"Let's get the fuck outta here!" someone shouted.

One of the thugs tried to get back to his feet. Max jumped over another body and swatted him in the chest with his bat.

Rey's blood turned to ice when he heard his mother cry out, "No! No! No!"

One of the gang members had taken hold of Miguel, wrapping his forearm around his neck. Miguel sobbed uncontrollably.

"I'll break his fucking neck!"

His mother reached out for him and was kicked in the face.

The gang member screeched, "Put your fucking guns down now! You want him to die? I don't give a shit. I'll kill him right now!"

"Max, don't," Rey said, seeing his brother creep alongside him.

Max stopped.

"Drop the bat, asshole," the kid said.

It clattered to the ground.

There were only a half-dozen Nine Judges left, but they had Miguel. Everyone laid their weapons down.

Getting back on their bikes, one of them said, "Come on, you know what all that noise just woke up."

Miguel struggled against his captor but it did no good.

"Don't even think of taking a shot at us," he said. "Or I'll cap his fucking skull."

Rey's mother shouted incoherently in her desperation. Alexiana and Gabby held on to her as if the laws of gravity had been suspended and they had vowed to keep her earthbound.

The remaining gang members turned back to the way they'd come, with Miguel held tight, unable to break free. His face was a frozen mask of unmitigated terror. Miguel's mouth was open wide in a silent scream, just like he'd sometimes cry out when he was upset as a baby.

"Miguel," Rey sobbed as he watched them ride out of sight.

85

The moment they took Miguel, Gabby's tears stopped. The pain, the fear was so great, it was as if her entire system had gone into suspended animation. She saw her mother shouting but couldn't hear her. She knew she was holding on to her mother's shirt but she couldn't feel it in her hands.

Her ears couldn't stop ringing. Each gunshot had felt like a punch to the center of her head.

Buck was standing over her father, saying something to him. Her father was facedown in the street, not moving.

She looked over at the cart with Dakota.

Her stomach should have lurched. She should have cried out.

Again, there was nothing.

It was hard to see Dakota through the thick layer of blood. She was dead. She had to be. If she wasn't, she would be soon. Rey was in the other cart, tears streaming down his face.

Max stormed over to her. He asked her something, but she couldn't decipher the words. Reading his lips did little to help her. He held out his hand and she took it. She watched her mother melt into Alexiana's arms.

Those men had taken her brother.

Why? What had Miguel done to them?

She understood, as horrible as it was, why they'd shot Dakota. She had fired first, at least Gabby was sure she had.

Her father was still on the ground. Buck was on his knees, shaking his shoulder.

Gabby pulled away from Max, took two faltering steps, and threw up.

86

"Dan. Dan. Jesus, Dan, can you hear me?"

Buck sounded as if he were miles away, calling for him across a violent ocean. Or maybe it just felt like an ocean. Daniel could swear that he was floating on the waves, but where? Were they at the beach? He couldn't remember going to one. And where was everyone else? And most of all, why was Buck here? He liked his neighbor, but he never considered him "family time at the beach" material.

He was afraid to open his eyes. There was a chance the sun was directly overhead. Staring right into it would hurt like heck.

If he turned to the side, faced the direction he thought Buck was calling from, he'd break the floating spell and dip under the water.

Why don't I feel wet? Or cool?

In a flash, he was afraid. Worst of all, he wasn't even sure what he was afraid of.

"Dan."

He opened his eyes. His fear ratcheted up a notch.

There was no brilliant flash of sunlight. Only darkness. It was a darkness so oppressive, he could literally feel its phantom pressure against his face.

He tried to speak. Someone groaned beside him.

Was that me?

His body started to rise. Something wrapped itself around his chest. He tried to keep his eyes open, but his eyelids fluttered like a bird's wings.

There was that odd, stilted groaning again.

All motion stopped. He was no longer floating on water or being pulled into the air like a leaf.

Daniel concentrated as hard as he could to keep his eyes open and focused.

Buck's wide face peered down at him.

"Thank God," his neighbor said, exhaling a warm, tangy breeze over his face.

"Buck? What's going on?"

The muscles of the big man's jaws tensed, tight knots pulsing. "You've been shot."

Daniel gave a short, pained laugh. "Come on, really. Why are you hovering over me?"

"Can you feel your left arm?" Buck asked.

Someone was crying close by. It sounded like a funeral. How did he get from a beach to a funeral? Buck said he was shot. Was he dead?

"I . . . I think I can." He tried to move his arm, but the limb wouldn't listen to his brain.

"I'm just gonna lay you back down, Danny. Give me a sec to get you some water and the first aid kit."

Daniel's stomach dropped as if he were in a rapidly descending elevator. Buck set him down.

As clarity trickled into his consciousness, a sharp, burning pain radiated down one side of his body. He scraped his tongue over his teeth to dispel the taste of pennies that threatened to make him gag.

Who was crying?

"Dad."

Daniel tilted his head as far as he could.

Max!

And there was Rey, his eldest son, being held up by his middle son. Why did Max have blood on him?

"Are you hurt?" he asked, his voice alien, unnatural.

Max shook his head. There were tears in Rey's eyes. Rey never cried, even as a little kid. He'd take a digger on the sidewalk, get back up, and trundle along as if nothing had happened.

But he wasn't the one sobbing. No, there was someone else.

"Where's Mom?" he croaked.

Both boys turned their heads to the right. Daniel couldn't contort his body to see where they were looking.

"They took Miguel," Rey said.

The words were like a punch in the gut. His lungs clamped shut and in a painful flash, everything came rushing back.

The gang.

Dakota . . . she shot one of them. Then all hell broke loose.

A sting, or better yet, a searing hot poker pressed into his flesh. Then nothing.

They took Miguel.

No!

87

"Liz, I need your help," Buck said.

The woman was understandably distraught. There was nothing Alexiana could say to soothe her.

Her husband was seriously hurt and she was the nurse. He hoped to God she would be able to set aside her grief for the time it took to make sure he was okay.

Buck knelt close to her. Elizabeth's eyes were bloodred. "Dan's been shot. He's awake. I think they might have gotten him in the arm, but there's a lot of blood. He needs you."

She stifled back a sob and rubbed her eyes with the back of her hand. Without a word, she took the first aid kit from him, stood up quickly, nearly swooned, and rushed over to Daniel. He was surrounded by Rey and Max and now Gabby.

"How bad is he?" Alexiana said.

Buck's heart was still doing a mad march. Within the shock of all the chaos that had erupted was a warm flood of relief that Alexiana somehow made it through unhurt. He cast a quick glance at the cart, blood dripping from the multiple holes in Dakota's body, collecting into large, crimson puddles.

"I don't know," he said, helping her to her feet. They embraced, Buck burying his face in her hair, savoring the smell of her, the life still within her. If they thought they had been in Hell before, they were dead wrong. Maybe Dante was right. There were multiple levels to Hades. The question now was how many they'd have to traverse to find Miguel.

Elizabeth had cut off Daniel's sleeve and poured alcohol on his upper arm. Daniel didn't even wince. His kids watched over him, Gabby clutching Rey's hand.

"We should see if she needs any help," Buck said.

Alexiana didn't want to part from him any more than he wanted to leave her. They walked arm in arm.

"What can I do?" Alexiana asked.

Elizabeth dabbed an angry-looking red entry wound with some gauze. "The bullet went right through," she said. "Can you thread that needle?" Alexiana dug into the first aid kit for the sutures.

While Elizabeth sealed the entry and exit wounds, Daniel stared down Yonkers Avenue, back to where they'd first seen the gang.

"Hurry," he said. "We have to go."

Buck said, "Dan, maybe we should rest up a moment. You were just shot."

He shook his head. Buck was taken aback by the cold, hard look in his once-passive neighbor's eyes. "No. The longer we wait, the smaller our chances of finding him become. I don't want my son to be with those animals one second longer than he has to."

There was no arguing with him. Besides, he was right. They had to get a move on.

He looked to Alexiana. "Honey, I have to do something with Dakota. I can't just leave her out here like that."

There was no time to bury her, even though there were a couple of good places to do so right in front of them. A grassy embankment that led to an old watering hole was just across the street. They didn't even have a shovel, which was ironic considering she was lying lifeless in a shopping cart pilfered to hold shovels and all the things they'd need to make a decent final resting place for her.

"What about the cars?" Alexiana said. "At least it'll keep the animals away from her."

He kissed the top of her head.

The driver's side door to a Dodge minivan was wide open. He reached back and slid the side door open.

Wrapping Dakota in a sheet and blanket, he carried her to the minivan.

He said the handful of prayers he knew in his head as he laid her in the middle row of seats.

You didn't deserve this. But you died protecting a family you'd never met until two weeks ago. I hope I have half your courage. Rest now, Dakota. Rest.

When he closed the door, Daniel was on his feet. Alexiana gasped. Buck looked down.

Dakota's blood was all over him, from his chest down to his thighs.

88

No one wanted to continue using the shopping cart where Dakota had been killed, so they loaded all of their supplies in the remaining cart. Max and Rey pushed it, Max doing most of the work, Rey using it to stay upright.

"Buck, do you know what part of the city the Nine Judges are in?" his father said. He had the hand of his bad arm tucked in his jeans pocket. He'd traded in the bulky shotgun for one of the pistols.

"I just know it was South Yonkers," Buck said.

They passed a seedy motel on their left, heading to the access points to the Saw Mill River Parkway. Their pace had quickened considerably. Rey was finding it hard to keep his legs moving fast enough, but he'd be damned if he'd complain. They had to find his brother.

His mother had given his father some painkillers and he was already acting like nothing had happened to him. The bullet came from a small-caliber gun and missed any vital parts in his arm. Still, Rey was amazed by his father's resilience.

"They're down in Getty Square," Rey said. "You see them a lot around Chicken Island."

Chicken Island was a very old nickname for the central

business district of South Yonkers. Rey assumed that back in the day, they must have sold live chickens in the area. Nowadays, it wasn't exactly pretty, but it was always bustling with people and deals, legitimate or not.

His mother tuned to him. "How do you know that?"

"A couple of them went to my school, at least until they were expelled. I've seen them down there a few times. They always have black bandannas."

His father said, "That's where they took my boy. Gangs are territorial. If they had a safe place to ride things out, it would be there. Probably the sub-basement of one of the old apartment buildings. Some of them are built to withstand a nuclear blast."

"That's still a lot of territory to cover," Buck said.

"Not if there aren't many people around. We just need to find one of them and follow them to their . . . nest."

Rey's lungs hitched, and he went into another coughing fit. Thankfully, Max slowed down so he could catch his breath. Something big and wet and burning like acid rocketed up his throat. He tilted his head down and spat as hard as he could, desperate to get it out of him.

A gelatinous wad of blood and phlegm splattered between his feet.

Please, no.

He pushed the cart forward before his brother could see. The taste in his mouth was vile. He'd tasted blood before, especially when he played basketball and had been smacked or elbowed in the mouth.

This was different. It wasn't just blood. This was the vile flavor of disease, of something dying within him.

"You all right?" Max asked.

"Yeah, I'm fine."

"I can ask Mom for another one of those pills."

"I'll take one later. Let's keep walking."

The truth was, finding Miguel now kept him from

grieving for Dakota. He'd never erase the sight of her as those animals shot her over and over.

Maybe it was lucky that he wouldn't have to live with that memory for long. He was going to die. Nothing in his body could tell him any different.

But before he did, he had to know Miguel was safe. Of all of them, he was the only one who hadn't been bitten by the rats. Poison could be coursing through all of their systems now.

Miguel was the last hope for survival.

"Isn't that where we saw Grandpa?" Gabby asked their mother, pointing across the street.

"Yes, it is. I'm surprised you remember. You were only six when he passed away."

A big white colonial building that had been converted to a funeral home many decades ago loomed ahead. Rey remembered every moment of his grandfather's wake. It was the first and only time he'd ever seen his father cry. It scared him then. He didn't know what to do or say, so he'd left his father to himself. Now that he was older, he realized his father could have used his company at that moment, more so than maybe ever.

Instead, he'd gone out back with Max, exploring the two empty lots behind the funeral home. They were overgrown with weeds and garbage. He and Max had been especially fascinated by a moldy mattress with a woman's bra and panties sitting in the center. Why would someone leave their underwear there?

And then the cats came. Someone must have been feeding them, because they scooted into the lot the moment they saw him and Max, thinking they had food.

War-torn strays and mewling litters surrounded them, rubbing against their legs, meowing and purring. They felt bad not having anything to give the cats.

Max was thinking the same thing because he said, "Dude,

remember all the cats? I asked Mom if I could take that orange one with the one eye home and she said no way. I wonder if it's still there."

"I wanted the big black one with the green eyes. Only I was smart enough not to beg for a cat at a funeral."

Max stopped the cart.

"Holy shit."

"What?" Rey said.

"The friggin' cats. What if they're all still there?"

Rey's head swam as he fought back another wave of coughing.

He called out, "Mom, Dad, hold up!"

89

Elizabeth felt as if she were being pushed from behind by a hurricane wind. It took all of her restraint not to run, to leave everyone behind and see if she could catch the gang's trail. Her baby was alone, kidnapped by people who had no problem shooting a sick woman, not to mention her own husband.

Daniel had to hold her back when Rey asked them to stop.

"We have to keep quiet," Rey said.

"How come?" Buck asked.

Rey looked to her. "Gabby got me and Max thinking about Grandpa's funeral. Remember where you found us?"

She looked to the funeral home a block ahead of them. Try as she might, the whole wake came up a blank. It was as if she couldn't remember anything past the moment Miguel was taken from her.

"Remember when I asked you if I could bring a cat home?" Max said.

"Vaguely," she replied.

"The whole area behind the funeral home was filled with stray cats. It was like a hundred," Max said.

"Or at least it seemed like a hundred to us at the time," Rey added. "It's a perfect place for them to stay. And if they're still around . . ."

There was no reason to believe the cats wouldn't be affected just like every other animal had been.

"We better not take our chances," Daniel said. "Once we get to the corner, no talking. Walk as quietly as you can. We can take a breath when we get to the gas station the next block over."

Elizabeth kept her eyes on the double doors of the funeral home. Scanning the area to the left and right, she plotted potential safe zones. Unfortunately the pickings were slim. On one side were row houses, long abandoned and boarded up. On the other, small businesses—a barbershop, Peruvian deli, electronics repair shop—with metal bars pulled down over doors and windows. Crime was a serious problem in this neighborhood, and shop owners had to take every precaution.

"Daniel, do you recall there being any bicycle shops around here?" she asked as quietly as possible.

"I don't think so, why?"

"I'm beginning to think those gang members had the right idea. Staying on foot makes us vulnerable." What she didn't say was her weak hope that if they found one, they'd find the remaining members of the Nine Judges, and their son.

"I agree, but I don't know if Rey would be up for it."

"Max could ride with him on the handlebars, just like Rey used to do with Max when he was little."

And how she hated watching them do that, her mother's worry going into overdrive, picturing them both falling headlong off Rey's bike.

"If we see one," Daniel said, "we'll grab what we can. We'll also have to find a way to bring our supplies along."

"By supplies, you mean firepower?"

He looked down at the gun in his hand. "Yeah."

Elizabeth saw movement by the front steps of the funeral

home. She dug her nails into Daniel's good arm, stopping him. "Look," she whispered.

A white, orange, and gray calico nimbly crawled from the scrub beside the funeral home and sat in the middle of the top step, tail twitching, watching them with wide, pale eyes.

90

As soon as Buck saw the cat, he planted his feet, aiming the shotgun at the still feline.

Alexiana whispered, "Don't. You'll only attract others."

"If there *are* others," he said.

Daniel, Elizabeth, Max, and Rey pulled up behind him, keeping close.

Circling the wagons, Buck thought with little sense of humor.

Neither the cat nor the humans moved. Buck didn't take his eyes from the cat's, knowing there wasn't a feline alive that could win a stare-down. The calico didn't so much as blink.

"At least it's not attacking us," Max said. "Maybe the cats are immune."

"Let's just keep walking," Buck said. They took a few tentative steps. He kept his eyes on the cat. "Why the hell isn't it backing down?"

"What?" Alexiana asked.

"That cat should have broken its stare by now. It's like it knows something we don't."

"You're talking crazy, Buck, and we have enough crazy to go around now."

They walked ten more feet. The cat had to swivel its head to follow their progress. Buck looked away for a moment, and that's when he saw the rest.

Two metal fences flanked the wide steps leading into the funeral home. Behind each fence was a recessed, vacant lot. At first, Buck thought for sure he was seeing the reflection of the weakening sun as it lit upon broken bottles and other scraps of trash that had collected in the wiring of the fence.

But he was wrong.

Dozens upon dozens of sets of eyes peered at them from the lowest links in the fence.

"Your kids were right," Buck said. "They're all watching us right now. Rey, you think you can find one of the grenades? It should be near the top of that bag."

Daniel said, "You can't just lob a grenade at them. They're cats. The moment they see it coming, they'll be long gone."

"What do you suggest we do?"

"So far, they're just observing. We should keep walking. The old public bathhouse is right down the street. If the cats come after us, we can make it there and bust in the doors. We'll ride it out inside," Daniel said.

A strong breeze kicked up, blowing refuse down the street. It carried a sour odor, with a hint of stomach-churning sweetness. It reminded Buck of hiking through the woods, knowing that a dead animal was near. There were houses and small apartment buildings everywhere. Each potentially was the final resting place of at least one person.

Thousands of corpses were rotting around them, thankfully unseen. The wind came from the direction of the Hudson River and the most densely populated area of the city. Buck shuddered, contemplating how bad things were going to be ahead of them. And somewhere in the middle of it was Miguel.

"Fuck these cats," Buck muttered. "You all go. I'll guard the rear."

Buck pumped the shotgun, hearing the shopping cart's rickety wheels resume their forward progress. He'd be damned if he let a bunch of cats make him shit his pants.

The chain fence sang as the cats made their move, climbing the links with ease. They perched atop the fence like a row of hungry vultures, heads hung low, tails whickering.

His finger tensed on the trigger.

The calico padded down the steps, slinking to the middle of the street, where it stopped and once again stared back at him.

The other cats leaped from the fence, landing on the broken sidewalk without a sound.

91

Daniel's core froze when he heard Buck shout, "Here they come!"

He spun to face the funeral parlor. The street was lined with cats of every size and color, some missing parts of ears and tails, kittens winding around their mother's stiff legs.

Unlike the other animals they'd come across, cats were refined land predators. No matter how much man had tried to domesticate them, he couldn't completely obliterate their natural hunting skills.

"It's like we're deer in the woods," Daniel said. He moved Max and Rey behind him. "They're sizing us up, not making any sudden moves so they don't scare us off."

Elizabeth said, "We're not going to be able to shoot them all."

He eyed the bathhouse. It was a long sprint to the heavy entrance doors. There was no way they could outrun the cats if they charged.

Again the wind picked up, clogging their noses with that horrible stench. It seemed death had them surrounded.

"We can certainly try," Daniel said.

The cats at the head of the pack took a slow, steady step, then another. The rest followed suit.

"Buck, try to take out the leader," Daniel said, recalling the rules of the animal kingdom. Did cats follow alpha males? Who the hell knew anymore? They hadn't hunted people in packs before.

"You mean the calico?" he replied, his hips and shoulders in a square shooter's stance.

"Yes. If you kill it, the others may scatter."

Besides, it's high time we made the first move, he thought, striding over next to Buck.

Buck said, "Here goes."

The blast was deafening. The calico and four other cats near it flipped into the air, spraying blood and viscera down on the pack.

The cats scampered away from the calico's shredded body, shoulders hunched, most tails puffed out in terror.

Daniel couldn't fight the grin from spreading on his face. "I thought that would stop them."

Buck shook his head.

"Yeah, but they haven't run for the hills. Let's just back away. Give them time to consider how bad it would be for them if they step past that calico."

Daniel was about to agree when the pack exploded as a single ferocious unit.

He instead shouted, "Run!"

Elizabeth, Rey, Max, Gabby, and Alexiana didn't need further prodding. Gabby wobbled on her bike, ditched it, and ran. They moved as fast as they could, keeping to the left of the row of stalled cars, their only clear route of escape.

Buck fired again and more cats broke into ragged pieces. Daniel fired into the undulating mass of bodies, not sure if he'd even hit any.

The cats advanced, jumping on cars, slinking under others, and running between the vacant spaces.

Daniel caught a gray tabby under the chin when it leapt off the roof of an SUV, headed for him. The dead cat twirled like a baton, rotating off the hood of an old Chevy like a rogue helicopter blade and dipping out of view.

Buck grabbed his bad arm. Daniel saw the edges of his vision go fuzzy. "Run and get to your family. I'm going to try something."

The cats had begun to yowl, a bloodcurdling cry that carried one simple note—rage.

His neighbor pushed him away, shouting, "Come on, you homeless fuckers! Come on!"

92

Alexiana turned to see Buck standing his ground, shouting at the cats. Daniel was in a dead sprint, moving away from the swarming cats.

"You have to get Buck," she said, the sting of salty tears hurting her eyes.

"He said he has a plan," Daniel replied, breathless. His skin had gone waxen. She had to remind herself that he'd just been shot and lost a lot of blood. It was a miracle he was able to stand, much less run. He was functioning solely on adrenaline and painkillers. What would happen when there was no more left in his system?

She watched in horror as two cats jumped, latching on to Buck's shoulders. He twisted back and forth, trying to dislodge them.

"Buck!"

Alexiana ran to him, taking aim at the cats but quickly realizing she would only shoot Buck. Maybe she could smack them off with the grip of her Beretta.

She felt a sharp pain in her ankle. A black cat with a white ring around one eye darted out from under a car and swiped at her, its claw etching a deep gulley in her flesh. Alexiana brought her foot up and smashed down as hard as she could.

The cat was too quick, dashing under the car before she could connect.

Buck's shotgun roared, followed by a dull, metallic *thud*.

Another cat ran atop an unmarked delivery truck. It sailed in the air, landing on her face, claws out. She was lucky to get her hands up, catching the cat and flinging it aside, but not before its pistoning claws shredded her forearms.

Elizabeth shouted behind her, but she kept moving forward, to Buck.

Cats had fastened themselves to his legs, trying to bite through the fabric.

Ignoring them, he raised the shotgun and fired again.

This time, a tremendous fireball singed the eyebrows and eyelashes from Alexiana's face. A blue Toyota reared up as the flames shot out from its punctured gas tank. Untold cats screamed in agony as they were doused in fire.

She stared in mute horror as flitting fireballs ran in every direction.

Her ears popped, then all sound was lost as another car exploded.

93

Max had just bashed a pair of gray and white cats with his bat when the first explosion rocked the blacktop and sent waves of searing heat their way. He instinctively ducked low, feeling as if a blowtorch's flame was hovering just over his head.

The few cats that had made it to them scattered, their lust for violence overrun by blind panic.

He stood back up in time for the second blast. This one sent him on his ass. He collided with his brother, who spun to the left, landing hard on his side.

Next thing he knew, his mother and father were helping him to his feet.

"Are you all right?" his mother asked.

He wished he'd started counting how many times those same words had been said since the day they left the shelter. He gave her a quick nod. "Yeah, I'm not hurt."

Gabby touched a sore spot on his arm. "You're bleeding."

He looked down at it. "Just a scratch."

His little sister seemed so stoic. She was normally the crybaby of the family. There was a faraway look in her eyes, as if she'd put some distance between herself and their predicament. Either that or she was in shock.

Rey was wobbly but managed to stay upright by holding on to the cart.

"Where are Buck and Alexiana?" Max said.

The entire street was choked with thick black smoke. The billowing cloud pushed steadily toward them.

"I don't know," his father said. "But we have to get away from that smoke."

Max saw flashes of flames within the smoke. It smelled like gasoline, burning tires, and plastic. The smell made his lungs seize and he thought he was going to gag.

His mother looped her arm around his. "Come on, Max. We have to go."

They walked as fast as they could without losing Rey, the toxic fog right on their heels. It rose high in the air, the flames crackling as they consumed everything in their reach.

"Over there," his mother said, pointing at a sandstone church ahead. It was just off the direct path of the smoke. His father lifted Rey and placed him atop the supply-filled cart. Now they could really run.

To his surprise, the church doors weren't locked. He pushed them open so his father could wheel the cart inside, slamming them closed once his mother and Gabby were inside.

He looked up in time to see the shadow of the oily fog pass over one of the ornate stained-glass windows. It smelled mercifully like candle wax and incense inside the cavernous church. That and something else he couldn't identify.

Max joined his parents and siblings at the head of the aisle.

What he saw made him rub his eyes in disbelief.

94

It had only been a few years since Gabby had made her First Communion, and she was still enthralled by the ceremony and mysteries of the Church. Jesus nailed to an enormous crucifix loomed over the altar. She made the sign of the cross and bowed her head.

The pews were filled with people.

She scanned the backs of their heads. No one turned to look at the visitors. Even the priest in his white robe remained in supplication at the marble stairs leading to the altar.

"Oh my," her mother said, placing a protective arm around Gabby.

"What, Mom?" she asked, for the first time in weeks feeling some small measure of comfort. When she was in school, she couldn't wait to make her Confirmation. Prep would begin the next year. She already had her Confirmation name picked out—Genevieve, a patron saint of Paris.

"Stay here with your mother," her father said, walking down the aisle.

"No, I want to go with you," she said, breaking free from her mother's grip.

She looked at the row next to her, expecting to see families in silent prayer or maybe welcoming smiles.

They were dead.

All of them.

Sick people must have come here, seeking God's help, passing away in the one place they felt safe.

"I told you to stay with Mom," her dad said.

She was frozen, afraid to look anywhere but the floor.

"It's all right," a voice called out, echoing throughout the church walls. "There's nothing to be frightened of. We can't shield our children from the truth. Not anymore."

The priest had gotten up and was now walking toward them.

"These people," he continued, "died in peace and filled with hope. They knew there was nothing left of this world to cling to, so they accepted their future, a much brighter one at that."

Gabby shifted behind her father. The priest was tall and thin with skin the color of paper. What little hair he had was over his ears, and his bald skull was dotted with brown spots.

"I'm Father Bodak. You're welcome to stay as long as you like."

He carried a smoking pot on the end of a long, gold chain. White, acrid smoke wafted in the air.

"Are you the only one alive?" her father asked.

The priest smiled. "Not at the moment. Now there's you and your family. I keep incense burning for obvious reasons. I'm afraid I might have to lock the doors someday soon. The church will be unsafe for anyone who already isn't afflicted."

"How is it that you're not sick?"

"There's a sub-basement under the parish house. I spent the first few days down there, at least until I needed water and food. Truth be told, I'm not well, but the disease in me has yet to win out. How are you and your family? I heard the explosion. Is anyone hurt?"

Gabby thought of Buck and Alexiana, wondering what had happened to them. Were they like the people in the pews?

"We're not sure," her father replied. "We have friends who were with us. They were near the blast. We couldn't see them through the smoke."

Father Bodak spread his arms wide. "Come, we can talk in the narthex. This is perhaps not the best place for your daughter at the moment."

95

Father Bodak introduced himself and Elizabeth said, "I'm Elizabeth Padilla, you've met my husband, Daniel, and daughter, Gabriela. These are my sons Max and Rey."

She saw the flash of pity in his eyes when he looked to Rey. He'd been surrounded by the sick and dying for weeks and knew the signs. The thought of losing Rey, on top of her pressing need to find Miguel, was almost too much for her heart to bear.

"We won't stay long," she said. "Just until the smoke clears. We have to find my youngest son."

"Were you separated during the explosion?" Father Bodak asked, lines of concern deepening at the corners of his mouth.

She couldn't stop the tears from springing to her eyes. "No. He was taken from us."

Daniel said, "Father, have you heard of a gang called the Nine Judges?"

The priest nodded gravely.

"Of all the good and wonderful people that God has taken, *they* are still in abundance. They came to the church a few days ago. I hid in the confessional and watched them steal everything they could carry. Senseless."

"Do you know where they are?" Elizabeth asked, hoping that somehow divine guidance had led them here to provide the answers they desperately needed.

Her stomach turned to lead when he said, "I'm afraid not. I only know that they had been a growing concern in the neighborhood for quite some time."

"What about people in charge?" Daniel said. "Have you or any of your parishioners, before they passed on, heard official word of what happened? I can't believe that our government would just leave us to ourselves. No one could wipe out an entire country in an afternoon."

The priest placed the smoking censer on the floor and folded his arms. "No one knows what happened. At least no one who has come to me. Everyone I've met has been sick and frightened. Before I became a priest, I spent three years in the army, stationed at Fort Hood. I find it just as hard to believe that there hasn't been any kind of military response, especially in the way of aid. With no ability to communicate, it's impossible to know what's going on beyond the immediate area. They could be in the next city over, and we'll never know unless we speak to someone who has seen them with their own eyes. Whoever did this knew our darkest fears and brought them to life."

Elizabeth couldn't stop staring at the rows and rows of still corpses. Did they die praying? Was there some measure of comfort at the end? Or did they pass away embroiled with fear, or with the impossible weight of grief, having lost the ones they loved most? Would it show on their faces— hundreds of death masks forever frozen in their final moments of emotional agony or ecstasy?

She didn't dare walk among the pews to find out for herself.

"If you're hungry, I can offer you food and water. There is plenty to go around. Most people who came here brought their provisions. Unfortunately, they passed on before they could make use of them," the priest said.

"We don't want to impose," Daniel said.

"You're not. I know that I won't have much use for them soon enough. I keep everything upstairs where the choir and organist would sit. I'll bring some down."

"Max, help Father Bodak," Elizabeth said. Her son rested his bat against the wall and followed him up the creaking stairs.

Gabby wrapped her arms around her hips. "I don't want to stay here."

As welcoming as Father Bodak was, Elizabeth couldn't stand the thought of being among the dead for much longer, either. She ran her fingers through Gabby's curls. Her hair was a ratty mess and her finger snagged on the knots.

"We won't. Just have a little something to eat to keep up your strength. We'll leave when the fires die down. It won't be long. I promise."

She thought of Buck and Alexiana. When the car went up in flames and smoke shot out everywhere, they'd been swamped. Being so close, she was sure there was no way they could have made it. But if they had, they were out there now, most likely hurt, and exposed. They had to leave, if only to find their neighbors, their saviors.

She glanced at Daniel, who reassured their daughter that they would leave very soon. Until then, it was best not to look at the pews, harder still to ignore the pervasive smell that hung lower than the rising incense.

96

The bad man who had hurt Miguel by squeezing him so hard he could barely breathe threw him to the ground. Miguel landed on his knees. He cried out from the pain.

"Shut up, crybaby!" one of the other bad men barked.

They'd taken him somewhere by the river. He could see the dark waters of the Hudson River at one point as the bikes scooted by the nice restaurants and the park that his parents took him to sometimes when the weather was good. They kept pedaling until they came to a run-down apartment building. It looked like half of it had been through a fire.

The gang rode to the back of the building, and one of them rapped on a dirty steel door nine times. Someone opened it but Miguel couldn't see who. Riding down dark, narrow hallways, they cruised through the opening of a steel cage, where he was deposited like a bag of sand.

Miguel bit his trembling lower lip, his tears making it impossible to tell who was who.

The room they had taken him to smelled bad, like old and broken things. It looked like it had been carved right out of the earth itself. A single lightbulb dangled from a chain in the ceiling. Old broken wood crates were stacked along one wall, along with dented metal garbage cans, their lids too warped to fit on top.

A man with an impressive seventies-style Afro stood over him.

"You going to keep quiet, Little Man?"

Miguel nodded quickly. He had never wanted his mother and father so badly in all his life. He was so scared, he'd peed himself on the ride to this dark place, and he felt ashamed.

"Good. You do what we say, we'll give you something to eat later."

He tossed something on the floor that landed with a hard *smack*. Miguel reached out for it, running his hands over the surface, fresh tears cascading down his cheeks. It was one of those plastic mattresses they use in cribs.

"Lie on that if you want."

The steel door slammed shut and a chain looped through it. The gang member snapped a lock in place.

Taking a breath was becoming a chore. He'd learned long ago that the moment he started struggling, he had to use his inhaler. There was no toughing it out, at least not until he got older and his lungs were stronger. He took his inhaler out of his pocket and took two quick puffs.

Miguel curled atop the mattress, thinking about his family, wondering what the gang was going to do to him.

And in the gloom, he thought of the rats. They lived in basements and horrible, dark places like this. If they came, there was nowhere for him to go.

Worst of all, there was no one to save him.

97

Father Bodak understood without having to be told that they needed to be on their way. Daniel kept a close eye on the elegant stained-glass windows, the image of John the Baptist baptizing Jesus searing into his memory. As soon as the smoke from the burning cars thinned out and the shadows bled from John and Jesus's faces, he knew it was time to go. He'd never felt so creeped out in all his life. If he survived, he was sure this church, all churches once being a great comfort to him, would haunt his dreams until his end.

"You could come with us, Father," he said. "Maybe we can find someone who can help you."

The priest gave a tired smile. "I need to be here, not just to pray over my parishioners, but to be here to help any others who may come. Maybe there will be other families like you in need of rest and food. Or more like them"—he motioned with his head toward the pews—"who need comfort and absolution."

"The captain always goes down with his ship," Daniel said softly, bringing a knowing nod from Father Bodak.

"Except this one is unsinkable," the priest said.

Elizabeth asked him to pray for them, and they dipped

their fingers in holy water, making the sign of the cross before they left the church.

"Thank you, Father," Rey said, Max giving him support. "Can you also say a prayer for a friend of ours? She . . . she died trying to save us."

He handed the priest a folded piece of paper. When he undid the folds, Daniel saw Dakota's name written in pencil.

"I will, once a day, every day."

Daniel opened the large doors, facing the dusk. The smoke had all but blown away, but the acrid smell remained strong as ever.

"If you find your boy and need a safe place to stay, please come back. The parish house will be yours, along with all of the remaining supplies."

Elizabeth pressed her hand into his. "Thank you. God bless you."

"And God be with you. I know you'll find your son safe."

Daniel stood at the top steps, contemplating their next move. It would be dark soon. Without lights anywhere, there was no telling who or what would be lying in wait for them.

But Miguel was out there, and there was no way they could wait to find him any longer than they had to.

Father Bodak closed the door behind them.

"Do we head for Chicken Island?" Elizabeth asked.

"It's a good place to start," he replied. "When we get close, we could find a store or something to hide in and stand watch. If they're down there, we'll spot them and trace where they're coming from. But first, let me look for Buck and Alexiana, alone."

The last thing he wanted was anyone to see their friends in pieces or burned or both. That explosion had been massive. He didn't hold out much hope of finding them alive.

He ran to the road, scorch marks tattooing the street and

surrounding cars. Pieces of cat had flown as far as a hundred feet. "Buck! Alexiana!"

There was no reply. Flames still crackled in the demolished cars.

"Buck! Can you hear me?"

He couldn't see them anywhere.

But he did see something else.

He stopped, walking backward slowly, steadily, keeping his eyes on the massive sentinel standing guard over the remains of the two-car blast.

98

Buck woke to the ringing of tiny bells. Hundreds of them. They sang and rang until his head felt as if it would split in two.

Christ, he hurt. This was worse than that car accident when he was working as a taxi driver at nights to pay for college. Then, he'd only broken his collarbone and fractured a rib or two.

This was all-over pain. No bone or organ spared.

"Oh fuck," Buck groaned, painfully rolling over from his stomach to his back. The air was filled with white smoke. The setting sun reflected off a long striation of clouds.

The cats!

He bolted upright, the rush of blood making his head swim. Eyes wide, he scanned the immediate area for any skulking cats. He saw the burning cars, frames blackened, tires melted, windows devoid of glass.

That sure made them scatter. I'll have to remember that for the next time. Just have to stand a little farther away.

Memories of what had transpired came back little by little, like pictures being flipped by a slow hand.

Two car doors, severed from the frame, had fallen one atop the other just a foot from where he lay. They would easily have flattened him if they'd landed just a little bit closer. He'd have to jump to get over them, and his body was in no shape for leaping.

His heart began to gallop. Where was Alexiana?

"Alex? Alexiana?"

It was a struggle to get to his feet, and once there he thought for sure he was going back down. His body swayed. He had to lock his knees to keep from tumbling over.

Turning as best he could, he saw her curled up against the back bumper of a Jeep. Its rear window had been pebbled inward.

Buck stumbled to her.

"Alexiana, wake up. Honey, it's me. Come on, baby."

With a heavy grunt, he managed to take a knee, cupping her face in his hands. Her pulse pounded beneath his quivering fingers.

"Thank you," he whispered, angling his body so he was next to hers. Pushing the hair from her face, he tapped her cheeks lightly.

"Alexiana, can you hear me? You're going to be all right. I just need you to open your eyes."

With night fast approaching, he had to get them to relative safety. He was in no position to carry her. If they were going anywhere, it would have to be with both of them on foot.

He fumbled through his pockets, hoping the bottle of water he'd stuffed in one was still there. It wasn't.

Where were the Padillas? If they weren't hurt, why weren't they around? *If I hurt them with my half-assed idea to kill those cats, I'll never forgive myself.* There was enough in this new world out to get them. It sickened him to think he might have been their undoing.

But he couldn't check for them until he got Alexiana to her feet. He kissed her forehead, then the tip of her nose, her lips and chin, the way he did every night before they went to sleep. She had been a godsend to him, restoring his faith in women and love and the possibility of a happy future.

Buck was about to attempt lifting her up, hoping that getting her body in motion would signal her brain to wake up, when her eyelids fluttered open.

She stared straight at him, her body gone rigid as a two-by-four.

What he saw in those eyes scared the hell out of him.

99

Rey knew he should be scared—downright terrified and for more than one reason—but numb didn't come close to describing the way he felt. Dakota had been murdered right before his eyes. Miguel, the sweetest kid in the world, snatched by gangbangers. Buck and Alexiana were somewhere out there, probably dead.

The wheezing in his lungs grew worse with each passing hour. It was easier to spit up blood now that the night had fallen. He didn't know how much longer he could go on.

Just give me until we find Miguel. Don't let me die without knowing he's okay.

The shopping cart's front wheels lodged on something, and his chest struck the handlebar.

"What the hell?" he muttered, pulling the cart back with a jerk.

Max said, "Nice rat."

The dead rodent lay on its side. "Hope there aren't any more living ones nearby," he said.

It was getting too dark to see. The only time he'd been outside in this kind of inky blackness was when his father took them on a camping trip to the Adirondacks. And even then they had a fire and several lanterns.

"Maybe we should go back," Max said to their parents. "That dog is probably gone by now."

"I was able to see past the dog," their father said. "Buck and Alexiana were nowhere to be found."

After leaving the church, their father had gone to where Buck had blown out the car's gas tank. Shattered bits of car littered the street and rooftops of the surrounding cars and trucks. An imposing bullmastiff rooted around the debris, sniffing for food. When the dog spotted him, it turned to all of them with a head that looked like it belonged on a pony. The mastiff bared its teeth, daring them to come any closer. They called out for Buck and Alexiana but got no answer. Their father contemplated shooting the dog, but was worried the sound would attract more predators, so they headed south on Yonkers Avenue.

Rey held out slim hope that they were alive and had moved on once they recovered from the explosion. They might be searching for them at this very moment.

Something chittered overhead, the sound fading in and out.

"Bats," Rey said.

Gabby gave a tiny shriek, covering her hair with her hands. Max pulled her to his side. "Stay close to me, Gabby. I won't let them get to you."

He swung blindly with the bat, slicing the empty air when it sounded like one was swooping close.

Luckily, it sounded like a single bat, and not the usual swarm they'd been experiencing. Rey wondered if he'd be able to shoot it like skeet when it flashed by the blazing moon that had just edged its way from behind the cloud cover. His arms were so weak, he doubted he'd be able to hold the rifle up high enough to try.

A dizzying wave of cold and nausea passed through him. He coughed in reaction, retching another gout of blood.

"Spitting is gross," Gabby said, oblivious to what had just come out of him.

"Gotta get the bad stuff out," he said. "That's the only way I'll get better."

She didn't reply and he couldn't see her face in the dark. The geometric shadows of the high-rise apartments ahead stood in contrast to the moon-softened glow of the Hudson behind them. They picked their way cautiously around the cars, sticking to the road, using the useless hunks of steel as cover.

Miguel was close. So were the Nine Judges.

Now it was just a matter of finding the hole they called home.

Rey willed his legs to move, his heart to maintain a steady rhythm, his lungs to take in and expel the fresh night air. All automatic systems had been switched to manual.

Keep going. Keep going. Keep going.

100

They made it to the intersection of Yonkers Avenue and South Broadway without incident. Daniel wasn't about to blow a sigh of relief. They still had some blocks to go before they made Chicken Island. St. Mary's sprawling church was to their left, the courthouse right across the street. He couldn't count how many times he'd driven this way, off to pick up whatever was on Elizabeth's list for the drugstore. Just earlier that day—God, had it only been hours ago?—Dakota had talked about White Castle. The fast-food joint was just a few blocks away.

All the stores were closed now and pounds of uncooked murder burgers were left rotting in sealed storage walk-ins.

"You want to press our luck?" he asked his wife in the same hushed tone reserved for libraries and church services.

"Yes. We don't have far to go."

It seemed as if the same bat had been following them all along. He kept wishing it would come close enough for a formal introduction with Max's own bat. With the way things had gone, he worried that it was a scout, calling for others to attack.

"We all want to get Miguel back, but you and I have to

consider Gabby and the boys. Rey doesn't sound good at all. I can hear every breath he takes. Gabby's scared of the dark, and Max needs to rest. How about we go around the corner and find a little store or someplace to settle in for the night? If the Nine Judges are around, they'll definitely pass by this area."

"It won't take much for us to get a little closer," she said, peering into the dark. A couple of times, they'd both clipped their hips and thighs on the edges of cars, stumbling over unseen objects left in the street.

Daniel touched Elizabeth's arm and felt her go rigid. "I'm worried about something else."

"What?" she said with a hint of exasperation.

"Nocturnal animals. What we haven't seen during the day is what will be waking up now."

"Honey, I don't think the raccoons are going to be lurking about in the center of the city."

"That was before everything went dark. It's been weeks. There's nothing here to scare them away anymore, and a lot of food left around. I saw quite a few turned-over garbage pails today with the plastic bags shredded. It's not safe out here."

She turned on him with contained fury. "It's never going to be safe out here, day or night. I'm not stopping until we find Miguel." It was a side of her he'd never seen and it worried him. "If you want to stop with the kids, you can. I won't hold it against you. In fact, I'll feel better knowing you're all safe."

"And what will you do if you find him, surrounded by that gang? You can't take them out by yourself. You have to stop a moment and think."

He was glad he couldn't see the look she was giving him, because he sure could feel the weight of it.

"Daniel Padilla, if you think for one second—"

She was cut off when Rey hissed, "Mom, Dad, listen. Do you hear it?"

Daniel felt his spirit falter.

He could hear exactly what was coming their way. They had to run.

101

Alexiana watched Buck's lips move, but she couldn't hear a thing. Not his voice. Not the crushed Budweiser can behind him tumbling along the street. Not even the breeze that caressed her face.

I'm deaf!

A scrabbling panic struggled for control. She bit down on her tongue to keep from screaming. Buck flinched, his face a mask of concern and confusion.

She touched at her ears, rubbing her lobes. Her ears didn't even feel like they were a part of her body. They belonged to someone else, that someone now in possession of her ability to hear.

Hurrying to her feet, she looked around at the destruction. Two smoking wrecks were bleak reminders of what Buck had done to save them. It was disorienting, seeing the small flame that still burned in the trunk of one of the cars but not being able to hear its familiar crackle. The sun was in for the night. She wondered how long she'd been unconscious. On the bright side, the feral cats were gone.

The explosion must have done something to her ears. She'd been to concerts so loud, it took days for her hearing to return to normal. But she could always still hear. This time, the silence was complete. It didn't feel temporary at all.

Buck's hands reached out for her. She studied his face, watched the gyrations of his mouth to no avail. She'd never been any good at lip-reading. Tears bubbled up out of frustration as much as fear.

"I can't hear!" she said, saying the words but having no idea how they sounded.

He steadied her shaking hands by grabbing hold of them. Taking a deep breath, he spoke to her.

Did he say, can you hear me?

She shook her head.

His mouth opened wider. *Can you hear me now?*

No.

He snapped his fingers right next to her ears. Nothing registered. He looked devastated when she said, "No. I can't hear a thing."

Buck wrapped his arms around her, pressing her head to his barrel chest. By the vibrations in his chest, she could tell he was saying something.

When she pulled away, wiping her tears with the back of her hand, it was easy to see him say, "I'm so sorry."

She pressed a finger over his lips. "You have nothing to be sorry about. You saved us . . . again. I love you."

He told her he loved her, his eyes red and wet with tears of his own.

Alexiana grabbed his arm. He kept talking. She pointed behind him. When he turned, he stepped in front of her. There was a tap on her thigh. Looking down, she saw his hand twitch.

The gun!

Her Beretta was still in her back pocket. She put it in his hand.

The massive dog put its front paws on the hood of a Nissan Sentra. It stood taller than Buck. She saw its black lips curl back from bloodstained teeth and knew it was sending out a warning growl.

The gun recoiled in Buck's hand. Alexiana saw the rose-red bloom at the dog's throat as the bullet burrowed its way through the dog's flesh and muscle.

Then something hit her from behind, and she screamed as hard as she could.

102

Max heard the steady *clop* of horse hooves before he saw them. He spun just in time to see a tight pack of racehorses barrel down the street, angling around cars and nimbly overstepping any and all objects scattered about the blacktop.

"Dad, we have to get somewhere safe. I watched them at the track when those bombs first hit," Rey said. "They're vicious. They were attacking people in their cars, tearing them apart."

His mother muttered a quick, "Jesus, Mary, and Joseph."

There looked to be five in all, black and brown Standardbreds that could outrun any man and had the power to go through walls if need be.

Max looked to the small shops to their left. Most had iron grates pulled down and locked tight. Across the street was a parking lot.

The horses rode hard, galloping closer. They hadn't spotted them yet, but Max knew it was only a matter of seconds until they did.

Frantically looking down the row of darkened shops, he shouted, "Over there!"

An old vacuum repair shop was at the corner. It was the one business not encased by protective grates.

"Go!" his father said.

The horses sounded as if they were right on top of them as they made a beeline for the repair shop. Rey somehow managed to keep up. Max pulled Gabby so hard, he worried he might dislocate her shoulder.

Better that than being left to face those horses.

One of them let loose with a heart-stopping whinny. It sounded like nothing in nature—more of a demonic wail from the bowels of Hell.

Max jumped in front of his father and swung the bat, smashing the glass door to pieces. His mother made sure Gabby went inside first, then Rey. "Get in, Max," she said. When he saw her eyes go wider than dinner plates, he spun around just in time to face a brown stallion as it used its head to pound his shoulder, spinning him to the ground.

That was followed by a sharp *crack* as his father shot at the horse behind it. The crazed animal made an ugly, high-pitched shriek, swerving to avoid them.

Max's shoulder throbbed. He tried to lift his bat, but the arm that had been smashed by the horse tingled with pins and needles. Every nerve in his shoulder thrummed.

His mother jerked him through the broken door. His father backed inside, his shotgun pointed at the retreating horses.

"Get to the rear of the store," he shouted. "They're coming back."

"Let me help you, Dad," Rey said, hobbling to the front door. He used the rifle as a makeshift cane.

"No, help your mother find a back room, something with a solid door."

Hefting the bat with his good arm, Max said, "Why don't you give me your rifle?"

Gabby yelled at the top of her lungs as a horse leaped over a fire hydrant and hurled itself headfirst through the shop's main window. It skidded to a gangly halt, ramming the small counter, sending the old but solid cash register sailing.

The horse flailed as if it were on ice, unable to regain its balance. Its huge head snapped back and forth, nipping at anyone who made a sound, missing them by inches.

"Shoot it, Daniel!" his mother shouted.

"I can't!"

Max saw that if his father's shot went wide, he'd hit his mother and sister. He ran to the horse, shouting something unintelligible, even to his own ears. He swung the bat upward and the knob connected with the horse's bottom jaw with a stomach-lurching crunch. Before it could react and try to take a chunk out of him, he caught it again on the side of its head. Blood fanned the nearby wall.

Working like a possessed one-armed machine, Max delivered blow after blow until the horse's legs went out from under it and the rest of its body followed.

There was no time to gloat. Rey howled, "Here come the rest!"

He and his father opened fire into the onyx streets. The beat of the horses' hooves quickened.

Max shouted, "Mom, there's a door over there," pointing to a red door beyond the rows of unrepaired vacuum cleaners. She ran with Gabby.

He turned to face the shattered window and saw death riding for them.

103

Alexiana's garbled cry startled Buck. She was on the ground, shouting something that didn't make sense.

The mastiff dropped as if it had been deboned in a flash. *One less thing to worry about.*

He hurried to lift her up. There was a bleeding gash on her forehead, the fresh blood in contrast to the dried blood and other cuts all over her head and face. Pebbles of safety glass glittered in the wound.

"What happened?" he said, enunciating as best he could so she could read his lips. It was dark as a cemetery at night, but the glow from the fading car fires gave an orange cast to her face.

"Hit me," she replied, looking everywhere.

"What hit you?"

"I don't know."

She was shouting, but there was no way for her to know that. For the moment, he was just grateful they could communicate. There would be plenty of time for feeling guilty over what he'd done to her later.

He grabbed her hand. "Come on, let's go."

They ran around the dead mastiff, heading to an intersection that would take them through a shortcut to South

Broadway. Daniel once told him his father went down that street to buy live chickens and goats so he could butcher his own meat. It cost a lot less than buying meat prepackaged in a supermarket. All you needed was the know-how and the stomach for the work.

If they followed that route, they could take South Broadway all the way down to the Bronx border. That would bring them closer to the city and, with any luck, official help.

But Daniel and Elizabeth were surely headed the other way, looking for the hideout of the Nine Judges. He was relieved to not see any of their bodies by the wreckage. His only worry now was that they hadn't left the scene of their own volition. What if the Nine Judges, alerted by the explosion, had come riding to the scene?

He squeezed Alexiana's hand to get her attention. He pointed to the way to the Bronx, then over past City Hall toward Chicken Island.

She tugged him along to where the Padillas would have gone.

"All right. I just wanted to make sure we were on the same page."

He wasn't sure she understood everything he'd said. He'd have to find paper and something to write with. It was easy enough to break into any store.

A putrid, bitter odor washed over them, making him wince.

Skunk. One of the little bastards had just sprayed real close.

Maybe I should find a place to stay until daylight. Lord knows, we both need to give our bodies a rest. If we're lucky, Alex's hearing will come back a little, too.

There were no residences nearby, just stores and restaurants. At least a restaurant would have some food.

The skunk smell seemed to double in pungency.

"Crap, there has to be a bunch of them," he said. Alexiana

wasn't facing him and didn't react. He wished to God and Allah and Vishnu that he had a flashlight, but the ones he'd brought were in Rey's cart and that was nowhere to be seen.

Scanning the ground, he kept a wary eye out for puffy, white-streaked tails. The skunks were close, of that there was no doubt. His eyes watered from their scattershot spray. Breathing through his mouth only made him taste it as well as smell it.

Alexiana tapped him frantically on the shoulder. He looked up.

Now he knew what had knocked her to the ground before.

The skunks were quite visible in the dark, as were the raccoons, the bandit-faced critters as big as beagles. But they weren't at their feet.

No, they had taken higher ground, the better to see eye to eye. On the hood and roof of every car they stood, black eyes trained on Buck and Alexiana. He checked the shells he had left for the shotgun in his shirt pocket.

This was not going to end well.

104

Daniel didn't waste time. A passive man all his life who believed in stricter gun laws, he couldn't pull the shotgun's trigger fast enough. His damaged arm pulsed with agonizing throbs from the recoil. The four remaining horses were straight from an apocalyptic fresco: wild, flowing manes; manic eyes; and unbridled power. He caught one in the center of its bared chest. The shells did nothing to slow it down.

Rey shouted, "Go for their legs." He took a shot at the tangle of powerful legs but must have missed.

His son was right. As incredibly strong as they were, their legs were vulnerable.

The only problem was, they were too late. Daniel was knocked aside as a black horse dove through the shattered window. Max and Rey were scattered to the other side of the shop, falling among old vacuum cleaners.

The rest of the horses followed on an unyielding path to the rear of the store. Daniel's side ached. He'd been hit so hard, he thought for sure there had to be internal bleeding. Shaking it off, he looked to make sure Max and Rey were all right. For the moment, they were hidden in a pile of vacuum cleaners, but he saw them struggling to get themselves free of the mass of broken appliances.

"Stay where you are," Daniel yelled.

Now that they had contained themselves in a small space, the horses went wild. They smashed the counter to splinters, knocked down shelves and spare parts mounted on pegs on the walls. It was absolute mayhem. They whinnied and stomped, oblivious now to the humans they had sought so desperately to attack in the first place.

A brown horse with white on its nose and ankles turned to face Daniel. This close, he could see thick, dark fluid leaking from its eyes and smell its foul breath. Its mouth opened wide, revealing blunt, dangerous teeth.

He aimed low, taking the horse by its knees. It fell immediately to the floor, its head shattering the tile floor on contact.

Daniel jumped at the sound of another shot. Rey fired twice, missing the mark at first, but clipping the hind leg of a chocolate stallion enough to send it sliding into a glass display case. Shards of glass exploded as if a bomb had been placed inside. A slash of heat burned Daniel's arm. A straight crimson line appeared on his forearm as if by magic as his flesh split apart.

One of the remaining horses made a beeline for his sons. He couldn't dare shoot it without hitting them. Max rose from his hiding place, shaking off a vacuum cleaner whose handle had attached itself to his arm. He swung his bat one-handed, hitting the horse across its nose. It plunged ahead, fastening its teeth on his shoulder.

"Aaaaaaaggghhhh!" Max screamed.

Rey tried to help but collapsed—either his foot was caught in the tangle of vacuums or his energy was spent.

Daniel spotted the other horse coming toward him and fired. One of its front legs disintegrated. Its forward momentum kept it coming. He jumped over its carcass as it skidded by.

The horse wouldn't let Max's shoulder go. The bat fell from his hand.

"Get the hell off my son!" Daniel shouted, knowing full well the horse didn't give a damn about him. All any of the animals knew was the lust for flesh. He placed the barrel of the shotgun against its side, and fired. Blood and gore shot out like water from a busted fire hydrant, covering him from head to toe.

Still, it wouldn't let go of Max. Whatever disease had been eating away at the brains of the animals, it was powerful enough to override their instincts and keep their bodies moving even when they were catastrophically injured.

Striding forward, he jammed the gun under its neck, pulling the trigger again. Daniel's ears rang, a high-pitched chime that dominated all other sound. This time, it did let go as its head flopped back, barely attached to its neck.

The weeping laceration in Max's shoulder needed stitches. His son stood on steady legs, biting back the pain.

The sound of broken, dying horses was enough to raise the hairs on Daniel's arms.

"All right, Max, just hang in there. We'll get your mother to fix you up. Why don't you sit down?"

Max nodded toward the open window. "I'm not getting comfortable here, Dad."

Rey's coughing helped Daniel find him within the rubble. He latched on to his arms and pulled him out. Something hot and wet flew from Rey's mouth, covering Daniel's thighs. He was already drenched in the spray from the horses. It was impossible to discern what Rey had just coughed up.

"Just hold on to me, Rey. We're going to find your mother and sister."

With Rey on one arm and Max the other, Daniel couldn't carry his shotgun. It didn't matter much anyway. He was down to one shell.

Woozy himself, Daniel half-carried his boys to the back of the shop, stepping around the writhing horses.

105

Buck knew that by nature, skunks and raccoons were docile, shy, terrified of humans. Nature had been turned on its ass in their insane new world, and this was proof.

The gathering of night-loving, garbage-picking critters bared their sharp teeth at them. Poised as they were on top of the surrounding cars and trucks, they were in a perfect position to let fly at Buck and Alexiana in some sensitive places, their throats and faces in particular.

Most of the raccoons were fat and bloated. They'd probably been feasting on so much food left to waste, it was a miracle they'd been able to clamber up the side of a car. If they leaped at them, gravity would take hold before they found their mark.

The skunks were another story. He never realized how vicious they could appear, their enlarged rat faces pinched with predatory hunger.

Alexiana trembled against his back. He couldn't imagine how this was for her, unable to hear, the rest of her senses in disarray.

It was hard to tell in the dark, but there looked to be well over twenty raccoons and skunks in the audience.

"What madness is bringing you two together?" he said to

the nearest raccoon, a raggedy beast of a thing whose claws scratched away the surface of the car's paint.

What the hell did they drop on us that could turn Mother Nature into the devil's army? Buck thought.

He took a tentative step, and the animals inched forward, hissing.

Well, they're certainly not going to let us walk on by.

Turning to Alexiana, he said, "Stay as close as you can to me." When she gave him a look that said she didn't understand, he hooked her hand under his belt. "Don't let go. You understand?"

She nodded yes.

Jesus H. Christ. I have to run through a gauntlet of fucking storybook animals. What's next? Do I have to shoot Bambi?

Flexing his hand on the grip of his pistol, he took several deep breaths, getting ready for a mad dash down Yonkers Avenue. Raccoons and skunks were pretty slow. Unless the gas used to make them crazy also gave them super strength and speed, they'd make it to the KFC down the block. Buck could shoot out the lock and they'd have a safe place to hide for a while. If they were lucky, and luck was no longer their friend, the stench of spoiled chicken would be held in check by the tight seals on the industrial refrigerators. If not, they were going to be in for a long, stomach-churning night.

But before they could take their first step, he had to show the critters there was reason to fear him. Sure, they had the numbers, but he had the firepower. Not enough to take them all on, but enough to make a point.

The report of distant gunfire echoed from the area beyond City Hall.

The animals' attention was pulled away from him and Alexiana. He craned his neck around and kissed her quick.

"Here goes."

Buck shot the fat raccoon perched on the hood of a Honda

Civic and ran, Alexiana tethered to him. He shot twice more, hitting two skunks that looked like they were ready to sail off the roof of a Ram truck. They burst into a pink mist.

He ran as fast and hard as his tired and battered legs would take him. They made it through the surrounding creatures quickly. He turned back and saw them on the street now, less-than-aerodynamic bodies trundling from side to side in pursuit.

More shots rang out. He wondered if it was the Nine Judges letting off steam, dealing with their own animal control issues, or worse—finding the Padillas.

With a comfortable distance between themselves and the animals, Buck gave the glass front door to the KFC a try. To his shock, it was open, which was a very good thing. If he had to shoot it open, the glass would have shattered and there'd be no way to keep the animals out.

He slammed the door behind them, dragging a pair of heavy garbage pails over to wedge against it. The first skunk hit the glass with a heavy *thump*, followed by the rest of its unlikely crew. The pane shook mightily, and he was sure the glass would break.

Alexiana clung to him, panting.

An odor worse than smelling salts hit him square in the nose.

It wasn't chicken.

106

As soon as his father opened the door at the end of the shop, Rey slipped from his grip, collapsing on a carpeted floor. Max turned on the small Maglite he'd been carrying in his pocket.

Rey's mind went into a panic as his lungs fought for air. It felt as if he was drowning. Flailing on the floor, he gasped for breath.

Max was by his ear, saying, "Rey, are you choking? Can you breathe?"

Rey tried to shake him off. He needed to concentrate. Take in as much air as possible. When he did, his lungs twitched, making him cough. Something thick and acidic lodged in his throat and this time, he thought there was no way he'd dislodge it. He tried to swallow. It didn't move. Nothing could get past whatever had crawled into his throat.

"Dad, Rey can't breathe!"

His brother's voice sounded as if he was in another room. Hands clutched at his arms, lifting him up.

He saw his father's face, and his panic doubled. The fear in his father's normally stoic eyes told him he was in trouble.

"Hit his back," his father said.

Rey's spine shuddered as Max pounded as hard as he could.

What meager oxygen that was in his lungs was trapped, and there was no way to replenish it with new. He wanted to scream, to cry, to say something to his family. To die in a blind panic seemed so unfair after everything they'd been through.

"Breathe, Rey, breathe," Max said, his voice up several octaves.

His father nudged Max away, looping his arms around his chest. He felt intense pressure in his gut, just under his rib cage. The vile thing in his throat shifted and he struggled to draw in a breath. His airway was still blocked.

"Dad, help him!" Max was near hysterics.

His father tugged again. Rey's mouth opened in a pained O, droplets of blood spewing on Max. His brother either didn't notice or didn't care.

"Stay with me, Rey," his father said. "We're going to get it out."

His father locked his hands together to form a large fist and he drove that fist under his diaphragm.

To Rey, it felt like a peeled, hard-boiled egg rocketed up his esophagus. It flew from his mouth, his teeth raking the hot, oily surface, splashing his tongue with diseased tissue and fluid. Max stepped aside like a matador as it splattered on the carpet.

That first breath, even though it was hot and stale, felt like a gift from heaven. His father held him like a rag doll as he drew quick breath after quick breath, like a man dying of thirst dipping his head into a cool spring.

"Slow down, Rey, or you're going to hyperventilate," his father said, rubbing his back. "A little slower. That's it. Try to hold it in for a bit. Just like that. You've got it. Nice and slow."

"What the hell is that?" Max said, pointing at the mass of bloody tissue that had expelled from Rey's mouth.

"Not now, Max. Here, help me set him down. And while you're at it, take a seat, too. Does your shoulder hurt?"

As Rey settled onto the floor, he watched Max as he angled his neck to see the bite on his shoulder. His shirt was shredded, and there was a ton of blood running down to his jeans. Max touched it tentatively, curling his lip.

"Not so bad. Feels kinda numb."

"It'll hurt later," his father said. "I'll go back to the cart and see what's in the first aid kit."

Rey wanted to say something, to thank his father, assure his little brother that he'd be all right, but it was impossible to make the words sprout from his damaged respiratory system. Now that he had settled down, he took in their surroundings. The little room was an office, with a battered metal desk and chair, a couple of filing cabinets, and a movie poster of *Foxy Brown* in a cheap frame, hanging at a crooked angle.

He slapped Max's thigh, sweeping the room with his hand, shaking his head.

His brother and father realized at the same moment what was very wrong with the room.

Max said, "Where are Mom and Gabby?"

107

Buck tried to get Alexiana to sit in one of the plastic booths, but she was terrified to let him out of her sight. If something happened to him and he called for help, she'd never know it. She dug her fingers into the collar of his shirt and did her best to say, "You're not leaving me."

He said something, but in the dark, she couldn't read his lips at all.

The stench inside was unbearable. Someone had died here.

The raccoons and skunks, realizing they couldn't get past the glass door and windows, started to filter away. The skunks hadn't sprayed because they weren't afraid. They were off to find food or other survivors dumb enough to be out in the streets at night. At least during the day, you could see what was coming before they were right on top of you.

The dining area of the KFC was empty. The trash bins overflowed with garbage and chicken bones. Her sneakers stuck to the floor with each step. A sign over a particularly large mound of garbage and food waste bore a smiling Colonel Sanders likeness, with a word bubble that said: *Please, keep our restaurant clean.*

Buck tugged on the loop of her jeans and she followed him to the counter. The stench was even worse here.

They both leaned over the stained white counter. Alexiana couldn't stop the bile from splashing the back of her teeth.

Four bodies in an advanced stage of decay lay on the maroon tiled floor. A mother, father, and their two young girls stared sightlessly at the ceiling. It looked as if the flesh was melting from their bones. Each had a red, cratered hole in their temple.

If they were alive, why would they kill themselves? And why here?

Buck hopped over the counter, careful not to step on them. Alexiana's heart stopped when he stomped into the darkness. He returned quickly, carrying an armful of KFC polo shirts. He placed one over each of their faces. While he did that, Alexiana said a silent prayer.

She couldn't stay here all night. Not knowing—

Casting a quick glance out the window, she saw there were just a few of the animals left loitering about. She pointed them out to Buck, who nodded and squeezed her shoulder.

Once the last one left, they had to find another place to stay.

108

Elizabeth kept her back to the steel door, arms wrapped around Gabby. She heard every shot inside the shop and the pounding of the horses as they went wild. They both cried, clinging to each another, hoping beyond hope that Daniel and the boys would somehow make it through all right.

She faced a slick, filthy concrete wall that had to be a dozen feet high. It smelled like old piss and mildew. Steps filled with litter led to the back of the shops and the next street over. They didn't dare go up those steps. There was no telling what could be waiting for them. Elizabeth's heart chilled at the thought of her and Gabby on their own.

It seemed selfish to even pray at this point. For all she knew, thousands of people were suffering behind closed doors at this very moment, each breath possibly their last.

There was a loud crash, and the horses cried out with high-pitched wails that made her shiver.

"Mommy, I'm scared," Gabby said, tears rolling down her cheeks.

"I know, honey, I know."

"I want Daddy."

Gabriela hadn't referred to them as Mommy and Daddy

for the past year, ever since she'd turned double digits. Overnight, they'd become Mom and Dad. The same had happened with Rey and Max, so they were prepared, but it hurt a little more this time because she was their only daughter.

"He'll be here, soon, Gabby. Just close your eyes and keep your arms around me, okay?"

Max shouted something, followed by a series of loud thumps. Elizabeth fought hard to keep her composure. As much as she wanted to let her fears loose, her daughter needed her to be strong.

"Do you remember the time you were learning to ride your bike in Coyne Park?" Elizabeth said. Gabby nodded her head against her mother's stomach. "We all took turns holding on to the backseat and running with you down the little track until you were ready to go on your own."

"And Miguel sat in the grass clapping," Gabby said.

"That's right. He wanted to try it without training wheels, too, but he wasn't ready for that yet. You tried and tried, and each time we let go, you were all right for a little bit, then you started to wobble and eventually you and the bike tipped over to one side. Your father and I were so amazed that no matter how many times you fell, you never cried and you never said you wanted to quit."

"That's because I wanted to ride like Max and Rey. I knew that if I cried, they would laugh at me."

They jerked at the jarring sound of gunfire. Elizabeth held her breath, sucking her tears back.

"No, sweetheart, they wouldn't have laughed at you. They wanted you to be able to ride without training wheels so bad, they were happy to stay at the park all day until you could do it. You were getting so frustrated. And what did Max do?"

Gabby sniffed, so stiff in her arms. "He got on my bike to show me how easy it was."

"That's right. And then he started doing tricks, like

standing on one pedal while he cruised around the track, then kneeling on the seat."

"Then he saw Bridgette Lanza coming from soccer practice on the other field, and when he waved at her, he fell off the bike," Gabby said.

Elizabeth smiled at the memory. "I still don't know how he managed that double somersault and ended up on his feet as if it was exactly what he'd meant to do. He didn't even get a scratch. He made you laugh, and I think he impressed Bridgette just a little bit that day. And the best part—"

Gabby completed the thought, "The best part was I was able to ride all by myself right after that. Max wasn't afraid, even of falling. I thought if I wasn't afraid, I could ride without training wheels, and even if I fell, I'd be all right, just like Max."

"Just like Max." Elizabeth pressed her lips on top of her daughter's head.

The furor in the shop suddenly died down. Elizabeth listened hard, but either no one was moving inside or the metal door was too thick to hear anything under a dull roar.

Gabby looked up at her with wet chestnut eyes. "Can we see Daddy, Max, and Rey now?"

Elizabeth held up a hand. "Just a moment. I have to be sure it's okay to go back inside."

And if the boys weren't okay? What would she do then? How would Gabriela react if she saw her father and brothers seriously hurt or worse?

She waited another minute. Silence.

"Don't let go of my hand," she said to Gabby.

She wrapped her hand around the cold knob and turned. It didn't budge. She pulled at the door, but it remained immovable.

"I think it's locked," she said. She used both hands, but the knob was unyielding.

Elizabeth was about to knock on the door when she felt Gabby tug at her shirt.

Following Gabby's gaze to the top of the stairs, she let go of the doorknob and clasped her hands around her daughter.

Dear God, no!

109

Alexiana didn't need to speak to tell him they couldn't stay in the KFC, and she didn't need to hear to know when it was time to follow Buck out the back door. If they stayed there any longer, he didn't think he'd ever rid his nose of the pungent, sickly sweet smell of those fruiting bodies.

Even now, out in the night air, he could smell that poor family as if they were walking right beside them.

Now there was the matter of where to go. The decision was easy.

City Hall.

The building sat on a hill, making it just about the highest vantage point in the downtown area. He and Alexiana could break inside and get to one of the highest floors. When daylight came, they'd be able to see anyone walking about, even across the Hudson on the Jersey side. There was a chance they could find the Padillas, or help, or even Miguel.

Buck motioned for Alexiana to stop. For a flash, she went rigid with expectation, fear washing over her face. He reassured her that, for the moment, they weren't in danger. He just needed something.

The front door to a red Jeep was wide open. Buck crawled into the back and pulled up the seats. In the seat well was the car's jack and a crowbar. He snapped the crowbar from its plastic holder.

"The new key to the city," he said, grunting as he contorted his body around the cramped space.

"We're going to stay there," he mouthed close to Alexiana's face, pointing at City Hall. She nodded and pressed his hand. They jogged across the jam-packed street, skirting around the building to the front steps. Buck was exhausted. What he wouldn't give for a ski lift to take them to where they needed to go. He paused a moment to catch his breath.

He couldn't wait too long. There was no telling what fresh hell was lurking about. Grabbing Alexiana's hand, they headed up the stairs. The tall front doors were open. Either no one had locked up when the shit hit the fan, or they weren't the first to think of using the old building as a temporary safe harbor. Inside was darker than outside.

"Fucking great," Buck said under his breath. "This whole place could be crammed with lunatics."

It only took a couple of weeks of deprivation of man's creature comforts to devolve him to a near-animal state. The more pampered a society, the faster they crumbled. Aside from stocking up on supplies for the end of the world, Buck had studied a lot of psychology. *Know thy enemy, and thy enemy is thee.*

The crowbar in one hand and his pistol in the other, he led Alexiana into the dark unknown, searching for a stairwell.

110

There was a moment when Daniel thought for sure he was having a heart attack. His heart was already pulsing to a dangerous beat after battling the racehorses. Realizing that his wife and daughter were missing escalated things to the breaking point. The pain in his gunshot arm burned like a hot poker being driven under his flesh. He found one of the painkillers Elizabeth had put in his pocket and chewed it.

"You boys stay here," he said. "I'll go find them."

Max and Rey were a mess. Rey's sickness was winning its battle over the heavy-duty antibiotics Elizabeth had been giving him. And Max, tough as he was, had been beaten and bitten to the point of collapse. The bleeding in his shoulder had stopped, but it had also sapped his strength.

Daniel went back into the store. It looked like one of Buck's grenades had gone off inside. Horses and busted vacuum cleaners were strewn everywhere.

No, they couldn't have gone past them, back out the store's front. So where the hell were they?

He turned around and felt his body deflate when he spied the battered silver door hidden behind wooden shelves crammed with labeled boxes of parts. It must lead to the back of the shop, outside, where Elizabeth and Gabby would be far from safe.

Gripping the handle, he gave it a turn and pulled. The door was wedged shut. The wood frame had warped over the years and was now a too-comfortable fit for the door itself.

"Elizabeth, can you hear me?" he said with his mouth close to the door. He knocked on it twice for good measure.

Two soft raps came back in reply.

"Elizabeth? Gabby, is that you?"

He knocked again, harder.

And again, two tiny knocks were all he got back.

Why aren't they answering me?

"The boys are all right. You can come in now. I'm going to pull on the door. I just need you to push."

Daniel pulled, but he couldn't feel them pushing on the other side.

Something's wrong.

He darted to the back room. "Max, Rey, I have to go back outside."

Max struggled to get up. "I'm coming with you."

Daniel held out his hand. "No, you're not. Your mother and sister are in the back of the store, but the door won't open. I'm going around to get them. Keep this door shut until we come back. I'll knock twice, stop, then twice again so you know it's us. You got that?"

They nodded their weary heads. Rey's eyes fluttered open and closed. The poor kid was just about asleep.

Daniel handed Max the .38 that he'd been keeping in his back pocket as a last resort. "Only shoot when you see what you're firing at."

Max took the pistol, laying it beside him.

Daniel couldn't believe he was giving his fourteen-year-old a gun, but there was no arguing the necessity. He ran out of the shop, leaping over one of the dead horses, turning left on the sidewalk in search of an alley.

111

The slow ascent up the pitch-black stairwell was getting to be too much for Alexiana. It was one thing not to be able to hear the echoes of their shoes scraping against the metal steps. It was another not to be able to see, as well. It felt like being inside a sensory deprivation chamber.

She kept four fingers looped around Buck's belt, felt his back heave like an overworked bellows. He wasn't a young man anymore. The most physical activity he usually did was to bring the food shopping bags in from the car. He'd held up so far, but she was worried about him.

And now she had to worry about his psyche. Knowing him, he blamed himself for her hearing loss. For all either of them knew, it would come back, though with each passing hour and nary a single sound, not even a distant ringing, she feared the worst. He'd done what he had to do to protect them, knowing the blast could have killed him. He'd told her to stay back, but those feral cats! She couldn't watch him struggle like that alone.

Buck stumbled and almost pitched forward. Alexiana tugged hard, steadying him.

The only saving grace was that they hadn't encountered

any animals or people. What if their footsteps had awakened a den of sleeping rats, who were at this moment slinking up the stairs to them?

Shuddering, she tried to keep her thoughts positive. There was no way of knowing how far they had ascended. Buck obviously wanted to get close to the top. This wasn't just about finding a safe place to rest. It was about being able to see what had happened around them, and potentially where to go next. The higher they went, the better.

But she knew that if they didn't stop soon, her flesh was going to crawl right off her bones. The lack of sensory input and the niggling fears gnawing at the back of her brain made every nerve in her body hum.

What brushed against her ankle?

She must have blurted something out because Buck stopped. When the feeling didn't return, she tapped his back to tell him to keep going. It might have only been a scrap of paper or her own out-of-control imagination. Anything was possible when you were deaf and blind. The combination took panic to an entirely new realm.

They continued walking, slow and steady, one of her hands on the rail, the other on Buck. When they came to a landing, Buck felt around for a door. A sliver of darkness lighter than the pitch they'd been in almost made her shout out with joy.

Walking into a long, carpeted hallway lined with doors, Alexiana thought her legs were going to go out from under her. A heady cocktail of relief and exhaustion bowled her over. If she hadn't been holding on to Buck, she would be on the floor.

He used the flat end of the crowbar to pry open the door of an office at the end of the hallway. Inside was a metal desk, circa 1970s government-issue, its surface covered with plastic In and Out trays and an ink blotter. Several battered chairs on casters and a bookshelf lined with more cactus plants than books took up the rest of the meager space.

Alexiana collapsed into one of the chairs, hanging her head between her knees. When she looked up, Buck was sitting, as well, though he'd rolled his chair to the window.

112

The naked man sat on the top step making slow, measured movements. Moonlight glinted off the meat cleaver in his right hand. His body was so filthy, it was impossible to tell his race. His uncut penis poked out of a nest of wiry black hairs. He coughed, blood cascading from his mouth and running down his deflated chest. Elizabeth could tell he'd once been in very good shape, but the sickness had been wasting him away, muscle by muscle.

When Daniel called to her through the door, the man smiled with crimson teeth and put a finger to his lips. *Shh.*

Gabby tried to hide behind her. Elizabeth heard her tap on the door soft enough so the crazy, sick man couldn't hear.

Daniel was trying to jerk the door open, to no avail.

"What do you want from us?" she said to the stranger.

He sucked on his teeth, one hand smearing the blood across his chest. He had close-cropped hair and the makings of a beard, flecks of white here and there. His wide nostrils flared with each breath, as if he was trying to absorb as much oxygen as he could with each inhalation. Something rattled in his chest, wet and rheumy. Elizabeth had heard that sound countless times in the hospital when patients came in with pneumonia.

Somewhere between running into the shop and out the back door, she'd lost her gun. She had no way of defending herself. All she could do was occupy him and wait for Daniel to arrive.

"Are you hurt or sick? I have medicine inside that could help you," she continued. "I'm a nurse. That's a lot of blood you're coughing up. You need help."

He spat on the step between his feet, dragging the knife over the concrete. The sound made Elizabeth's hair stand on end. The man stood up with a grunt and took a faltering step toward them.

"Please, don't hurt us. Just put the knife down. There's nothing we can do to harm you. I only want to help. Why don't you tell me your name?"

The man didn't respond, just pinned her back with his demented stare. Gabby whimpered behind her. Elizabeth whispered from the side of her mouth, "If he comes down here, I want you to run past him as fast as you can. Your father and brothers are right around the corner."

"I don't want to leave you, Mommy."

"Just do what I say, okay?"

If Elizabeth had to let him stab her to death, so be it. All that mattered was that Gabby was safe.

The man's voice, that of a drowning man, startled her. "I don't want you," he said. "I'm going to fuck your girl's brains out. And you get to watch."

His head reared back and he let loose with a wild man's scream. With his knife raised high, he ran down the stairs.

113

Miguel listened to the men down the dark hallway laughing and yelling, sometimes arguing. They were playing some kind of card game and there would be loud accusations of cheating, followed by the frantic sounds of scuffling. Things would die down, and then everything would start up again.

He pulled his knees as close as he could to his chest, resting his chin on his kneecaps.

Earlier, a boy who looked to be Max's age threw a warm bottle of water to him, along with a box of raisins. He didn't say a word, just tossed him something to eat and drink and left.

He was so scared, he couldn't stop crying. He tried his best to keep his sobs low, so the bad gang people wouldn't hear him. Maybe they would forget he was even here and he could find a way to open the gate.

His mom and dad would be here soon. He had never been so sure of anything in his life. They wouldn't leave him here. He pictured their faces, and Max and Rey and Gabby, thought about family vacations or just sitting in the living room watching TV. If he closed his eyes and concentrated hard enough, he could even make himself believe that he was back home and they were laughing, watching *The Big Bang Theory*. He didn't understand half of what the people on the show were talking about, but hearing his family laugh always made him chuckle along with them.

He sat between his mother and father on the couch, watching *The Big Bang Theory*, sipping on a Capri Sun, and waiting for Gabby to get popcorn for all of them at the commercial break.

114

It was downright surreal looking over the city and not seeing a single light. Not even a stray fire. It was like looking into a mine chamber. He could see across to the cliffs of the Palisades and over as far as the Tappan Zee Bridge that connected Westchester and Rockland counties.

How many cars are on that bridge that will never make it to the other side?

The Tappan Zee Bridge was infamous for jumpers. So many people had stopped their cars in the center of the span and taken nosedives into the strong current of the Hudson that they had to erect higher barriers and post signs advising people to call the suicide hotline.

Of course, that wasn't enough to stop a person set on killing themselves, but he guessed it made the county feel like they'd done all they could. Buck wondered how many people had jumped compared to the Golden Gate Bridge. And what was it about bridges that appealed to the suicidal?

"You're getting maudlin," he said aloud.

His feet were propped on the windowsill and he sat as far back in the chair as it would go. Alexiana was asleep in the chair next to him, her head on his shoulder.

He should probably get some sleep while it was still dark.

Everything would be different when the sun was up. They'd have a course of action, a solid direction to take.

At least that was the hope. If there'd been any kind of military assistance, they would have had generators and lights. If they could just spot a pocket of people, a group they could join, everyone looking out for one another's backs, that would be enough.

And then there was Miguel and the Nine Judges. He couldn't live with himself if he didn't try to find the boy. If the Padillas had survived the night, and in his gut he knew they had, they would be close. Even before everything went irretrievably haywire, they'd become his adopted family. He wasn't going to abandon them. He held no ill will toward them even if they had up and left after the explosion. The smart assumption would be that he and Alexiana had bought the farm. They had a son to find, kids to protect. They were the future, even before the shit storm. Buck was a relic. Alex was a saint fool enough to hitch her wagon to him. He chuckled, rubbing his eyes with his knuckles.

They would need to get more ammo in the morning. The police station was just across the street. Surely they'd have left something behind. Then they needed food. There was a greasy diner close by. They'd raid the pantry for canned food and water. What were the odds of one of those oversized diner cookies wrapped in cellophane still being good to eat? His stomach rumbled at the thought.

Buck stroked Alexiana's hair, taking in the natural scent of her, sans fruity soaps and perfume. He never loved her more than he did at this moment. Resting his head against hers, he closed his eyes and thought of better days.

115

Daniel heard a man scream, then Elizabeth and Gabby. Heart ramming his chest, he sprinted toward the sound, jumping over and nearly falling into a pile of plump trash bags.

Gabby's steady squeals were a beacon. He skidded into a chest-high fence. Looking down, he saw a filthy, naked man pushing Elizabeth against a wall. Gabby was being crushed behind her.

"Hey!" Daniel shouted to distract the man.

He looked up at him, and Daniel knew this man had checked out a long time ago. One eye twitched, madness burning behind it. Daniel also saw the cleaver in his hand, his wife holding on to the man's wrist to keep it from plunging into her neck. There was blood everywhere, but he couldn't tell who it belonged to.

"Get the hell off my wife!"

He ran around the fence, keeping his eye on the man, looking for the break to the stairs.

"I don't want your wife," the man replied coolly, a devil's grin on his grimy face.

Daniel had never felt such rage before.

He hopped over the fence, howling with his own newfound madness. His foot caught the edge of a step and his legs went out from under him. His bad arm thwacked the concrete, igniting sparks in his head. He skidded down the remaining steps on his back.

The man laughed at his clumsy rescue and turned back to Elizabeth.

"Come on, lady, no sense hogging that hot little piece of ass. Haven't you heard? It's a new world. Everybody gets to fuck whoever they want!"

He drove the knife into her. Elizabeth twisted her body, the knife grazing her upper arm, slicing open a red, wet smile on her flesh.

"Get away from her!" Elizabeth shouted.

Daniel was back on his feet. He saw Gabby's terrified eyes as she tried to make herself as small as possible behind her mother's back.

There was no way this bastard was going to lay one finger on her.

Daniel lunged at the man, grabbing the short hairs on his head, pulling him back until he could hear the roots start to give way. The man spun around, slashing at him with the cleaver. It whistled through the empty space between them, just missing Daniel's chest.

Spotting his one chance to end this quickly, Daniel reared back and caught the man as hard as he could in the balls. Air and blood exploded from his mouth, all over Daniel. He staggered into the wall, his hands cupping his shattered testicles.

"Run, get out of here, now!" Daniel said to his wife and daughter.

Elizabeth tugged at his arm. "Come on."

"I'll be with you in a minute. There's an alley just over there. Follow it until you get to the next street. Head for the repair shop and go to the back room. Knock twice, stop, and two more times. The boys will let you in."

"But, Daniel—"

"I said go!"

Elizabeth gave him a pleading look, but he was past giving in to anything but what he felt needed to be done.

"Come on, Gabby. Daddy will be right behind us," she said, ushering her up the stairs.

Daniel turned to the naked man, who had taken a knee, coughing. Thick gobs of phlegm and blood spattered the ground.

He was sick, just like Rey.

But there was a sickness far more cancerous in the man's brain. Daniel couldn't just walk away, knowing he'd still be out here, waiting for them. And if not them, another innocent family, or child.

"What's the matter?" the man said in a high, pained voice. "You don't wanna share?"

Daniel picked up the cleaver, wavering it in his hand, judging its weight.

"Put your hands over your head," Daniel said.

The man grimaced. "You broke my fucking balls, asshole. Go fuck yourself."

Daniel stepped between his writhing legs. "I said put your hands over your head."

A thick gob of red spit hit Daniel in the chest.

Daniel sliced the man's forearms, one after the other, filleting the flesh down to the ropy muscle. His arms retracted as he yowled.

"Thank you," Daniel said, bringing the cleaver down on the man's genitals, cleaving his penis and scrotum in half. Thick gouts of blood gushed from the fatal wound. Daniel hacked again, this time at the man's inner thigh, hoping to find a major artery. On the third try, he did. A fountain of blood cascaded over his head with a sharp hiss. He jumped back to avoid the spray.

The man's pain was so extreme, he couldn't even get a scream out as he twitched on the floor, limbs jittering.

Daniel watched and waited for the man to die.

116

Rey jerked awake as if he'd been pulled by a lifeguard from a riptide. He grabbed Max by the arm.

"Where is everyone?" Rey asked, eyes darting around the semi-dark, alien room.

Max sighed. "Pop went to get Mom and Gabby. They went out the back and the door is stuck. They should be here any minute."

"What about Miguel?"

Max brought his face close to his. "You don't remember about Miguel?"

Rey tried to think. Something didn't feel right. He wanted his family. What was he supposed to remember about Miguel?

"No. Is he with Mom, too?"

Max stared at him, his lips pressed into a tight line. Finally, he said, "Yeah, she took him and Gabby outside."

"They'll be here soon?"

"Yeah."

Rey took in a deep breath. He expected to cough. When he didn't, he took another, and another. Faster and faster, he couldn't get enough air into his lungs. It was if they'd been starved and were finally allowed to feast.

"Dude, slow down, you're going to make yourself pass out or something," Max said, placing his hand on his chest.

"No," Rey said. "It feels good . . . to breathe."

His heart marched a double beat, overflowing with life-giving oxygen as it soared through his veins.

Everyone would be back soon. He couldn't wait to show them how much better he felt.

117

Alexiana woke up because she thought she heard something. Opening her eyes, she realized it had just been a dream. She still couldn't hear a thing, not even Buck's snoring. The man buzzed away like a band saw every time he closed his eyes.

Now that she was up, she really had to go to the bathroom. She couldn't remember the last time she'd peed. Had it been two days ago? It couldn't have been. She was definitely dehydrated. She would have to drink as much as she could tomorrow.

Gently, she pulled away from Buck, taking the Beretta from her back pocket. There were two bullets left. She hoped to God she didn't need to use them as she went into the hallway in search of the bathroom. Her foot hit something, sending it gliding across the carpet.

It was an iPhone. It must have fallen from someone's pocket when they rushed to get out of the building. People used to camp out for days waiting for the new version to come out. Now it was just another piece of useless trash. On a whim, she tried to turn it on. The display screen remained dark, vacant.

Dropping it to the floor, she jumped back a step at the huddled, shadowy figures at the end of the hall.

Her first bizarre instinct was, *Are they ghosts?* She'd been a sucker for all those ghost-hunting shows on TV and the programs about celebrities and their paranormal encounters. Buck said that stuff was eating IQ points, one episode at a time.

The shadows moved closer, and there was a sudden burst of flame. Alexiana raised her gun. Something waved in the air, a black stick, or were they arms? The floating fire came closer, illuminating what was behind it.

She put the gun down.

A teenaged girl carried a metal bowl. The fire was contained in the bowl, scraps of paper thrown in as a makeshift flashlight. Behind her was an older man and a woman who could be her mother. The girl and woman both had long onyx hair, aquiline noses, and deep-set eyes.

The woman's lips moved. Alexiana shook her head. She said, "I'm sorry, I can't hear," hoping it came out right.

The trio looked past her. Alexiana spun around. Buck stood in the hallway, gun in hand but pointed at the floor.

Has it come to this already? Any interaction with another living person must be done at gunpoint?

"Buck, no," Alexiana said. She felt his hand on her shoulder.

The girl brought the bowl of fire closer, bringing her features into sharper clarity. Her young bronze skin was marred by streaks of dirt. The crescents of her fingernails were caked black.

The man and woman behind her were empty-handed. They had no weapons. All three wore shorts, and in the flickering firelight, Alexiana saw red welts and rashes on their knees and legs. They had not had it easy.

Alexiana put her gun in her back pocket to show them she meant no harm. She hoped Buck was doing the same.

The girl spoke, motioning for her to follow them.

When the trio turned to go back down the hall, Alexiana walked right behind them. If it was a trap, the blame would be on her.

118

Elizabeth shook with relief when Daniel emerged from the alley. She and Gabby had gone as far as the front window of the repair shop. Two of the horses were still alive, though unable to get back on their legs. Gabby refused to walk past them, worrying that they would bite her.

Elizabeth saw the fresh blood on Daniel's clothes. He gave her a look that begged her not to ask. Whatever had happened back there with the crazed man was between Daniel, the man, and God. She wondered if there would ever be a time when he could talk about it—or one when she would be ready to hear it.

"Why aren't you inside? It's not safe out here," he said, keeping his voice low. It seemed even the act of breathing was loud enough to wake the dead. Of course, after the cacophony in the shop, anyone with working ears would know something major had just gone down and exactly where it had happened.

"Gabby's afraid of the horses."

Their only daughter didn't cry, but Elizabeth watched her body stiffen every time she looked through the smashed window.

Daniel lifted her to his chest. "Don't be afraid. They can't hurt anyone anymore. Just close your eyes. I'll walk you through."

Gabby wasn't the only one afraid. One of the horses, blood frothing from its mouth, twitched its powerful head up and down, back and forth, anxious to get its teeth into anything that came near. A tall metal shelf had fallen across its back, a barrier between them and the nipping, dying horse. They skirted behind it, stepping over the still body of another. Its front legs had been splintered, one side of its head caved in.

"The boys are back here. There's a storage room we can stay in until the morning. I'll go to the deli across the street and get something for us to drink in a bit." He let Gabby back down on her feet. "I forgot something."

He ran to the tipped-over shopping cart and came back with the first aid kit.

Elizabeth's heartbeat stopped. "Are the boys hurt?"

"One of the horses locked its teeth into Max's shoulder. It bled a lot but I think it looks worse than it is."

She grabbed the plastic box from his hands, jogging to the closed door of the back room. She knocked just as Daniel had told her. The door opened on a squeaky hinge. When she saw Max's bloody face, she rushed inside to sweep him into her arms.

"Oh my God, Max, are you okay? Your father said you were bit. Show me where."

It was hard to tell with all of the blood—most of it, presumably, belonging to the slaughtered horses.

"It just got me in the shoulder," he said, tugging his shirt down from his neck. "It wasn't enough to stop me, though. Me, Pop, and Rey held off four crazy horses. I'll bet no one's ever done that before."

There are a lot of things happening that have never been done before, Elizabeth thought with a corpulent weight of sadness she could feel in her body as much as her soul.

The bite was at the front and back of his shoulder. It

wasn't deep, but it looked painful. Once the adrenaline wore off, Max would feel it—not that he'd ever admit it. No, her middle son was too proud for that.

"I'm going to pour some alcohol, then peroxide on it. You want to hold my hand? It's going to sting."

He gave her a weak half smile. "You can do it. I'll be fine. It's not like this is the first time this week."

The antiseptic washed the blood away. Daniel shined the Maglite at the wound so she could clean it properly.

"Good thing we have a nurse on call," Daniel said, chuckling.

"With four boys in the family, someone had to have medical training," she said. Max didn't even wince as she packed the wound with gauze, wrapping tape over it and under his armpit.

"There, it'll do. We have to keep that clean. Take that shirt off. We'll find a new one tomorrow."

Max chucked the shirt into the far corner of the room.

Elizabeth pushed her hair behind her ears. "Now, Rey is due for antibiotics."

When she looked to Rey, who had been on the floor, his back propped against the wall, she found Gabby draped over his chest, crying.

"Gabby, stay off his chest. He's had a hard enough time with breathing and coughing."

Her daughter looked up, a stream of tears rushing from her red, swollen eyes.

"Mommy, I don't think Rey is breathing!"

119

Buck kept his hand on the gun in his pocket, just in case. These three looked as harmful as ladybugs, but he wasn't going to take any chances. The man looked to be about the same age as him, but he walked with a severe limp and his back was hunched slightly. The woman held on to his arm, guiding him down the hall.

They stopped in what was once a break room—refrigerator, microwave, two coffeemakers, two toaster ovens, and a couple of tables with hard plastic chairs. The windows looked out on the new riverview apartment buildings and the Hudson. Another set behind him gave a bird's-eye view of the north and west of the city, all the way to the Saw Mill Parkway.

One table was filled from end to end with open cans, empty water bottles, and sports drinks. They must have been staying here awhile.

The woman helped the man into a chair. The girl opened a cabinet and added more scraps of paper to the fire to better illuminate the room.

"Amazing," the man said. He had kind ginger eyes beneath unruly, graying brows. "You're the first people to even attempt coming in the building since we got here. I guess people aren't bothering with complaints or marriage licenses anymore." His body shook as he snickered. "I'm sorry, I've already forgotten how to be polite. My name is Vishal Patel. This is my daughter, Rita, and my granddaughter, Sailaja."

Alexiana smiled and nodded. Buck said, "I'm Buck Clarke and this is my girlfriend, Alexiana DeCarlo. We had an incident earlier. She hasn't gotten her hearing back yet."

"We saw the cars explode," Rita said. "We watched the whole thing. After the smoke cleared, I wanted to come down to help you, but—"

Buck waved his hand. "No, you did the right thing, staying here where it's safe. Did you see the family who was with us?"

"Yes."

"Did you see what happened to them? We've been separated ever since, and I'm not sure if they're okay or not."

"They went to the church when the smoke got bad," Sailaja said, offering them each a glass bottle of iced tea. Buck popped the cap and drank half of it in one swallow. He hadn't realized how thirsty he'd been. "We couldn't see you anymore at that point, but we watched them run to the church. We went there a few days ago. It was bad."

Buck pulled out a seat for Alexiana and sat next to her. He looked at the family across the table, folding his hands together. "What was so bad about the church?" He thought of the Nine Judges using it as a hideout. His stomach dropped.

Vishal said, "It's a cemetery. There's an old Polish priest there. He takes in the sick so they can die in absolution before the cross. The pews are filled with the dead."

"Jesus Christ."

"I don't think he's with us anymore," Vishal said.

For the first time since it had happened, Buck was grateful Alexiana couldn't hear.

"Your friends didn't stay long, though. When the streets cleared of the smoke, they set out. They went back to look for you, but there was a tremendous dog guarding the area. I think it was saving you for a meal for later," Rita said, loudly crunching an empty plastic bottle. "They must not have seen you, because they headed this way. We lost track of them, but we heard shots and a lot of shouting."

Buck had heard the shots, as well, and hoped the Padillas were in no way a part of it. Like everything else, it was a hope that might as well have been spit into a hurricane.

"I don't mean to be too personal," Buck said, "but how is your health? Were you in a secure shelter when the . . . the . . ."

"World came to an end?" Vishal finished for him. "Close, but not close enough, I'm afraid. We've been able to keep ahead of the fate that's befallen everyone else, but I don't think we can ultimately outrun it."

120

Daniel pulled as hard as he could at his hair, walking in a tight circle while Elizabeth wailed, rocking Rey in her arms. This couldn't be happening! Had they been spared a quick death only to be taken one by one? Were they being punished for surviving, for staying together even when their world was torn apart?

Silent tears stained his shirt.

Max kept repeating, "He said he felt good. He was breathing better. He felt good."

Gabby latched on to Elizabeth's back, both of them on the floor with Rey. His eyes were mercifully closed. Daniel didn't think he could take seeing death's gray veil over his first child's eyes.

"Why? Why?" Elizabeth chanted, her tears falling into Rey's hair.

Like Daniel, Gabby was beyond words. All they could do was cry.

Images of Rey as a baby played like old home movies in his mind—Rey gnawing on the third Pack 'n Play they'd had to buy in a year, Daniel nicknaming him the shark because of his sharp teeth. Rey on his first day of kindergarten, so stoic until he and his mother left the classroom. Oh, how he cried. Elizabeth melted into Daniel as they walked outside past his classroom, their son's howls echoing down the residential street. His thirteenth birthday, when they gave him the mountain bike he'd been asking for and how his face lit up. Graduating from grammar school, how proud they all were. Getting ready to graduate from high school, one step closer to becoming a man.

All of it leading to this place, in a dusty storeroom, a broken family left behind as Rey went to a place that had to be better than here.

I have to get air, Daniel said to himself, believing he might have said it out loud, as well, but everyone was so wrapped up in their own grief, they wouldn't have heard it if the horses came back to life and resumed their attack. Jerking the door open, he walked unsteadily down the hall.

Through the haze of his tears, he saw the first tawny rays of the sun chasing the shadows back into dark corners and their daytime hiding places.

What would they do with Rey?

And where was Miguel?

Daniel felt his resolve waver, whatever stores of strength he had left bleeding from every pore. He staggered over the lip of the broken window, collapsing on his rump on the sidewalk.

He wept, great, heaving sobs that caromed off the surrounding buildings, his grief whispering into thin air.

Cry for Rey. Can't let Max and Gabriela see you like this. Cry until you feel you can stop it. Because you have to. Your baby is close. We can all mourn for Rey—later. Miguel is still here. Dear God, you can't take him from us. No. He's alive, and alone and scared. We'll find him.

We'll find him.

121

Once Buck realized there was nothing to fear from Vishal and his family, he'd let his guard down and somehow fallen asleep in the supremely uncomfortable chair with Alexiana leaning against him. Rita's crunching on dry cereal woke him up. The sun sat alone in a cloudless sky.

"Good morning," she said softly so as not to wake anyone else up.

Buck covered his mouth as he yawned. "Would you look at that sky! From here, you'd almost think nothing was wrong with the world."

He managed to angle himself out of the chair and gently lay Alexiana's head on the table.

"Poor thing is wiped out," he said.

"You went through a lot yesterday," Rita said. "It's a wonder you're even alive."

He motioned for her to join him just outside the break room, where they could talk freely. She carried the box of cereal, offering him some, which he gladly accepted. He'd never been a cereal guy. At this moment, it tasted like a five-star breakfast at the Ritz on an expense account.

"Alexiana and I have to find our friends. But before we do that, I'm going across the street to the police station to see what firearms they left behind. If there's one thing I've learned, you can't be outside unless you're armed. I'll bring back something for you, too."

Rita shook her head. "We don't believe in guns."

"It's not a question of belief. The truth is, without them, you don't stand a chance. Between the animals and people like the Nine Judges, you wouldn't last half a day out there without protection."

She smiled, and it seemed so out of place, he didn't know how to take it.

"We're not leaving. My father started a fever the other day, and my daughter began to cough yesterday. When the explosions happened, we were in the basement of our store, getting things ready to bring upstairs. We owned an Indian grocery store on Lawrence Street. We went upstairs to see what had happened, and when panic broke out, we locked and shuttered the doors and went back to the basement. But we'd been exposed. At the time we thought nothing of it, but we were outside when the smoke filled the streets. We've lasted this long only because we got away from it quickly."

Buck sighed, both hands on her arms. "It might just be that that little bit of exposure won't be enough to . . . you know."

"It was enough. We saw what happened to the others. There's no escaping it. You and your girlfriend are a miracle, a gift to us. If you hadn't come here, we would have assumed there was no hope." She gave him the box of cereal. "Before we came up here to get away, we heard that the military had extraction boats in Hastings. My father would never make the journey, not in his condition, and we won't leave him. If you find your friends, you may want to go there. I haven't seen any activity on the Hudson, so it may have been wishful thinking. But I think if anyone will find help, it will be you."

Buck grimaced. "What makes you say that?"

Sailaja had woken up and went for a can of Hawaiian Punch. She gave Rita and Buck a little finger wave.

"Because you're survivors, and you're healthy. And now you have my faith. Don't break it."

He'd never been an emotional man, but he had to fight like hell to swallow back the lump in his throat and hold back his tears. These were good people, content to spend their last days in a break room atop City Hall. Nothing seemed fair or right anymore.

Rita shooed him away. "Now go and hurry back. I'll keep an eye out for your friends."

122

Max went with his father to the YMCA across the street in search of blankets. Neither spoke, and they avoided eye contact as much as possible. His mother and Gabby were in the storage room with Rey, beside themselves with grief.

He died leaning on me and I didn't even know it. Did he say anything or ask for help? I know I was zoning out. I'm so dizzy. You can't leave me like this, Rey. You can't—

The redolence of death smacked them in the face the moment they entered the building. The dead were everywhere—in their rooms, lying on beds, fallen on floors, face-down in the hallway, as if they'd made a last, hopeless dash for help that would never come.

A high-pitched buzz gave him hope that electricity had been restored. Max flipped a light switch but nothing happened.

"It's flies," his father said.

Max looked down the hall. Flies were everywhere, feasting from one body to the next. He swatted them away, sickened by the thought of being bitten by one that had just sucked the juice of an infected corpse.

His father darted into a room, emerging with a couple of

clean shirts in dry cleaner's plastic. "Put one on and use the other to cover your mouth," he said.

The blue button-down dress shirt was a little long in the arms, but it fit close enough. He ripped the white dress shirt in two, handing half to his father. They had left the sports equipment behind. A hockey helmet only offered a false sense of security.

"No blankets in there?" Max asked.

"There was a man on it," was all he said before moving down the hall.

Max had never been in a Y before and had a preconceived notion that all Ys were glorified flophouses. This one, despite the bodies, looked to have been pretty clean and ordered. It was actually kind of like a mini-hotel. Most of the doors were locked.

"Hand me your bat," his father said. "I don't want to have to explore the upper floors. We have to get back to your mother and sister."

He tried a door handle. When it didn't turn, he heaved the bat at the knob with a ferocity Max had never seen in his father. It clattered to the floor and he kicked the door open.

A black man with a frazzled Mohawk was curled up in a ball on the floor, underneath the window that looked out onto the neighboring wall of the Subway sandwich shop. His oxygen-deprived, decomposing flesh had turned a color that seemed utterly unnatural for a human being. A puddle of dried blood trailed from the corner of his mouth.

The man's bed was made. He must have collapsed, never even making it to the bed.

"These will do," his father said, stripping off the sheets and tan blanket. He handed the bundle to Max and they headed to the exit. The sooner they were out of here, the better.

They paused on the top steps of the Y to make sure no

Nine Judges were about. It wouldn't do to be seen, not yet anyway. "We're good."

The horses in the shop were all dead now. Flies, drunk on the never-ending feast that Yonkers offered, settled into the exposed meat of their hides and jellied eyes.

His mother and sister sat on their knees on either side of his brother. Rey's eyes were closed, and his chin rested on his chest. Max could easily believe he was just taking a nap.

The four of them gently moved Rey so they could wrap him in the sheets, then the blanket. The tears had stopped for the moment, but they all sniffled every few seconds. There was no place to bury him, not here in the center of the city. They would leave him here, do what they could to seal up the door, and come back for him if and when they found help.

His mother prayed over Rey's body, and there was an un-spoken resolve to be strong, to hold it together. While she said a full rosary, they held hands, he was sure each lost in memories of Rey as much as he was.

When she was finished, they stacked everything they could find against the door to make it difficult to get through.

As they stepped out of the shop, his mother said, "Where should we go?"

"We want a good view of the area, so we should go to that restaurant on the water. It's up high enough and is all glass," his father said.

It was decided. They jogged to the waterfront, heads swiveling in every direction, hoping not to be seen. There were no words to be said. Max worried that if he tried to speak, he'd break down. Rey would want them to find Miguel above everything.

Max imagined Rey running by his side. It didn't ease his pain, but it did give him the strength to keep moving.

123

Alexiana had been terrified when she woke up and didn't see Buck. Sailaja had already written a note for her, handing it over the moment her eyes flickered open.

Buck will be right back. He went to the police station to get supplies.

She mouthed *Thank you* and haltingly got up from the chair. Her entire body felt as if her bones had been fused together. The act of standing was like rending each bone apart from one another.

Vishal offered her a bottle of water and a selection of granola bars. She took the water with a smile, but declined the bars. The pain from sleeping in that horrid chair overrode her need to eat, though she knew she would have to force something down sooner rather than later. She had to keep up her strength.

Communication with the Patels proved frustrating. They'd have to understand. She hadn't even been deaf for twenty-four hours yet. It was disappointing that none of her hearing had returned. She would have had some hope of recovering that sense if even a little had come back while she slept.

You're not that lucky, she thought. *But you are still alive, which would seem a hell of a lot luckier if the prospect of living were a little brighter.*

Buck wasn't going to give up on the Padillas, and neither was she.

Leaning her forehead against the window, she stood next to Rita, gazing at the empty streets. There wasn't a plane in the sky or a boat on the river. It looked like a perfect day for sailing.

A beautiful day shining on a destroyed city with more corpses than the living to taint the fresh air.

She stepped away from the window, taking a walk down the hall to work out the kinks in her back.

I have every fucking right to be morose.

Alexiana watched Vishal bend over, coughing hard into his hand. The scene looked hauntingly familiar.

I hope Rey is holding up through all of this.

124

Elizabeth refused to let go of Gabby's hand as they made their way to the boardwalk. They kept to the shadows and pressed close to buildings, wary of prying eyes or unwanted visitors.

It was strange, all this time hoping to find other survivors, now praying they came across no one before they got to the elevated restaurant. YO2 had opened around the time the Yonkers waterfront project had completed the first phase of revitalization several years ago. Gone were the burned-out buildings, half-vacant project housing, and decrepit businesses and factories. In their place were a beautiful new boardwalk, family-style and upscale restaurants, a park and playground, and new high-rise apartments, all right on the banks of the Hudson River. What was once an area to be avoided at all costs—unless you were in need of drugs, prostitutes, or other illicit items—became a favorite destination overnight.

It looked like the coveted waterfront was about to become the jewel of the city, and then the economy collapsed. The new restaurants and hot spots couldn't weather the storm, shuttering their doors in rapid order.

But not YO2, a celebrity chef–owned eatery that didn't

compromise its high-priced menu. Most amazing of all, people kept coming, and it was now the most popular restaurant in the city.

It was on the boardwalk, right above what had once been the dock for the Yonkers Water Taxi, a service that ferried people to and from the city. That went bust in short order. She and Rey had meant to try it one day but never found the time.

"This place looks like it's sealed up tight," Daniel said as they gathered by the elevator that led to YO2. Stands of binoculars were mounted along the edges of the dock. Elizabeth remembered taking a roll of quarters down here last summer so all of the kids could take turns scanning the boats on the water and New York City's skyline to the south.

Behind the elevator that went directly to the freestanding structure that housed YO2 was a set of stairs they could take. She wondered if any elevators in the city would ever run again. "Max, let me have your bat," Daniel said.

"I wonder why no one bothered to break in before," Elizabeth said, the cold caress of an early morning Hudson breeze cooling her cheeks. Gabby's hand was hot and sweaty in her own, but she was *connected*.

Max said, "Maybe whatever blew up happened down here first. People didn't have time to loot."

As they ascended the dark stairwell, Daniel in the lead, he said, "You're probably right. Hundreds of thousands of people live in this area, and all we've seen is one crazy person last night. Whoever did this to the city knew exactly what they were doing."

The double glass doors at the top of the stairs were indeed locked, but they were no match for Max's bat. Elizabeth cringed when the glass shattered, hoping the noise wouldn't travel far. The dining room was set for dinner service. Impeccably white tablecloths, fine dinnerware, and cutlery all in perfect alignment. Wilted wildflowers decayed in vases in the center of each table.

"We'll find them from up here," Daniel said.

The restaurant was all tinted windows, giving them a 360-degree view of the downtown area. The best part was they could see out, while anyone from the ground couldn't see in.

"Gabby and I will watch from over there," Elizabeth said, pointing to a table for two to their left. She gave Gabby's hand a gentle squeeze.

If they found the Nine Judges, how would they get Miguel away from them? They were low on ammunition, hurt, and exhausted. If they had done something to her baby, she wasn't sure she wanted to go on. They'd had to leave the shopping cart with most of the supplies because the horses had demolished it and a good deal of its contents. She worried that her spirit would simply dissolve. And what would become then of Max and Gabriela?

Stay angry. They have your boy. But they won't for long. Sooner or later, they'll come out of their rat's hiding hole.

Miguel will be waiting for us. Somehow, we'll make them pay.

125

When Buck returned with little to show, winded from walking up all the stairs, Rita rushed over to him. Alexiana sat with her nose inches from the window, peering at something intently.

"I think we spotted your friends," Rita said. "I saw a man and woman with what looked like their son and daughter running to the waterfront."

He walked as fast as he could to the window, nudging Alexiana. She pointed to an area by the boardwalk.

"Our friends have two boys," Buck said. "One of them has been sick, so we found an old shopping cart to move him around. Did you see him?"

Rita chewed at a fingernail. "I'm sorry, there was just the boy and the girl."

Buck tapped his girlfriend's shoulder and asked her, enunciating as best he could, if she spotted Rey. She looked confused until he said the boy's name. She shook her head, then grabbed a piece of paper and a pencil.

I saw them, too. He's not with them.

Buck felt like a rapidly deflating balloon. Rey's absence could mean one of two things. He was either too sick to move on, so they set him up someplace safe while they searched for Miguel.

The other option was too heartrending to consider.

"Did you see where they went?" he asked.

Alexiana scribbled.

That expensive restaurant. Y something.

Of course. Aside from City Hall, it had one of the best views in the area. If the Nine Judges were here, they'd see them.

"We have to go to them," Buck said. He opened up a canvas Stew Leonard's shopping bag to show Alexiana the Glocks and clips he'd managed to find at the police station. Most of the place had been picked clean. He wasn't going to tell her that he had to take them from a couple of dead cops, their bodies bloated and feeling like jelly as he maneuvered them to check their holsters.

Vishal rose from his chair with his granddaughter's assistance. "I'm glad you found your friends. Please, you're welcome to bring them back here and stay with us. There's more than enough food and water to go around. I think our city employees did more eating and drinking than actual work."

Buck shook his hand. "Thank you. It's damn good to know there are still decent people left in this city. We have something very important to do, and if we can find their boy, I think we'll head to Hastings to see if the rumors are true. I promise, if we find help, we're coming back here with them."

Smiling weakly, Vishal patted his hand. "I'd tell you to take my beautiful women with you, but they're as stubborn as I am. I'll pray you make it safely, and hope I'll be here when you return. Good luck."

They exchanged hugs and Buck walked out of the break room with his arm around Alexiana. He gave her one of the

Glocks and a spare clip. The jog down the stairs was a hell of a lot easier than the walk up. They had to hurry. He didn't want to get to the restaurant after the Padillas had left. If they were going to take Miguel back, they'd need every bit of help they could get.

126

The morning was anything but quiet. What Daniel saw as he watched from behind a table meant for romantic dinners for two made him wonder just how they'd gotten this far with any of them alive.

He called Elizabeth to the window when he spotted a middle-aged man and woman as they emerged from the Bank of America two blocks over. It looked as if they had been hiding out in the ATM vestibule overnight. When Daniel saw the blood on their shirts, hands, necks, and faces, he made a point to tell Max and Gabby to stay where they were, keeping watch on the opposite side of the restaurant. Sure, they had seen more than any child—or adult, for that matter—should in any lifetime, and they would see worse things to come, but if he could spare them from one more horror, he would.

"What is it? Do you see Miguel?" Elizabeth asked, her eyes sparkling with dread. If it was Miguel and he'd asked the kids to keep away, it had to be bad.

"No, it's not Miguel," he said quickly, pulling her closer. "Look, survivors."

Her hand flew to her mouth. "They look awful. Maybe

you should go downstairs and bring them here. At least they'll be safe and there's food and drinks."

"That's what I was going to do. Until I saw that." He pointed to the next street over.

"Oh my God."

A pack of feral dogs, twice the size of the one they'd faced on McLean Avenue, had gotten the scent of the couple. They were in full predator mode, prowling the street, heads low, backs arched, headed straight for them.

"We have to do something," she said, digging her fingers into his arm.

"We don't have enough firepower to hold back a pack that big."

"Then we have to warn them."

"How? If I break the glass, that pack will come right for us."

She looked at him, and in her stare he saw tired despair. Her gaze stirred feelings of failure within himself—failure to keep his sons safe from harm, failure to find Buck and Alexiana, failure to find any answers as to what the hell had happened to them. He had to do something, anything.

"I'll try to warn them."

"Hurry!"

Daniel sprinted across the restaurant, ignoring Max and Gabby's questions. Clanging down the stairs, he hit the main door, squinting into the sunlight. He couldn't see the couple from his vantage point.

Leaping onto an SUV, he cupped his hands over his eyes, searching for them. Was he too late?

No. There they were. The dogs must have been right around the corner.

"Hey!" he shouted. "Go back to the bank!"

The couple froze, heads turning every which way, searching for the source of the command.

"There's a pack of wild dogs coming for you! Run! Go back to the bank and bar the door!"

The man yelled, "Where are you?"

"Just run!"

Daniel's heart stopped when the dogs began to bay. They turned the corner in a tight formation. Daniel punched the side of his thigh. Damn! He'd been too late.

The couple put up their hands in defense and disappeared underneath a pile of fur and teeth. The sounds of their screams made Daniel's gut clench.

He teetered on the verge of running to them. Maybe if he fired into the pack, the sound of the gun would startle them and they'd retreat.

It was too long a shot. The animals were no longer what they once had been. The dogs outside the bar had been ruthless, relentless.

He walked back to the restaurant on numb legs.

128

Elizabeth couldn't bear to watch anymore. She turned to look at her children, her remaining children, and wondered, *What are their lives going to be like? Is this it? Running and hiding, fighting and dying? How could we be abandoned like this?*

Daniel came back inside, huffing and puffing.

"Pop, what happened?" Max asked.

Daniel shook off the question. He said, "You see anything?"

Gabby spoke up, "There was a whole bunch of seagulls. They were down by the nature barge. You remember the place you took me and Miguel for story time once?"

"I do."

"The seagulls were circling, with more and more of them joining the circle. I looked around the barge, and I saw this big dog, like a Saint Bernard. It was hurt. It could barely move. They started diving at it, and it couldn't even bark to scare them off. Then they all landed on it."

"I'm sorry you had to see that," Daniel said, stroking her hair.

"That wasn't all. Dad, they carried it away. There were so many with their beaks stuck in its fur, and they flew with it!

I watched them take it over the water, then they let it go and started swooping into the water."

Elizabeth's jaw clenched. No matter where they looked, a fresh hell was ready to erupt.

"Honey, why don't you go in the kitchen and find some canned food. Max can keep watch for now," she said.

"Can Max come with me?"

"Yeah," Max said, placing a big-brotherly hand on her shoulder. "You'll need help with the can opener anyway."

When they left the dining room, Elizabeth allowed a few tears to fall. Daniel wiped them from her cheeks with the back of his finger.

"I couldn't watch after—" she started to say.

"It's better you didn't."

She hugged him fiercely. "I just want to find Miguel. I don't care if we have to live in a filthy root cellar for the rest of our lives, scavenging for scraps. I want us together and safe."

"We'll find Miguel, I promise. And I'll find something a little better than a root cellar." She felt his breath against her neck.

Daring to look out the window, she went stiff as a board.

"What's wrong?" he asked, breaking their embrace.

She pointed out the window. "Look. It's Buck and Alexiana."

Their neighbors squatted behind a van, just half a block away from the feeding dogs. Elizabeth tensed. *What if the dogs see them? We can't just sit here and watch. We have to do something.*

A waterfall of relief cascaded over her when she saw them sneak away. They watched Buck and Alexiana run, hunched over, heads low, in the direction of the train station.

"Daniel, you have to get them."

When she turned, he was already checking the clip of

their remaining pistol. He spotted a metal pole, probably used to prop something up, behind the bar.

"I'll be back. Just keep looking for Miguel or the Nine Judges. And don't let Max follow me."

"I will. I won't." She kissed him, tasting the salt of his sweat. She listened to him clambering down the stairs and went back to her watch.

129

Alexiana was shoved hard in the back and went to her knees, her palms skidding on the concrete. The flesh of her hands burned. When she tried to get up, a foot on her lower back pressed her down.

Buck was still standing, staring at the gang member, the lower half of his face hidden by the black bandanna.

Who are they still hiding from? There's no one left to call the police. For all we've seen, there aren't any police to call. Of all the people rotting in their homes, how the hell do these pieces of trash rate survival?

With the masks on, she couldn't fathom what they were saying. One of them, his eyes glassy, bloodshot (*I'm sure they've managed to find all the dope they can smoke*), crouched close to her, looking her in the eye. The bandanna moved in and out as he spoke. When she didn't—couldn't—answer, he kicked her in the shoulder. Bright flares of agony flickered in her periphery.

Despite the pain, she pushed with her arms to get up. The foot returned to her back, shoving her hard, knocking the wind from her lungs.

"Buck!"

He looked toward her, his face an unreadable mask, which

meant he was planning something. Normally, she would have begged him to just do what they said, endure whatever crap they felt like dishing out, and let them move on when they were bored.

Things were no longer normal. Somehow, this gang had eluded the winds of death that swept through the city. Maybe she and Buck had been spared to finish what had been started.

Buck spoke, and the gang member who had kicked her jumped to his side, yelling into his ear.

Alexiana inched her hand into her pocket. She'd moved her pistol to her front pocket for some unknown reason earlier.

Maybe none of them were in control of their own actions anymore.

Her fingertips touched steel.

130

"You are one dumb motherfucker," the gang member said. His chestnut head was shaved down to his irregularly shaped skull. *How many skull fractures does it take to get a noggin like that?* Buck thought. *Or was his mother on drugs when she was pregnant?*

Their bikes leaned against the stairwell leading to the train platform. It looked like they had just come from raiding the station. Plastic shopping bags were laden with packaged snacks and cans.

"What made you think you could keep on steppin' after we took your kid?" he said, jabbing Buck's chest with a finger that felt as if it were made of iron.

Buck's jaw clenched, and he fought hard to keep his voice even. "What made you think we were just going to let you take our kid?"

Lumpy Head laughed as another of the gang jumped over to him, shouting a string of curses so close to his ear it hurt.

"Little Man is safer with us than with your raggedy asses. Where are your other friends? We heard a lot of bad shit going down last night. Those horses are fucking crazy, man.

If they come for you, you ain't got much of a chance. But then, you already know that, don't you?"

Every muscle in Buck's body constricted. God, he wanted to land a haymaker right in this punk's mouth.

"Yeah, your little crew is a lot thinner, which shows me you weren't fit to watch over your own. We have jobs for Little Man to do. And see, we watch each other's backs."

Buck sneered. "Oh, like the ones we killed by the overpass? The ones you turned tail from and left behind? I'll bet right now some dogs are shitting them out so the flies can eat the rest."

All of the air exploded from him as he was hammered in the stomach. Acidic bile lurched up his throat, spluttering from his lips. Matching blows landed on each kidney. His eyes rolled up in his head, and he faced an inviting darkness.

Still on his feet and swaying, Buck wiped the vomit from his mouth with the back of his hand.

"You're awful tough when you're surrounded by your little lackeys. You afraid of a man forty years older than you?"

Lumpy Head punched him in the chest. Buck felt his heart actually stutter.

"What the fuck you say?"

Fighting to keep his breath, to keep from falling over, Buck looked down at Alexiana. Her hand was in her pocket and he could see her elbow bend slightly.

Keep their eyes on you!

"I used to eat chickenshits like you for breakfast when I was in the navy. You're not original or special. Dick skins like you are in every port. You're tough as nails when you outnumber a guy, but you shit your diapers when it's one-on-one."

Lumpy Head turned to his posse. "You hear this guy? Holy crap, he must have woken up and decided today was the day he wanted to die."

The gang laughed along with him.

Buck spat, a green glob that landed on Lumpy Head's chest. "You all may kill me, but you'll have to live knowing you're weaker than an old man."

The barrage of blows came before he could brace himself.

131

Before he'd left, Daniel took a quick peek at the scene with the unlucky couple. The dogs had dragged off most of the pieces. The few that were left scrabbled for the remains.

They probably took their prizes somewhere they could eat in peace, then sleep.

He thought he should be safe if he turned left, keeping two blocks between himself and the dwindled pack, staying downwind of them. His body was bone-weary, yet he ran. Buck and Alexiana were close. He had to find them.

Running past the two boardwalk restaurants to the left of YO2, he turned right, the public library dead ahead. Dipping into the shade of the train overpass, his foot caught on something solid and he pitched forward, a bottle shattering underneath him when he hit the ground.

Shards of glass dug into the flesh of his belly. Moaning, he turned onto his back, inspecting the damage.

The glass was green and had mercifully broken into small bits.

"Heineken," he muttered, pulling them from the fabric of his shirt and skin, leaving behind red spots of fire. "I knew I didn't drink you for a reason."

He could have disemboweled himself. The overpass was filthy. Infection would be sure to follow.

Daniel gasped, clambering away when he noticed what he'd tripped on.

A homeless man, little more than untold layers of overcoats and facial hair, lay on his back, dead, old bloodstains smearing his cheeks. His eyelids were open, but something had eaten out the eyeballs themselves.

Picking up the pole, Daniel resumed his run, ignoring the remaining glass in his stomach.

As he turned the corner, he looked straight down to the station.

There were Buck and Alexiana. They were surrounded by Nine Judges. Alexiana was already on the ground, and Buck was sinking to his knees under a vicious beating.

He ran to them, heedless of the danger. His first instinct was to shout, but it was probably best if he could take them unawares.

When the gunshot cracked, he froze.

132

It was strange, bordering on dreamlike.

Alexiana felt the kick of the gun when she pulled the trigger. She saw the fountain of blood erupt from one of the gang member's backs as he fell forward, tumbling over Buck.

Not hearing the shot or the pained scream of the gang member somehow removed her a level from the scene. It was like watching someone else from behind soundproof glass.

Everyone backed away from Buck, training their cold eyes on her.

She fired again, an echo-less plume of smoke and fire. The bullet grazed the bald guy's head, taking his ear along for the ride. His hand shot up to the hole where his ear had been, and he shouted something at her, spittle flying from his lips like a rabid dog.

"Fuck you," she said, pulling the trigger again. This time, he leapt to the side and she missed him entirely.

Something cold and hard pressed into her cheek. She looked up. The one with the bloodshot eyes held a gun to her face. If he was giving her any parting words, they were lost to her.

She wanted to reach out for Buck's hand, to feel him one more time, but he lay unconscious, too far out of her reach.

Make this something that will haunt him for whatever short time he has left, she thought.

So she looked to her executioner and smiled. His eyes narrowed, the bandanna moving again.

Alexiana kept smiling, accepting her fate, unnerving the man who would take her from this world.

She waited for the pain, hoping it was short-lived.

Instead, he pulled the gun from her face and began firing over her head.

133

Daniel pressed his back against a Town Car across the street from the train station. He thought the gang members would run when Alexiana shot at them, but that wasn't going to happen. Unfortunately, she'd only killed one and wounded another. That still left three, and one of them was going to get his revenge.

He used the hood of the Town Car to prop his unsteady arms, took aim, and fired at the gang. One of them jumped as if he'd stepped on a hornet's nest. He pirouetted away from the group, clutching his leg.

The rest turned to Daniel, guns in outstretched hands, pulling their triggers as fast as they could. He ducked behind the car, pulling himself into a ball by the rear tire. Bullets thunked into metal like fat raindrops on a tin roof.

When there was a pause, he popped his head up. Two of them were reloading as they marched to the car.

Dammit! Now what?

He was no crack shot. He'd have to make a run for it, hope their aim was as bad as his own. It was one thing to take a shot at an immobile, defenseless woman. It was another to take out a moving target.

Sprinting from the car before they could reload, he headed

north. The last thing he wanted to do was have them follow him to the restaurant. There was another shot and he ducked, almost losing his stride.

The gang member who had been standing over Alexiana crumpled to the ground, hands on his crotch. She'd shot him right in the balls.

"Yo, fuck this shit!" one of them shouted, and soon they were all rushing for their bikes, pedaling away in the direction of the new waterfront apartments. Daniel watched them go, his heart thudding.

Alexiana! Buck!

He ran to them, dropping to the ground by Alexiana.

"Are you hurt?" he said. Her face and upper torso were covered in blood.

She looked at him with uncomprehending eyes. She must be in shock. "Let me check to see if you've been shot. We've been so worried about you."

Alexiana waved him off, crawling on her hands and knees to Buck. The big man was trying to get up, groaning and coughing.

"Buck, maybe you should stay down," Daniel said. "You might have internal injuries."

His neighbor gave a wet cough, spitting where he couldn't see. "If I do, I'm fucked. I ever tell you you've got perfect timing?"

"I don't know how perfect. Alexiana might have been shot and I think she's in shock."

She melted into Buck's arms, her back heaving with strange-sounding sobs.

"It's not shock, Dan. She's deaf."

134

Max was the first to spot his father, Buck, and Alexiana limping toward the restaurant.

"Gabby, where are those seagulls?"

She ran to the other side of the dining room. "They're still by the barge."

"Ma, look," he said, jabbing a finger at the glass.

"Oh, thank God," she said, collapsing into her seat.

Then he saw the Nine Judges, riding their bikes like the devil was on their asses. His mother saw them, too.

"Mom, don't lose them," he said, heading for the stairs.

She yelled at him. "Do not leave this restaurant! You stay here, Max, until your father comes back. He's almost here."

Gabby turned to him with wet eyes. "The seagulls saw them."

Max pleaded, "Ma, I have to help them get inside." His hand folded around his bat.

It looked like Buck was hurt bad. His father and Alexiana carried him between them. If those seagulls started diving, they wouldn't be able to ward them off and get inside the restaurant. After eating several cans of fruit and drinking his weight in bottled water, he had energy to burn. He could help them. Why couldn't she understand that?

She spoke without looking at him, her eyes glued to the gang members. "I told you to stay here, and that's final."

He hopped from foot to foot, looking to Gabby, who studied the motions of the seagulls. Peering at them, he couldn't believe their size. Those things must have been eating like kings. They were huge!

There was no sense asking. He ran for the stairs, ignoring his mother's angry shouts.

His sneakers clomping on the boardwalk, he immediately spotted his father and neighbors. They were just by the roundabout, going slow. The first seagull cawed, swooping over their heads. Alexiana pulled out her gun, aiming at the sky.

"Dad!"

His father looked at him, alarmed. "Max, get back in the restaurant."

"It's the seagulls. They're coming."

"Get inside!"

A seagull that looked like a medium-sized dog with wings slammed into the back of Buck's head. He lost his balance, taking his father and Alexiana down with him. A trio of gulls, sensing easy prey, descended.

Max dashed to them, the bat cocked over his shoulder. He swung, connecting with one of the seagulls while the other two pecked at his father. He caught each of them in their sides, their bodies spinning end over end across the pavement like feathered hockey pucks.

"Come on," Max said, offering a hand to his father. He helped him to his feet, preparing for more.

"All right," his father said. "We'll stay close together."

It was only forty or so yards to the safety of the restaurant. The rest of the gulls came for them. Alexiana shot blindly, hitting nothing but air.

As they stumbled to the restaurant's entrance, Max slashed back and forth with the bat, taking the gulls out as fast as he could. Some managed to get through, driving their sharp beaks into them.

It was madness. The gulls kept coming, more determined than ever. So many had latched on to them, it was as if they were wearing living coats of crazed sea birds.

Making it to the boardwalk and under the overhang of the restaurant kept more from finding them easily. They swatted and punched, trying to shake off the seagulls.

As they peeled off, Max made valiant parting swings, hoping to make them think twice before they came back for more. The last of them departed from Alexiana's hair as they slammed into the stairwell door.

"I'm going to start calling you Bat Man," Buck said, grimacing. "We need to get you a secret identity and a cool car."

They took the stairs slowly, collapsing onto the padded love seats in the waiting area.

135

Elizabeth rushed to them the moment they entered the restaurant. The Nine Judges had slipped out of sight, but she knew where they'd gone. She flashed Max an angry look that didn't faze him in the least. Daniel, Buck, and Alexiana were bloody messes.

"Gabby, get me as many bottles of water as you can carry."

"Yes, Mommy," Gabby said, scampering to the bar.

She wrapped her arms around her husband. "You're hurt. What happened?"

He kissed her lips, her cheek, her neck. "A lot. Buck and Alexiana were being beaten up by the Nine Judges. She took most of them out."

Elizabeth touched Alexiana's arm. She looked like Carrie at the prom. She opened her eyes and smiled. "I am so glad we found you. I was afraid—"

"She can't hear you," Buck said, wheezing. "She lost her hearing when I set off those cars. What she didn't lose was her courage." He draped his arm over her, wincing, nuzzling her hair.

Gabby deposited five bottles of water on the floor.

"We have to clean you up, find out where you're all hurt," Elizabeth said.

The pebbled glass in Daniel's belly pockmarked him with surface wounds. The seagulls only managed to add more scratches on top of the lacerations that already crisscrossed their flesh like tribal tattoos. She breathed a heavy sigh when she realized the blood on Alexiana was not her own. While she worked on them, Gabby bringing her a fresh supply of towels to sop up the blood, Buck told them everything that had happened since they'd been separated. In turn, she broke the news about Rey, tears running of their own accord down her face.

"I'm so sorry, Liz," Buck said. Every move he made seemed like pure agony. She was pretty sure he had some cracked ribs, if not something worse. He'd taken one hell of a beating and he wasn't a young man. "Rey was a great kid."

"Thank you," she said, concentrating on removing the blood from Alexiana's arms. "I saw where the gang went."

Daniel sat straighter in the love seat. "You did? Where?"

"Past the new apartments. I saw them turn into one of the older buildings on Rathmore. They went in the back, and then I lost sight of them. But they have to be in that building."

"That makes perfect sense," Buck said. "Those old buildings are solid as hell. A lot of them have fallout shelters in their basements. Cold War construction and fears. Figures cockroaches like that would be there."

Daniel held out his hand to Gabby, who helped him from the love seat. "You want to help me get some food for everyone?" He turned to Liz. "We're going to eat and rest. When the sun goes down, we're heading to Rathmore and we're getting Miguel back."

Elizabeth wanted to go now. Knowing her baby was just a few blocks away brought a leaden weight on her chest.

But Daniel was right. They were in no shape to go

anywhere at the moment. Plus, in the light of day, they could be easily spotted.

Buck said, "Miguel is alive and well."

"How do you know?"

"They basically told us. Called him Little Man. Said they had plans for him."

"Plans, what kind of plans?"

Buck closed his eyes. "They didn't say. I was glad to get that much out of them. At that point, I needed to keep them busy so Alexiana could make them realize the error of their ways. The good thing is, I think they're scared of us now. We've taken out a handful of their members. They thought you and Dan were out of the picture. When he showed up, that got them thinking."

Daniel came back with an armful of cans, placing them on a white-clothed table. "Eat up, everyone." Gabby brought over forks and napkins.

While Elizabeth chewed on a cold, white potato, she couldn't keep from thinking this was their last supper. She forced every morsel down, each swallow helped along by one word.

Miguel.

136

As the sun began to set, it was decided by the adults that Gabby would stay in the restaurant when everyone went to find Miguel. The thought of being alone terrified her.

"Mom, Dad, please let me go. I promise I'll stay out of the way."

Her father sat on a nearby chair so he could be eye to eye with her. "It's not a matter of being in the way or not. Where we're going will be dangerous. I can't risk having you there."

She felt the steady burn of tears building up. "But Max is going."

Her mother said, "What gave you that idea?"

"Because he said he was."

Her father looked to her brother, frowning. "Max, I need you to stay here with your sister. If something should happen to us, she'll need you to protect her."

If something should happen to us.

The words, spoken aloud so matter-of-factly, made her tremble all over. If something did happen and they didn't come back, what would she and Max do? Keep walking until the next group of animals tore them apart? Stay in here until there was no more food and water and die of starvation and dehydration? Max was strong and brave, but he was still just a kid, her goofy big brother. How could he take on this new and dangerous world with her?

Gabby said, "What if we came with you but hid in a building across the street?"

"We don't know how secure any of the buildings are on Rathmore. At least here, we know you'll be safe. We'll even set up a barricade on the outside when we leave," her father replied.

She felt her mother's steady hand stroking her hair from behind. "I know it's scary, honey, but we have to protect all of our children."

Gabby turned on her mother. "The way you protected Rey?"

The moment it came out, she wished she'd never said such a horrible thing. *What is wrong with you? It wasn't Mom and Dad's fault that Rey got sick.*

But wasn't that the point? Even parents couldn't protect their kids anymore. Every monster in every closet and under every bed had been set loose. Protection was an illusion.

Her mother's face went cold and still.

"You'll stay here with Max," she said, walking away.

She watched Buck whisper something in Max's ear, and saw him hand her brother a gun, which he quickly placed on the chair next to him, moving it under the table with his foot.

Now the tears did come, and nothing her father said could make things better. Max pushed the love seats against the door as soon as they left with Buck and Alexiana. He went to the window, settling into a chair, propping his feet on another.

"You want to watch them?" he asked. She could tell he was angry, forced to babysit when he knew he could help get Miguel out of the gang's hideout. She dabbed her tears with the corner of a tablecloth.

"No."

137

When the man with the missing ear had opened the cage door and yanked him from the mattress, Miguel was sure he was taking him out to hurt him . . . or worse. One side of his head was caked in dried blood, rivers of it snaking down his neck.

"Time to earn your keep," he'd said, digging his hard fingers into Miguel's arm and pulling him along.

"You're hurting me," Miguel said.

The man pushed him against the wall, and next thing he knew, there was a gun pointed under his chin.

"Do I look like I give a shit?"

Miguel was afraid to shake his head, and terror had made his voice disappear. Something hot bloomed in his pants. The man looked down and smiled, but it wasn't a happy smile.

"Aren't you a little too old not to be potty trained?"

He put the gun away and pulled Miguel along, his shoulder blade aching, near the point of dislocation.

Miguel thought it couldn't get worse than this.

He was wrong.

The one-eared man said he had a job for him to do. Miguel didn't dare ask. If he said the wrong thing, he'd have a gun back in his face.

They walked up the apartment building's dark stairs. It smelled of untold ethnic meals, mildew, and something Miguel had only smelled when the wind blew a certain way when he and his family were walking after they left Buck's shelter. Stopping on the second floor, the man kicked and kicked at an apartment door until it sprang open, slamming into the interior wall, motes of plaster spiraling in the stale air.

He pushed the bandanna over his nose and mouth. Miguel wondered why he'd do such a thing until the overpowering odor nearly knocked him over.

"Now, get in there and look for food," the man said, handing him a supermarket bag. "When you're done with the kitchen, look in the medicine cabinet and bedrooms for prescriptions. You know what those bottles look like, right?"

Miguel eyed the gun that was back in his hand. He nodded quickly.

The man planted his foot in Miguel's behind and shoved him into the apartment, slamming the door closed after him.

"Knock when you're done," he said from the other side of the door.

The first apartment had been beyond terrible. Miguel couldn't help throwing up in the hallway. He went to the kitchen on unsteady legs, filling the bag with cans and boxes of cereal. When he came to the living room, he threw up again on an empty rocking chair.

An old man and woman lay on the couch, dead, decaying. There were so many flies on them, it was impossible to see their faces. Miguel ran past the couch, flies buzzing after him. He threw any amber pill bottle he could find into the bag and dashed out of the apartment, careful not to look at the man and woman.

The door flew open when he knocked.

The man eyed the full bag, as well as the vomit on his shirt.

"That's some sick fucking shit, right, Little Man?"

Miguel was too nauseous to reply. He handed the bag to the man, who pulled another one out of his back pocket.

"One down, a whole lot more to go," he said, turning to the next apartment and kicking down its door.

And so it went for Miguel, the growing heat intensifying the smell as he raided apartments for supplies, always under the watchful eyes of the dead and the constant hum of feeding flies.

138

Each breath felt like a ragged knife was being raked across his chest. Buck volunteered to take the rear and watch their backs, because he knew he couldn't keep pace with Liz and Dan. Alexiana hung between them, always looking back to make sure he hadn't dropped to the pavement.

Just do this and you can rest for as long as you like, buddy. No chores, no clocks, no nothing but sleep.

The pessimistic side of him, which had been growing in strength the longer they wandered the city with no sign of hope or help, said, *Might as well push it, old man. You're probably not making it out of here alive, so what's the point in resting?*

Rathmore Street was the demarcation line between the gentrified waterfront and the lost cause. There had been plans to tear this entire neighborhood of crumbling apartment buildings down, but the money dried up and people lost interest. The pavement in the street even changed the moment they stepped onto Rathmore, smooth blacktop giving way to cracks and potholes big enough to bathe a toddler in, the old cobblestones visible in some areas.

It was dark as hell, but Buck remembered it always being this way. When streetlights blew out here, the city didn't see the need to replace them. The people who lived here preferred the dark.

Daniel and Elizabeth pulled up behind an old Buick with no tires across the street from the apartment building they'd seen the Nine Judges enter. It was five floors, a good number of the windows boarded over. Other windows were open, curtains billowing out with the night breeze. It was hard to believe that people actually called the place home.

"We have to be extra-careful about critters down this way," Buck wheezed. "Before the animals lost their minds, this area was home to more rats than you could count in a lifetime."

Dan held his pistol between two hands, studying the building. "Then we'd better not wait out here long."

Before Buck could tell him it was best to wait a few minutes to make sure they hadn't been spotted, Daniel and Elizabeth were off and running down the side alley, headed for the rear of the building.

"Damn," he hissed, grabbing Alexiana's hand and following them, crouched as low as he could without passing out from the pain in his ribs. Dan held up his hand, ordering them to stop.

Voices filtered through the alley.

"I don't know how much longer we can stay here, man," someone said. "I'm gonna go crazy if I don't get me some pussy."

"All that shit we had stored inside, we forgot bitches," another replied. "I hear you. Maybe we should head up to some of those nice hoods, like the ones they got in Briarcliff and shit. It's a new world, you know what I'm sayin'? We need to step up to high-class bitches."

The men laughed, their humorless chuckling fading as they walked inside. A door slammed behind them.

Buck wondered how many of the gang members were left.

It seemed hopeless to pray for a manageable number. Was anyone even listening anymore?

Alexiana tapped his arm.

The back courtyard of the building looked out on a vacant lot, the high grass sloping to the banks of the Hudson River. The grass moved and sounded as if it were alive. Something was coming—a whole lot of somethings.

"It's now or never, Dan," Buck whispered. "Pretty soon, we're going to have company."

The old gate separating the properties rattled as what Buck assumed were furry bodies passed through it.

"I guess it's a sign not to hesitate," Dan said. He made for the back door, the women on his heels. Buck followed, keeping one eye on the yard. They were all inside the door before he could see what had gotten their scent. He wedged the door closed.

"We'll have to leave through the front," he said.

They had enough to contend with. He had no desire to see what would be waiting for them in the back.

139

The gang had left battery-operated lanterns at varying intervals on the floor, trails of light leading to their left and right. They were in a main room right now, a place where the super would have stored things for the building at one time, leading to a laundry room.

Daniel's senses recoiled. There were soiled, threadbare mattresses everywhere. The smell alone told him this was a place where people came to get high and screw. The Nine Judges were obviously not fans of Home and Garden TV. They heard more people talking, but it wasn't possible to tell where the voices were coming from.

"Do you want to split up?" Elizabeth said.

"No," Daniel replied, his voice as low as it could go. "We need to stay together. I think we should go where we *don't* think the gang will be. If we're lucky, we can find Miguel without confrontation."

"We're due for a splash of good luck," Buck said. "So, which way do we go?"

Daniel chewed on his lower lip. His nerves were tingling so much, he wanted to jump out of his own skin. He was a software developer and web designer, for Christ's sake.

Rambo he was not. But Rambo he would be if that's what was necessary to get his son back.

"Left," he said. "I think the ones talking are to the right."

He could see how this was a perfect fallout shelter. It was like being in an underground tunnel system, like the vast catacombs under Grand Central Terminal. He'd gotten a tour of them many years ago from a friend who worked for the MTA. They carried bats. When Daniel asked why, his friend simply said, "Rats."

"How big do they get down here?" Daniel had asked.

"Fucking huge. The people down here can be worse. Some of them haven't seen the outside for years. When they see the bats, they back off."

Luckily, they had seen neither rats nor underground dwelling people. But the strangeness of the day had never left him.

As they carefully made their way down the hallway, various rooms opened up, dark and piled with junk. Some of the rooms were barred with locked cage doors. They must have been places where residents stored things like their bicycles, baby carriages, and other outdoor items.

They came to the end of the long hallway. Daniel looked through the grimy window in a door that had been rusted shut, spying a crumbling staircase. If any gang members went through here, they had to be strong as an ox to get the door to budge.

The path of least resistance was not in the cards for them.

"Buck and I will take the lead," he said. "If you shoot, be careful and know exactly who you're shooting at. We don't want to hit Miguel by accident."

Holding him back for a second, Buck said, "The only way we get Miguel back is if we take them hard and fast. Don't give them time to react."

Daniel's gut clenched into a burning knot.

"Trust me, I won't."

He led the way down the hall. One of the rooms ahead glowed brightly. They could see shadows cast on the wall of people moving about. They crept to the edge of the wide door frame. He looked back at Elizabeth. She was surprisingly calm.

This is what we've become, Daniel thought.

He held up his hand, counting down from five. Buck, Elizabeth, and Alexiana nodded.

Taking a breath, Daniel swung into the room. There were a half dozen of the Nine Judges, drinking warm bottles of beer, sitting on overturned plastic crates. Several lanterns and boxes of Slim Jims were on a folding card table in the center of the room.

"Where's my son?" Daniel demanded, his gun wavering between two of the gang members who had risen from their crates only to take a few wary steps back. The air was hazy, smelling of skunk weed.

"Hey, man, don't shoot, all right?" one of them said, glassy eyes wide and unfocused.

"The boy you took, where the fuck is he?" Buck said.

"We don't know nothing about no boy."

Elizabeth shouted, "Bullshit! You tell me where my son is right now or I'll shoot you in the stomach. You know how long it takes to die from a gut shot? The pain will make it feel like forever."

Suddenly, one of the gang members, a man in a dirty white T-shirt with a scraggly, wiry beard, smiled.

"Oh, you mean the little kid we got doing corpse duty?" he said.

Daniel was almost overcome by an urge to shoot him in his grinning face.

"Where . . . is . . . he?" he said, his finger tensed on the trigger. Maybe they should just shoot them all and search the building for his son without having to worry about interference.

The gang member pointed to a spot over his shoulder.

Daniel slowly turned around, his gun still trained on the bearded bastard.

The man with the lumpy head stood in the doorway, holding Miguel by his shirt collar, practically lifting him off the floor.

He wasn't alone.

140

Elizabeth screamed for a variety of reasons. There was her son, his shimmering eyes filled with dread. Beside him were four heavily armed gang members, rendering their surge impotent. She didn't dare shoot, lest everyone follow suit. No one would survive in the cramped space, least of all Miguel, the only innocent among them.

"Give me my son," she said.

"Put your guns down," the strange-looking man with one ear grunted, lifting Miguel higher. She saw the red burn where the shirt cut into her son's neck. She desperately wanted to run to him.

Everyone was too stunned to move.

"It wasn't a question. I said to put your motherfucking guns down. If you don't want to do what I say, I can always choke Little Man right here until you get the point."

Elizabeth let the Beretta clatter to the ground. Daniel and Buck did the same. When Alexiana saw what was happening, she followed suit.

"That's more like it. Now, I think we should all be honest with each other. Like, for instance, I tell you the truth when I say you're not getting out of here. Not alive, anyway. But not until we've had a chance to let off . . . a little steam. Besides, we've got a little unfinished business to tend to."

He eyed Elizabeth and Alexiana hungrily.

"Y'all could use a little washing up, but that's what we have Little Man for. Shit, we'll even let your men watch. I see that shit all the time on YouPorn. Middle-aged white men gettin' off on watching their wives with a black man."

The Nine Judges laughed, a thin veil cloaking their sick desire.

"Now, take off your clothes."

"Give me my son," Elizabeth said.

"Clothes first. Your son can wash you up all nice for your reunion, get in all those places we're gonna explore."

She trembled with burning rage.

"You touch my wife and I'll fucking kill you," Daniel said, lunging for the man.

Two of the Nine Judges tackled him from behind, delivering savage blows to the side of his head. Daniel remained facedown on the dirty floor. Another man grabbed Buck, wrestling his arms behind his back. He struggled as much as he could, but he was no match for the larger, younger, unhurt gang member.

"Don't worry, old man, your time will come. Seems your little group has done more damage to my crew than all that shit the terrorists dropped on us. You gonna have to pay for that. Well, after we have a little fun with your girl. How an old sack of shit like you got such a fine piece of ass is beyond me."

He strode to Alexiana, jamming the barrel of his gun to her forehead. "Now, I said to get naked."

"She can't hear you," Elizabeth said, the words bobbing in her throat. "She's deaf."

The gun swiveled in her direction. "Then you're just going to have to show her what to do. Let's see what that MILF body looks like."

As she pulled up her shirt, she heard Buck sob, "I'm so sorry, Lizzy."

Her fingers fumbled with her bra. She unhooked it, covering her breasts with an arm.

"You're gonna need both hands to take off them pants," the man with one ear said.

"Mommy," Miguel sobbed.

"Shut up, Little Man!"

"Look away, baby," she said, undoing the button of her jeans. Miguel looked at his feet, teardrops splashing on his sneakers.

Alexiana stepped out of her panties just as Elizabeth kicked off her jeans. She was a few years younger than her and had never had any children. She was a runner and had a lean, fit body. That body would work against her, as Elizabeth could already hear the gang talking about taking her first.

Elizabeth reached out to take her friend's hand.

The sound of a belt being undone behind them made Elizabeth clench. She was smacked in the back by a hard, calloused palm. Bent over, the crotch of a man's jeans pressed against her while hands grabbed her breasts hard, pinching her nipples. When she looked to her side, she saw the same thing was happening to Alexiana.

Don't give them the satisfaction of hearing you beg or cry. As long as we're alive, there's still a chance.

"Those are some sweet asses," one of them said. That comment was met with husky grunts of agreement.

"Forget cleaning them up," the one-eared one said. "I'm taking the first turn."

Elizabeth cried out when she saw Miguel thrown to the ground. He hurt his knee, wrapping both hands around it and crying.

"No!" she said, struggling to stand. The man behind her

clasped the back of her neck, forcing her down. Alexiana tried the same.

The man with one ear unzipped his pants in front of her face, dangling his hardness an inch away from her lips. "You never know, you might even like it." To the one holding her, he said, "Keep her just like that. I want to try some white meat first."

Elizabeth was about to call out for Daniel when the ear-splitting blast of a gun brought everyone to a standstill.

141

Alexiana shouted an incomprehensible cry when she looked to the doorway, something hot and wet splashing across her naked back. When the men lost their grip on her, she fell forward, her chin scraping along the filthy concrete floor.

The gang members, all in various forms of undress, couldn't find their pants, much less their guns.

Gabby's mouth moved as she shot one after the other. At one point Alexiana thought she saw her say the word *Mommy.* Max came running up behind her, his sweaty hair covering his uncomprehending eyes.

When one of the Nine Judges lunged for Gabby, Max hit him across the jaw with the bat, shattering the bone. Alexiana was grateful she couldn't hear it.

Buck had gotten free, shooting the one who had held Elizabeth.

It was utter carnage.

And it had all been started by the same sweet girl who had sold her Girl Scout cookies every year and used to have her over for teatime with her stuffed animals.

Alexiana's heart broke for the little girl.

This could never be undone. She'd be a different person from here on. Maybe there just wasn't room for purity anymore—at least not if one wanted to survive.

142

Daniel came to at the sound of gunfire and initially thought he'd been plunged into Hell.

Gabriela had followed them to the apartment building and done the unthinkable.

"Gabby, stop!" he shouted above the din.

His voice gave her pause, and she looked to him as if she'd just awakened from a dream.

"Daddy," she said.

He staggered over to her and took the pistol from her steady hand, pulling her to his chest.

"We told you to stay at the restaurant."

All of the gang members were dead or dying. He saw Max and Buck take down the two she hadn't shot. The man with one ear who had been poised to rape Alexiana lay on his back, the bullet having taken out his left eye and cheek.

"I was scared," Gabby said. "So I took the gun that Buck had given Max off the table and went out the back steps that were in the kitchen."

"She was gone so fast, I had to run to keep up with her," Max said.

Elizabeth had quickly thrown on her clothes and scooped Miguel into her arms. She wept uncontrollably. Buck positioned himself in front of Alexiana so she could dress.

"We have to get out of here," Daniel said. Blood was everywhere, a rippling pool soaking their feet.

As they stepped into the hall, they heard the steady rumble of footsteps.

Miguel said, "There are more of them. They stay in two of the second-floor apartments." His voice was on the edge of panic.

Daniel asked Gabby, "How did you get inside?"

"Through the front door. It wasn't locked. Then I came down the steps over there." She pointed to an exit sign down the hall. It appeared that there were three sets of stairs that led to the basement. One was blocked by the rusted-shut door. The other was currently filled with Nine Judges on high alert.

Daniel urged everyone forward to the stairwell Gabby had used. "Everyone, run as fast as you can up those stairs and head straight for the restaurant."

Elizabeth latched on to his shirt. "You're coming with us."

"I will. Just give me thirty seconds. Don't ask questions, just go!"

Buck pulled her along. Miguel had his arms wrapped tight around her neck.

Daniel ran to the back door leading to the courtyard. If his timing was off by even a few seconds, he wasn't going to make it to the restaurant. But it had to be done. They didn't have a chance of not being seen and followed to the restaurant. The only way to prevent that was to create a diversion.

Squaring his shoulders like he was back on the high school football team, he body-slammed the door leading to the back courtyard. The smell of the sewer and wet animal smacked him in the face.

Rats had been piling up against the door, eager to get their sharp teeth into fresh meat.

He turned and ran back into the basement's hallway, thousands of squealing rats tumbling over each other's bodies to get at him.

The rest of the gang was at the bottom of the stairwell. Daniel opened the door to the one his family had used just as the gang spilled into the hallway on high alert. All of them were brandishing guns and looked anxious to use them. He slammed the door shut just as they spotted him, leaning against it with all his body weight.

"Oh shit!" one of them screamed.

Through the head-high window in the stairwell door, Daniel watched the rats make a beeline for the gang. They started shooting, ear-numbing blasts that couldn't drown out the hungry cry of the rat horde. The gang sang a chorus of profanities as the rats swarmed over them.

A chunk of the bottom half of the door Daniel stood behind was missing. Rats came pouring into the opening.

Taking the steps two at a time, he hit the lobby at full speed. It wouldn't be enough to simply outrun the rats and the gang. He needed to do one more thing.

He almost lost his footing, running over the uneven tile in the lobby. He undid his belt as he ran, the unceasing screeching of the rats setting his nerves on edge.

The double doors of the front entrance swung wide open when he hit them. A quick glance down the street gave him a brief respite. His family, Buck, and Alexiana were nowhere in sight. They must have really been running hard.

A few rats made it through the doors before he could close them. They clung to his pants, eagerly burrowing their teeth into the denim. Ignoring them, he unlooped the belt from his jeans and strung it between the handles of the double doors.

Notching the belt as tight as he could, he pulled on the doors. They barely budged.

Kicking off the rats, he sprinted to the darkened street, his heart banging hard enough to dim the edges of his vision.

He smiled when he heard the first gang member hit the fastened door, followed by a scream.

143

Gabby ran from her mother's arms the moment her father walked into the restaurant. She tackled him with such force, they both fell into one of the love seats.

"I'm so sorry, Daddy, for not listening to you," she said into his neck. "And I'm sorry I . . . I . . . I . . ."

"Shhh-shhh-shh," he said, running his hands through her hair. "Tonight, you were braver than all of us combined. You saved our whole family."

"But I shot people."

"You did what you felt had to be done. We're all here now because of you."

She pulled back, staring into his eyes. He looked so tired. But his love for her never looked brighter. "Do you think God will be mad at me?"

He pressed his lips to her forehead.

"God is who sent you to us, baby. You're one of his most special creations."

Her mother, Miguel, and Max joined them on the love seat. They were never a group hug type of family, but at this moment, they needed to be with each other, to bond in every and any way possible.

Max whispered in her ear, "Rey would have been proud of you."

They all had looked up to Rey. Through everything that had happened, she had forgotten about her older brother, and it made her feel guilty and sad.

She looked to Buck and Alexiana, who sat on chairs holding hands, watching them.

"You're part of the family, too," Gabby said, motioning them to join her. Buck and Alexiana stood over her, a hand on each of her shoulders.

"I think we all need to get some sleep," her father said when they broke up, everyone wiping tears from their faces. "Anyone have anyplace they need to be tomorrow?"

Six faces looked back at him, puzzled.

"Exactly. It's going to be a sleep-in day. Let's organize these love seats and use tablecloths as sheets and fold them up for pillows."

They set about making beds for everyone. Despite his protests, it was agreed that Buck take the biggest love seat. They didn't say it, but they all knew he was hurt pretty bad inside. Sleeping on the floor was not an option.

When Miguel asked, "Where's Rey?" her mother and father took him to the other end of the restaurant and sat him on her mother's lap. They talked quietly for a couple of minutes, then Miguel broke down crying. So did Gabby. She even saw a tear in Buck and Alexiana's eyes. It took her brother almost a half an hour to settle down. When he walked over to her, his eyes were swollen and pink. He looked like the most tired kid who had ever lived. He plopped onto the carpet, rubbing his eyes.

Gabby sat cross-legged on the floor next to him. "You want to sleep next to me?"

His eyes lit up. Back home, when things had been normal, he'd always asked to sleep in her room, though most times she told him to go back to his own.

"Do you think Mom and Dad will let us sleep between them?" he said.

"There's no way you're not," their mother said, snapping a tablecloth.

They ate a little and drank cans of orange and tomato juice. No one spoke much. Buck was the first to close his eyes, and his snoring was quick to follow. It gave a strange kind of comfort to all of them, and pretty soon everyone was asleep.

144

Max couldn't remember the last time he'd slept so long. Before, when everything was normal, there was always a reason to wake up earlier than he wanted to—school, baseball practice, baseball games, chores, family outings, tutoring (he hated math and science and it showed in his grades).

When his eyelids finally pried themselves apart the day after they'd rescued Miguel, he was surprised to find Gabby was the only one awake. She sat in a chair looking at the Hudson River.

"You missed the seagulls," she said.

"Oh yeah?" Max rubbed the sleep from his eyes, stretched his damaged shoulder.

"They found a bunch of cats down by the park. Took a few of them and flew too far for me to follow."

He wanted to ask her about last night, but couldn't find the right words. How did a big brother go about asking his little sister how she felt about blowing away a roomful of gangbangers? Would she cry? Or scream? Or retreat so far into herself, she might never come back?

It was better to leave it alone . . . for now.

"You eat anything yet?" he asked instead.

"I found a box of croutons. There's some left," she said, pointing to the open box on the table. He sniffed the contents.

"Whoa, that's a lot of garlic. I'll pass."

Miguel was the next to rise, and he had no problem crunching on garlic croutons. The kid was starving. Max wanted to hug him. He'd never realized how much he loved his pest of a little brother until he'd been taken from them.

When their mother and father woke, Max could tell by the color of the sun against the Palisades that it was getting late.

"We're going to stay here awhile," his father said. "There's no need to rush back out there. Plus, we all need the rest."

It was funny, after weeks in Buck's shelter, Max didn't think he'd ever want to be confined in one place again. The restaurant was comfortable, though a little on the hot side by the afternoon, but most of all, safe.

"We need more food," Max said.

"You're right. And more to drink than water and liquor. You want to come with me on a supply run? There's a deli just down the street. We can see if there's anything left," his father said.

Buck and Alexiana were starting to wake up when they left. It was a fast run but plentiful. They'd have actual cereal for breakfast tomorrow.

And so it went for close to a week. It was Gabby's idea to watch for the daily routines of the animals that now owned the city. They used waiters' order pads to log which type of animal, the size of the pack, the estimated time they were spotted, and where. The horses were the most breathtaking to watch, even though they knew they'd been altered somehow into barreling killing machines. A group of ten former racehorses galloped across South Broadway once a day in the morning. Buck explained to them that a group of horses was called a *team* or *harras*.

Then there were the feral dogs and cats. They kept to the shadows during the heat of the day, the dogs sniffing around about dusk and the cats shortly thereafter. The rats, contrary to their nature, were a constant, especially down by the water.

In all that time, they'd spotted three human survivors, all of them the worse for wear. It had been easy to see that they were sick, very sick, by the blood on their faces, their shambling walk, and their vacant eyes. One collapsed on the street, a wiry man of indeterminate age. He was dead by the time Max and his father got to him. Another man was overcome by a pack of dogs, right on the boardwalk. Within an hour, a smear of blood was the only evidence he'd been there. The last, an older woman with wild gray hair, shuffled to the park, sat on a bench, and while looking at the sunset, pulled a gun out of her purse and shot herself.

That was it. As far as they knew, they were the only people alive who hadn't succumbed to the illness.

Max and his father went out during the times when they were sure the animals were at rest or in other parts of the city. They found a pair of discarded bikes in the park, not far from where the woman had killed herself—her body had been removed overnight by the animals.

They gathered more food and drinks, clothes from a local department store, and they even went to St. Joseph's Hospital. The stench of the dead prevented them from going inside. It was no longer a place of healing. Like the church they had stayed in, it had become an enormous mausoleum. They did find a sign taped to the glass doors leading to the emergency room.

THERE IS NO CURE FOR THE CONTAGION.
PLEASE STAY IN YOUR HOMES. IT IS NOT SAFE

*IN THE HOSPITAL. WE WILL NOT OPEN THE
DOORS FOR ANYONE.*

They broke into a small gun shop tucked between a barber-shop and a Dominican deli, loading up several bags with handguns and bullets. It was a sad fact of this new life that they couldn't be caught without firearms.

Back in the restaurant, they rested, ate, and healed. By divine Providence, the building had been built with windows that could be opened so the summer heat didn't melt them. They kept all of the windows open slightly, but not with a large enough gap for the birds to get through.

Buck's warbling wheeze got better when he breathed. They were sitting at the largest round table in the dining room, eating out of cans, when he said, "Alex and I met a family in City Hall before we reconnected with you."

"Were they healthy, like us?" Max's mother asked.

"No. They still looked to be all right, but they had the beginning of the sickness. They told me they'd heard that people had been going to Hastings, that there might be help there."

"Hastings isn't far at all," his father said, drinking the juice from his can of pears.

"No, it isn't. I'm game to give it a try if you all are. As nice as it's been sleeping my days and nights away, I'm starting to get antsy," Buck said.

His mother smiled. "That also means you're healing up." She placed a reassuring hand on top of Alexiana's, who simply smiled while everyone spoke. Gabby would write what they said on a pad for her.

"If we just follow Warburton, it'll take us there in a few hours if we take it slow and careful," Buck said. "There's nothing left here. There has to be someone else alive out there. If Hastings is a dead end, I say we keep going north.

The farther we get from Manhattan, the better our chances. At least that's what my gut is telling me."

When Alexiana read what Gabby had written, she patted Buck's shrinking round stomach and said in her new, faltering voice, "That's a lot of gut. We should listen to it."

It was the first time they'd all laughed in weeks.

145

This time around, everyone, including Gabby and Miguel, carried a gun. Elizabeth hated the idea, but the pros outweighed the cons. No one was safe, and it had been painfully proven that the adults couldn't always protect the children. She fretted constantly about what Gabby had felt she had to do, knowing her little girl would be little no more. She'd been quieter since that night, aloof, more serious. It broke her heart as much as knowing her child had saved them made her glow with pride.

They had all changed.

She just wasn't sure if it was for the better.

They left the restaurant in the early afternoon, when it was hottest. The heat seemed to keep the animals away from the streets.

Their first stop was City Hall to check on the Patel family. Buck and Daniel made the trek to the top floor while everyone else waited in the gloomy lobby. When they trudged back down the stairs, Buck looked to Alexiana and shook his head gravely.

"All of them?" she asked.

"Yeah."

They left City Hall, their spirits lower than when they'd

entered. Elizabeth had been hoping the Patels would have agreed to go with them. They even had a new shopping cart they'd taken from outside the nearby ShopRite for the old man. Adding new people, good people, to their group would have been a positive sign as they searched for help.

Passing the DMV and the historic Philipse Manor House, they turned left on Warburton.

"I'd trade my life to have Rey here with us," Elizabeth whispered to Daniel. The sun was especially brutal today. Perspiration dripped from every pore.

Daniel pulled her close as they walked, the heat from his body making her feel somehow safe. "I would, too. That's why we're all going to live for him. I dream about him every night. Just last night, I talked to him on that bench on the boardwalk by the park. It was night and the air was cool, like early fall."

"What did you talk about?"

"I don't know. I can never remember. But I can always recall that he was in my dreams. It's strange, I know."

She kissed his sweaty cheek. "It's not strange at all. In fact, now I'm jealous."

Miguel bumped into her thigh. She hadn't let him leave her sight since they'd gotten him back.

"Look, there's the park where you took us to hear that old people music," he said, grinning.

Untermyer Park was famous for its gardens, and it hosted free concerts in the summer. Wanting to expose the kids to all kinds of music, they took them there all the time.

"I'm surprised you heard anything," she said. "You spent most of your time there running around catching fireflies with your sister."

What they'd never told the kids was that the park was also infamous as the meeting place for the satanic cult that the serial killer the Son of Sam belonged to in the 1970s. When Rey found out about it online one day, he'd said he couldn't wait to go back there. Its sordid history suddenly made it not boring.

"We'll be in Hastings soon," Buck announced, his eyes on the sky. A few hawks had flown overheard, but they'd ignored them so far. One thing they'd noticed from their vantage point in the restaurant was that there had been fewer animals each day. Daniel theorized that when they ran out of people to attack, they were going after each other.

"Once we get to the Riverview, I'll know we've left Yonkers behind," Buck said.

"What's the Riverview?" Elizabeth asked.

"That's a catering place where Alex and I met at a mutual friend's wedding," he replied with a smile. He kept her hand intertwined with his the entire walk. After everything, no one wanted to be separated from one another.

The scattered wreckage of a single-engine plane littered a rolling hill, bits of the wings and fuselage covering the train tracks below. How many lives had been lost from planes simply dropping out of the sky when the EMP bomb detonated?

They passed some very nice condos overlooking the water, and then there was the Riverview, along with a sign welcoming them to Hastings. The sun was starting to wane.

Daniel said, "We should find a place to crash for the night."

Buck nodded. "I hear you, Dan."

They went four more blocks before coming across a little pink house, just like the John Mellencamp song. Elizabeth was pretty sure she still owned the 45, crammed in a box with all of her other records in the attic. Buck broke the lock on the front door. There were no corpses waiting for them inside. There were five beds, as well as an oversized couch and love seat.

"What do we do tomorrow?" Max asked after they secured the door and picked their sleeping spots.

"Head to the town square and see what's up," Buck said. "If no one's around, we'll know we should keep moving on."

Elizabeth wondered if that was what their life had become—long treks and empty towns.

146

The heavy pounding at the door brought Buck to a heart-hammering state of panic.

"Open up," a voice shouted through the door.

The Padillas had taken the second-floor bedrooms. Buck and Alexiana had discovered the couch was a convertible and opted to stay downstairs. She slept with her back to him, blissfully unaware. He shook her awake. As she rubbed her eyes, questioning him with a look as to why he'd awakened her, he pointed at the door, pantomiming someone knocking.

Footsteps thundered above them.

It was still dark outside.

"Shit," Buck hissed, stubbing his toe on one of the convertible's metal legs. He fumbled for his gun, deciding it was probably best to have two. Whoever was outside didn't sound all that friendly.

Daniel and Elizabeth hustled down the stairs.

"Stay back," Buck whispered. "Whoever it is, I don't want them to know how many we are." He tossed a pistol to each of them, as well as Alexiana, urging her to join Daniel and Elizabeth, out of the sight line of the front door.

We're in for a long, bad haul when we can't trust the living any more than the crazed animals, he thought, smoothing the hairs against his skull. He peeked out the front window.

There were five men, strong alpha types with square shoulders and hard jaws. Each held a lantern in one hand and a bat in the other. He also spotted the butts of a few guns sticking out of their pockets.

"Dan, go upstairs and cover me from one of the windows. Make sure no one sees you."

"Got it." Daniel hurried up the stairs, treading as lightly as he could. Buck heard him urge the kids to stay in their room. Max started to protest, but his father got him to quiet down.

The knocking resumed, four meaty-fisted pounds.

Buck swung the door open quickly, taking the man off guard. His black hair was in a buzz cut and he wore a track-suit filled to bursting with muscle. The four men behind him looked and were dressed pretty much the same.

What is this, a night watch uniform?

"Sorry to wake you," the man said in a tone that said he wasn't the least bit apologetic. "One of our people saw you come in earlier. I thought it was best we check things out now rather than wait until morning."

Why was that?

Buck put on as much charm as he could muster. He didn't like the look of these guys at all. Hastings was a place for the upper middle class and soap opera stars, not posses of white bodybuilders. "You guys are a sight for sore eyes. I haven't seen another human being who wasn't on death's door for weeks now. Please tell me I've gotten past the infected zone."

The man's face softened a bit. "I wish I could. Some of us were lucky. We'd prepared. Looks like you did, too."

"Had a bomb shelter under my house and yard. It did its job until we were overrun by rats. Been walking ever since."

The man at the door grimaced, as did a couple of his cronies. "Those damn things are everywhere. Vicious as hell.

I found a nest the other night. We dumped a bunch of gas on them and burned them up."

They looked at each other in an uncomfortable silence. Buck broke it by saying, "I'm Buck Clarke. And you guys are . . ."

"Vin Haslett. That's Nicky, Joe, Emmet, and Rob."

The hard men with the bats and guns gave him perfunctory nods.

"Did I do something wrong stopping in this house?" Buck asked. "It was late in the day, and I was beat. If it belongs to someone still aboveground, I'll leave right now. It's just that I didn't think anyone was left, you know?"

Vin shook his head. "No, you can stay. I have no idea who owned this place. You alone?"

"My wife is here, too. She's hard of hearing. She didn't hear you knock."

"We just needed to check. Some strange people have come through in the past couple of weeks. We had to make sure you were on the level."

Buck noticed that the tension in Vic's shoulders had eased. He leaned the bat against his thigh.

"Tell me, do you know what happened? Who did it? Have you seen or heard anything?" Buck asked.

Vin scratched the stubble on his chin. "Not a thing. I do know that the same thing happened on the Jersey side, too. We had some stragglers who made it over the Tappan Zee Bridge here last week. All communication is out. Some people think it was God, you know, the whole apocalypse thing. I can tell you know better than that."

"I sure would hope God has nothing to do with this. Do you have a lot of survivors? I can tell you, in Yonkers, there are none that I've seen who are left upright." He left out the part about the Nine Judges.

"A few. We have to be cautious now. It's a different world. I didn't mean to frighten you."

Buck waved at the air. "No, I understand."

"You should get some sleep. We have a kind of makeshift HQ at the A&P down the road a ways. If you want, you can meet up with us in the morning."

"That would be nice," Buck said, smiling. "I was getting tired of feeling like Charlton Heston."

Vin cocked his head.

"The last man on earth," Buck said. "Never mind. Sure, we'll definitely see you at the A&P."

Vin nodded, a tight smile on his lips. "Sounds good. See you then. Good night."

"Good night," Buck said, closing the door and feeling as if he'd exhaled for the first time since he'd opened it.

147

Daniel couldn't go back to sleep. He, Buck, and Elizabeth had discussed everything in the kitchen. It was too difficult to write and read notes in the dark, so Alexiana went back to the couch. Buck would fill her in later.

"I admit they looked like a lynch mob at first, but like us, I think they're just wary of anyone who comes around. Shit, I had a gun in each pocket myself, with you ready to take them out if they made any sudden moves," Buck said, his elbow on the table, head resting in his palm.

"He didn't say how many survivors?" Elizabeth asked.

"No. Said he had a few. Hastings has money. People with money have the ability to protect their asses. There's probably quite a few people who were able to ride out the storm," Buck said.

"So, do we go to the A&P, or just head to the next town? They know as much as we do. Maybe people farther up the line have had a better time of it," Daniel said, picking at a nail.

Elizabeth said, "I vote for the A&P. If anything, we need to give the kids hope that there is life out there. The things they've had to see and do. I just want to show them something positive."

Daniel slid his arm across her shoulders and kissed her cheek.

"And that's another reason why I love you. I agree. Maybe there'll be some kids their own age. I'm not saying we make this our home, but if the community is doing well, it can't hurt to stay awhile."

Buck rapped on the table. "That settles it. We walk on over after breakfast. Now, if you don't mind, I have a dream about a certain bar on the beach in Key West I need to get back to."

Max was still awake when Daniel and Elizabeth went upstairs. He explained everything to his son, who had grown twenty years in just one week. He worried how Max would react, but was pleasantly surprised when he said he thought it was a good idea.

"It'd be nice to see someone else who isn't infected or out to kill us," he said, half-joking. Daniel ruffled his hair like he used to when Max was much smaller.

"Get some sleep," he said.

Elizabeth had no trouble snuggling up to him and falling back to sleep.

Daniel just couldn't shut his brain down. They'd finally met people, and they still had no answers. The empty space of not knowing was growing bigger and more urgent. There had to be a logical reason why his oldest son had died, why an entire city and its neighboring towns were no more. It was like being told someone you loved was missing and never finding a body, never getting a lead. A question without an answer was like a festering tumor. Each day, it grew and grew, until it consumed every thought, every cell.

They were no closer to an answer, and no closer to an end.

They still had to watch for animals and live a step above cavemen.

The more he thought, the less sleepy he became, until the sun bled through the gaps in the blinds and splashed on the foot of the bed.

148

"You want dry Wheaties or dry Cheerios?" Max asked Miguel when he came down for breakfast. Buck and Alexiana were already awake, sipping on glass bottles of warm Starbucks Frappuccinos.

"Cheerios," Miguel said, his hair every which way. Buck told Max to keep the blinds and shades drawn, but he could see it was going to be a sunny day. He even heard a few birds chirping by the kitchen window.

I wonder if they'd attack us, too, if they saw us. He poured a bowl of cereal for his brother.

His father and mother surprised him by coming up from the basement.

"They have a ton of jarred preserves," his mother said. "Now I wish we had some bread to put it on."

Gabby came clomping down the stairs at the same time.

"We're going to meet a group of people today," his mother said to Gabby and Miguel. For a flash, they looked terrified. "They're like us. They're not sick."

"I think we should still carry our guns," Max said. "Even

if the people are nice, we still have the animals to worry about."

His father looked as if he was going to correct him, then he looked to Buck and his face changed. "You need to keep them out of sight. I don't want these people to get the wrong idea about us."

"What, that we're not stupid?" Max said, biting into a Pop-Tart.

"Watch it," his mother warned.

"I'm just saying."

"Well, don't."

Oddly, his mother's brief moment of anger made him feel like things could get back to normal again. His not being in trouble all the time was beginning to feel . . . troubling.

"I don't want to go," Gabby said. She wasn't whining, wasn't sullen. She said it as a simple matter of opinion.

"I know it's scary, honey," their mother said.

"I'm not scared."

She opened a wrapper of Pop-Tarts and began nibbling at a corner.

"I'm bringing my bat," Max said.

"It's permanently stained red," his father said. "Leave it here. You can take it with us when we decide to leave Hastings."

Max bit the inside of his cheek to keep himself from saying something stupid. He understood his parents' point. Alexiana walked by, gently touching his shoulder. Was she letting him know she was on his side?

Buck tucked a gun in each pocket. He'd found an old Mets cap and pulled it onto his head. As goofy as he'd looked with the cowboy hat, it had fit his large personality. The Mets cap felt downright alien sitting on top of his head.

"I think I'll go outside and shed a tear for the old country," he said. Over the last few weeks, Max had learned that Buck had a limitless number of ways to say he needed to pee. Miguel giggled.

"And save me one of those Pop-Tarts. I need the sugar."

Max placed one on a plate as Buck was opening the door. When he heard Buck say, "What the hell's going on?" his stomach sank.

149

The moment Buck saw the crowd of people gathered outside the little pink house, he knew this was no welcoming committee. He half-turned to fake going back inside so they couldn't see him slip his hand into his pocket.

"You lied to us," Vin said, a metal pipe resting on his shoulder. Behind him this time were the four goons from the night before, as well as a couple dozen men and women, all holding blunt instruments, none looking like they held the light of Christian kindness.

"Hey, Vin, I'm surprised to see you here," Buck said, buying some time. "I don't understand what you think I lied about."

Vin broke out in a wolfish smile.

"You said it was just you and your wife. You and I both know that wasn't the truth."

Buck inhaled. "Now, you can't blame me for that. I didn't know you from Adam. You come banging on the door in the middle of the night looking like you were itching for a fight. We'd dealt with a gang in Yonkers a week ago. I had to be careful."

"I'm disappointed, but my beef isn't really with you. Give them up, and you'll be fine."

"Give who up?"

Vin spat on the lawn. "The fucking Arabs you came in with. It's their kind who destroyed everything. Just hand them over."

Buck stared hard at the man, ignoring the others. "You must have lost your mind. The people I'm with aren't Arabs, not that it matters. Even if they were, they weren't the ones who dropped those bombs or released that poison. Besides, even you don't know who did this to us. It could have been the goddamn Canadians for all you know."

Vin took a step toward Buck.

"I'm not asking. We saw all of you. Our eyes don't lie. You think we don't know Arabs when we see them?"

Someone jostled Buck aside. It was Daniel.

"You've all made a mistake," he said, hands held up as if the police had guns trained on him. "I'm an American, just like you. My family came here from Puerto Rico before I was born."

"Bullshit," a woman wearing a *Walking Dead* T-shirt and cargo shorts said.

"My family and I have gone through the same hell as you. We lost our son. Our lives will never be the same, just like you. We're not your enemy."

"Sure looks like it," someone muttered.

Buck saw the crowd was getting jumpy. Hands tensed around weapons. This was going to easily get out of hand.

Vin said, "That's pretty much what the last Arab said to us, except he said he was from Pakistan or some shit like that. You're all natural-born liars who have no value on life."

"My name is Daniel Padilla! Does that sound Arabic to you?"

Someone laughed. "They can make up any name they want." Buck couldn't see who'd said it. His finger slipped past the trigger guard.

"I know you have a woman and three kids," Vin said. "I

need you all to come out now. If not, we'll just take all of you."
He sneered at Buck. "In fact, that's just what we should do."

Daniel said, "You're not touching my kids."

There was a moment of silence as Daniel's words hung over the justice-hungry, misinformed crowd. Buck knew for sure there had to be parents in the mob. Surely they could sympathize. Maybe Dan had found the secret code to defuse the situation.

Daniel continued, "I understand your anger, I feel your pain. I want to lash out and find someone, anyone responsible for who did this to our country. But I know I can't just vent that anger blindly. I love my children, and I'll be damned if I let anything more happen to them after all we've been through to get this far."

Buck and Daniel flinched when someone fired a gun into the air.

150

"Don't listen to his lies!" a woman screamed.

Elizabeth shouted to her kids, "Get away from the windows!"

Grabbing a gun off the living room table, she ran to the front door just as the mob was making their advance.

"Take all of them!"

"Alive if you can."

"Not for long!"

Buck got tangled on his own feet and fell backward into the house. Daniel held his ground. "Get back. I told you you're not touching my family!"

No one was listening. They'd been harboring hate for so long, it was going to be unleashed on their family no matter what Daniel said. Mob mentality had taken control. There would be no reasoning with them.

So Elizabeth did the only thing she could do.

Stopping next to her husband, she shot the man nearest to the front steps. The bullet caught him in the mouth just as he was calling Daniel a "no-good sand nigger." He collapsed onto the woman close behind him holding an ax, red paint flaking off the head. She fell onto the ax, the blade slicing into her side.

For just a second, everything seemed to stop. The mob paused, the gunshot and the woman's cries momentarily shocking them. It passed quickly, their clamoring and anger increasing tenfold.

"Daniel, we can't let them in," she said.

"I know."

He grabbed the gun he'd tucked behind his back, firing off three quick shots in a small arc, hitting the front row of the mob. The siding of the house popped as shots were fired back at them.

Elizabeth felt something sting her arm and her fingers went numb. Blood splashed her face. She lifted her other arm, shooting wildly into the crowd. Daniel grunted and dropped to a knee.

Buck was shouting, "You sons of bitches! You sick sons of bitches," as he tried to drag Elizabeth and Daniel back into the house. Alexiana had a grip on Daniel's shirt. His stomach was a spreading, crimson stain. Still, he tried to shoot back, but his gun was empty.

And so was hers.

Hands grabbed Elizabeth's legs, pulling her down the two front steps. Daniel was dragged next to her into the mob. She could hear her children screaming for them, hear Buck's anguished cries, blocking out the wild epithets and threats to kill her right now. Someone kicked the side of her head and her vision tripled.

"No!" Daniel screamed, breaking free to throw his body over hers.

Then there were other screams, panicked yelps. Elizabeth couldn't see what was going on through the tangle of legs around her. If it was at all possible, it sounded as if things were about to get much, much worse.

151

Buck couldn't believe his eyes. From out of the side yards of the houses across the street, a hundred or more animals came swarming into the mob, alerted and excited by the commotion. Dogs, cats, muskrats, raccoons, even a family of wild turkeys, ran for the mob. The animals were rangy, blood-caked, and ravenous.

"They brought them here!" a man with a handlebar mustache cried, pointing at Liz and Dan as they lay bleeding in the grass. They'd taken out seven of the mob, their bodies twisted and lifeless. Buck had to get them back into the house.

"Alex, I need you to cover me," he said, handing her his gun and motioning toward the window. She nodded, knocking the glass out of a window.

"Mom, Dad!" Max shouted, running to the door. Buck had a hard time holding him back. "If you can, get the hell out the back door with your brother and sister."

"No. I won't leave them."

"I'll get them inside. You have to protect Miguel and Gabby."

Max stood panting, humming with indecision.

Half the mob was fighting off the animals, the other half

resuming their march on the house. There was no time to even think of his next move. Buck sprinted for Daniel and Elizabeth while Alexiana fired into the crowd. A woman who had a dog latched on to her leg spun as a bullet caught her in the collarbone. The dog was happy for the assist, as were its companions that tore into her.

Buck hit the ground. "I've got you."

Daniel's head rose. "Save the kids," he said, blood dribbling from his mouth. "Please, save the kids."

Elizabeth was under him, barely conscious and bleeding in several places. Buck tried to get a good enough grip on their shirts to drag them back into the house. A fist came crashing into his mouth, breaking his handhold on the Padillas. Flipping backward, he saw a seagull come nosediving for him. It missed, bashing into the chest of the man who had punched him.

"What the fuck?" Buck said, scanning the pandemonium.

It was hard to tell where the mob began and the wild animals ended.

He didn't have long to watch before a bat crashed into his knee. "Fucking Arab lover," one of the goons from the night before spat. Something pulled him deeper into the mob's violent core. He couldn't tell whether it was man or beast.

Alexiana yelled for him. "Lock the door!" he shouted back.

When he looked back, he saw it was too late. Three men had grabbed her, shoving her to the ground, letting a handful of muskrats get at her as they clawed and nibbled at her face. Her cries were unimaginable.

Buck tried to get to his feet, but the mob pushed down on him, driving every molecule of air from his lungs, the weight increasing so he couldn't breathe. A black Labrador snaked its way to him, fangs bared. He prayed he'd pass out before he felt the first bite.

152

After Alexiana had run from the house to get Buck, Max slammed the door shut. A couple of rats had made it into the house. He made quick work of them with his bat.

Miguel and Gabby were eerily quiet, but heavy tears made snaking rivers through the grime on their cheeks.

"I want Mommy," Miguel said. His chest heaved frantically, an asthma attack fast approaching.

Max looked out the window. His parents were lost in a sea of angry humans and hungry animals. There were more gunshots, some at the larger animals, others at Buck, Alexiana, and his parents. Birds of every feather swooped down, pecking at anything that moved, feeding on the bodies that had fallen.

They talked about Hell in church and school. Everyone had a similar vision of it—fire and cratered canyons, black smoke and the cries of the damned. And lording about it all, a cloven-hoofed Satan, ram horns reared back with sinister laughter.

That was a fairy tale.

Max knew, this was true hell.

He had to protect Miguel and Gabby, but how? He was one kid against everything that wanted inside the house. With so many animals around, they wouldn't stand a chance going out the back door.

"What do we do?" Gabby said, holding a gun.

"Put that down," he said. "It won't do us any good."

Something slammed against the front door. A mirror in the living room exploded as a bullet shattered the glass. Miguel screamed.

When Max ducked, he saw the answer. It was a horrible one, but perhaps the only one.

Buck's remaining grenade sat in an ashtray by the couch. Max had seen enough movies to know how to use it. You pulled the pin, threw it, and took cover.

The only way to stop this was to lob it into the crowd.

The same crowd where his parents, Buck, and Alexiana were, helpless, probably dead, but very possibly still alive.

He picked it up, looked to his brother and sister.

Gabby wiped her tears. "You have to do it." She covered Miguel's chest with her arms, trying to settle his breathing down. Miguel pressed his inhaler, but nothing happened. That had been the last one.

"But what about Mom and Dad?" Max said. The grenade felt like it weighed a thousand pounds. His arm suddenly felt weak, lifeless.

Gabby slowly shook her head. Even if they were still alive, what could they do to fix their wounds? They both knew their parents had been shot, more than once.

It was the *only* thing to do.

Max couldn't let the mob or even the animals touch Gabby or Miguel. It was what his parents would have wanted. He'd get them out of here, find a safe place, and stay there. Someplace where there were no people.

Miguel struggled for air while Gabby spoke softly to him, just as their mother had.

Stifling his tears, Max gripped the front doorknob and flung it open. Outside was utter madness.

He pulled the pin, releasing the lever.

"Fuck all of you!" he screamed, throwing it into the center of the mob.

Slamming the door closed, he yelled, "Get down!"

The explosion came faster than he thought it would.